THE
PORTRAIT
ARTIST

THE
PORTRAIT
ARTIST

DANI HEYWOOD-LONSDALE

BLOOMSBURY PUBLISHING

LONDON · OXFORD · NEW YORK · NEW DELHI · SYDNEY

BLOOMSBURY PUBLISHING
Bloomsbury Publishing Plc
50 Bedford Square, London, WC1B 3DP, UK
Bloomsbury Publishing Ireland Limited,
29 Earlsfort Terrace, Dublin 2, D02 AY28, Ireland

BLOOMSBURY, BLOOMSBURY PUBLISHING and the Diana logo are
trademarks of Bloomsbury Publishing Plc

First published in Great Britain 2025

A catalogue record for this book is available from the British Library

ISBN: HB: 978-1-5266-6995-7; TPB: 978-1-5266-6996-4;
EBOOK: 978-1-5266-6997-1; EPDF: 978-1-5266-6998-8

2 4 6 8 10 9 7 5 3 1

Typeset by Integra Software Services Pvt. Ltd.
Printed and bound in Great Britain by CPI Group (UK) Ltd, Croydon CR0 4YY

To find out more about our authors and books visit www.bloomsbury.com
and sign up for our newsletters

For product safety related questions contact productsafety@bloomsbury.com

For Mum and Dad

July 1831

Sir H. Ellis,
We have discovered a most wondrous treasure, a
marvel to surpass all gems and oddities. We are on
our way home with it now. The vial sits snugly in
my breast pocket as I write this. You shall behold
it soon... It is, without a doubt, our most prized
discovery.

Yours,
T. P.-H.

PART ONE

Kunekune Pig

Autumn 1890

The grey door on Charing Cross Road sits amongst the gentlemen's clubs and brandy houses like a forgotten woman, plain and reticent. It is clean and tidily kept indeed, but is an afterthought amidst its gritty yet resplendent neighbours. On this dusty morning when there is a chill upon the square, the early sun has no favourites when casting shadows.

But out of all the grand shops and imposing houses in this part of London, the grey door is the precise destination of Jonathan Hammond. He walks with his head down, chin tucked into the folds of great black lapels much too thick to be fashionable in early October. Past the clockmaker's at No. 68 on Pall Mall, the Traveller's Club at No. 49 – he knows these buildings by the bases of their iron gates and the pebbles that have collected round them. He could walk this route with his eyes closed and often has in his dreams. Upon reaching Trafalgar Square, the lions and Admiral Nelson are as wonted company as the armchairs in Mr Hammond's sitting room.

There is a spring in his step – the kind that children have when sucking on a pear drop – and indeed the upturned corners of his mouth are just visible. This quickens his pace despite being four hours earlier than necessary.

Unbeknown to the world, Mr Hammond has recently aided in the acquisition of Hans Holbein the Younger's *Ambassadors*, and its debut in the nation's collection is to be announced at midday. It is his first year in post as assistant to the Gallery's director – a distinguished director, it must be noted, for Sir Frederic has obtained a Botticelli, a Canaletto and a Velázquez during his tenure. Mr Hammond is lucky to shadow such a giant. Gone are the days when del Piombo's *Lazarus* was the diamond of the collection and the art spanned all of one townhouse wall. Upon securing the ropes and lighting for *Ambassadors* the previous afternoon, Mr Hammond had waved his cigar around like a maestro, gliding between the rooms and naming the paintings out loud – miming, even, pretend conversations that would take place on the morrow. He shakes his head now at the gaiety, the silliness, turning the corner to the Gallery's inconspicuous side door.

At first, Mr Hammond does not notice the parcel. He grips the key in his pocket as he approaches the steps and admires the extension as he always does. Inside, the Barry rooms are tall and elegant with an octagonal gallery that inspires awe from even the harshest of critics; from the street, it is an ordinary and unspectacular edifice.

He is on the pavement in front of the arched door and nearly knocks the parcel with the toe of his boot before realising that it is there.

'How very curious.'

It is a large parcel wrapped in crinkled brown paper, the kind you get meat wrapped in at the butcher's, though this parcel is much heftier than a couple of pounds of bacon. It balances flat against the door at eighteen inches by thirty-six – a familiar lean, a recognisable thickness around the perimeter. His expertise is not needed to know what it is.

Mr Hammond tilts the painting forward delicately as if leading a woman in a dance. There is no address, no name, not a single mark on the brown paper in front or behind. For one moment, his curiosity is eclipsed by annoyance as he remembers the impending pressures of the day to come. He does not have time for tomfoolery on the best of days.

'Well.'

He unties the twine in a huff and peels back the top left corner. The tearing seems to echo down the empty street and in its harshness, Mr Hammond cannot help but feel that the fate of the day has been altered, that he has awakened something long asleep.

It is a gold frame, thick and ornate. The corner of the painting is a smoky grey-green which, as he tears the paper further, reveals

4

itself to be a country sky pricked with the tops of oaks. These are not mere brushstrokes. Even this sliver of the painting is alive with pigments buffed, scraped and prodded, carved and manipulated, with a silkiness like fog on water. Mr Hammond kneels and brings his nose close to the paint.

It is not possible.

He straightens and peels back a bit more, this time directing the tear towards the centre of the painting, which reveals the most uncommon of sitters. He bends close again. A sweetness, it is undeniable.

Trapping the folds of paint are layers of syrupy beeswax. It is not the fashion to mix oils with wax, be it on canvas or wood panel. The Egyptians heated beeswax and added coloured pigments before painting their panels and portraits; few masters dabbled with this method in recent centuries. This painting before him, however, uses beeswax in a different manner. He is familiar with the method. The wax is sloshed onto the wood and dried before the paint is layered on top; only then is it pushed, pulled and chiselled, to mesh and mould into one velvety medium. He has seen this technique used by only one artist. To think that this could be… well, it is nigh impossible. It has been fifty years since the last one appeared on the doorstep of the Academy, and under the darkest of circumstances, just like the ones before it.

Mr Hammond unbuttons his coat and flaps its sides like a pelican. Crimson blooms on his cheeks and a sheen of sweat causes his collar to wilt. Mr Hammond is an art consultant with an impressive clientele: Lord Ian Montague, Sir Ashley Wright, Sir Nicholas Williams-Wynn; he organises and hangs exhibitions for the private British Institution; he has been responsible for maintaining the royal collection of pictures for the royal family itself. But never has he handled, never has he been so close, never has he dreamed…

No. It is not possible.

With one final pull, the paper is shed. It is a true masterpiece, even a layman would recognise the fact. The subject of the painting in all its glory is still baffling. But Mr Hammond is not looking at the face before him, is not admiring the million strokes through wax that bring the hair alive. He stares only at the bottom right corner where a signature is printed in pale yet bold brandishing. The *Ambassadors* is all but forgotten. Mr Hammond knows he should not disturb the canvas, but he raises a quivering hand and with a touch as light and gentle as gossamer, he brushes the name with his fingertips.

PONDEN-HALL

He draws in a sharp intake of air and holds it within himself, stills his lungs that beat upon his heart like a bass drum. It is all he can do to stop himself from weeping.

1

The Oyster Rooms on Duke Street is a refined and respected restaurant that sits back from the dusty din of carriages and omnibuses like a pearl between grey cockles. It is a purveyor of oysters to the Queen herself – to the Prince of Wales, too, who is a loyal customer on its quieter days. The restaurant's front windows are narrow and dark; those outside wonder who is dining by candlelight in the middle of the day, and those inside sit snugly in safe shadows with lobster tails and lemons.

Any meal at the Oyster Rooms is indulgent and often coated in a haze of wine. Solomon Oak supped here many times in the sumptuous years of his life whilst discussing paintings, when slurping through oyster platters was a simple and ordinary luxury. Once upon a time, he would have been recognised in any London square, sometimes even followed by Ponden-Hall zealots desperate to know more about the painter and his secrets, which they believed Oak himself fastidiously guarded. He is relieved to be invisible to them all now.

He is late for this meeting which has coaxed him out of his home in Oxford and away from his daughter. Jonathan Hammond, his old student: too loyal and persistent in his adoration of Oak to be offended by silence. Still too stubborn, as well, to accept when Oak says *No* for the fourth time. It was Hammond's final note that inspired pause, written almost as a postscript in hurried scribble as if it were a desperate addition before stuffing it into the envelope: *Your expertise on Ponden-Hall is needed at the Gallery*. Well. It had worked. Now that he is back in the metropolis, however, he regrets his curiosity.

The streets are congested this late morning so the route to the restaurant zigzags across the city, past the French quarter in St Anne Soho, past the Rookery of St Giles-in-the-Field where the pubs and lodging houses appear more impoverished than Oak remembers. At last, the carriage trots to a stop in front of the Oyster Rooms and as he descends, Oak pulls his coat tightly around him as if to ward off the grime and stenches of London. He flinches at every stiff groan of a carriage wheel, at every sharp whoop or profanity that is shouted from coachmen, pie men, hawkers. It is a wonder that he lived here on and off for thirty years.

Although he has not dined here since its relocation from King Street, the button-backed booths and red velvet cushions are as familiar to Oak as his own study; the dim lighting is a comforting cloak.

Jonathan Hammond is seated in the deepest corner behind the bar where a smattering of mollusc paintings hang around his head like a halo. His whiskers are finely groomed as they always are, although his hairline and its startling recession are impossible to ignore. Young Jonny Hammond. His forehead has grown in size and sheen like the crown of a boiled egg.

'Professor Oak,' he says, standing – knocks a fork to the floor, bumps the water glass. 'Professor, it is truly good to see you. I have taken the liberty to order a bottle of red wine and warm potted shrimps to begin.'

'Thank you, Jonny. You remember well.'

Hammond passes a menu to Oak and observes him over his own. Can this be his idol? The intellectual who inspired – emboldened and *roused* – Hammond to pursue a life of art and academia? The once famed art historian is pinker and pudgier than he was at their last meeting and his white, untamed hair furls about his eyebrows and his ears. A layer of dust and lint rests unshaken across his coat collar; the shoulders bunch in odd places and the seams appear lopsided – more moulded to its hanger than to the soft body beneath it. Just below the left lapel are the crinkled and brittle remains of a spider's legs. He never did care much about grooming, Hammond notes, though this state of unkemptness would confirm any rumours that the great Solomon Oak has become a mad and zany recluse. Oxford, it seems, has preserved his old professor with a neglectful hand. Indeed he looks more like an eighty-year-old than a man of sixty-five with these deep, gathered pouches under his eyes.

'Are you well, Professor?' Hammond asks. 'I must admit I am surprised to see you in front of me. They said you'd never come. It is wonderful to see you after so long.'

'You sent me five letters in five days, Jonny. What could I do?'

'Ignore me as you have done for the past decade.'

'You know that is not personal, my boy.'

'I do know that.'

Hammond smiles and beckons the waiter to their table.

'The dressed crab for me, if you please,' says he. 'And a dozen West Merseas for my friend.' Winking at Oak, he adds, 'If you do not finish them, I shall help you.' Hammond's cheeks are flushed and the smile is plastered too wildly across his face.

The menus are swept away. Oak takes note of the time.

'How is darling Alice?' Hammond asks.

'She is very well, thank you. A hive of energy, that girl of mine. I have given up trying to stop her from helping Missy with the chores – you remember Missy, our daily? 'Tis unorthodox, I know, but you can imagine their closeness after everything, and I see no real harm in it. She is too keen perhaps on venturing into town to help with the grocery shopping or poking about the flower stalls. Risky businesses of that sort—'

Hammond laughs. 'Risky? Oxford is not London, sir. A few flower peddlers—'

'No, no, Jonny, you've not seen some of the seedier stalls in the market these days. She is too eager to walk Missy halfway down the street, too excitable to answer the door. Why, just the other day I overheard her having an elaborate conversation with the postman! Nearly half an hour. Of no importance either – she was asking him about his routes and his favourite doorknockers.' Oak sips his wine and shakes his head. 'I suppose it is partly because I keep her close, but – well, she will finish with her studies soon.' He leans forward, a glint in his eye. 'I have arranged a surprise for her. Do you remember Magnus Bird?'

'Bird... yes, he was two, three years below me, was he not?'

'The very man. He has agreed to take Alice on as a governess for his two children. As soon as she finishes her exams.'

'Why, how marvellous! Is that… would she…' Hammond hastens through his memories of Oak's daughter and recalls a bright, fiery little thing. He would have pictured Alice Oak to become an outspoken businesswoman or an advocate for female poetry like those rebellious spirits in New York; a governess on Portman Square, he would never have dreamed. Hammond shrugs, for people do change and she was so little when he last saw her. 'She is very lucky indeed.'

'She will be well kept and safe,' asserts Oak. 'That is most important.'

It is natural to be asked about his daughter, and she is often the topic of choice for the few people Solomon Oak sees in these sluggish days of his life, but even now, ten years later, he wonders if it takes great consciousness and effort to not bring up his firstborn. He wonders if the milkman, the butcher, the student in the park who he taught many years ago think about his daughters Emma and Alice in tandem, as he does.

'She is eighteen now, you know. Last March. I even had a cake made.'

Hammond shakes his head. 'Eighteen. It is a wonder. She is a wonder.'

Of course, Oak knows this – is baffled by this girl who is his flesh and blood. He misses Laura, his wife, but the pangs of grief at the onset, which were once so acute, have dwindled over the years to a dull ache. Their romance, swift and unexpected as a noon tide, was such a surprise to Oak in his forties that he could only close his mouth and be swept away. Their courtship seemed to bloom so fast that he could only feel one emotion at a time, which was, more often than anything, grateful. She played the organ and had an appetite for frescoes. She had a heart for charity and volunteered with the Workhouse Visiting Association in London. Twenty years his junior, she was an angel – fleeting and purposeful, like the figures in Caravaggio's paintings who appear before their earthly charges for a few wondrous moments and return to paradise. When Oak imagines her, which tends to be in the quiet moments of waking, it is with a golden arc around her small, bowed head like da Forlì's *Angel* in the Vatican; she is never nude and perfect with coils of flowing hair like Botticelli's *Venus*, nor is she swanlike and regal like Parmigianino's *Madonna*. But she is young and beautiful and full of grace, which is more than Solomon Oak ever hoped for, even for the briefest of years. And she had given him two children. Would she have left so early – left such delicate charges in his care – if she knew that their firstborn would follow her into the heavens before reaching adulthood?

Their potted shrimps in butter and nutmeg arrive with toast. It has been a long while since Oak has eaten so richly; at home, he eats hard-boiled eggs with pickles and peppers and the tiniest pinch of salt when Missy is not looking. Oak is certain that he will soon be asked for an inconvenient favour, yet for some reason, he feels that he is standing on a precipice taking his final breath before a fall.

'Why have you called me here, Jonny? Your last letter mentioned Ponden-Hall. I know you are not so wicked to lure me from my home on false pretences.'

Hammond swallows and takes his time dabbing the butter off his beard. He licks his lips, which are mildly wine-stained with a flaky red ring around his teeth; this, coupled with his tapping fingers and unfounded enthusiasm, makes Hammond resemble a Shakespearean fool rather than the esteemed assistant director of England's National Gallery.

'There was…' begins Hammond. 'Last week…'

He fiddles with the tines of his fork.

Something has happened. Oak has not been summoned to deliver a lecture or write a paper as he presumed.

Hammond is careful with his words when he speaks again. 'When I arrived at the Gallery last Friday, there was a painting on the doorstep. It was wrapped in brown paper and tied with string.'

Oak is silent.

'It was early,' he continues. 'I am certain that no one else saw it. I brought it in immediately and hid it in the broom cupboard between the Barry rooms. Only Sir Frederic knows about it.'

There is a stirring deep beneath Oak's ribs, a fleck of tinder waiting to catch. He is startled by this; he had thought that any kindling or hunger for such a possibility was dampened long ago. He cannot speak.

'The signature looks real,' says Hammond. 'And the painting – it is exquisite.'

There is a fire in Oak's heart – it is undeniable – rising and expanding like an aeronaut's balloon.

'I was right, then.' It is more a croak than words.

Hammond nods. 'You were right. He is still alive.'

'What will Sir Frederic do?'

'He refuses to make any decision or announcement until its authenticity is confirmed.'

And Oak understands. Gone are Hammond's polished manners. He sits before Oak once more like a fervent university pupil looking up at his erudite professor for the answers.

'And if it is authentic?' asks Oak.

'Well then. There will be no keeping it from the papers. It will be madness from here to the furthest valleys in the kingdom. Just like before.'

All jitters and apprehension have evaporated. Oak traces the rim of his bowl in reticent thought; his exhaustion and tiredness have lifted like a spring chill.

'They will come in droves to see it,' he says finally.

Hammond drops his head into his hands. It is what he dreads most. It is, he knows, inevitable.

'And it will be a fully fledged manhunt.' Oak drums his fingers on the table and shakes the curls surrounding his brow. 'Undeservedly so.'

For the first time, Hammond's grin is sincere. 'You still don't believe any of it?'

'Of course not.'

'But the bodies, Professor.'

'Show me one, Jonny, and I would *consider* the tales.'

'You know very well that DeLacey was buried at sea.'

'And the others?'

'Never found.'

'Ah, well, that is convenient, isn't it.'

Hammond snorts a concession and tops up their glasses. 'If a stubborn academic like you continues to disbelieve—'

'Disbelieve what? Stupidity and superstition.'

'You know what the people think. These paintings possess something of...'

Hammond pauses here. Oak knows what he is thinking, knows how preposterous it sounds, and yet they are both aware of what transpired sixty years ago. Hammond was not yet born and Oak was a mere boy during the decade of Ponden-Hall's works. They have read all of the articles: the craze of the public, the obsession and the fear.

He cannot help it: 'Is it wonderful, Jonny?' asks Oak.

This is the Solomon that Hammond knows – a vestige of the man who once wept for the beauty of a shade of vermilion on a leaf. 'My dear professor,' Hammond says, 'it is a marvel.'

It has been a long while since Oak has felt palpable excitement to see a piece of art. The recent works of Impressionism do not provoke him, yet if he says this out loud he is criticised for being snobbish or pretentious. He swishes his wine in a whirlpool and lets it swirl to calm. 'And in the past week, have you heard anything? The sitter's obituary? Any rumours?'

'There will not be an obituary,' says Hammond.

'Not another ragamuffin?'

'No.'

'What then?'

He leans forward over the tableware and Oak mimics him, as if pulled by an invisible string.

'It is a pig, Professor,' says Hammond, bemused.

'A pig.'

'Yes.'

'How curious indeed.'

Oak is ravenous. He is thrilled at the prospect of a dozen oysters and only out of politeness does he refrain from scraping the hardened butter from his bowl. It is a foreign sensation, having an appetite again.

'They will never find it,' he says. 'The pig, I mean.'

'Oh, but there will be claims.'

'Of course there will be. And if this is a true Ponden-Hall,' Oak continues, 'it means he is eighty-two.'

'Yes.'

'And if it is a true Ponden-Hall, I will not seem so buffoon-like to my critics. He has been alive all these many years. Did not die from some deal with the devil or kill himself to be with those he loved.' Oaks shakes his head. 'I knew he was not finished. He has something yet to say.'

'So it seems. Perhaps you will receive heaps of apologetic post. Perhaps you will start teaching again.'

Oak smiles and smooths the linen napkin across his lap. 'No, my boy. Those days are long behind me.'

2

Oxford train station is abuzz with hawkers and lingering coachmen even though it will be another hour before the next train arrives. It is the postprandial hour of the afternoon when merchants loll about in a sleepier rhythm and the sugars from jellies and pork pies have peaked and begun their denouement. At this hazy and liminal time of day, Alice Oak makes her way to the broom-seller who sits cross-legged on the kerb outside the station's main entrance. The road is not busy, not at this hour, which is lucky because Alice barely glances over the swing of her scarf before crossing.

She moves with a confident skip, her assuredness born more from naivety and impatience than experience. She holds her head high, chin up, and feels as if she glides along the square like a ballerina. In truth, her legs are little and sturdy, and the bounce betrayed in her step is more reminiscent of a puppy than a graceful *danseuse*. Her mop of hair is full and unruly, both regal and wiry, the one physical trait inherited from her father; it is restrained daily in a plait that, whilst tight, is still long enough to reach the soft curve of her lower back. The rest of her – dark eyes, small mouth often pressed into a determined line, petite frame in a wool cape purchased years ago but pristine with trimmed lace – is all her mother.

The train station is not on the stubby list of locales that Alice is permitted to visit in her weekly routine. Thus, most of her trips here take place in the wee hours of morning or long after sunset, with an excuse to fetch fresh milk, or in the hours after supper when her father locks himself in his study with tea that grows cold on the mantel. For the first time in a long while, the great Solomon Oak has gone to London, leaving his restless, sheltered girl on her own. As

Alice winds her way to the kerb, she finds that she does not miss the darkness and the quiet of her usual visits. She cannot help but study and stare at a mother and her two young children; a small group of painters who are touching up the lamplights and railings; the flower cart and nut peddler; the snoozing drivers in their carriages.

'Miss Oak,' says the broom-seller, tipping his hat.

'Good day, Barnabas. Are you well?'

'Sales are slow.'

Alice frowns and fumbles in her coat pocket. 'For your pains,' she says and offers a farthing.

Barnabas wheezes through the gaps in his smile. 'You don't even know if I have anything for you, girl.'

'Do you?'

The broom-seller winks and, with trouble, hikes up his trousers to reveal long socks and a narrow envelope tucked inside.

Alice shifts to block the sight from passers-by — a pair of skipping siblings; the pie man hawking one final steak and kidney pot; the same group of painters, who have migrated to a closer railing. Is not one of them much younger than the others? Dressed too smartly to be painting a lamp-post? Absurd, in fact, to paint in tails and a top hat.

'There's no need to be so dramatic, Barnabas. If I may, please.'

The envelope is not properly sealed. It is a short message.

Alice exhales and puffs her cheeks.

'No luck, eh?'

'No indeed,' says Alice. ''Tis my fourth rejection, as you well know.' She tears the paper in half and stuffs it into a pocket. 'My thanks, as always, Barnabas, for being a trusty conduit. Have you heard of any others?'

'Not what you're looking for. If you want a job, girl, you need to be willing to step out into town. Plenty of houses would take on a kitchen maid or laundress. Or with your education, surely you could tutor.'

Alice shakes her head. 'It would not do. If I started tutoring some of the university families, Father would hear of it and he simply cannot know. He cannot know that I am even looking.'

'I don't see why. A girl has to grow up sometime.'

The positions that Barnabas refers to are long-term commitments, and Alice is seeking temporary employment to earn as much money as she can over the next few months. She does not confide her true motivations to the broom-seller: her yearning to go to the continent on a grand tour in early summer. Only Peter, her old classmate and now the bookshop apprentice, knows of this longing. She is, despite the cocooned life she has led for a decade, more like her father than anyone thinks; the spark for art and history and rambling through European cities may not have been roaring and bold in Emma, her older sister, who preferred to travel and explore through the pages of her books, but it is there in Alice, just as bright and eager to be nourished as her father was when he was eighteen.

Alice sighs. 'Thank you, Barnabas. I will be in touch soon.'

She has only walked to the corner before she feels a light touch on her elbow.

'Pardon, Miss.'

Alice is not used to being confronted on the street – is not used to being seen at all – so despite the phantom fingers that linger on her sleeve, she casts glances behind both shoulders before looking the boy in the eye. It is the young painter, black polish on his cheeks and paint smudges on the scalloped flaps and brass buttons of his stylish long coat. Alice is startled, for the boy is older than she imagined – just a few years older than her, perhaps – and his eyes, whilst bright, are piercingly dark.

'Forgive me for disturbing you, but I could not help overhearing your conversation,' says the boy. 'You are looking for a job?'

Alice straightens. Perhaps it has not been wise of her to risk these meetings in the daylight after all.

'Oh no, you must have misheard,' she says. 'I am still a student.'

'I know of an opportunity if you are interested.'

'I am not. Thank you. Good day.'

'It is in town but in the evenings. Always after dark.'

Alice crosses her arms and nods towards the lamp-posts, still glistening from fresh paint. 'I have had no painting experience. And I am slightly embarrassed to admit this, but I do not do very well with heights.' She recalls a memory of climbing up the apple tree; she and Emma, impatient, had flown their kite in the back garden despite Solomon's promise to take them to the Meadow later in the afternoon. Alice had scampered up the trunk and released the kite with ease, only to find herself paralysed once she looked down. It was the only time she recalls Solomon needing to save her. She crinkles her nose at this disappointment. 'So you see, I could never climb ladders and polish posts—'

'Oh, it is not a job like that, Miss. This is not my job either. Do you see that hansom there? Parked with the speckled piebald near the columns? It is mine. I am a coachman for a great house north of Oxford. 'Tis the master of the house who is looking to employ a bit of extra help.'

The boy is unflinching and speaks kindly. He stands erect with elegant posture, but he is slight in build and only just taller than Alice. There is a rosy energy about him – a glow to his skin, as if he has spent long, recent days in the sun. Alice cannot place his accent: a posh lilt, but different from the landowners and professors she has heard in her father's circles.

'What sort of job?' she asks.

'Deliveries. Lifting parcels mainly, organising them in the carriage to make my life easier. Perhaps keeping the inventory in order on the odd day here or there.'

Alice has tended to the post at home and occasionally helps Missy sift through old receipts. This is the extent of her administrative work, and more often than not, the tasks are abandoned and unfinished paper nests on the console table, for Alice grows bored.

'No previous experience is necessary,' the boy says. 'And you will always be with me to guide you.'

'In town, you say? But after dark?'

'Yes, Miss. Mostly around Jericho. A handful more central with one or two in the surrounding villages. The deliveries don't take long with a nimble hansom like mine.'

This is an attractive prospect, for if Alice works in the evening hours after supper, the chances of being spotted by acquaintances and neighbourhood gossips are slim.

'How often?' she asks the boy.

'Three times a week, but the days are flexible as long as the work gets done.'

'I have lectures in the day and eat an early supper with my father. If I could have a few hours to study in between eating and work, that would be helpful.'

'I never start before 8 p.m.'

Alice will concoct a scheme that requires her out of the house. An evening tutorial in the labs, perhaps. A sudden interest in astronomy. Her father will be hesitant to let her go but he will concede in the end as long as Missy accompanies her. Missy will keep her secret, especially once she understands what the money is for. She has always encouraged Alice to pursue her ambitions, has she not? This is largely because Missy believes Alice's own mother would have supported such behaviour, Laura Rollo Oak having been a woman who pushed boundaries herself – and with charm too. Missy can only assume Alice's ambitions would have been entertained… and Alice will take advantage of this conjecture.

'And for how long will this employment carry on?' she asks the boy.

'This, too, is flexible but at least through the spring.'

'Tis perfect. 'I would be very interested in the opportunity,' says Alice.

'Very good. In two Mondays then? I will collect you here at the station.'

'Thank you.'

'My name is Lou,' says the boy with a bow.

There is something out of kilter about him but Alice cannot land her finger on what it is. She can feel him studying her.

'My name is Alice. Alice Oak.'

'I shall see you in two weeks.'

'Sorry, might I ask – if you drive that hansom, why were you working with those men?'

'Oh, I do all sorts of jobs. I like to keep busy. I park here at the station to offer lifts, and on the slower days, I offer my services to people who need an extra hand.'

'What liberty you have.'

'Indeed. I have helped with some extraordinary chores. Once, I transported a pregnant goat and her farmer from one end of the town to another. The first kid was halfway out by the time we arrived.'

Alice is appalled. 'In the hansom? Your master did not mind?'

Lou shrugs. 'It was immaculate by the time I drove it home. The master has no need for a driver these days, so I am at my leisure to do as I please and meet who I wish. Train stations are a treasure trove for people-watching and people-meeting.'

This makes Alice uncomfortable, but she cannot help but envy Lou's independence.

'Monday then,' Lou says. A nod to Alice's dress. 'Oh, and you might want to consider wearing bloomers. The deliveries are often on muddy paths and I find it easier to manoeuvre the crates without the pesky weight and constrictions of a skirt.'

'I… I beg your pardon?'

Before Alice can comprehend what this advice implies, Lou presses a wad of notes into her hands.

'I bought my bloomers from Nichol's on the High,' says Lou. 'The only place you'll find them in Oxford. There are bound to be more in the years to come as more women take up cycling. But until then, unless you want to venture to London, Nichol's is the place.'

'But—'

Lou has already begun to walk away. Alice skips to keep up.

'You might consider wearing a shirtwaist, as well,' says Lou. 'Cotton or linen are both comfortable.'

'A what?'

'A shirtwaist. Unlined. Much better for moving freely. Do you play tennis?'

'Tennis? Why, no, I— Wait!'

But Lou is crossing the square. Alice jogs at pace to catch up and narrowly misses being knocked over by an approaching coach. The crowds have grown in just the past fifteen minutes with a rising commotion of galloping hooves and chatter.

'They come embroidered, too – lace and frills, if you desire such details,' Lou continues over her shoulder, 'but I prefer simple hems.'

'Please wait!'

Lou stops, expectant.

'I apologise, I just…' Alice clutches a stitch at her side and exhales heavily. 'I am surprised, that's all. I did not realise—'

'I know,' says Lou and rubs a smudge of dust off her lapel. She smiles. 'No matter. It happens all the time and it will certainly happen again.'

'It is no wonder that you seemed… Why do you…?' Alice colours. 'How funny that I… Well, with your hair tucked up like that, I—'

'I look forward to having your help and company,' says Lou, straightening her top hat. 'Monday evening. Do not be late.'

With a final nod to Alice, Lou is lost amongst the crowd, which now flows like a swelling tide. Alice can only gawk. In a daze, she remembers the notes in her hand and studies them – a hefty amount, too generous a sum to give a stranger. She should not accept this, of course, but when she scans the throng of travellers and peddlers and carriages at Oxford station, Lou is nowhere to be seen, has quietly, gracefully melded into the bustle of the day as only a woman could.

On her way home, Alice takes a detour to Thornton's Bookshop on Broad Street. The bell jingles as she sweeps through the door and Peter Bridge pops up from behind the register, having been perusing a box of freshly delivered anthologies.

He glances at the timetable on the counter.

'What are you doing here, Alice? 'Tis not Tuesday or Thursday.'

'I know. My father has gone to London and I find myself at a loose end,' she says. 'And anyway, I have some exciting news to share.'

Peter's bewilderment gives way to curiosity and he beckons her out of the doorway with a suspicious smile. His cheeks are always peppered with freckles, but on this day, pink from a fire just slightly too early for the season, they glow in abundance. Alice softens when he smiles. If he were not so strictly part of her weekly programme, not so much a part of the furniture and bookshelves of Thornton's, perhaps she would view him as a pleasing, attractive, if sometimes pernickety, specimen of the opposite sex. But he is only Peter, an old friend from childhood summer walks, an apprentice at her favourite bookshop, who indulges her in her whims and daydreams of art and jaunting abroad.

'Go on then,' he urges her.

'I have been offered a job.'

'At last! Doing what?'

'Deliveries.'

Peter crosses his arms. 'Deliveries?'

'Yes. Well, it seems that way anyway. To be honest, I do not know much about the position, but it will be in the evenings so Father will be distracted, and they will employ me through the spring – a perfect timeline for my journey to the continent.'

'And you will conduct these deliveries afoot?'

'No, no, my employer has a hansom. She is a woman, if you can believe it.'

'A woman coachman? I have never heard of such a thing.'

'Yes, I was surprised myself—'

'Why would a woman drive a coach?'

'I think it is a perfectly respectable job for anyone.' She dares not mention Lou's perplexing attire.

'And the wage?'

Alice colours. 'I… do not know the particulars of that either.'

Peter's scepticism is plain upon his brow. 'So you have agreed to work for a stranger in the evenings, and you do not know how much you will be paid.'

Alice bristles. 'She is not a stranger. She is called Lou and she works for a grand house in Oxfordshire.' She draws out the wad of notes from her pocket and waves it in Peter's face. 'And look here. I have not even started yet and she has given me an ample amount of money so I may dress the part.'

'Where will these deliveries take place?'

'I… around Oxford, of course.'

'And what will you be delivering?'

'Oh, Peter, do stop fixating on the trivialities and be happy for me!'

He throws his hands before him in supplication. 'Forgive me! I am of course delighted for you. It's just… well, you are a brave and stubborn creature, Alice Oak, but you are not the most careful. You never have been. One of us needs to question these things.'

It seems that she is for ever rolling her eyes at him. 'Well. I think it is the perfect opportunity. I need to earn money in some way. Not all of us have rich uncles to whisk us away to France.'

Alice traces the spines on the closest shelf with her index finger. The leather is so sturdy and polished, unfrayed and smooth to the touch, unlike the old and tattered volumes in her father's study. The entire shop smells of vanilla and earth – *the chemical compositions of the pages*, Peter has taught her.

'Perhaps,' Peter offers, 'you and I will be in Paris at the same time. Uncle says we will depart shortly after Easter.'

Alice squeezes her eyes shut and shakes her head. 'Oh, I cannot bear the thought. First Elinor moves to Edinburgh to be married and now you are off to grander cities and fancy company. If you are due to be gone after Easter, I shall aim to depart then as well.'

'I have something to show you,' Peter says. From behind the counter where they keep special acquisitions for their wealthier clientele, Peter draws out a crisp sleeved periodical. 'It arrived from Paris two days ago. 'Tis an art publication with criticisms and articles on the Impressionists.'

'Oh, Peter...'

'Do not bend the corner! Our client has not yet seen it. He is in London until November. But look here on page ten.'

'Why, 'tis a piece by Eugène Dumont!'

Peter does not conceal his pride. 'Mr Thornton allowed me to help him in this acquisition. I wrote to the bookshops myself. The old French don was much pleased.'

Alice skims the dark ink, perfectly imposed on the page by rubber printing plates. 'May I take it home?'

'Take it home?'

'Just for a week, Peter! I am slower in French.'

'You are off your chump, Alice Oak. I could lose my job if I allowed you to take it.'

'You said yourself that your client will not return until next month. I will take the best of care with it.'

'With all due respect, Alice, I cannot fathom the state it would be in after a week in your keeping.' Peter's laugh betrays nervousness, for he cannot tell if she jests. 'Now give it here.'

'You are a rude boy, Peter Bridge. How else am I to learn about the French painters? And by Dumont himself.'

Her mood soured, Alice pulls her coat about her and turns from the desk.

'We could read it now, together,' Peter offers in conciliation. 'Or come round to my father's this afternoon. Benjamin Chaddleworth is coming to tea. You would be most welcome to join us.'

'Oh, I cannot think of anything worse, Peter. Benjamin can barely look me in the eye if I run into him at the market.' This is not an exaggeration. Just last week, Benjamin, one of Alice's few friends from school before her father pulled her out to be educated at home, had knocked an entire tower of cheese to the floor in his haste to leave the shop upon seeing her. Like the others – and they were all so young – he had found Emma's death confusing to navigate, but how to act around the surviving sister was almost worse. At first, they offered pity and moved in awkward circles around Alice. In time, they avoided her altogether.

'No, no,' sighs Alice. She is halfway through the door. 'I have an errand on the High that must be completed before Missy is wise to my absence. Good day, Peter. I shall see you on Tuesday, as always and for ever more.'

3

Post luncheon, the National Gallery hums like an apiary. Art enthusiasts and art students roam its tall corridors and burgeoning wings,
admiring the museum's growth, critiquing its stocky architecture
and deliberating over and over again which masterpieces should
really belong there instead of at the Academy. Every room has at
least a dozen quiet onlookers, and the not-so-quiet ones pronounce
facetious opinions on how Hogarth's satires were painted in bad
taste or how Turner's request to always be displayed next to Claude
should for ever be honoured.

In the midst of these gatherings, Jonathan Hammond, Solomon
Oak and the director of the Gallery himself, Sir Frederic Burton,
huddle in the Gallery's largest broom cupboard, tucked away between
the Barry wings. The parcel, hastily re-wrapped in its brown paper
and string, balances against a stack of buckets and brushes. Oak
kneels before it, trying to conceal a trembling that has nothing to do
with a medical condition. He is about to behold the impossible – the
unattainable work of someone believed to be dead.

'The same size as the peacocks, I would guess,' he says to no one
in particular.

'We could compare them side by side with a print if it would be
helpful,' says Sir Frederic. 'Once the visitors have gone.'

'It won't be necessary.'

The paper and string fall away like silver maple after a frost, and
perched before Oak is a painting of exquisite detail and beauty. He
stares at it for many minutes, his hand on the frame as if comforting
an old friend. The daring use of viridian that cuts the frame, the
faded stones to mimic the use of smalt, a lone stroke of ultramarine

on the bridge of the snout; the eye darts around this calculated path, always moving, always moving.

Oak exhales a quivering breath and it is an effort to keep upright and stabilise his breathing. It has been fifty years since the last one, when Oak was only fifteen, yet here he is, still buckling in awe of these strokes, these perfect pulls of paint through wax of this master. It has always been the textures of Ponden-Hall's works that stand out: waxy peaks and perfectly pooled globules, so rich and tactile compared to other portrait painters. Oak has always been drawn to these works for their textures – and their intimacy. Man or beast, Timothy Ponden-Hall's gift lies in how he depicts his sitters: a knowing expression, an intimate moment captured between painter and friend; the audience feel as if they are part of the moment, part of the space. Oak has always found greater company and comfort in these paintings than he has from his flesh-and-blood friends. How is it possible to feel such intimacy with the sitter of a painting?

And what is more, Ponden-Hall's sitters are all deceased. Within days of each painting appearing on the steps of the Gallery, an obituary would surface or news of an animal death linked to the paintings would circulate. It was this strangeness, this mystery, that drew in Oak most of all and catalysed his fascination in his school years; what was the painter trying to say? Why devote such mastery to these particular sitters? Now that he has experienced his own grief, first with his wife and then, more profoundly and more excruciatingly, with his daughter, he is drawn to the paintings even more. In his heart of hearts, he wishes that Ponden-Hall could have painted Emma, could have memorialised her in this bold and intimate space.

Although the paper still covers the bottom right corner, Oak turns to the men and says, 'It is real.'

Hammond exhales into his hands, which are palmed as if in prayer over his lips. Sir Frederic, too, releases a heavy breath and sinks against the door. He knows what this will mean for the next few months, possibly years.

'You're certain?' he asks.

'Yes,' says Oak. 'And you are too. You can feel it. The warmth, the life, the detail. See how it emerges from the canvas through the wax. Only Ponden-Hall could extract life from an unwieldy medium so successfully.'

Hammond shakes his head. 'Fifty years. And he returns with a pig.'

'Why?' asks Sir Frederic. 'Who would commission a common farm pig?'

'A Kunekune,' says Hammond, 'if you read the inscription on the back. I have been in touch with the Pig Association. There are no records of such a breed in the country.'

'Brought back from one of his expeditions then,' says Oak.

'And not registered. He was always eccentric. Why this? Why now?'

'This is where we go blind.' Hammond rubs his eyes with the butts of his hands. 'There are no obvious connections between the paintings. Not after the woodpecker and the orphan boy. This is no different.'

'Part of his deal with the devil.'

Hammond snorts. 'The papers will spin it like a top. By the end of this, they will crown Ponden-Hall as Satan himself with horns and a forked tongue.'

'But it is not just any pig,' says Oak. He has freed the painting and hangs it on a hook meant for aprons and towels.

In their cramped space, it is difficult to step back and study the painting from a distance. The three lean into the far wall, elbows and great lapels overlapping as if in a Punch cartoon.

'Notice the composition,' says Oak. It is impossible to go on without sounding as if he is at the front of a lecture hall. 'Do you see how the pig faces us? His upturned nose, his white eyelashes, those tassels hanging off his jowls like a wattle. One crooked tusk. An ink blot over one eye. The scattering of smaller spots below the ear as if someone has shaken a pen. A grump, if I were to guess based on that scowl. And old, too — look at the wisps poking out of his ears, white as salt. This, gentlemen, is a very specific pig. Why has Ponden-Hall not given us a profile? Side-on would give us a rotund belly, its height, its scraggly tail. But side-on, you see, could be any pig. This pig is as distinct as you or me, and he meant a great deal to Timothy.'

''Tis a pig, Professor.'

'I mean it. It is one of Ponden-Hall's most distinguishable qualities in his work. There is deep affection in all of them. Art reflects the artist's mind, the artist's mood. This is a pig — a simple farm animal to be slaughtered or reared. And yet look at the painstaking time he has taken to portray him. Each wiry hair is pulled out of the wax and oil, is moulded, nudged and carved from an unruly medium at once thick and syrupy, at once solid and stiff. It is like discovering figures in a block of marble – rescuing them from an immutable cage.'

'It is a work of brilliance,' says Hammond. 'But you cannot compare this to Michelangelo's sculptures.'

'And why not? The idea is the same. The figures exist in catatonic, trapped forms. The artist finds them and sets them free.'

'Who is the pig, then?'

'That,' says Oak, 'we may never know. But it gives us a hint about Ponden-Hall's whereabouts. Look at the background: a stable of sorts, corrugated-iron roof, patches of cow parsley and buttercups at the base of every fence post.'

Sir Frederic grunts and throws his hand towards the painting's skyline. 'Aside from London, that could be anywhere in England. It could be in Hampstead Heath!'

'It could be,' says Oak.

'The great Timothy Ponden-Hall: slinking about under our noses,' posits Sir Frederic, 'taking dips in the ponds and hosting dinner parties for the architects and authors all this time.'

''Tis a famous retreat for artistic types,' concedes Hammond.

'Even if he did skulk about Hampstead, how do we know this wasn't painted years ago? Fifty years, gentlemen – we forget the longevity of his mystery.'

'It was painted within the week,' says Oak. 'Just like the last ten, this will have been painted one day, maybe two days after death. If you are close enough to the canvas, you can smell that the paint is still fresh. The turpentine is sharp.'

They know this is true. The agitated pink in Sir Frederic's cheeks gives way to the pallor of pea soup and his moustaches hang limp past his lips. Hammond, too, grows wan and the perspiration on his nose and wrinkled forehead glistens in the broom cupboard's patchy light.

Sir Frederic's voice is gruff when he speaks. 'It is impossible to separate Ponden-Hall's paintings from the conversation of mortality, Solomon. Even if you do not believe in the rumours, the rest of the country does. These could be simple death portraits, yes. But they could be more.'

'Even you say there is an unnatural quality to them,' says Hammond. 'The texture – the sheen of the oil—'

'—is beeswax. As natural and ordinary as a walnut. You remember, gentlemen, that this is a form of encaustic painting from the ancient Egyptians that mixes the pigments with hot wax. Nothing more. I could give you an entire lecture on the process one day, if you'd like, but I assure you: there is no miraculous or mystic elixir in the painting. Not in any of them.' Oak glances from one to the other, his curls bouncing. 'You are both well-educated men, certainly two of the most intelligent academics I have ever worked with. Surely, you cannot fall for this puffery. Such nonsense and fodder are for the seedy dens on South Bank, for the unsavoury public houses in the East End.'

These barbs fall short of their mark, for it is known that men from all classes and cultures in society have been taken in by the Ponden-Hall tales. Yes, the maids in their sculleries, the Burmese and lascars on the West India Dock, the Guards officers in their Chelsea barracks, the Chinese in Pennyfields and Poplar are all purveyors of the tales, but in fact, the keenest believers are those who reside in laboratories and holy domes.

'If it is like all those years ago, he will be hounded down like a fox,' laments Sir Frederic. 'Why will he do this to himself? Why has he returned at all?'

'I believe he wants to be found.' Oak stands before the painting once more and leans close. The subtle sweetness emanates from the canvas with its biting tint of vinegar. 'This is his swan song. I have always said that there is a story behind his work – one that is not yet understood by any of us. Perhaps he wants it shared before the end.'

'What will you do, Professor?'

The old art historian straightens and cleans his spectacles on the pleat of his waistcoat. 'What do you mean?'

Hammond treads delicately. Although he has brought Oak to verify the painting's authenticity, the question he is about to pose has been dancing around their discussions, only waiting to tumble into the light.

'This reappearance of Ponden-Hall is surely sign enough that perhaps, if you were interested, you could finish your book,' he says. ''Tis an opportunity nobody thought you would have.'

Sir Frederic frowns at his boots.

Hammond regrets his boldness, but it is too late.

'I think not,' says Oak coolly. 'There was no interest ten years ago and nothing has changed.'

'You were revisiting it when we last spoke.' Hammond can hear the soft crunch of eggshells beneath him. He does not want to hurt Oak, does not want to cast him back to his deepest moments of despair. Indeed, Hammond remembers it well – was there to watch his revered professor be struck down by inconceivable tragedy. And yet he pushes, because perhaps this is the magnum opus that Solomon Oak deserves.

'And then I changed my mind,' says Oak. He gathers his coat about him and stands as tall and dignified as possible before donning his hat. 'I must catch the last train, so I shall leave you. I hope my services have proved useful.'

'Consider it, Solomon.' Sir Frederic is gentle but firm. 'If you are so adamant that Ponden-Hall does not play with the occult, you can salvage his name. I am confident that an attractive agreement can be made. If you work alongside the Gallery to help us find him, you would receive a generous stipend. And access to the paintings whenever you want, of course. You can tell the story you have been wanting to tell.'

'And that story – the true story – would not sell, not compared to the witchcraft and hocus-pocus that everyone wishes to be real. If I wrote that book, it would be a story about a gifted artist who mixed beeswax with his pigments and resorted to the life of a recluse. It would be wonderful because his *art* is wonderful. Nothing more. I am afraid that is not enough to satiate the desires of a public obsessed with immortality.'

'But if it is the truth—'

'Since when do people care about what is true?'

'I have a cousin in publishing, Solomon,' offers Sir Frederic. He has never forgotten Oak's donation to the Gallery or the many times he stood in for lectures when more famous guest orators left the museum in a bind. 'Perhaps the first print-run would not be so size-able, but they rarely are. Take the book *Frankenstein*! Just five hundred copies in the original release and look how its success has ballooned.'

Oak grunts. 'A novel. And one with monsters and the like.'

'Then think about Timothy,' says Sir Frederic. 'Perhaps if you found him first, you could discover the truth about all those tales. Explain the motives and meanings behind the masterpieces. If anyone could find him, it would be you. You have studied his work more closely than anyone. He is your life's work. *He* is what you should be writing about… not dilly-dallying in your garden writing contrary papers on the French painters.'

Although this final spur is delivered with the best intentions, it does indeed cross a line and both men are immediately sorry for it. But Oak is unmoved.

'Not every man is meant to leave behind a legacy,' he says at last. 'I have quite accepted that by now. Good day, gentlemen.'

On the train journey back to Oxford, Oak has the first-class dining carriage nearly to himself. He sits at the first seat closest to the door. The cool draught from the windows is a comfort to him, and whilst the other two travellers shiver in their coats and cast disgruntled glances at the conductor, Oak is thankful for the sobering effect it has on his racing mind. He is not tempted by the slew of luxuries on offer: salted toffees, polished plums, roasted walnuts, a slice of candied apple next to a plump and flaky pork pie. Oak orders a sherry, which he does not drink.

By the time the train grinds into Oxford, Oak has solidified his decision to pursue Ponden-Hall's story no longer. It is true that no other art scholar, historian or biographer knows Ponden-Hall's art as Oak does; it is also true that no one else is interested in knowing it because the art itself, for most, is the least interesting element of Ponden-Hall's work. No, it would be a fruitless endeavour to revisit this project. Any glint of enthusiasm or fire he felt looking upon the new painting has been smothered, doused with the excuse of old age and the quiet acceptance of a mediocre career. If he cannot leave behind a great legacy of blood and bones, why should it be any different with his work? Oak is relieved to turn away. He will retreat to his comfortable and quiet home on Mansfield Road, and he will watch the word spread like wildfire through the cities and country-side that Timothy Ponden-Hall is alive and toying with immortality once more.

4

As the final sand granules pass to the bottom bulb of the hourglass, Grace Dodd unbinds the straps around her wrist, nods to the semi-circle of gentlemen who have been drawing her for the past two hours and flounces to the door, bare bottom swaying like a peacock's plumes. The men are all over twenty years of age, most of them married, as is preferred for participants in the course, but she feels their eyes on the dimples of her back, the curve of her scapula, the fleshy side hang of her breast. Only once she is out of the drawing room does she relax her spine and roll her head from side to side. She unpins her hair, which has been twisted and bunned, and allows the curls to fall around her shoulders.

She gathers her chemise, purple and silk, along with the finest dress she owns, and takes them to her favourite room in the Academy. Here after a sitting, she wanders and thinks about nothing in partic-ular for a drowsy hour, sometimes more. Here, she begins to dress. With visitors gone, the Academy feels tall and hollow. The air is always crisp and clean and smells of nothing, as if the paintings lap up the perfumes and powders and musk of the day's visitors. They hang one atop the other like stacks of sugar cubes, tilting forward off their hooks as if they will topple with the locking of a door. But without the crowds of admirers, even the paintings cannot fill the space and Grace Dodd feels like the mistress of the room.

'You have been most elegant this afternoon. Oh dear, pardon me.'

Charles Dawson, keeper of the Royal Academy, enters the room from another arched doorway. Grace Dodd jumps, her dress halfway arranged hanging about her waist, breasts falling fully out of the chemise that is just too small. Although Mr Dawson apologises for his interruption, he does not look away. A blush rises to his cheeks and he rocks between heeled boot and toes. He is nearing forty with a plump wife at home and two young girls. His bushy sideburns hint that the rest of his head might have had more hair in the dawn of his manhood, and his eyebrows frame his face not unpleasantly. He is the sort of once-handsome rogue turned tired husband that Grace would once have targeted for a ruse. She no longer runs such schemes, although she is poorer for it. Her collection of jewellery and feathered hats has not been refreshed for some time and this, too, is an injurious shame, for she enjoys keeping up with the seasons' fashions. Oh, how envious she was upon seeing a new hat walk out of Liberty, wider than any of hers, trimmed with ribbons and curling flowers and topped with an entire stuffed swallow. Grace continues to be sweet with the seamstresses there and is certain that she could acquire one. But no. She will see these habits of her new life through.

'It was difficult to maintain the arched back,' she says.

'You did splendidly. A real picture of *Grace*.' Mr Dawson chuckles at his own joke.

'Same time tomorrow then?'

'And most probably the day after as well. 'Tis a difficult pose to capture.'

'Then that is my contract for the week.'

She sits three times a week during the autumn and winter months for Mr Dawson's most popular course. The wage is meagre, but it is enough coupled with her brush and canvas duties, and although the position comes with the reputation of being a whore, Grace can look herself in the mirror and know that she is doing honest work. How ironic, she thinks, considering that her past life of swindling portrayed her as an upstanding woman.

'I wish you would consider sitting more,' says Mr Dawson.

'Your male models are equally prepossessing, even though they may not be so popular with your students.'

Mr Dawson sighs. 'I am truly sorry to interrupt you, but I wanted you to know that this time next week and most probably the one after, I will very likely have need of this room.'

'At this time? After hours?'

'A special favour. Just on Monday evenings.'

Grace raises her eyebrows. Mr Dawson is not famous for favours. 'For whom?'

'You are aware of the new Ponden-Hall, I presume.'

'Of course. One would have to live under a rock *not* to have heard of it. Why, it is all the students in class can talk about and it is on the front of every paper. Just yesterday in the pub, I overheard the barmaid speaking to a group of gentlemen about this pig and what it might mean. Is there any word as to where Ponden-Hall might be?'

'None at all – which is precisely why my guest may be coming. He is to deliver a lecture soon.'

Grace's eyes flicker. 'Who is he?'

'Solomon Oak.'

'The art historian?'

Mr Dawson nods. 'The very one. He has not actually agreed to anything yet; he is being a bit stubborn about the whole matter, according to Sir Frederic at the Gallery. But I do believe he will come around. Oak is, as you must know, the closest thing to a biographer that Ponden-Hall has. He is one of the few who believed Ponden-Hall was still alive – suffered for believing this, in fact, when the paintings stopped fifty years ago and he continued to write about him as a modern master, shaming anyone who fuelled rumours of unnatural methods. Then about ten years ago, one of Oak's daughters died. Influenza or something. The poor chap has rarely been seen in public since; he has written the odd article condemning the Impressionists for their vulgarity, but as you know, more and more of the public have changed their minds about this – people are less critical and many are even celebrating the movement. If Solomon Oak was out of favour with his praising of Ponden-Hall's work before, he is certainly unpopular now.

'Anyway, it sounds as if the Gallery has asked him to deliver a series of lectures on Ponden-Hall's paintings – a sort of summary of his life's works to put the entire mystery into context. Sir Frederic is hopeful that the revisiting of Ponden-Hall's earlier works will shed some light and we will discover something new. Clues perhaps that have been missed.'

'Clues that will lead to Ponden-Hall?'

'Clues that will explain anything, I think. The explorer–painter has many secrets. And now that a new painting has appeared, those secrets are hotly pursued. Anyway, I just wanted to give you notice.'

'So he will spend time with my favourite painting.'

'Yes. Although I believe he is most interested in the portrait of DeLacey. The first lecture would naturally be devoted to that piece.'

They turn to face the largest wall of the Gallery where, in its centre, three paintings have been granted breathing space, unlike the others. Ponden-Hall's first, second and tenth paintings, all framed in strips of gold and walnut wood, hang untouched by other works like a row of prized jewels. The tenth painting, his final painting left at the Academy fifty years ago, is titled *Woman in a Sunhat*, a portrait of Ponden-Hall's younger sister. She sits with fair head tilted in an elegant dress of white linen, the beeswax dripping in and through the folds of her V-collar.

Since she first set foot in the Royal Academy many years ago, Grace Dodd has been drawn to this painting. 'Something about her mouth,' she had explained to Mr Dawson. 'As if she is about to say something.' Which is ironic because Adelaide Ponden-Hall was a mute, for ever in the wings of her famous explorer family's lives. Even this fortifies the invisible thread that pulls Grace to the painting and inspires a strange kinship, for Grace Dodd knows what it feels like to live in the shadows.

''Tis one of his most beautiful works,' says Mr Dawson.

Grace nods. 'His paintings of women – this one and *The Potter's Daughter* – are particularly exceptional. I do not know much about Timothy Ponden-Hall,' Grace muses, 'but it seems he has painted them with great respect. A true gentleman.'

Mr Dawson scoffs. 'You couldn't be farther from the truth. The tales of his wildness and promiscuity are nearly as legendary as his art! He was a hound, madame, with an insatiable appetite. For women *and* men is the rumour. You can imagine the strain he caused the family. The Ponden-Halls were an aristocratic bloodline with generations of famed explorers. Timothy's grandfather sailed with James Cook and there are records to suggest that a Ponden-Hall even accompanied Sir Francis Drake in the 1500s. They have always been a respectable family – adventurous and seafaring, yes, but never *wild*, as Timothy came known to be after the death of his parents when he was only a child. Even his foray into painting deviated from what he and his family were known for.'

'I knew he was an explorer first,' says Grace, 'but I was unaware of the magnitude of his family's fame.'

'The Ponden-Halls were always in the society papers for their journeys abroad and engagements at home. Only when Timothy stepped into the limelight did their family name become entrenched in gossip and rumour – the parties, the extravagant wealth brought home in treasure chests, the scandalous relationships.'

'A character of intrigue then,' says Grace, her smile teasing. 'I would much rather read about inappropriate relationships and foreign riches than the boring supper parties of the stuffy upper class.'

Grace's admiration of the rogue irritates Mr Dawson. 'You jest, madame, but I don't believe it would be too overstated of me to say that Timothy Ponden-Hall was the singular cause of the family's downfall. When he disappeared with Hugh after the shipwreck – his final excursion, as you know; an abrupt and tragic end to a prom-ising seafaring career – his grandparents were heartbroken. In the 1840s on her deathbed, his grandmother wrote a public plea for him to reveal himself and come home, to claim his inheritance and continue the Ponden-Hall legacy as a respectable man. Of course, Timothy never responded or resurfaced. He began to paint these death portraits in hiding, leaving them to be found in the dead of night. When Julian and Elizabeth Ponden-Hall died, they left their entire estate to him. To this day, it remains unclaimed, untouched.'

Grace no longer smiles. She is thoughtful for a moment before she proffers, 'Perhaps Timothy Ponden-Hall is interested in something beyond the material. I am myself only just beginning to explore this idea.' But Charles Dawson is not the one with whom she would like to traverse this thought, so she manoeuvres back to the impersonal. 'And now Timothy Ponden-Hall has returned. How tragic that he suffered such loss at such a young age; no wonder he was fascinated by death and immortality. We would do well to acknowledge the passing of time, though. One does grow up, you know. Why, I am a very different person at thirty-five than I was at twenty-five, with notably different interests!'

This vocalisation of her age sours on her tongue. She knows that in the eyes of some men, she has aged past the prime of her beauty.

She does not remember what she dreamed she would be as a little girl; her memories from childhood revolve around reading with her father and the great sadness she felt when she and her mother left him and ended up in an almshouse. She has lived on her own for so long. Grace dusts her hands and fluffs her hair. She is a free woman who honestly earns her keep and this is all she desires now.

'Might I escort you home?' Mr Dawson asks.

'Don't be daft. And be seen with me on the Strand? You have daughters to consider, Mr Dawson.' But she offers him a half-smile, which accentuates her dimples. 'I have another hour's work here to do anyway.'

'Oh, of course,' he says, 'I do forget your secondary commitment.'

Together they meander through two more gallery rooms to an inconspicuous cleaning cupboard at the back of the Academy. A bucket of paint-soiled brushes has been dumped outside the door.

Grace sighs. 'My industry awaits. I will see you tomorrow, Mr Dawson. A good evening to you.'

When Grace is alone in the washing closet, she cups her tender wrist. It stings raw where the straps have cut into her, holding her arm in a stationary wave for four, maybe five hours. She is certain that the neck of the hourglass is a hair too thin, so that time slows, singular granule by singular granule. She is fatigued. Sometimes she pretends that she is sitting for George Romney or Thomas Gainsborough. But the fantasy only distracts for the first half-hour before it dissolves into pain and a chill around her delicate parts. She will dust her wrist with powder and wrap it in linen at home.

So it is Solomon Oak. She has known for three days now that someone would come for the Ponden-Hall paintings. A letter had arrived with the milkman; the accompanying pouch had clinked against his metal churn as he filled her jug. When asked about the mysterious delivery, the milkman avoided her eyes and shrugged before passing on to her neighbour. The letter itself was addressed to her in boldly flowing script, instructing her that a man would soon come to examine the Ponden-Hall paintings and that she must plant an idea in his mind about the map in the DeLacey portrait. Grace is not one to take orders from an invisible master. She does not like being ordered about at all. Yet she is also not one to turn away from money, and the pouch is hefty with gold.

Now, she lengthens her neck and teases out her dark curls so they cascade around her shoulders like a shawl. Her dress feels heavy tonight, the wide pleated skirt and bustle unnecessary weights that pull at her arms as she begins to lather the paint bristles with lye. Grace has noticed that some women have started to do away with their crinolines and bustles altogether; her finest dress will soon be out of fashion. Her stomach sinks at the thought.

The paint from this evening is thicker and stickier than usual, claylike and stubborn. What she needs is a tub of boiling water to loosen the clots. Gathering the brushes into a heap, she folds them into a linen sheet to bring home to her quarters in Covent Garden. Concluding the job at home means that she will need to return them in the morning for the next class session. A small imposition, but it does offer an opportunity to confront Professor Fairbanks, a lecturer on Renaissance art who is using the premises, for he has once more rejected her application to take his course. Her past three attempts have been dismissed, allegedly owing to full registers, but Grace knows that it is her lack of a formal education that mars her appeal. Professor Fairbanks is no famed virtuoso himself, but he converses with Grace as if she is a dung beetle and is quick to look shrewdly upon her nicked hands from scrubbing brushes and stretching canvases. And here she thought such proximity to the field, however lowly, might serve as an advantage.

One day, Grace thinks, she will be welcomed to study Renaissance art and there will be no need to suffer menial work. Gripping the bucket of brushes in one hand and cradling a voluminous jar of walnut oil in the opposite arm, Grace glides down the cobbled lane, sumptuous bell skirt swaying beneath the weight of her burdens, an ex-swindler turned honest, irredeemable charwoman.

5

Alice crumples the front page of the Sunday paper and piles it into the kindling basket. The rest of the bundle she takes to her father in the study. It has been four days since Sir Frederic's public announcement and every paper, penny press and tabloid journal has brandished the story across its front pages like a royal sash. It is the plum of every conversation, teetering on the lips of university professors and lamp-lighters alike, for this is not only about art but also the intrigues of immortality and long-lost secrets as well. And whilst it could be argued that townspeople are savouring their final days of autumnal walks in these crisp October afternoons, wandering the streets to admire the elegant turn from emerald to gold, Alice swears that more passers-by have drifted to Mansfield Road, particularly pausing to behold a leaf or unremarkable rock across from their very house.

As a result, their curtains on the ground floor are drawn at all hours of the day, and even more than usual, Solomon spends his time tending to their little garden which, though surrounded by a high stone wall, is not shielded from the gossip that rises over and plonks itself into his ears. *Solomon Oak has known where the painter has been hiding all this time. Do you think Oak has struck his own deal with Ponden-Hall? He must be in his sixties now – I, too, would be thinking of immortality. Do you reckon Oak's garden is sizeable enough to house a pig beyond this wall? The pig could be his, aye?*

Oak is quiet and irritable, which inspires Alice and the daily to render themselves invisible. Even Alice's tutors have paused their visits, honouring – for the first time in Alice's memory – a harvest holiday which some schools take so that pupils can help with the harvest.

This leaves Alice at a loose end. She is restless at the best of times; without her tutorials, she restrains herself from climbing the walls. At first, she tries to help Missy. In one moment, Missy whips out the sheets and then flours the butcher's block to knead bread; in the next, she polishes the silverware and takes an inventory of the larder. All this she accomplishes with the finesse and speed of a humming-bird. Alice is keen – desperate, even – to assist, but after rusting the linens and serving a loaf of bitter bread for tea, she surrenders to Missy's claim that every book in the study needs dusting, and that it is probably best not to leave them in stacks on the stairs as she clears the shelves.

Alice, then, is left to fill her hours in the study next to her father, who does not wish to discuss any matters related to Ponden-Hall, Ponden Hall's artwork or any artwork at all, which leaves the barrel of discussion points rather bare between father and daughter. Oak paces the room often, pauses and frowns. It is a repeated routine that Alice dares not break. She has not told her father about the delivery job; she has yet to think of an excuse to be out on some evenings, but at this rate, Oak will hardly notice if she is gone for a week – a welcome change from his typical hawk-like scrutiny of her whereabouts.

Missy brings in the tea tray with an assortment of kippers, cheese sandwiches and apple tarts. Beside the teapot is a staggering pile of letters.

'Is this the filtered pile?' Alice hisses, eyes bulging.

Missy is unwavering, hands clasped upon her apron. 'It is, Alice. All sealed with a signature or come from official businesses as requested.'

Oak's sip of his tea is long and deep. He takes up the ivory letter cutter and slits through the first envelope as if he is slicing blight from an orchid. His eyes flick back and forth only a few times before he tosses it into the fire. Alice reads each letterhead sideways before the popping embers catch and they curl into smoke: *The Midland Naturalist*, *The Victorian Naturalist*, *Science Gossip*, *Popular Science* – all scientific journals of sorts, varying in credibility, reputation and favour. There are a few letters written from churches in London, their calligraphy abundant with ringlets and richly inked crosses.

Oak gesticulates to the letter before him. '*Recreative Science: Intellectual Observation,*' he reads aloud. 'What observation is *not* intellectual? Can you believe there are ten thousand of these confounded publications?'

'We can toss them out, Father,' says Alice. 'You need not read them.'

'Dear Mr Oak, due to your exceptional scholarship on Timothy Ponden-Hall – oh, now they are invested in my work, I *see* – dah dah dah, we would like to offer our financial assistance in your pursuit of the painter – endless pots of money, have they now? – on and on, tada tada tada, if only you would partner with us upon your journey to discover the truth about Ponden-Hall's elixir.'

Oak flips the stationery and examines its botanical border and illustrations of American buffalo. 'More and more amateur scientists who are keen for the natural world but know nothing about it. Look at this drawing of a llama – the ears, the jaw. It has no scientific basis.'

He rubs his eyes and slumps back against the cushion. 'I am not against science but the haste to progress it is counterproductive. One cannot rush these things.'

There is a knock at the front door.

Alice glances at the clock: ten minutes past teatime. 'Who could be calling at this hour?'

They are silent in the study and listen to the rustle of Missy's skirts, the bolt of the door and its baritone creak. Whilst Oak has received a torrent of post, nobody has had the gall to call in person. Oak hopes that word of his dismissal and disinterest in the affair has spread far and wide. He is willing to barricade himself in his study for as long as it takes.

Missy returns to the study flustered and appeals in hushed urgency, 'There is a Mr Edward Bromage here for you, sir. I have tried to turn him away but he insists on seeing you. He is in the foyer now.'

Oak's memory is as sharp as a bread lame. 'I do not know an Edward Bromage. What does he want?'

'He will say no more to me, sir. He is determined to speak to you.'

Oak straightens, smooths his waistcoat and motions to Alice to clear the books from the chair opposite near the fireplace. 'Another teapot, Missy, if you please. But no mention of supper.'

'And the curtains,' she murmurs, throwing them open to cast cold, brilliant sunlight upon the books and maps and prints. Her light footfalls disappear down the corridor and are eclipsed by a slow, lumbering tread that causes the floorboards to groan.

Edward Bromage's person fills the entire doorway. Not only does his top hat knock the doorframe, but his shoulders are broad and round and his belly bursts forth like a hydrogen balloon. His face is jovial enough, although his eyes seem to have a perpetual squint, which could be from years of hearty laughter, or a keen habit of scrutinising men higher up than he is. The study shrinks as his bulk crosses to the desk and he holds out a hand to Oak, who only half-rises to clasp it before resuming his seat.

'Edward Nicholas Bromage of the Royal Society,' says the guest, whose portly fingers cause Oak to wince. 'You are exceedingly kind to take my call.'

'I was under the impression that I did not have much of a choice. May I offer you a cup of tea?'

'Now, now, Mr Oak, I don't think you realise who I am or who I represent. I can assure you that I am no common businessman. My diary is booked up to December with appointments with men who want my attention – want the *Society*'s attention. And here I am coming to you in your very home. Now, tea would be lovely. Or coffee if it is available? I like a strong cup in the afternoon to keep me going.'

Missy, who has glided in with an additional tray, nods at Oak before surreptitiously dragging a side table up against Bromage's chair; the chair legs, carved into Grecian female figures, are buckling under his heft, bending as no caryatid has ever done who upholds the Parthenon. Missy will not allow Oak to be humiliated in front of this stranger; although the beans have not yet been ground this week and the cloth is still out to dry, she will busy herself and produce a full chamber of coffee before Bromage has finished his tart. Alice bites her lip to suppress a laugh as she realises that Missy has brought out a platter of buns, seed cakes and a bag of leftover sweetmeats gifted from the neighbours three days previously. It is a feast fit to feed ten guests for afternoon tea, but Missy has assessed their visitor's appetite. It is difficult not to take notice of Bromage's stomach, for the buttons down his middle look fit to pop like a parade of corks.

'I don't want to beat about the bush, Mr Oak. You have been contacted by several others, no doubt,' says Bromage. 'What have they offered you? I am here to offer you more – tenfold even. You see, you have not even given a number and I already multiply it. The

Royal Society will pay what it must to find Ponden-Hall and unlock the secrets of the elixir.'

If he notices Oak's tart face, he does not let on.

'What have the others proposed? That they shall use the elixir for virtue? To preserve the natural world – our flora, our animals, our oceans and skies? To increase the lifespan of common man? I reckon you've been propositioned by the church, too. To destroy it, no doubt. Lock Ponden-Hall in Reading Gaol and return the reigning of life to God!'

'All of those things and more,' says Oak, 'and I shall not be involved in any of it.'

'Because you have not heard the *right* proposal.' Bromage sits with his legs apart, hands resting on his thighs, which gives him an ovular silhouette against the mantelpiece like a smug Humpty Dumpty. 'We at the Society believe in acquiring knowledge through experimental investigation—'

'I thought men of the Royal Society were interested in pure and authentic *science*, Mr Bromage. Why on earth is the Society interested in this painting?'

'Well, Mr Oak, I will be plain with you. The Society promotes excellence in science as you say, and I will admit that a fair number of my colleagues… *disagree* with my interest in Ponden-Hall's work and are less than satisfied with the grant I have received to pursue this. But they are wrong. If the painter has tampered with an elixir that can change the course of life and death, why, I cannot think of anything more interesting or relevant to discuss in scientific circles! They will see. They might disagree now, but I hold sway yet if you understand what I mean.'

'I do not. If you are at odds with your associates, I can only presume you have a wealthy father. With all due respect, Mr Bromage, it sounds as if you favour sensationalism over rigour like all the others.'

'The Society favours experimentation in order to progress science, and I believe if said experimentation is sensational, so much the better.'

'I do not understand what experimentations you speak of, Mr Bromage,' says Oak. He is tired of such talk and has read it all in the letters he has discarded.

'You know very well what Timothy Ponden-Hall and Hugh DeLacey were searching for on their last expedition, Oak. And they found it – the elixir of life, and they were bringing it back when their ship sank to the bottom of the ocean. They survived and the vial did too. Come now… all of those paintings appearing on the steps of the Academy followed by obituaries? It is no coincidence. He has done something to those sitters… has tampered with them in some way. Do you know what this could mean for science? For humanity? It alters life and the afterlife and any philosophical discussion around it.'

'Mr Bromage, you march in here with grand propositions and confident schemes assuming I believe in the elixir in the first place. This bedlam that has taken over the country is nonsense. It is all for nothing.'

'The elixir exists, Oak. There was a note, you well remember, sent to the principal of the British Museum. On his final expedition, he was bringing home his "most prized discovery" – Ponden-Hall's own words! A vial sitting "snugly in his—"'

'—breast pocket, as he wrote. Yes, yes, I know the letter just like everyone else.' Oak breaks off the corner of a biscuit and does not bother to chew with his mouth closed. 'You do not understand Ponden-Hall as I do. Ponden-Hall is immortal, yes, but not because of a mythical potion brought back from the ends of the earth. He is immortal through his art, as are his subjects. He knows this. He was always proud and boastful of the artefacts he brought home. That the world has latched on to his excitement over this supposed vial simply speaks of humanity's fear and obsession with death.'

'And I suppose you are not afraid of death?'

'No. We shall all die.' Whilst death is never far from the shallows of his thoughts, Oak is not used to speaking about it. This conviction that death is final, inescapable, is as sharp on his tongue as a sour plum. He believes and laments it in equal measure. Emma will not return, nor will his wife; that his own death may reunite them one day is a balm that indeed releases him from any fear of dying. 'There is no point believing in supernatural interventions,' he reiterates. 'Death is inevitable and we must accept that.'

Bromage rubs his thighs. His beady eyes fix on Oak as his moustache twitches like the hands of a clock.

'Perhaps you are right,' he says. 'Perhaps there is no elixir. But Ponden-Hall has secrets, that you cannot deny. If there is an elixir or hocus-pocus or a deal with the devil, it is an opportunity too valuable to miss. If that elixir disappears with Ponden-Hall and the rest of his secrets, we will know how close we came to conquering death and for ever regret not grasping the chance to do so. Do you not wish to find him before it is too late?'

'I wish to find him so I might compliment his genius. He is a modern master, Mr Bromage. There is something – I know not what – that connects the paintings together, and yes, I would like to find him simply to understand. But that is the work for someone else – someone younger. I have accepted for some time now that Ponden-Hall's legacy is no longer intertwined with my own. I do not need to leave a legacy behind. I am content.'

Alice has heard her father say this on many occasions, yet its sting does not lessen.

Missy returns, victorious, with a piping hot saucer of coffee. She stands at Bromage's elbow to offer it with care, but he leans forward with great effort. The seams of his topcoat strain taut like the hairs on a bow.

'I believe,' says Bromage with a beguiling smile, 'the *story*, as you say, behind the paintings centres around Hugh DeLacey. Ponden-Hall's best friend: fellow explorer, confidant, schoolmate…' he raises his eyebrows, 'lover perhaps? DeLacey dies at the green age of twenty-three, allegedly having caught pneumonia. His entire life ahead of him – a wealthy, famous, attractive young man grinning up at the daisy roots in his prime. What if Ponden-Hall knew that he could preserve his lover in some capacity, could grant him immortality at the peak of his life?

'That vial was greater than any of their previous spoils, surpassing even the kraken's tentacle that they had brought back the previous year from the Barents Sea.'

Oak closes his eyes and smiles gently. 'A rather sizeable octopus, that was all.'

'DeLacey's body appeared two weeks after the shipwreck and didn't have a single mark of decay upon it. How does one explain that, Oak? Cold as a winter pond, the papers said, but as rosy, stern and beautiful as if he were merely sleeping.'

'Show me the body now, then. Let us see this pristine and princely corpse – but alas, it is buried at sea. How troubling that we cannot confirm its persistent beauty—'

'Buried at sea out of reach from men of science – men of respect-able intentions and convictions!'

Oak bats this away as if it were a fly. 'An utter convenience.'

With the coffee passed on, Missy putters about the trays collecting napkins and sweeping crumbs into piles with her fingers, and elbows Alice when she notices that the girl is gawking. Alice clutches the damp cloth thrust upon her and takes extra care to dab up little spills on the table, rubbing teacup rings in a slow, exaggerated fashion.

Bromage continues, 'And then the painting appears on Pall Mall. The first one. A perfect likeness, a masterful depiction, with Ponden-Hall's signature bold in the corner for all to see. He has tampered with DeLacey's fate—'

'How? I was not aware that fates pranced around for all to see so that it is clear when they are tampered with.'

'The body—'

'Very well,' says Oak, clasping his hands before him. 'Assuming the nonsense about DeLacey's body is somehow true, how do you know that it was not merely embalmed or expertly preserved? 'Tis a question more for chemists than for wielders of magic potions. The Egyptians preserved their dead; surely, someone in our century could do the same and surpass their skill.'

Bromage opens his mouth to respond but nothing comes. Instead he studies Oak with beetle eyes and scratches his thigh, causing the coffee to slosh over his other hand. Oak does not budge. He is relaxed and unthreatened. Edward Bromage has underestimated the steadfastness of Solomon Oak.

'The body preserved and the soul immortalised,' Bromage finally says. 'There was the cigar smoke on the docks. *Cinnamon, leather, a fiery black pepper,*' he recites. 'That was the rhyme from the paper. DeLacey had a favourite cigar which was said to smell of cinnamon, leather and pepper brought back from islands in the Caribbean. The day they took his body to sea, the smell was all over the docks. He was there, Oak. To see himself off.'

Oak scoffs. 'A child's nursery rhyme published in a penny dread-ful. I am sure my daughter remembers the rhyme as well.'

And she does. Alice, like her father, has a deep love for Ponden-Hall, though not Ponden-Hall the painter but Ponden-Hall the explorer. She thinks, now, of her childhood built on the stories of Ponden-Hall and DeLacey, and how she and Emma used to recreate their expeditions in their bedroom with the pole of a broom for a mast and linen tablecloths for sails.

'Even the most obscure tales are inspired by truth,' says Bromage. There is a glint in his eye. 'If Ponden-Hall has discovered a way to cheat death, it should be shared and further explored. It could be dangerous, yes. Or it could be mankind's greatest discovery since fire. The Society will find him, Oak. But we could use your help. If anyone can work out where Ponden-Hall is, it's you.'

Oak's smile is slight and sad. He turns to his bookshelf, where a stack of notebooks has collected cobwebs and dust.

To Bromage he says, 'You are very flattering. It is clear that you have read the first instalment of what would have been my book; you will have found these chapters in the Bodleian's archives, no doubt. You are probably one of a readership of ten. That Ponden-Hall's relationship with DeLacey lies at the heart of it all is one of the theories I propose. You have embellished it a bit and dressed it up with supernatural treasures. But I recognise my own ideas, Mr Bromage, even dressed up like a pantomime dame. It has not worked. I will politely decline now and see you out.'

'I have been given a generous grant, Oak. I am very persuasive. I said it at the start and I shall say it again: name your price. We can pay a kingly sum.'

'No, thank you.'

With a clatter of china on oak, Bromage is on his feet with surprising agility. 'Then I have wasted my time. I told them I had heard you were a stubborn old man, but I had no idea of your arrogance. You are a fool if you cannot see that Ponden-Hall is worth more than his art. You cannot see past trite flicks of paint when the power to conquer mortality is before you!'

'Thank you for your visit, Mr Bromage.'

'We have powerful men backing our endeavour. If we need to start experimenting with diluted quantities of the elixir before the pure source is found, we will do so.'

'Whatever do you mean?'

'I need not remind you that as of one week ago, a new valuable specimen sits in the National Gallery. My, how science has progressed in the past fifty years; it would be fascinating to see what could be discovered with a fresh sample.'

'You will not touch that painting.' Oak, too, now stands, knuckles white upon his desk.

'I told you we have very influential friends. If the painting must be dissected for the greater good, I think the Gallery can make that sacrifice—'

'You would find nothing but beeswax and oil!'

'Their profits have tripled in the past day alone; I think people would pay even more to see it deconstructed.'

'Sir Frederic would never let this happen.'

'Sir Frederic will not have a choice.'

At the study door, Bromage pauses, wheezing from walking at pace. 'Every man wants a legacy, Oak. Do not pretend you will not despise yourself when your beloved Ponden-Hall paintings are explained by men of science.'

They can picture Bromage's hulking mass ploughing down the corridor and through the front door, can hear his heavy, indignant stomps descending the steps to the street beyond, and then all is quiet. The click of the bolt is a welcome, decisive relief.

With Bromage gone, the house totters off-kilter. It is hours past Missy's usual departure time but she lingers, scrubbing the cutlery, serving a supper of cold pheasant, fluffing the cushions in the study window seat that have not been sat upon since she has worked there. Her husband will be home from his counting house now, but he is a sweet soul and will wait to sup with her whenever she returns. Drawing out her needles and spools, Missy begins to tackle a pile of linens and moth-nibbled jumpers. All of these chores can wait for morning, but perhaps somehow, her tidying the bits and bobs around him will help bring order to Oak's mind, which has been rattled like a jar of beans.

He remains in the study, but has moved from his desk to the sunken armchair before the fire. The curtains are closed once more, though the waning day brings with it a purple light that glows through the imperfect meeting of cloth and sash. Oak has resigned himself to retirement – to a quiet life where he can roam the canals, read stacks of books with a bowl of peaches at his elbow or visit the rooms of the Ashmolean when his thirst for art must be satiated.

And yet he is unsettled.

He is furious at the prospect of the painting being dissected for science; he feels nauseated, in fact, when he imagines a scalpel being taken to the wax and oil. If Bromage's threat materialises and the painting is, in fact, in danger of being deconstructed, Oak knows that he himself must be there to oversee it all. Only he would keep the preservation of the painting the top priority; anyone else – even other historians and researchers – would not be so vigilant, would likely sacrifice the integrity of the piece for a measly scrape of beeswax.

Oak is angrier still at the thought of Ponden-Hall being found, old and slow in these final years of his life, only to be bothered and harassed for a thing of legend, for a tall tale. But most of all, Oak despairs at the thought of Ponden-Hall being remembered for such balderdash, for the stuff of fairy tales and myth, whilst his art – the mastery and mystery of it all, each stroke, pull and prod of the wax – is forgotten and dismissed. Timothy Ponden-Hall is trying to tell the world something, Oak is sure of this, and it is not a truth revealed about immortality. If it is left to Bromage and his Society, or anyone else for that matter, the message will be lost. Oak is in anguish at the thought.

Bundled in his overcoat and top hat, Oak steps out onto his front porch and inhales the cool air with greed. A dampness lingers; there will be rain. He must walk. He has always been a flaneur of sorts – the aimless wandering is a comforting method of escapism. The knots in his mind unravel themselves in time with the click of his boots.

No matter in what direction he sets off, Oak finds that his feet always bring him to the Covered Market. He is drawn to the arcade of haphazard stalls with their bright signs and strange aromas. It is under construction, and its cast-iron and timber roofs – which will be painted salmon pink, according to market gossip – will be refitted before the rain and wind of winter properly descend.

Oak avoids the market in the daytime. Its sawdust floors are trodden upon by hurried wives and picky servants replenishing their stocks of butter, fresh cream, apples and greens for the week; feral children duck in and out of doorways, sweeping quick fingers into opened sweet jars and pastry domes; there are humble carpenters, blacksmiths and grinders alongside well-to-do bankers and lawyers, all dipping into the market for a fresh thumb of coffee and plum turnover or the comforting grease of sausage rolls and pasties. Whilst there has been an upsurge in respectable stalls – garden produce, cut flowers, candied nuts and plump fruit – the odd unsavoury stall of seedy jewellery or garish bric-a-brac continues to draw a scruffy clientele.

Now, as the sky dims and the street-lamps are lit, only a handful of stragglers linger about the market. Butchers wash their blocks and move their hooks of hanging hams inside. The hulks of larger cuts – beef, pork, lamb, all with their trotters and bone on the line – are wrapped and re-peppered to keep the flies at bay. Across from them, the fishmongers wipe their knives, sweeping salt and scales to the floor before they slide rows of fish into coolers.

Past the butchers and poulterers, Oak winds his way to the centre of the market where the roof is vaulted over a handful of speciality shops. The mix of cheese, coffee and fish is pungent even in the airy space, but Oak is used to it. He stands at the centre of the crossway as he always does and looks up. He is no expert on architecture, has not formally studied it since one course at university, but he knows enough to appreciate this building: its roof trusses, capped pilasters, moulded cornices.

A child's cry brings Oak's attention to a closed spice shop. Against the door, a father leans his bicycle and attempts to hold his kicking, screaming son against his chest. There is a whir of slapping hands and feet, more octopus than child, before the father gives up and puts him down.

Oak is reminded of Emma's own defiant face and turns down the opposite alleyway.

Rain patters on the tin above. At the end of the passage, Oak looks out onto the high street where the benches glisten wet and lamplights flicker against an increasing fall. Yes, he is restless. His chest heaves and his breaths come rapidly even though he has not exerted himself. He has not felt such energy in a long time and in a flash of wild abandon, he imagines himself jumping into the Thames and swimming all the way to London – to the Billingsgate market or to the Limehouse docks, where he would be greeted by sailors from Zanzibar and Sumatra. How amusing it would be to ascend out of the Thames like a water nymph and flit through Victoria Embankment Gardens, down the Strand past Nelson's Column and atop the closest lion to guard Ponden-Hall's painting from Bromage and his pompous Society.

How can an old man put a stop to such proceedings? Revisiting a broken promise to Emma seems too much to bear, and yet here he is considering it. His hand finds the familiar dip in his breastbone and rests there, atop the beating within. A chance to fulfil a promise, a silly one made to an excitable nine-year-old girl by a doting father. *We shall finish the book together*, he had said. *And share Ponden-Hall's story with the world.*

A thunderous crash behind him snaps Oak out of his reverie. Outside a cookery shop, two columns of wicker baskets have fallen onto a table of iron pans and tin pots. Oak scans the darkness for the source of the calamity. As he takes a step backward onto the street, out from behind the tumbled baskets emerges a figure, small but bold.

It takes Oak a moment. At first, it is like seeing a cherub, familiar and comforting, yet fleeting and unplaceable as if from a work studied long ago. From which painting does she descend? And as the girl materialises from hazy frescoes and oil and chalk into a fibrous, breathing being, Oak sees that she is his own. His second-born.

'What are you doing here?' Oak asks.

His relief mingles with remnants of his restlessness as he beckons Alice to him. 'It is dark out – you should be at home. How many times have I told you that a young girl should not be unaccompanied after dark. And you'll catch cold in this rain.'

Her hands find her hips. 'I am eighteen now, Father, you would do well to remember. And anyway, 'tis lucky I followed you out. You forgot your umbrella.'

The sight of his sturdy umbrella under his daughter's arm touches something deep within Oak's belly. Tiredness sweeps over the retired art historian. Arm in arm beneath the umbrella, they turn for home. Past the dark fishmongers' and butchers' shops; past the coffee roasters and bakers; through the alleyways behind pubs that smell of barley, apple skins and rotting limes. It is not until they reach the corner of Mansfield Road, the lamps in the study and sitting room glowing warmly through cracks in the curtains, that Oak speaks.

'I am going to find Ponden-Hall,' he says.

Alice does not betray her excitement but gently squeezes her father's arm, still interlinked with hers.

'I owe it to her and to him. A legacy.'

Alice nods. She guides her father up the stairs and into the foyer before the rain begins to pelt down in one final torrent. She will put the kettle on and listen to her father's plans late into the night. This was once Emma's role – teasing out ideas and churning through memos far past their bedtime. Alice will scribble notes and pose questions, drag out old lithographs and maps that her father will tap and scrutinise. And whilst Alice is grateful to see her father spirited and impassioned, grateful for her father's opportunity to complete the monumental work in his life, the wound is freshly felt. For once more, Alice is the quiet second, the living blood and bones of a grieving father.

6

Overlooking a field of lingering buttercups out towards the arboretum and pigsty, one bay window of the great house remains for ever open. Its curtains, embroidered apple blossoms and peacocks on the finest silk from Marseilles, are never unpinned from their hooks, whilst the layer of muslin that hangs lightly from the valance dances and lifts with the wind. This layer is meant to keep out the beetles and moths of autumn, but in fact, it hangs year-round to soften the inpouring light.

Upon the window seat sits a silver tray. The biscuits are stale and the bonbons have hardened, whilst the tiny mounds of cacao powder have blown in all directions to mix with the dust collected over a fortnight. A cold saucer of tea, barely touched. An empty plate with a few scattered crumbs – remnants of a sandwich or a more indulgent pastry roll.

The feature of the room should be the majestic inglenook fireplace that spans the length of one entire wall. Its mantle beam is from one tree, thick and richly stained. Upon the hearth, on a row of flags, smoothed over a century by warmth-seeking toes, lives a row of old wine barrels, now full of logs, kindling and dried tangerine peels. A scent of cinnamon hangs about the stones although nothing is presently alight in the fireplace.

Elaborately framed maps and nautical charts, yards wide, adorn the walls, which rise up to a vaulted ceiling. Gold barometers and brass compasses are displayed in their retirement, proud and polished with a permanent fog as if they are still at sea. Glass-encased ropes in beautiful, twisted knots hang in one corner of the room, whilst a floor-to-ceiling shelf is home to a gaggle of instruments: taffrail logs, depth sounders, sextants, a Hadley quadrant. To a landlubber, they could be tools out of a medieval doctor's bag.

There are also endless shelves of books, leather-bound and gilded. There are taper candles held afloat in old spools, brass lanterns, and a monstrous brass-and-wooden chandelier raised and lowered by a pulley.

In corners of the room are bundles of folded easels. They lean into each other like lovers in dark corners at a masquerade.

Yet despite these quirky collections, the focal point of the room is a majestic mahogany table, upon which sit hundreds upon hundreds of metal tubes and pig's bladders filled with paint, alongside vials of dry pigments and wooden bowls of beeswax. Ochre, russet, ultramarine and crimson; rose madder, ecru, taupe and gold. Jars of oils – linseed, walnut, poppyseed – sit amongst bottles of mastic and dammar varnishes. Whilst the rest of the room has gathered cobwebs and dust bunnies, the contents of the table are pristine and immaculately kept. Every paintbrush is washed and dried as if newly fitted.

The lone easel erected next to the table is sturdy but simple. It is decorated with no elaborate carvings or gold fastenings. And yet given its location at the heart of the room, it possesses a gravitas. Brilliance is created here, it humbly communicates. No canvas can be seen throughout the room. Aside from the forgotten tray, no evidence of recent disturbance can be seen at all. It is as peaceful as a crypt.

Until the door is unlocked and two women enter. One, an elderly figure who stoops as she walks, gathers up the tray and pauses to take in the view. The other wanders around the room, her hands clasped in the small of her back. She ignores the layer of dust but straightens a map of the Norwegian Sea which has tilted towards the fingers of Iceland.

'You are certain we are to close the room?' asks the younger.

'Yes.' The elder is nearly back at the door. Although she is slow, the tray does not rattle. 'There will be no need to paint again for a few months, yet. You know what to do.'

The younger woman nods and in one swift motion, she casts a gentle muslin sheet over the table and all of its tubes, bottles and brushes.

They exit together and with the soft click of a key, Ponden-Hall's studio is put to rest once more.

7

Solomon Oak takes a room in South Kensington at the end of October. Through a friend of an old colleague, he has been given a flat on the first floor, simple but generous in size with tall, imposing windows that look out onto Exhibition Road. From the dining room, Oak watches the men unload his carriage – trunks of books, shirts and tweed jackets that have not been aired in an age. He has no plans to socialise in the city, yet he is practical enough to know that he will be invited to the odd luncheon, possibly even a dinner party if he is not cautious with the company he keeps.

'Your tea, sir,' says Missy and places his favourite cup and saucer on the table before him.

Missy has insisted on coming with Oak to help with an initial tidy of the flat – to unpack his clothes, dust the curtains, stock the tiny kitchen and place orders for meats and vegetables to be delivered throughout the week. She will then return to Oxford, a prospect that simultaneously terrifies and excites Oak: it has been years since he has cooked for himself or even made himself a cup of tea. The thought of being in his own company, however, without a shadow puttering after him to ensure that he is comfortable at all hours of the day, is a tempting relief. And he has never lost his appreciation for cold meats and bread.

Alice will remain in Oxford where she will be safe and sheltered from the pressures and demands of London. Oak has not thought of the details. But Missy will look after her, he is sure of this. He frets about his grown daughter even this morning despite the comfort that Missy will be back with her before the robin's autumn song this eve. He has not yet told Missy about his arrangement for Alice's governess position; it will be a marvellous surprise for them both, and he is certain that Missy will praise his pains to keep the girl safe.

There is a rapping at the door, which has been propped open with the umbrella stand, and before Oak or Missy can respond, the flushed face of Jonathan Hammond pops into the room.

'Anybody home?' he asks.

'Come in, Jonny. We were just sitting down to a cup of tea.'

Hammond takes in the tidy piles of Oak's belongings. Less than one would expect for a month's stay in the capital but more than a weekend's suitcase. Hammond is satisfied. 'Is your accommodation suitable, Professor?'

'Very much so.'

'I must say once again, I did not believe that you would come. I was shocked, in fact, when they told me.'

'I am still a bit stunned myself,' says Oak. He offers Hammond a plate of cheese straws and cashews. 'Emma would have wanted this.'

Hammond perches next to his old teacher on the window ledge and peers out onto the street.

'I won't bother you long – I just wanted to call in and see how you were getting on. And I thought I might ask... I thought perhaps you might have had a chance to consider... well, Sir Frederic is wondering—'

'I will deliver the lectures,' says Oak.

'You will?'

'I will.'

Hammond exhales and leans forward to grasp Oak's hand in his own. 'That is marvellous news, Professor, thank you. It means we can offer the press and the public a credible source of information, an official event of repute. It has been mayhem here – fake academics, lesser art historians than yourself, priests and scientists *preaching* in the square at all hours of the day! They all have their theories about Ponden-Hall.'

'Of course they do.'

'They will pay good money to hear you speak. Enough, I am sure, to fund any publication—'

Oak shakes his head and pats Hammond's hand as if appeasing a child. 'I am not concerned with money now, Jonny. I have returned to London to revisit Ponden-Hall's works and to celebrate them with whoever is willing to listen. I will do five lectures.'

'Five?'

'Yes. A series on DeLacey, the animal portraits, the orphan boy, the potter's daughter, and his sister Adelaide.'

It is a logical sequence but Hammond's frown betrays his disappointment.

'I think Sir Frederic was hoping for ten, a lecture for each painting. Or eight, at least.'

'I will do five. The series shall be titled, *The True Immortality of Ponden-Hall: His Life and Loves in Wax and Oil*.'

'The "*true* immortality"?' Hammond reddens. 'Now, Professor, there is no need to poke the bear.'

Oak bites into a straw and shrugs. 'It is the most accurate name for the series.'

'Well, anyway, we can discuss the particulars later. Sir Frederic told me this morning that the funding for your research has just been approved. And you shall have access to the paintings and archives of both the Gallery and the Academy after hours as you requested.'

Oak nods. 'Access to the paintings is most important. And I shall borrow a room at the library for some reading, I think, but aside from that, I have brought everything I need with me right here.'

'Well then.'

For a moment, as they sip their tea and watch the bustle of Exhibition Road below, both men are infused with an optimism which neither will voice into being – a silent hope, thinner than the wings of a dragonfly and infinitely more fragile, that perhaps they will find the painter. Perhaps, even, he will be grateful to be found.

'Isn't it wonderful to think that just under forty years ago, in front of these very windows, the kraken tentacle was carried in a glass dome to the Great Exhibition,' says Oak. 'Imagine it, Jonny: the trove of extraordinary artefacts from Ponden-Hall and DeLacey's expeditions – crimson diamonds, bronze leopards, the vertebrae of giant fossilised reptiles – but their greatest acquisition and favourite amongst the public: the kraken tentacle.' He traces the road with his little finger. 'Up this very street. It was displayed on a modest table between Rimmel's perfume fountain and a barometer run by leeches. I saw it with my own two eyes. I was a young man then at the start of my career.'

'It must have been a sight.'

'Oh, it wasn't. A beautiful octopus, yes, but nothing more. Nothing peculiar.'

Hammond eyes his stubborn professor, who returns the reproach with a wink.

'But what *was* extraordinary was the buzz that accompanied it. Wonderfully electric. You could feel the thrill and mystery with each glance cast over a shoulder. DeLacey had been dead for twenty years then; Ponden-Hall was in hiding. It was only after the Exhibition that people started wondering if he was dead himself. And brewing in everyone's mind, leaping off everyone's lips was the nosy hope: "Is Ponden-Hall amongst us?" Oh, I scoffed at the time. Of course he would not be there, risking being sighted so he could see his prized kraken leg admired and gawked at by the masses. But I have wondered since then. Perhaps even the great Ponden-Hall needed affirmation – needed to see the world's reaction to his marvel. Perhaps he was there all along and we simply did not see him.'

8

The pantaloons are a wonder. Alice is convinced that they are the best invention since the wheel. She moves this way and that, swishes the airy ballooned cotton between her thighs, stretches the ruched cuffs above her ankles. How freeing and comfortable they are! Hands on hips, Alice stares down at her legs in admiration as she sways back and forth, wiggles her knees. She now owns two pairs from Nichol's as well as a linen shirtwaist – no frills, no lace – and still, she has notes to spare. The balance she had offered to return to Lou, of course, but was met with a hasty pat on the hand and a nod to put them away.

Lou. Who is this woman who folds her hair away under a top hat? Who drives a hansom at her leisure around Oxford and beyond and serves as a stableman for the gentry? Peter's reservations linger in Alice's mind, but as always, she believes he is overthinking. Lou is a woman of intrigue, yes, certainly like no other woman that Alice has ever encountered, but she is not dangerous.

At nine in the evening in the mouth of a crisp, autumnal bite, Alice rubs her arms, focuses on her pantaloons and tries her best not to study her surroundings. She nearly did not come. At the bottom of her road, she had stopped and almost turned right round to be subsumed back into her usual Monday evening routine of reading and sneaking a biscuit or two from the larder. The job is not promising, for what does Alice know about deliveries and keeping inventories? And Jericho, she knows not at all – and the more she sees of it, the more she is inspired to skip back to the fire and bolt the door, rather than wait for the spooks of October to best her nerves.

Yet still, Alice waits.

Lou has piqued her curiosity. Alice has thought of little since meeting the coachwoman. She has ruminated on how Lou has achieved her station, on what paths she has roved that have led her here. Indeed in Alice's honest moments, she wonders if she herself can lead such a life of roaming and sovereignty. And so Alice waits for Lou to return, purely with the selfish intention to learn more about her.

In truth, she is in one of the most isolated corners of Jericho: dark, yes, but very much safe from passers-by, never mind cruel spooks. They have parked Lou's hansom at a gap in the wall that separates the few houses and smattering of industrial sites from the riverbank. The bank is muddy after the day's rain. Alice tries to stand on a bed of fallen leaves to spare her boots but she sinks anyway in her nervous rocking.

Lou has gone down to the river. For twenty, perhaps thirty minutes, Alice has waited in the cold. She dares not call out. When she is certain that Lou will not return – that the coachwoman has fallen into the river or has been assaulted by a team of thieves – voices emerge from the bank. In the pale glow of Alice's lone candle lamp, Lou and another figure materialise.

'We have a problem,' says Lou, brushing past her to the carriage. She continues talking over her shoulder. 'We haven't used this offloading point since the storm. Several branches have fallen and are blocking the path. An entire tree has come down further along. The parcels are quite large this evening; we'll need to clear the path before we bring them up. And Georgie mustn't linger here much longer so our work must be swift.'

'Bring the parcels up?' asks Alice. 'Where are they?'

'On me canal boat.' Georgie's voice is deep and rich like a cello. He is a burly man dressed all in grey – breeches that hold up sturdy trousers and knee-high rubber boots fit for shrimpers or clam diggers. Even in the darkness, Alice can see that his clothes are old and worn; they lack the crispness that her own coat and collar betray.

'Alice and I will clear the path if you unload the crates,' says Lou.

'Done.' Georgie is swallowed up by the darkness before Alice can enquire more.

'Here,' says Lou, thrusting a pair of gloves into Alice's hands. 'We must be quick.'

Alice is ready to put them on – how frigid the air is – but when she sees that Lou wears none, she pockets them and follows Lou in haste.

The path is completely blocked by an unruly pile of branches. An easy task, Alice muses, to clear the way and move them, until she attempts to lift one. The offshoots and nests of leaves paw at her face as she bends to grasp the base; they leave scratches on her nose and twigs and debris in her hair. Never mind the obstacle of picking up the branch; its heftiness is deceptive – an elephant in a cloud. Alice will never again take for granted the ease and grace with which a branch luffs against the sky. How does such density appear so weightless, so delicate?

Next to her, Lou glides from the path to a clearing as if delivering bouquets of posies. Alice watches every move, hoping to magpie any trick that brings ease. Lou hoists the heaviest bulk of each branch onto a shoulder – often the gnarled and sinewy ends that have snapped away – and drags them through the bed of leaves to the new pile. She is careful and measured with her movements, and whilst she is slow, she is the picture of grace.

Alice will not have it. She is determined to hold her own, and is certain that the more branches she transports, the easier it will become. But on the contrary, her hair only becomes more tangled in the offshoots with the branches pinioned awkwardly against her body. In the soft moonlight, she can see the zigzagged gouges in the mud, uneven hacks where she has dragged the fallen limbs alongside her own clumsy feet. She ignores the straight row of smooth, light footprints next to hers on the path.

The joke extends, for throughout it all, Lou works in a coachman's livery, head ensconced in fine silk hat and all. Despite Alice's new garments from Nichol's, Lou is more polished than her, for there are also the top boots, and the buttons of the frock coat are plated to match the mountings of the hansom. Why Lou has remained in livery to conduct such menial labour is baffling to Alice. And she still cannot decipher Lou's age, for Lou's small and sprite-like face in the moonlight and diminutive stature betray more youth than woman.

'Bend at the knees.'

'I beg your pardon?'

'If you bend your knees and leverage the branch onto your shoulder like this… when you stand, the weight will be borne with much less effort.'

It is a simple morsel of advice, one that should be obvious for someone who has studied physics. The problem is that studying is all Alice has ever done; every splinter lodged into the heels of her soft palms reminds her of this.

'Ah,' says Alice. 'Yes. Yes, I did consider that manoeuvre. I think I have worked it out, though — it has to do with the angle of the branch, you see, and how I hold it against my body.'

'Very well,' says Lou.

Alice holds her head higher after this, and holds her breath with each heave so as not to betray the sheer exhaustion and discomfort she suffers.

Alice can tell by the turn of Lou's chin that she wishes to converse more. But the coachwoman holds her tongue. Alice, too, has a slew of questions but does not want to appear idle — or nosy — on her first night. For half an hour they work in silence, passing each other like ships.

Once the path is cleared, they descend to the dock. It is small, no wider than five feet, and as Alice lowers the lamp to examine her footing, she can see in the pale glow that the edges are rotting away. The last thing she wants to do is step onto the soggy platform.

'Come, Alice,' whispers Lou. ''Tis already late and Georgie must get home.'

In the open air and out from under the trees, the sliver of the moon casts a stingy light. Alice's eyes adjust slowly. At Lou's feet are seven large crates — great hefty ones reminiscent of her father's travel trunks, but cheap; she can see the splintered edges silhouetted in the light but still refuses to put on Lou's gloves.

'We are to bring these up the bank?' she asks.

'And into the carriage.'

'Right. Of course.'

Alice bends to pick up the first parcel. It is heavier than it looks and the weight is unevenly distributed, for the right side causes her to buckle. She bends this time at the knees, feels her pantaloons tighten around her hams as she bounces a couple of squats in preparation. She is able to lift it but she is off balance and the slippery slats cause her to falter. The crate crashes with a thud, sending a shudder through the dock which confirms its rickety foundations. Alice is amazed that it has not fallen straight through.

'All in control,' Alice announces to the dark. 'I was just testing the balance. The leverage. Quite good, quite good.'

In the end, she drags the chest the rest of the way down the slimy mooring and up the bank. Lou and Georgie follow with a crate between them – and pass Alice, in fact, on the final ascent with apologetic comments on how they cannot break the momentum. Twenty minutes later, they stand panting before Lou's hansom, with great heaving breaths like white smoke under the moonlight. From a deep pocket, Georgie pulls out a flask. He only half-raises it to Alice, assuming that she will politely decline.

'Actually, I would love a sip,' says Alice. 'Thank you.'

'So what brings you to work with us this evening, Miss Oak?' Georgie asks. 'Lou says your father is a professor. This isn't the labour for daughters of scholars.'

The damson vodka burns Alice's throat but she harnesses a cough. She is uncertain of the motive behind this question; is it in jest or sincerity? 'And why not?' she returns. 'All honest work is good work. So my father has always told us.'

'Your father knows of your employment then?' asks Lou.

Here, she casts her eyes to the carriage wheels. 'Not exactly.'

'I figured as much from your conduct in Oxford.'

'You need the job for something,' says Georgie.

'Well…' she says measuredly. She sees no harm in telling these strangers. In fact, perhaps saying it out loud will make it more real. 'I would like to visit Europe. And my family's finances, whilst suitable to keep us well, would not extend to such a trip.'

'A Grand Tour,' says Lou. 'How traditional.'

'*You?*' asks Georgie. 'A Grand Tour?'

Alice prickles at his candidness. 'Yes, me. Women have travelled to Europe before. I plan to go at the start of summer. There is a series of lectures I would like to attend in Paris.'

'Will you go alone?' asks Lou.

'That is my intention, yes.'

'Well. I suppose travelling to Europe on your own don't require too much baggage. Pack light, hey?' Georgie's eyes twinkle as he sips his vodka.

The twitch of Lou's upper lip is hardly perceptible. 'I think it is a winning idea. An impressive ambition, Alice. Such tours have fallen out of fashion in this century and I do think the young have suffered from it – a lack of real culture. It is one matter to study the arts, but to see them in person is really quite extraordinary.'

'You are an art enthusiast then,' says Alice. She is surprised but pleased – feels, for the first time this evening, a glimmer of enthusiasm, that perhaps she could offer something interesting to say. 'Do you favour a time period?'

'The Renaissance masters. How they painted those great domes and frescoes and pillars in the time they did them... the minute details on every cherub's curl, even on a ceiling three hundred feet high. One can only stand meekly and stare in awe.'

'You have been to the continent then?'

'Oh, yes. A few times.'

Alice has been brought up knowing it is grossly impolite to stare, but stare is what she does at this bewildering woman before her. 'How... I do not mean to be rude, but I never would have thought that—'

'A coach driver would have the means to travel? On the contrary, Alice, we are a wily breed. The menial employment I have taken on ships, in taverns, on coaches to see myself through... well, the first glimpse of every new city is worth it tenfold. And all honest work, mind you. I pride myself on that.' Lou hesitates before venturing, 'Surely your father's recent work on the Ponden-Hall revival could send you to Europe twenty times over. To India and the Orient, even.'

At this, Alice is regrounded. Her father is an important man, a famous man in this saga, and even this sliver of a secret life that Alice has pursued for herself cannot be separated from the great Solomon Oak. More than anything, Alice is uncomfortable at Lou's presumptions.

'I would be very surprised if he makes any money at all with his new involvement,' she says. 'He is not doing it for the money.'

Lou straightens her hat and shivers. The air is crisp now that they have stood in one place for too long and the perspiration from their labour is cool upon their skin. 'Understood. Come, we must go. We should deliver what we can before midnight.'

'A pleasure to meet you, Miss Oak,' says Georgie. And tipping his cap to Lou, 'A pleasure as always. Again in a fortnight.'

'Indeed. Thank you, Georgie. I hope your son's cough improves.'

Once situated in the hansom, Lou grips the reins, yet stays her command to whip them forward. They sit side by side, an oddly intimate setting for a pair of strangers who are about to extend their company in the deepening hours of night. Alice is bruised and battered, her trousers and boots sullied as if she has crawled through a pigsty. The questions she has for Lou roil within her but in this state of physical prostration, she can only huddle into her coat and be still, waiting for the icy winds to lash at her cheeks as they gallop onward.

'And your preferred time period, then?' Lou's voice is calm, unhurried.

'I beg your pardon?' asks Alice.

'Your preferred period of art. I told you I favoured the Renaissance masters. We did not discuss your own.'

Alice grows pink. 'Well... I am actually an admirer of the French Impressionists.' She is grateful for the numbing cold, for without it, her neck and cheeks might radiate through her scarf like a stove. 'Monet's bathers, Renoir's boats... the bold way they contrast oranges and blues. Oh, my father would scoff if he knew how I truly felt! The countless times we have discussed the "loose and lazy" splotches of colour over breakfast. I believe he deeply dislikes them. When in fact, I actually love them. How extraordinary to extrapolate a woman's hat or a skiff paddle based on one purposeful stroke. In the real world, we see masses of colour and light and our brains connect the dots to complete the forms. Why should painting not mimic this experience?'

Upon realising that she has raised her voice, Alice bites her lip and sinks further into the sprung seat.

Lou only laughs. 'And why would your father scoff?'

'Oh, he thinks it is all a bit of nonsense. He is more of a traditionalist, you see. He, like you, reveres the Renaissance geniuses. Of course, I appreciate the magnificence of that period as well, but I do not believe that these French painters are destitute of talent. They are trying to achieve something different. I find it exciting. There is a lecture series by Eugène Dumont that I would like to attend in the summer. He is an expert on the Impressionists.' And then, fearful that she has spoken too boldly, 'I mean… of course I am not as educated or well-travelled as you or my father, so perhaps 'tis only a matter of time before I, too, will feel that they are lacking.'

'No, no,' says Lou, and her top hat shakes in the moonlight. 'Tastes can develop, certainly, but at any given time, one's opinion on art is always valid. 'Tis the point of art to stir us whether we have studied paintings for fifty years or are looking upon our first painting. Be confident in your tastes, Alice. But do be open to the notion that they are wilful and unpredictable and will almost certainly change.'

And with this conviction, Lou whips the horse forward. For the rest of the evening until Alice is delivered to her front door on Mansfield Road, they discuss the innovation and untidy processes of the French Impressionists – the experiences they stimulate and how sometimes, the fibrous, textured, bold brushstrokes depicting a crab are more interesting and beautiful than the smooth, perfect shell of the real thing.

9

With the last of the visitors escorted out, Charles Dawson takes pains to drag a desk from the curator's office to the largest room in the Academy. Here, he plonks it down before Ponden-Hall's three masterpieces.

'Are you comfortable? A cup of tea?' asks Mr Dawson.

'This should be fine,' says Oak. He follows the keeper and loosens the scarf about his neck. When he sees the paintings, his entire being lifts. He moves forward as if to embrace them like old friends. The walls of the Academy, along with its hundreds of other paintings, fall away, and he is alone with these works of art. If he could, he would sit with them for ever.

Mr Dawson coughs. 'It is an honour to have you visiting us again, Mr Oak,' he says. 'I have much work to be getting on with so I shall retreat to my office. If there is anything you need, just knock. Anything at all.'

'I am much obliged to you, Charles. This should be just fine.'

Mr Dawson's footfalls echo in the high, empty chamber.

Oak stands before the portrait of Hugh DeLacey. He remembers his first viewing, just days after it appeared on the doorstep of the Academy in 1831. Since then, it has been a constant in his life, each viewing building upon every stroke, gash, wax globule in his memory. Even after Emma's death, it had been a source of comfort and familiarity. He can close his eyes and still envision every nudge and prod of paint.

He does this now, eyes closed as if in prayer. *Hugh DeLacey behind a desk. His hands rest calmly on a map and a single rose upon the rich mahogany wood. He is surrounded by trinkets and instruments from his travels: compasses, cigars, jars of cinnamon sticks, an astrolabe; they sit atop shelves or hang against the wall behind him. To his left is a hefty stack of letters, worn and faded from being read on a loop whilst away at sea. Crisp paper and full inkwells perch next to them so that DeLacey may respond to whomever he misses − likely several different women.*

The painting materialises, solid canvas and gesso, as Oak opens his eyes. It is real, as solid as human bone and more immortal. He can reach out and stroke it if he wishes. But he refrains as he always does. He will study the painting anew.

Before he can launch into a fresh examination, he is interrupted by a soft sigh. Oak turns to find a woman standing in the middle of the gallery in a dress of powder-blue muslin with lace-capped sleeves. Her collar is tall and boned, and her overskirt is swagged to show off the ruffled underskirt beneath: an expensive ensemble. Her hair is pinned to tumble down over one shoulder, long and puffed and in disarray − a mythological goddess stepping out of Botticelli's *La Primavera.*

'Grace Dodd,' says the woman with a subtle curtsy. 'I apologise for interrupting. Mr Oak, is it?'

'It is,' says Oak.

'Mr Dawson has told me about your… work tonight. I am a sitter here for the art students.'

Oak knows the reputation of sitters, their histories and their status in the world. He has never given them much thought − he is far more interested in the finished product of the paintings they inspire.

'I am a great admirer of Mr Ponden-Hall's *Woman in a Sunhat,*' Grace continues. 'It is my favourite painting in the entire Academy. I was hoping that I might sit with you to learn something of it; I know nothing about the artist, you see, aside from the tales I heard as a child. One does grow out of ghost stories.'

Oak unfurls a roll of paper on the desk and readies a pen. 'You are very welcome to stay, Miss Dodd, though I will not be admiring Miss Ponden-Hall this evening. My focus tonight is on Mr DeLacey.'

'Of course. To prepare for your lecture.'

Oak is surprised at her knowledge of this. It has been some time since strangers were interested in his work. Once more, he is relieved to be there after hours when he is less at risk of falling victim to the hounding of the clergy or bribery from the dogged scientific societies.

Oak wonders if he should have brought the cluster of biographies or his folder of articles. These writings, like the paintings, are woven throughout the memories of Oak's life like a tapestry. Perhaps revisiting them altogether will yield something new.

'Mr Oak,' persists Grace, 'the map on DeLacey's desk. What is it of?'

'The map? 'Tis difficult to discern – as you can see, it is obscured by DeLacey's fingers and the rose.' Oak reapproaches the painting and leans in. 'It will be one of their routes, no doubt. Perhaps the Barents Sea outside of Russia, as that was where they encountered the kraken.'

'Russia that size?'

'I do not think it is drawn to scale, my dear. It serves as a symbol more than anything else – a map to represent his explorer's heart. They did this with portraits at the time. Tokens and objects to capture a man's life interests. The map, here you see, alongside the rose, and the central placement of both, are meant to illustrate DeLacey's greatest loves: exploring and, many argue, Ponden-Hall himself.'

Grace's smile is conciliatory. 'Of course, you know his works better than I do. I just thought, from here, they might be a group of islands. Do not the Sandwich Islands arc across the ocean in that way with the largest island at the bottom?'

Oak frowns and examines the map. It is a frightfully small detail in the whole of the portrait. DeLacey's hands cover most of the flattened scroll. The map itself has not been painted with great care – flat strokes, thin navigational lines for seafaring eyes. Indeed, the lack of precision compared to the richness and vibrancy of the hands and rose does suggest that its location is a secondary element.

And yet. Now that Oak scrutinises the map closer, peeking between the fingers, are those not islands? From under his thumb, is that a standalone piece of earth or does it attach to a wider body of land below the wrist? Oak has not considered the location on the map since he first professionally examined the painting thirty years ago, and even back then, it was widely accepted that the map was one symbol of many in the portrait. He steps back with earnestness and takes in the painting as a whole. Yes, the map's features are sparse and general – more a caricature of a map than the real thing. If it were significant, Ponden-Hall would have made this clear. Oak is certain of it. Even so, he feels rattled, caught unawares by the simplest observation. A pebble of frustration is felt in his stomach and he is, for just one moment, gripped by doubt.

'I am certain that the map is a symbol in and of itself, Miss Dodd, and that its location is secondary. And as far as I am aware, Ponden-Hall and DeLacey never ventured as far as the Sandwich Islands.' Oak studies the young woman before him. He is bemused but is kind when he says, 'I am, however, deeply impressed with your geographical knowledge. It is an interesting idea, anyway. It wouldn't hurt to look into it, I suppose, as I revisit all of the paintings.'

Grace fingers the string of pearls around her neck in meek pride. 'I was once a pupil of a rather impressive history don. He adored his maps.'

Oak considers the necessary class and wealth which would enable such tutelage of a female student; this young woman before him with her questionable attire and status of Academy sitter does not betray a privileged upbringing, yet he pursues the thought no further. He will judge art and no more.

Grace's studentship under the history don is no lie, and she is surprised to find that the thought of him is still painful. Her knowledge of the Sandwich Islands, though, and its riddle in DeLacey's portrait come not from him. She has upheld her end of the bargain with the mysterious author of the letter; she can now pocket the pouch of coins without guilt.

It is late and she has done what she has come to do. She should thank the art historian and glide away, allow him to carry on with what is sure to be a long and exhausting evening. But Grace is surprised to find herself captivated by this old man: the passion that infuses his speech; the fortitude to discover something new; the tender way he looks upon these paintings. There is a story here, and for the first time in a long while, Grace Dodd finds herself intrigued. Another thought also crosses her mind: might a connection, *any* connection, however peripheral, with the famous Solomon Oak aid in her applications to study the history of art? He is a luminary in the field, and here he ruminates before her very eyes. What harm would it do, a further morsel of conversation?

'I beg your pardon, Mr Oak,' Grace interrupts him once more. 'I know you have much to do this evening, but I have always wondered something about Timothy Ponden-Hall and seeing that you are the expert on his work, I believe I would deeply regret it if I did not ask you whilst you are here before me.'

Oak is startled to find that she is still in the room, so immersed is he in his notes and long, breathless studies of the painting.

'Of course,' he says. 'I will answer if I can.'

'I understand that Timothy Ponden-Hall's paintings are steeped in rumour and fear as much as they are in talent and mastery. The new portrait of the pig has revived a sort of mania amongst the public. Why, one can hardly walk down an alley without hearing tongues wagging about the artist's unorthodox tampering with death. But despite these whispers, Mr Oak, I have yet to gather precisely what everyone is afraid of. What do they believe Ponden-Hall has done, Mr Oak? There are so many variants of the rumours that I hardly know where the truth lies.'

'Ha! My dear, if only more people were concerned about the truth.' Oak straightens and cleans his spectacles with his shirt cuff. He is impressed with this woman. How refreshing to see someone question and challenge the rumours so easily lapped up by the masses. 'Your question can merit a complicated answer or a very simple one. The simple, singular truth you should know about the Ponden-Hall paintings is that there is nothing suspicious or sinister about them. It was well known that Timothy was fascinated by death – obsessed by it, even, after experiencing the death of his parents at an early age. They died in an unexpected carriage accident, you see. And as an explorer, he would have encountered cultures who revered the dead and believed in immortality: the Mexicans, who buried their dead with possessions to accompany them in the afterlife; the Greeks, whose art on vases depicted scenes of lamentations to immortalise the deceased.'

'All fascinating,' marvels Grace.

'Quite. And so when Hugh DeLacey died after the shipwreck – his greatest friend, fellow seaman, alleged lover – Timothy painted him. I should think it is a logical elucidation: inspired by the Greeks and the wider world in their handling of death, Timothy believed that immortality lay in the continued remembrance of the deceased by the living. What better way to immortalise his best friend – and all beloved and dear to him – than through art?'

'That does not sound so sinister,' says Grace. ''Tis rather a sweet idea.'

'Indeed. Which is why it is an unbearable offence that this master of portraiture will be remembered not for his genius but for the twaddle that surrounds his work.'

Grace cannot help but smile. The disgust on Oak's face is plain. 'The twaddle, I presume, is the more complicated answer to my question. I should like to hear it, Mr Oak. Not to believe, I promise you, but to be entertained by it all. What do the public believe?'

A small deviation from the night's work will do no harm, thinks Oak. He is bewildered by her enthusiasm and equally tickled. For one moment, he is cast back to a scene in the nursery of their London home; Emma is not more than three or four years old, for Alice is asleep in the wicker cradle. Emma had laid out etchings of Filippo Lippi's unfinished fresco scenes in the Spoleto Cathedral, dragged down from Oak's desk with a blind hand. *She points to the figures and wants to know about them*, the nanny had explained, apologetic and fearful that Oak might be cross. But he was not. How curious that such a young child was interested in these Renaissance frescoes. When she saw that he was awed rather than angry, the nanny had advised, *You must strike when the iron is hot, sir. If a child shows interest in something, there is no better time to start teaching them.* Oak had lived by this advice with both of his children and the fruits had been abundant. Never did he have to cajole Emma into learning about Dutch Realism or bribe Alice to learn her letters; he simply followed their lead and was an eager teacher when they were ready.

Grace is not, of course, a child, and Oak is cognisant of her familiarity with at least the three Ponden-Halls before them. But her interest is refreshing and Oak is always eager to teach the untainted history of Ponden-Hall's body of work to a willing ear.

'You will do well to keep this in front of you,' says Oak, handing Grace a rumpled sheet of paper from his briefcase. It is a list of Ponden-Hall's paintings with their dates and locations of origin.

No. 1 *Hugh DeLacey*, 1831, The Royal Academy of Arts

No. 2 *John Mortimer – Butler*, 1831, The Royal Academy of Arts

No. 3 *Prince – A Spaniel*, 1832, The National Gallery

No. 4 *Gentle Polyphemus – A Piebald*, 1835, The National Gallery

No. 5 *The Three-toed Woodpecker*, 1836, The National Gallery

No. 6 *Harry – An Orphan Boy*, 1837, The Royal Academy of Arts

No. 7 *Anne – The Potter's Daughter*, 1837, The Royal Academy of Arts

No. 8 *Bluebell – A Dairy Cow*, 1837, The National Gallery

No. 9 *Peacocks*, 1839, The National Gallery

No. 10 *Woman in a Sunhat*, 1840, The Royal Academy of Arts

At the bottom of the page, penned in fresh ink, is: No. 11 *Archibald – Kunekune Pig*, 1890, The National Gallery.

'To understand the rumours, Miss Dodd, it is necessary to understand not only their peculiar revelations to the world but the goings-on around them.'

'Of course.'

Oak rubs his hands and begins to pace before his audience of one, the habits of lecturing quite sleepy but always there in his muscles and joints. 'Timothy Ponden-Hall and Hugh DeLacey were already famed explorers by the time they were twenty-three. They had been apprenticed on several expeditions in their late teenage years and had earned early reputations for their boldness, bravery and sometimes recklessness. They brought home the most enthralling treasures: pearls the size of skulls, double-edged swords from the East, stone masks too heavy to be lifted by one man. They were in the prime of life, revelling in the world's mysteries abroad and being celebrated – pursued in business, love and lust – when home in England.

'In 1831, on their way home from an expedition, their ship was swallowed by a treacherous storm on the coast of Cornwall. Only the bones of the ship washed up on shore along with the very broken bodies of Timothy and Hugh. It was a miracle that they survived at all, for the rest of the crew did not. They were admitted to the Cornwall Infirmary on the evening of the wreck, and the last hospital records show that both men had stabilised by midnight. In the early hours of the following morning, however, both men had disappeared. No nurses at the hospital witnessed any strange movement, and the guards were not disturbed by any carriage or horseman. The men had simply vanished.

'A couple weeks later, Hugh DeLacey's body would appear, as if by magic, at a morgue in south London with a note requesting that he be buried at sea.'

'How tragic,' breathes Grace. 'To survive the shipwreck only to die so soon after.'

'Mm. And shortly after Hugh's body surfaced, a portrait of him appeared on the doorstep of the Academy – the first painting by Timothy Ponden-Hall.'

It has been a long while since Oak recounted these events out loud. As much as he despises the rumours that surround them, the stories themselves of the wreck and how the first paintings appeared are thrilling to tell, especially to a riveted audience. He is reminded of the lively debates he used to have with his own children over these tales. With Grace, here and now, the evening has taken an enjoyable turn.

'At first, the public was merely surprised and baffled,' he continues. 'Timothy had always been a patron and supporter of art, but nobody knew of his exquisite talent as a painter himself. The portrait was lauded by all. Here the gossip began to stir, for it was strange that Timothy delivered the portrait and remained in hiding. *He is mourning*, everyone said. Of course, the portrait solidified the scandalous hearsay that the men were lovers. But the real prattle began a week after DeLacey's body appeared. The keeper of the morgue announced to the public that DeLacey's body had not decayed. Seven days after death, and the body was in perfect condition; DeLacey looked as if he was having a nap. And he remained this way until he was buried at sea.'

''Tis eerie, Mr Oak, you must admit. 'Tis most unnatural.'

Oak holds up a hand and concedes, 'If it was true, yes, it would be most unnatural. I never saw the body myself, of course – I was a child.'

'But others did.'

'Yes, they claimed to. But Hugh DeLacey's wish was honoured and he was given a sea burial, so we were quite conveniently unable to confirm the state of his body later on.

'Now then. How did links between DeLacey's body and Ponden-Hall's painting transpire? An article at the time recalled a letter sent by Timothy to Sir Henry Ellis, Principal of the British Museum, just months before the shipwreck. Timothy wrote that they were on their way home and that they brought with them their greatest discovery yet, kept snugly in a vial in his breast pocket. People thought they had found the elixir of life.

'You asked, Miss Dodd, what the public believed – what they still believe.' Oak's chuckle is tired as he rubs his face. 'Some people think that in his grief over Hugh's death, Timothy drank the elixir and in some macabre way, attained the ability to preserve the dead. Others believe he mixed the elixir into his wax and oil, which has immortalised the souls of his sitters and their physical bodies too, preserved in the state in which he painted them.'

'Immortality of the soul and physical preservation,' states Grace.

'That's right.'

'Mr Wilde's series in *Lippincott's* over the summer will not have helped matters then.'

'Certainly not!' Oak's laugh is deep and bitter. 'That fantasy tale could not have come at a worse time. You see, a great many of the public – the most superstitious of them – believe that Timothy struck a deal with the devil himself: an eternal life with those most beloved to him, preserved in paintings, but owned for ever by the fires in hell.' Oak massages his temples. 'I cannot speak these fantasies out loud without scoffing. I cannot suffer them, Miss Dodd. How can anyone believe such drivel? And in doing so, divert focus from the prodigious art before us?'

'They are fanciful claims, to be certain,' agrees Grace. 'And what of the other bodies?' she asks, scanning the list of portraits. 'Were they preserved as DeLacey's was?'

'Ah. Well, John Mortimer, Hugh DeLacey's butler, died later that year. He was an old man and had been completely devoted to Hugh since Hugh was a boy. Mortimer's obituary was anonymously submitted to a London paper and confirmed that he had been laid to rest in a private graveyard near his home. Two days later, his portrait appeared on the doorstep of the Academy just as DeLacey's had done, with Ponden-Hall's signature vivid in the bottom right corner. You can imagine the pandemonium that followed. Mad searches for the body ensued across the country. The problem was that Mortimer had no family of his own as he had devoted his entire life to serving DeLacey, so nobody knew where the body was buried. There was no one to ask.'

'They never found him?'

'Never. So it was impossible to verify if his body decayed in its natural order. Of course, many took this as confirmation itself – that the death was anonymously reported and the body buried in a secret grave. Ponden-Hall was behind this, they claimed; DeLacey's loyal butler and friend had been immortalised to keep him company in another life.' Oak shrugs. 'And the others have similar stories: the body of Harry, the orphan boy, was burnt in a terrible fire; Adelaide Ponden-Hall was buried in the family's private cemetery but this location is unknown to the public; and the body of Anne, the potter's daughter, was devastatingly one of many that was snatched by grave robbers in the Staffordshire area shortly after her burial.'

'This is almost inconceivable, Mr Oak,' says Grace. 'What poor fortune… all those bodies, disappearing or tragically destroyed.'

'You can understand, then, how easy it is for rumours to fester and grow. The rest of the portraits are of animals. You can imagine the number of letters claiming ownership of dead woodpeckers and dairy cows that did not deteriorate – all balderdash, all for fame! And throughout it all, these exquisite paintings are not given the prestigious and admirable status they deserve in the world of art. This is what pains me most, Miss Dodd. They call them death portraits; they call him the elixir artist who tampers with souls. But Ponden-Hall's truest genius lies in how he has rendered his sitters in beeswax, oil and pigments; they are as alive and evocative and bold as you or me in this space between memory and materiality. Timothy Ponden-Hall has immortalised them absolutely, but not in the occult way that everyone hopes. They are in our stories, perched upon our lips.'

Grace is silent as the art historian's fervent words cloud her mind, seep into the very powders and creams and essences upon her skin. She has always marvelled at Ponden-Hall's paintings, has always – in her past shadowed and deceitful livelihood – found light and uncomplicated probity in *Woman in a Sunhat*. It is with art, Grace reflects, that she can be most honest, can show herself bare and wanting to these portraits who will not pass judgement. Oak has complicated this space now. Grace has never considered the paintings' purposes beyond an aesthetic pleasure or the brandishing of wealth and power. She has never thought about the complexity between artist and sitter – or indeed the artist's wishes for how his audience sees his work and how they feel about it. She can bare herself to these portraits, but all this time, she has never thought to probe beyond the wax and oil and question what secrets the paintings bare themselves.

Grace shakes her head as if to push these complexities aside, for Oak is speaking again, is pacing again, and she is spellbound by these uncharted layers of intentions and love, manipulated on the canvas by the great Ponden-Hall. She must not miss a single detail of Solomon Oak's discourse, must not miss a single word.

DOWAGER OFFERS SMALL FORTUNE TO DRINK PONDEN-HALL'S ELIXIR

The Morning Post, January 1832

Dowager Countess Laura Graham of Hertfordshire has celebrated her seventieth birthday with a formal offer to Timothy Ponden-Hall for a drop of his famous elixir. The dowager, known in society for throwing extravagant Christmas balls, hosted a lavish party at the weekend which ended in an unorthodox toast: a sum of no less than ten thousand pounds to the explorer-painter for a 'tipple' from the vial.

Dowager Countess Graham said of her offer: 'It is not lost on me what a blessing it is to have reached this age. The world moves on and I should like to plod along with it for as long as possible. If Timothy Ponden-Hall is indeed in possession of the elixir of life, I implore him to share it. Ten thousand pounds is my offer, and I dare say I would be open to discussion if he asked for more. Just a drop. I would put it into a gin sling or an apple toddy and toast my late husband.'

When asked if she truly believed in the elixir's existence, she responded: 'And what if it doesn't exist? Timothy Ponden-Hall could give me a drop of water or a drop of poison if he wished and take my money. The outcome would be a reunion with my dear Thomas sooner rather than later. I have nothing to lose. And how marvellous if it *does* exist. I should have a jolly old time throwing parties for ever more. And I would get another dog.'

The dowager's offer follows the appearance of Ponden-Hall's portrait of John Mortimer, Hugh DeLacey's butler, last month on the eighth of December. The location of Mortimer's body is unknown, so rumours of his physical preservation cannot be confirmed. Like Hugh DeLacey's before him, Mortimer's portrait appeared at the

Royal Academy just days after his alleged death was anonymously reported to the papers. Gossip of immortality and Faustian pacts runs rampant in London due to the mysterious nature of both portraits and Ponden-Hall's prolonged absence from society.

Ponden-Hall has not responded to Dowager Countess Graham's offer and his whereabouts are still unknown.

10

Alice awakes as stiff and heavy as a stale seed loaf. Her face lies buried in sumptuous goose down, her body splayed as if she has fallen from a tower window and landed flat upon her four-poster. Her arms – are those her arms? Those great things of lead sewn onto her scapulae with tendrils of fire? They burn and throb as she rolls onto her back.

She is dying. This is what it must feel like – a chorus of muscle spasms up and down her sciatic, her lower lumbar, triggering the pulsating pain of every fibre in her biceps, triceps, whatever the muscle is that sheathes her shoulder blade; she can no longer remember the squawking of her natural science teachers. How to repair torn muscle, how to mend disfigured tendon: these are topics that should have been taught. They would have been far more useful.

Alice should not joke about death, she knows this, but the throbbing of these phantom body parts is excruciating. She is also starving. But most importantly, *her pantaloons*. She had left them in a muddied, crusted heap at the base of the bathtub late last night. It was all she could do to scrunch them off her legs and melt into the tub with relief. She must retrieve them now before Missy spots them and beholds the state of them.

Slowly, gingerly, she slides off the bed and slips into her dressing gown. She glimpses herself in the corridor mirror: hair askew as a rat's nest, limbs soft and pale as ever – which is infuriating, because how can so much pain emanate from her being and show not an inkling of evidence? When she leans in closer, she sees traces of scratches along the side of her face. A tiny nick on her chin. And ah – is that a bruise forming on her left cheekbone? Alice smiles in spite of herself. Well, at least that is something, some small vestige of her pains. *But Missy.* Her expression sours as she realises that she will need to explain these souvenirs if they do develop as the day progresses. What can one do? She will sort out the pantaloons first and worry about a story later.

Upon entering the bathroom, Alice is perturbed to find that the pantaloons are nowhere in sight. The tub is shining and the floor has been swept. Curse Missy's efficiency.

Alice hobbles down the stairs, leaning on the banister the whole length of the way. Breakfast is waiting on the kitchen table but Missy is nowhere to be seen.

With her body barricaded in cushions, Alice drains the pitcher of water and tangerine peels, devours the platter of cold meats and malt bread. And as she satiates her tremendous appetite, she sees them. There through the window, hanging on the stone porch, pristine, having been washed and scrubbed with lye, are Alice's pantaloons. The iron, she now notices, is warming on the stove. And before she can conjure up a believable tale – a slip near the river, a muddy horse ride with the neighbour – Missy bursts through the side door, arms full of produce and chrysanthemums and a parcel of buns from the market.

'At last you are up!' she chides, disappearing into the pantry. 'There are more sardines in that bowl there if you are still hungry. And more bread here.'

Alice freezes, unsure of how to broach the subject.

Missy bustles about the kitchen, arranging the chrysanthemums in her favourite glass vase.

'I know your father isn't fussed about having flowers in the house, but with just the two of us, I thought a bit of autumn cheer would do the room well.'

'Missy—'

'What do you fancy for lunch today? I can take out the salted beef if you are not bored of it.'

'Yes, that would be fine. But Missy?'

The daily looks up from plumping the flowers.

'I apologise about the trousers,' says Alice. 'I took a fall. I was going to clean them myself.'

Missy's eyebrow twitches as she takes a pan out for a stew. 'Perhaps a drier walk next time.'

'Yes. Certainly. Port Meadow was a mess of damp and mud.'

'I must say, though, that I am pleased to see you doing some form of exercise.'

Alice exhales. She will be able to evade the tricky matter this time. Really, Missy is absorbed with a great amount of work; of course she does not have time to dwell on Alice's exploits. 'Yes, exercise,' she says breezily. 'So important. Restorative to be out and about.' Alice stands, bread roll in hand, ready to escape to the study before she can be questioned further.

'The amount of mud on them...' The lilt of Missy's voice is just as casual. 'Odd when it did not rain until late yesterday evening.'

Missy's back is to her, so Alice cannot read her face. She chops the potatoes in a comforting rhythm. Alice had intended to tell Missy about her post with Lou but she had wanted to wait to ensure at least some success of the endeavour – a few weeks at least. Perhaps, though, this is the apt moment.

'Well. The city is in a bog, you know? Only Oxford would be a mud bath before a shower.' Alice takes a sip of water. 'And actually... well, a bit of exciting news...'

Missy's ears perk up and the chopping ceases. She turns around to face Alice and leans back on her hands upon the countertop. 'Well?'

'Well, Missy, the truth of it is, I... In a felicitous turn of circumstance, I have...' There is no point in dilly-dallying. Alice crosses her arms. 'I have taken a job. In the evenings with a coachman helping with deliveries – a coachwoman, actually, although I believed her to be a boy at first. She wears a coachman's livery. She seems an honest and dependable sort. It is just three days a week and only through spring. Now before you scold me and warn me about the company of strangers, I must insist on holding this position. I am trying to save some money, you see. For what, I would rather not share at this moment, but know that I have thought a great deal about my prospects after finishing my studies and there is something that I would like to pursue. And so... you cannot move my mind on this, Missy. It is very much set.'

Across the kitchen, Missy is still. She continues to lean on her hands and seems not to draw breath. Not a single muscle in her face twitches; her mouth is set in a neutral line. She is so still, in fact, that Alice wonders if she has heard her at all.

Alice swallows, chin protruding. 'Well? What have you to say?'

'Deliveries, you say?'

'Yes. No further afield than Oxford.'

'I see. And in the evenings…?'

Alice's resolve begins to wobble. 'Yes. I do recognise now that this might sound questionable, but the coachwoman's reasons for this are her own. I have… felt utterly safe in her company and we are doing no harm. We are merely delivering parcels.'

'What exactly are you delivering?'

'I… do not quite know, to be honest.'

Missy considers this determined young woman before her. Alice can feel her scrutiny, and she cannot tell whether the expression on Missy's face betrays pride or worry or a curious mixture of both.

At last, the faintest smile cracks Missy's reserve. 'Good for you, Alice.'

Alice is cautious, untrusting of such approval.

'It sounds rather thrilling,' says Missy.

Alice clasps her hands. 'It does, doesn't it! Why, last night under the glow of the moon, we went down to the river and collected a group of crates all the way from London. Her courier seemed a lovely man, too.'

Missy wipes her hands on her apron. 'I think the fewer details I know about the position the better, my dear. But of course… I *should* tell your father.'

'Oh no, Missy, you mustn't!' Alice scurries to her side and loops her arm in confidence. 'I will tell him, I promise. Just give me these next few weeks to ease into the position. Let me earn a bit of coin at least before he spoils it all. He is sure to disapprove, you know he will.'

Missy eyes the girl sideways. 'You are desirous to pursue something after your studies, you say? You have a plan, Alice?'

'I do. And I am certain that you would applaud it.'

'And this coachwoman… she is trustworthy?'

'I believe so, yes. She wears the finest of things, is very well spoken. Her master lives in a great house north of Oxford.'

'Well.' Missy squeezes Alice's arm. 'If you feel safe with her, I will trust your judgement, Alice. And perhaps I am putting too much trust in a stranger, but I would like to believe that a fellow woman would take care of a young charge like you.'

'She will, Missy. She has been.'

'Even so, you must be careful. You have never been very careful. And you will tell your father eventually?'

'I will! I promise you I will – just not yet. Perhaps when he is in better spirits upon his return from London.'

On her tiptoes and gripping the daily's arm, Alice teeters in anticipation. Her plea is silent and hopeful, and in this moment, Alice would offer this woman the world.

'Oh, very well,' accedes Missy. Her sigh is dramatic but she struggles to conceal upturned lips as Alice bounces beside her.

'Thank you, thank you, Missy,' Alice croons. 'And thank you for washing my pantaloons.' She squeezes Missy once more and nuzzles her face into her arm. Alice grabs another bread roll and means to steal into the study before she can be questioned more. Missy is a considerate and compassionate creature but she is not stupid; better to quit her whilst ahead. And with a cheeky turn in the doorway, 'They really are the most comfortable things, Missy, these pantaloons. I shall buy you a pair.'

Missy does not break rhythm; the knife is newly taken up and meets with the vegetables once more; she does not make eye contact; she bites a smile and slices through the final potato. The iron will be hot enough now.

For two weeks, Alice aids Lou in her night-time deliveries on Mondays, Wednesdays and Fridays. After each evening, two certainties solidify in Alice's mind: firstly, these deliveries – these strange parcels that rattle or slosh or weigh her down – are irrefutably suspicious. They must be questionable in content or supplier, for why else would they have to be delivered under the cloak of night? When Alice asked about this, Lou shrugged.

'It is just easier to not draw attention sometimes,' she explained. 'Some of my charges have been so invisible to society for so long that it is more comfortable for them to plod on in the shadows.'

Alice does not fully understand this. Lou's manner around work and how she speaks of people – these invisible charges of hers – does not suggest a character of moral degradation. But the coachwoman remains tight-lipped about their identities and what, precisely, she is bringing them. As an honest young woman from a respectable family, Alice cannot with a clear conscience continue supporting such work if it is indeed suspicious.

And yet. Despite the potentially dubious work, Lou has revealed herself to be kind, hard-working and curious about everything; in short, she is the most interesting – and confusing – person Alice has ever met.

On this day, a Friday, they will deviate from their typical evening portage and meet in the morning for a special errand – one that Alice would never consider if her father was not holed up in London preparing for his lectures. She knows nothing about the errand, only that it is a personal job for a friend rather than a client. Though the risk of being seen by someone of importance in Oxford society is unsettling, the prospect of spending the morning with Lou cheers Alice. She bounds down the porch steps with a lightness of foot and two caramels in her coat pocket.

Lou awaits her at the train station, pristine in her livery. It is the first time Alice has seen her in the daylight since their initial meeting. Her top hat is pushed back from her forehead, which reveals dark, unruly strands of hair that try to escape around her temples. It is clear that she has worked long days in the sun over the summer, for even now in crisp autumn, there is a healthy afterglow of rosy olive about her skin.

'We shall leave the hansom here for the moment,' Lou says, taking Alice's arm. 'Our first stop is just around the corner. Have you ever had a chocolate lime?'

'I do not think so.'

'Well, you are in for a treat. They are my absolute favourite. I can never have just one.'

'Are we off to a confectionery shop, then?'

'We are. The best one in town.' Lou smiles at Alice's bewilderment. 'Our visit is twofold this morning, Alice. A dear friend of mine has fallen ill and she deserves a bit of cheer. A little bundle from this shop will be just the ticket. And another friend's son has recently been employed here. I just want to pop in to see how he is getting on.'

'I see,' says Alice. 'Will he be expecting you, then?'

'Oh, no. I have never met the boy, in fact. His mother was a trader in London and has only recently come to Oxford. Only by chance did I run into her at the market last week and she told me about her son taking a job here. The shop has a new owner, you see, so I do not know him. And my friend's son… well. I would just like to see how he is settling in. My friend would be horrified if she knew I was checking up on him. Let us see.'

The confectionery shop is indeed a few yards around the corner, and as she feels so often whilst spending time with Lou, Alice is surprised and embarrassed not to have known about the sweet shop until now. As the crow flies, it must be fifteen minutes from Mansfield Road where she has lived her entire life. She and Emma loved cakes and puddings as all children do, but never expected to buy them. Their father, never one for excess or sugary indulgences, had treated them as adults in this pocket of life too; if sweets were offered at a dinner party, of course they could enjoy them. In the humdrum of everyday living, sweets were simply non-existent.

The shop is bright and colourful with tall sash windows so that any passers-by can see the brimming shelves of sweet jars, chocolate slabs, candied nuts and marshmallows. The shelves seem to go on and on. A back door hints that more delicacies lie within. In the centre of it all are grand golden scales, prepped to measure spoiling amounts of treats to be boxed, ribboned and swept home with a skip and a hop.

As they enter the shop, a thin, beady-eyed man chivvies out a pair of loitering children. He is counting or double-counting his ledger, for he nods at each entry as he progresses down the page and silently mouths sums.

'Good morning,' says Lou. 'Are you the new owner of this fine shop?'

The man squints at Lou and then leans out of the door and picks at his teeth, staring down a group of school children who count pennies and eye the lemon drops in the window. 'That's right. Wouldn't say new though. Old Brown hasn't run this shop for nigh on two years. Retired and buggered off to Switzerland or somewhere.'

Lou frowns. 'Well. It has been far too long since I have had an excuse to buy chocolates, then. Good for Mr Brown. He was a charming man with the most delectable sweets.'

'*That* hasn't changed,' says the shopkeeper. He snaps his fingers at the boy behind the counter and signals for him to dust the jars near the door. 'We've the best sweets in town. Try 'em and see for yourself. You have to pay, mind you. No handouts here – no *samples*, as Brown used to do. He had no head for business.'

'I see.'

Alice can tell that Lou is weighing something in her mind. The boy is of middling height with dark brown, freckled skin – a stark contrast to his bright yellow uniform. He also has a limp, Alice realises, and struggles to position himself in the narrow space between the door and the gap in the counter; he has to balance in a most unnatural way to polish the jars. Alice sees Lou studying him sideways before glancing at her pocket watch.

'Very well,' she says. 'We have quite a large order if you don't mind and are a bit pressed for time.'

'Oy!' the man calls to the boy. 'An order here.' He returns to his ledger and shows not the slightest interest in Lou or Alice.

Lou smiles at the boy. He has icing sugar dusted across his cheeks and on the edge of the fringe that hangs low over his eyes, thick and black. 'Please could we have a scoop each of pear drops, clove rocks and bonbons?'

'Certainly.' The boy nods and shuffles as best he can to each appropriate jar.

'And then perhaps two logs of marzipan – sliced, if you please. And a slab of fudge.'

'Of course.'

Alice has never seen such an abundance of sweets. Her mouth waters as she reads the label of each jar.

It is a large order as Lou foretold, but the boy's limp accentuates his effort and the order feels particularly excessive. Lou watches the shopkeeper sit idly for several minutes engrossed in his records. A small queue has begun to form.

The boy begins to slice the marzipan. He brushes his hair away from his face with his arm and fumbles with the knife.

'Perhaps a bit of assistance for him—' Lou proposes to the shopkeeper, but he ignores her.

'And the fudge?' the boy asks. 'Which flavour would you like?'

Lou appeals to the shopkeeper once more. 'Good sir, I do mean to spoil my friend, so perhaps a second pair of hands to help with the order?' When he still does not respond, Lou scans the trays of silky, perfectly poured fudge. 'Very well. Mary is fond of fudge. One of each will do.'

Alice gawks at Lou.

The boy pauses his slicing. Behind Lou, a woman raises her eyebrows and her daughter puffs her cheeks. There are at least thirty trays of fudge displayed and a few more cooling behind the counter.

At last, the shopkeeper is on his feet, a wide and wolfish grin plastered across his face.

'I… misheard you earlier. Let us make sure we don't forget anything, shall we?' he asks.

A resounding *ding!* echoes through the shop with each entry at the cash register – so many that it sounds like a song, and indeed the shopkeeper seems to dance with each punch as the total climbs and climbs.

'Will that be everything, sir?' he asks with a sycophantic bow.

'Almost,' says Lou.

The man sweats with glee.

'You do the fudge, boy!' he orders. 'And I'll take care of the rest. Don't skimp with the corner pieces. Extra ribbon is under the candied almonds. Wrap them double; the boxes will be heavy. And don't forget to weigh each one twice! Write them here – to the tenth.'

The boy bustles about as quickly as possible to compensate for his limp. His eyes bulge at the tray stacks of fudge, overwhelmed, and he begins with the closest batch and makes his way down the line – buttermilk, clotted cream, walnut…

'What else can I get you?' the shopkeeper asks.

Lou does not hesitate. 'A box of the brandy balls, please.'

Alice taps her finger on her chin. 'What about those? Coconut ice.'

'Those toffees – a few more of the ones with butterscotch,' says Lou.

'And the jelly beans,' pipes up Alice. 'And those oval mints.'

'Lemon drops too, if you please.' Lou rattles on.

The shopkeeper dashes around the shelves as the orders tumble out of their mouths, and Lou seems satisfied with his engagement.

'What's the occasion?' he sweetly asks.

'A get-well present,' says Lou. 'A beautiful friend of mine is unwell.'

'Mm, yes, yes,' he responds, but he does not really hear her. He licks his lips with each new *ding* of the order. A proper queue has formed out of the door now, and few passers-by linger at the windows to watch this spectacle – this obscene, indulgent order piled higher and higher on the counters, with boxes of peanut brittle, jellies and Turkish delight teetering like building blocks.

The boy continues to carve out generous chunks of fudge and places them on the scale with care.

'And that will be all, I think,' says Lou. 'Thank you.'

Only their foreheads can be seen above the towers of fudge now. The collection of treats is enormous – all prettily boxed – and plainly expensive, and the shopkeeper is greedy with delight. As he tells Lou the total, she does not flinch and rifles through her wallet to count out a stash of crisp notes.

The fall happens in slow motion for Alice.

After wrapping the final box of fudge – butterscotch and rum – in his haste to add it to the pile, the boy in his lopsidedness has misjudged his positioning in the cramped corner, now barricaded with parcels of sweets. His elbow knocks the closest stack, which triggers a violent jerk in the other direction, and in his attempt to save the boxes from toppling to the floor, the boy falls – it seems, in these seconds of molasses movements, that he floats between the ribboned boxes as if in jelly – tripping over himself and sending several bundles of fudge flying into the jars and glass domes on the counter.

A collective breath is drawn from everyone present. The twitch of the shopkeeper's eye, the dropped jaw of the little girl behind – these are details that Alice will remember later when she replays the scene in her mind as they ride away.

By instinct, she and Lou kneel to help gather the boxes. They have not split open; even the bows are intact and bounce back into place. The sweets inside will be as perfect and delectable as when they were carved out of their trays.

'Not to worry,' says Lou softly to the boy, who remains on the floor. 'It will make no difference to their taste.'

But her reassurances are unheard, for the shopkeeper is shouting at the boy with all his might, his face crimson and taut, his teeth bared as if about to spring for the jugular. The crowd thins. Those who linger turn away out of discomfort and pity for the boy. Globs of spittle burst from the shopkeeper's mouth as he continues to berate the boy for his clumsiness, his limp, the ineptitude of his race.

It is this final, offensive affront that springs Lou back to her feet.

Alice has never seen such revulsion on her face. There is fire in her eyes and her lips press to form a tight line. At first, Alice believes that she will in turn shout at the shopkeeper. There is a fierce restraint about her; her fists ball at her sides and although she is petite, a wild and vast fury is plain upon her face.

'I have never...' she begins. Then, looking the shopkeeper square in the eye, 'Do you treat all of your staff like stray dogs?'

The shopkeeper looks from the boy, to Lou, to the small audience on the street.

'I beg your pardon,' he says.

'I have changed my mind,' says Lou with an icy calmness. 'I would like to cancel my order.'

'You would like to... surely not, sir,' says the shopkeeper. He bustles about, straightening boxes and fetching new ones. 'I can cut fresh slabs of fudge. The middle pieces are best anyway. And look here, I can do an extra box of bonbons, what do you say?'

Lou shakes her head. 'No thank you. We shall be leaving.'

'The caramel toffees! A free box. The most coveted treat these days.'

Lou has snapped closed her purse and takes Alice's arm to lead her out.

'Two boxes then! Or a bag of chocolate limes—'

'No thank you.'

'You see!' shouts the man, turning back to the boy, who cowers behind the platter of marshmallows. 'Do you see what your careless-ness has cost me, you opium filth! You belong in Limehouse with the rest of them and their drug dens. This will come out of your wages, it will!'

'I should think not,' interjects Lou. A stillness settles upon the shop and those who lean in to hear what she might say. 'We are not leaving for a few knocked-over boxes. We shall take our business elsewhere because I refuse to support an establishment run by a cruel and intemperate bully like yourself.'

And to the shop boy: 'I was impressed with your care and attention to detail, young man. There is a cobbler on George Street who is seeking an apprentice. I should think you would be most valuable to him. And you would certainly be appreciated for your talents – the cobbler is a top, respectful man. Tell him Lou sent you. Good day.'

In the hansom, Lou turns to Alice, her anger still simmering on her cheeks.

'I was quite serious about spoiling my friend. The next best confectionery shop is in Witney. Let us go there.'

'All the way to Witney?'

'Mary should not be left wanting just because a shopkeeper is an ignoramus.'

Alice admires her fire and her principles. She is also more terrified of her now than she ever was.

On their journeys, even short ones, they have become used to an immensurable flow of conversation – used to talking over one another, in fact. On this ride, they are silent. Alice casts sideways glances at Lou, whose lips have settled into a thin line. Her expression is less a scowl now, the anger subsiding as they ride west at a clip. Eventually, her spine softens and Lou appears altogether exhausted.

'I did think the chocolate limes looked less than satisfactory,' Alice ventures.

Lou's smile is empty and unconvincing.

'It looked like the peels were still on them.'

Lou snorts.

Alice faces Lou. 'I did feel sorry for the boy. It was good of you to think about… well, the tasks he was having the boy do with his poor leg—'

'Never mind,' Lou says. She closes her eyes for a moment and shakes her head. 'We must not let people like that disappoint us. 'Tis a shame. I had heard rumours about his… manner towards certain people. I am only sorry they turned out to be true. The boy's physical disposition is unfortunate, to be sure. But did you hear what he called him? Opium filth.'

'He was referring to the drug dens in London, was he not?'

'Yes – a repulsive offence in itself to assume all Chinese men are sailors of ill repute. But the boy is not even Chinese! He is of Malayan descent. As I mentioned earlier, his parents were traders in London for several years.'

Alice has heard of Malaya in her geography lessons. It is in the far east near Burma and the Philippine Islands. 'I would not have known that he was Malay,' she admits.

Upon sensing her discomfort, Lou softens. 'No,' she says, 'but you would not assume his race or splutter insolent insults either.' She sighs. 'It is not just here. You will see it on the continent too – this superiority over others. Often over skin that is a different tint from one's own.'

Alice crinkles her forehead. 'We spoke of this once, my geography tutor and I. I asked why those from the Caribbean tended to be servants – pages or nannies or beggars. He said their poor status had naught to do with their race but rather upheld the existence of a hierarchy. He said it is a social division rather than a colour division.'

'Naught to do with their race?' Lou's eyebrows rise to the underbrim of her hat. 'And in this hierarchy of his, did your tutor acknowledge the *race* of each social tier? He would find quite an obvious pattern, I should think.'

'He did not elaborate much.'

'No, I suppose it all makes sense to him.' When Alice does not respond, she continues, 'I do believe most of the English are now opposed to forced slavery – why, I have never met a single Englishman who supports what they did in the American south. However, entrapment in a line of work is not always enforced by chains. One does not always choose the family or status one is born into, and we would be wise to admit to ourselves that individuals more often than not end up in the same social tier as their parents. Your geography tutor is correct in that there is a hierarchy that is largely accepted as immovable. But it does not mean it is right, and it certainly does not ignore one's race. Why, if your skin was not white, Alice, despite coming from a respectable family – famous even, in academic circles – I think you would find it a great challenge to find employment. You would find more in common with the outcasts or "vagabonds" rather than the "citizens", as Mr Mayhew called the distinctions.'

Alice nods into her scarf and is grateful that Lou cannot see her thoughts – her past frustrations in failing to find a job that suited her pernickety needs; her exhaustion many an evening after a walk along the river when she entered the kitchen with claims of starvation.

'And…' continues Lou, 'add to this the challenge of being a woman. Well. Women have always faced a steeper mountain, but a white woman will have fewer stones in her path. We must help each other, that is all. And regardless of how we look.'

Of course Alice is aware of the trials she will face as a woman, but this concept of womanhood and support she has never pondered – has never even considered it. The students she met through her father as a child were typically male. She has often pined for Emma in the quiet moments – when she first wakes up, when she eats lunch at the table alone, when she successfully skips a stone and has no one to marvel with – largely because she is lonely, but also perhaps, now that Lou has cast a light upon it, because a sister, a fellow woman, might help her make sense of this world, which seems to reveal more barriers as she grows older.

'I have much to learn,' is all Alice can say.

'Well. Such cognisance is a start.'

Lou is more cheerful after this. Alice remembers then that she must disappoint her next week.

'I almost forgot to tell you,' she says, 'that I will not be able to help you on Monday evening. I will be in London for my father's first lecture. I'm sorry – I had been meaning to bring it up but it kept escaping me.'

'How fascinating. And how wonderful that you will be there to support him. You must be proud.'

'I am.'

'How will you get there?'

She has not, of course, thought about such details yet.

'The train, I suppose,' Alice says.

'Would you like a ride?'

'All the way to London?'

Lou shrugs. 'I have some business to take care of there. Monday is just as good a day as any.'

The prospect of taking the train excites Alice, to be certain, but she has never made the journey without her father. Missy is due to escort her onto the train and an assistant will collect her at Paddington, but a long jaunt with Lou is most appealing, even if it means extending the journey by at least four hours.

'A ride would be lovely if it is truly no trouble,' she says.

'It would be a pleasure.'

'You should stay for the lecture.' Alice has not thought about such an invitation until this very moment, but upon consideration, she thinks that Lou in her worldliness and curiosity would be the ideal audience for Solomon Oak's return to academia. It is a risk to have her there, Alice knows this, but she would be a great comfort. 'You would be most welcome, but I'm afraid we would have to act as strangers. As you know, my father is not aware that I have taken this position with you. I think it would be best if he did not meet you – not yet, anyway.'

'Understood. I have a talent for blending into a room. Are you quite certain you want me there?'

'I insist. I believe you would enjoy the lecture – would probably appreciate it more than most. And I would be grateful for the company into the city.'

Lou scratches her head and never takes her eyes from the road. 'Thank you, Alice. I would like that very much indeed.'

11

On the eve before his first lecture, Solomon Oak sits amongst a city of books in the British Museum reading room. Grace has assisted him all afternoon, ferrying volumes between tables, scribing for him when his thoughts tumble out of his head too swiftly for his own fatigued hand. With her eagerness to help, her propensity for chasing relevant tangents and her unremitting slew of questions, Oak is reminded of Emma. Sometimes, when Oak must steer her back on course, reground her when she has vehemently disappeared down a rabbit hole, it is rather cruelly too familiar. For the most part, though, it is a comfort. Grace's sheer enthusiasm is invigorating and for that, Oak is grateful.

Now that she has left to clean the brushes and stretch new canvases at the Academy, Oak ruminates alone. The towers around him stack thirty, forty books high:

Histories of orphan asylums.

Recipes of poppy and nut oil compounds.

Logbooks of sailing vessels: arrivals, departures, curling lists of booty brought into British ports.

Biological records of woodpeckers and bovines of Scandinavia.

A family tree of pedigree spaniels dating back from the 1700s.

It is the logbook in front of him, however – one with records of all British expeditions across the Pacific Ocean over the past two hundred years – which claims Oak's full attention. This and a map. He flips his notebook open and unfolds a grainy etching of No. 1, *Hugh DeLacey*. His eyes dart from one to another to another: logbook to map to portrait.

It is curious indeed. Ever since Grace mentioned the possible link between the map and the Sandwich Islands, it has been playing on his mind.

It is true that Timothy Ponden-Hall and Hugh DeLacey never visited the Sandwich Islands. But Julien Ponden-Hall did with Captain Cook. Everyone knows this, of course – one of the more well-known links the family has to a famous explorer. What Oak has failed to consider in the past, however, is the date. There it is, 1778, next to a smudge of coffee or cigar ash:

Sandwich Islands, the crew of Captain Cook
31. J. PONDEN-HALL

Oak is more familiar with the Ponden-Hall family line than his own. This is no hyperbole, for the Oaks are not a proud line and no records date back before his own great-grandmother. Oak knows that Andrew Ponden-Hall, Timothy's father, was born in 1779. An idea begins to germinate in Oak's mind.

The more Oak studies the etching, the more he is convinced that the map sitting beneath DeLacey's fingertips is, in fact, of the Sandwich Islands.

Until now, Oak has believed – has said in his lectures – that the map in this portrait is a representative token. Of course when the painting first appeared, the map was scrutinised under a magnifying glass, but scholars compared it to closer land masses, more famil-iar seas linked to Ponden-Hall and DeLacey's excursions. It was no dramatic realisation to find that it was not modelled on a real place. It symbolised a knowledge and love of exploration, nothing more. Yet now, reconsidering this family link to the islands, Oak cannot dismiss this detail. It is certainly not coincidence. His curiosity blooms. He will thank Grace for this clue next time he sees her. The threads in his mind traverse one another in loose, frantic patterns in need of the ribbon to pierce them all, make sense of the tangle and pull them taut.

12

Lecture One: Hugh DeLacey

No. 1 *Hugh DeLacey*, 1831, The Royal Academy of Arts

On the night of Oak's first lecture, the National Gallery bombinates like a hive. The Central Hall heaves, for it is crammed with chairs from its triple-arched entrance to the velvet rope on the far side of the room which demarcates a narrow stage. It is a work of art itself, the hall, with a ceiling of golden leaves that arcs upwards like the upside-down bows of a ship before flourishing into an elevated glass rooftop. If the laws of physics rendered it possible, the Gallery staff would stack chairs upon chairs like sugar cubes, rows balancing on rows to allow for a larger audience. Lecture tickets sold out in half an hour. Already, shoulders rub shoulders as bodies squeeze between seats like jellied eels, and latecomers jostle each other in doorways. The air is thick with bergamot and lemon oil and sweat.

It has been a long while since Alice visited the Gallery. Luca Giordano's paintings still adorn these walls – *modelli* for the ceiling frescoes in a Florence palace, Alice remembers. Only ten of twelve here, as the other two are in private collections. *Allegory of Justice. Homage to Velázquez. Perseus turning Phineas and his Followers to Stone.* Her favourite.

But only Alice admires the oil studies this evening. The rest of the room only has eyes for the painting behind the rope. Necks crane. Bodies lean in like flies to light. Even the odd pair of opera glasses is spotted amidst the crowd, ivory and brass bobbing in a sea of hats and collars.

The legacy of Timothy Ponden-Hall transcends age, gender and class. An older generation in their cravats and spectacles have come to hear the great Solomon Oak speak once more. They have grown up with Ponden-Hall's paintings and story; they were there when the paintings first appeared as treasures left by a phantom hand. They have seen Oak rise to prominence, revered and praised for his scholarship. They have also seen him fall, for his blindness to the dark rumours, for his disinterest in the elixir and immortality. Tonight, they whisper amongst themselves, perhaps they will see him redeemed, a saviour to satiate their hunger for answers that have been buried over years and years. Like layers of beeswax and linseed oil.

Students of Alice's age are also in the audience, intrigued by this story that is more legend than history, hoping in their heart of hearts to be swept away by tales of adventure that enthralled them as children.

And between these two extremes of old and young are the doctors, priests, occultists. The scientists and clergymen. Writers of penny presses and editors of more respectable publications. Every single one a sleuth in his own right with a pen poised to flourish. In the front row, immediately before the podium, sits Edward Bromage. He leans forward onto his knees, round and full as a chocolate Bismarck, and although Alice can only see the back of his head, she is certain that Bromage is squinting, scrutinising the painting. When he does turn in his seat, he stares at everyone around him like a wolf amongst sheep who is too plump to make any rash movement.

Alice points him out to Lou and whispers about his intrusion into their home.

'Remarkable,' she says. 'What a glower he has. Do you suppose he practises in a mirror?'

Alice laughs.

'An intimidating specimen,' Lou continues. 'I believe a lesser man would have given him anything he asked for.'

'Yes, well, my father is very stubborn.'

'Principled.'

'Yes. Principled.'

Sometimes, Lou seems to understand her father better than she does, just from their discussions, from Alice's snippets of details about their relationship as they cart boxes to doorsteps in the thick of night. As they wait for the lecture to begin, the hall abuzz with chatter and speculation, Alice feels comforted to have Lou by her side. She sits next to her in her waistcoat and starched collar, the top hat off on this rare occasion, which allows her short but wild hair to frame her face. The boyishness is less prominent in this way; her features are so small, so dainty. Alice wonders why Lou feels less secure like this, de-costumed and beautifully plain. She is grateful indeed to have her company on this evening, and she must restrain herself from leaning in to whisper gossip and observations into Lou's ear too frequently so they do not look too familiar with one another. Lou was in bright spirits for the duration of the journey; she had stayed up all night reading old articles and essays by Oak which she had found in Oxford's public library. She praised Oak's eloquence, his expertise on the process of painting and ability to write about it, and most of all, his integrity. Now, she sits next to Alice, cheeks flushed with anticipation. Alice is pink with pride.

Jonathan Hammond approaches the podium. Alice cannot help but smile when she sees her father's old student. He is more stooped than when she last saw him but his moustaches are just as elaborate as memory serves. Alice has known Jonathan Hammond all her life, for he was in his final year at the university when she was born. He was Oak's prodigious pupil – not only his student but also his greatest admirer. And he was there for Alice's birth, her mother's death just days later and, eventually, Emma's too – a quiet crutch, a steadfast brace for Oak when grief had swallowed him whole. They are more friends than professor and student now, although neither man would admit this, of course. But Alice knows what Jonathan Hammond has been over the years for their family, and for this, she is warmed to see him. She will embrace him after the lecture and only let go with reluctance.

'Ladies and gentlemen,' Hammond says as the din mellows to silence. 'I would like to commend you, first and foremost, for nabbing a ticket for the evening. You will know that tonight is the first of five lectures to be delivered by Professor Solomon Oak on Timothy Ponden-Hall's original ten paintings…'

He waffles on as he always does but Alice does not hear. Her father has sneaked into the room from the back door and rocks, hands in pleated pockets, in Hammond's shadow. She has not seen her father for three weeks – their longest time apart. After the lecture, they will go to the South Kensington flat together.

Alice is used to seeing Oak from the back of lecture theatres. Too clever to be entertained by a nanny, and too troublesome to remain at home with the daily, she and Emma were given drawing paper and charcoal and plonked down at the furthest row of desks during Oak's evening classes. She would draw shipwrecks and aeronauts falling out of balloons whilst Emma created paper doves. And although they sat behind rows of students, their father seemed to loom before them at the lectern like a giant, his voice raspy yet authoritative, his gestures impassioned and strong, though only ever with one hand, for the other always remained casually in his pocket.

This evening, Oak's hair, untamed as ever, riots about his head as if he is in a gale. His coat and breeches are too large, and his spectacles dawdle on his nose ready to slip off. The great Solomon Oak indeed.

Suddenly, Alice does not want to hear this new lecture. She would like to gather her father, fold him up and tuck him into her pocket to take him back to Oxford.

But the room pulses with applause and Oak clears his throat – or tries to. The coughing fit is unexpected. Hammond begins patting him on the back and points for the porters to fetch water. But there is no need, for a tall and shapely woman approaches the podium with a full glass, gloved hand on her bosom in elegant concern. Her dark hair gathers about her shoulders, though even its thick and bandolined layers do not hide the low-cut faille dress with its lustrous sheen and loose ribbon.

'Now *really*,' hisses a woman beside Alice to her husband, 'at an event like this? And those sleeves at this time of year?'

Oak consumes the water in grateful gulps. When he has settled, he dabs his mouth with a handkerchief and squeezes the woman's hand. 'Thank you, my dear. Lovely to see you again.'

There are murmurs and blushes throughout the audience and Alice's realisation is slow and resonating as a church bell. To see her *again*. The woman offers a dimpled smile to the room with an unnecessary curtsy, and the embarrassment for Oak that fills the hall acutely settles in Alice's stomach, on the tips of her ears, in the pads of her toes. She has never considered her father's private life. Perhaps he has hidden away in Oxford too long and has craved London after all.

'Miss Grace Dodd is a sitter at the Academy,' says Oak to the audience. 'We met briefly the other night when I was revisiting the painting. She was rather unexpected but welcome company and has been helping me with my research.'

There are sniggers throughout the crowd. A few women shake their heads whilst others look to the buttons and hooks of their boots. Everyone in the audience knows what an Academy sitter is code for.

If Oak senses the discomfort, he does not show it. He takes a deep breath and stands tall at the lectern. 'Pardon me. Nerves, I think. Thank you, Jonathan. Many of you will know that I was hesitant to deliver these lectures. It has been a very long time since I have addressed an audience and I am flattered to see you all here before me. You will also know that I was one of the few... perhaps the only one over the past decades who believed that Timothy Ponden-Hall was still alive. Yet I never dared to dream that there would be another painting. He is, you see, giving me – giving *all* of us – another chance to understand the narrative behind his work.

'I have titled this series of lectures *The True Immortality of Ponden-Hall: His Life and Loves in Wax and Oil*. My intention is to revisit each work with a willing audience and frame them in the course of Timothy's life, to postulate why he immortalised *these* sitters – through his paints and the eternity of art above all else.'

There is an uneasy ripple in the crowd. A flicker of dislike.

Oak clasps his hands together. 'Now. I have always been a creature of habit. Let us begin this way, then, as I always began my lectures at the university. This is a difficult exercise, as you are all familiar with the portrait, but I would like you to try and see the painting as if for the first time. View it with fresh eyes. Look upon it with new enthusiasm.'

It is indeed difficult for Alice to do this; the painting is as familiar to her as a miniature of her own family. But study it, she does.

Hugh DeLacey sits behind a desk, his hands resting calmly on a map and a single rose upon the rich mahogany wood. Fragments of her father's lectures return to Alice in hazy pieces; it is like reaching through cobwebs to draw out gossamer – loose, wispy things that once took solid shape. What had her father said about DeLacey's expression? What was the significance of his puffed silk shirt? DeLacey stares out of the frame, his chin turned ever so slightly as if he has just been called, as if he has been interrupted at his work. But he is not angry. On the contrary, the confident gaze, the barely parted lips, the dark hair that escapes his sea cap – longer and more unkempt than would have been fashionable at the time – all suggest a moment of peace, a welcome distraction from his letters and maritime planning to look upon… who? Is it a playful look he gives his painter? Alice does not know, but upon this renewed study of the piece and seeing this enthralled audience stare in wonder, it is clear for the first time how striking and burly Hugh DeLacey is, how handsome Timothy Ponden-Hall has depicted this man.

'It is a flattering portrait,' says Oak. 'You can see how even in looks, DeLacey and Ponden-Hall complemented each other well. They matched each other in brawn, in height, in boyishness, only Ponden-Hall's hair was pale and straight as arrows. They were two sides of the same coin.

'Now before we turn our attention to the composition of the piece, it is worth noting Ponden-Hall's technique. You will see it refined with each painting he creates.'

Oak begins to pace again, and the more he talks, the straighter he stands, the louder his voice booms throughout the chamber, the more animated his right hand becomes as his left hand rests snugly in his pocket. In a matter of minutes, Solomon Oak has shed years of his life, and Alice sees her father come alive. Oak shrugs off a shroud of sleepiness that has collected over the past decade, a bear waking from hibernation.

'The masters of the past learned their trade by taking apprenticeships with their elders,' explains Oak. 'They ground colours, boiled rabbit skin, stuffed pigs' bladders, learned to layer and experiment with pigments and bowls of oils. Artists today – they do not do this. They learn at academies and schools in large groups, so that much of their work looks the same: their brush techniques, how to prime a canvas, how to mix colours that are already ground to fine dust before entering the studio.

'But Ponden-Hall has not been taught in this way. You can tell by his use of colour: the hues of ultramarine and ochre unmatched by any of his contemporaries; the richness of his browns and greens, like peas in soil; the gloss of the original canvas – you can see it here in the corner, the pains with which he has covered it with boiled rabbit skin and gesso. In this way – how he prepares his canvas and his paints – he uses the old methods.

'Now.' Oak spins around and raises a finger. 'He deviates from the masters – his own touch of genius – with his use of beeswax. The Egyptians used beeswax in what they called an encaustic process. They would melt wax and pour pigments into it to create multi-coloured waxes before ever touching the canvas. They used the coloured wax as paint, their brushes stiffening with each stroke as the wax cooled upon the board.

'Ponden-Hall, however, does not mix pigments into the wax.' Oak raises his hand so it hovers over DeLacey's puffed sleeve. He traces its outline, his fingers a hair's breadth away from the rippling layers. 'After priming his canvas, Ponden-Hall sloshes beeswax on top, creating an uneven surface. He never smooths it out – do you see here? How the wrinkle of the sleeve is elevated compared to the cuff? He allows the wax to pool and drip to create a natural texture on the canvas. Only then, once the beeswax is poured and settled, does he add paint. He paints over the wax and then manipulates it – chisels it, pokes it, pulls it to draw out the forms within, all the while blending the oils and buffing the substances together. This is what brings his subjects off the canvas. They are textured, breathing works of art. Look at DeLacey's hair. Every strand meticulously coaxed and pulled out of the wax. It is a tactile process, a minute version of sculpting in addition to painting.'

Oak draws his hand away from the canvas. 'It is as if, in the wax, the figures have always been there. You can see, I hope, the skill and brilliance required to create such portraits. He depicts his sitters in living, breathing likeness, yet he has discovered and freed them from a mass of wax and oil as if they were there all along. 'Tis the work of genius.'

The hall is silent. Attentive.

It is like riding a bicycle, lecturing, Alice remembers her father telling them. You could avoid setting foot in a lecture hall for years, but put the right painting in front of you with an audience, and the pure desire to teach someone about it – to discuss the shared human experience of being moved by art – and lecturing becomes as natural as breathing. Alice has taken for granted her life filled with masterpieces and original Ponden-Halls; one does not notice or appreciate air.

'And now the painting itself,' continues Oak. 'Our eye is drawn to DeLacey himself in the first instance. But then we follow the lines of his arms to his desk, and we notice that he is surrounded by meaningful trinkets; it shows us what DeLacey valued and how Ponden-Hall viewed him. Take the rose and the map below his hands, for example. Scholars have used these symbols to support their strong belief that DeLacey and Ponden-Hall were lovers. The map on the desk' – here, a flicker of a pause – 'mainly obscured by his hands, represents their years of travelling and exploring together, whilst the rose, an obvious token of love, is intimately intertwined within his fingers. Despite the stack of supposed love letters in the corner of the desk, it is the map and the rose that DeLacey guards closely.'

Only Alice sees it, for only Alice knows Oak well enough: the tottering of a thought upon the old man's lips. She can see her father considering, the quick currents of his brain in contemplation.

'Curiously,' says Oak slowly, 'the map is one of the Sandwich Islands.'

There is a quieting of pens scratching paper as the writers in the hall look up. Even those new to the saga are aware that this is new information. The way Oak presents it. The way everyone in the room has leaned forward.

'Only recently have I confirmed this, with the help of Miss Dodd.' He nods to her. The audience prickles once more; some of the elderly shake their heads in open judgement. 'It has been widely accepted that the map is more symbolic than anything else and that the place it depicts is secondary.' He purses his lips and then brushes the thought away with his hand as if flicking a feather. 'It most likely *is* secondary. A place chosen as a mere symbol to represent his love of travel.

'Now then. If we follow the lines, it leads us in a circular upward swing around the space. At the edge of the desk: the vial – perhaps the rumoured elixir brought back from their latest adventure. Or perhaps it is only rose water—'

No one is fooled. Oak licks his lips and takes longer sips of his water; his left hand has come out of his pocket and he fidgets with the buttons on his waistcoat. This new information has rattled the great art historian, and whilst the audience continues to take notes, half of their minds are reaching back to history lessons and penny presses in search of the new connection. *When did Ponden-Hall and DeLacey venture to the Sandwich Islands? What business brought them there?*

Alice knows that her father will have asked himself these very questions. And perhaps he already knows more than he has chosen to share. If the information is so precious, why not keep it a secret until more could be revealed? She will be bold and ask her father all of these questions tonight when they are alone in the flat.

Oak's voice is all but gone by the time he finishes. His natural rasp is coated in dust that cannot be watered away no matter how much he drinks.

'I have been asked to deliver these lectures with the hope that a previously unseen piece of the puzzle would reveal itself,' he concludes. 'That a detail might hint of Ponden-Hall's intentions *and* perhaps his whereabouts. I make no bold claims tonight except this: I do believe that after all these years, Timothy Ponden-Hall wants to be found. The Kunekune pig gifted to us is no indiscriminate surprise. Like the three-toed woodpecker and the peacocks, this is a beast from abroad. There are no records of such pigs here in England; he would have brought it home – a favourite foreign creature, a new pet. It makes me wonder: for how long has Timothy Ponden-Hall been abroad over these past fifty years since his last portrait? To where has he ventured? Perhaps his long silence will fit tidily into the narrative after all, whatever that may be.'

Here, Oak pauses. He has promised Jonathan that he will focus purely on the painting tonight and not on his own judgements of the public's motivations and interests. No remonstrations; no scoldings.

But he cannot help himself.

He takes a deep breath. This is what he truly wants to say.

'I only hope that the right man finds the artist so that he is treated with the respect and dignity he deserves,' states Oak. 'If you wish to find him for any other reason, shame on you. Shame on you all—'

'*Thank you*, Professor Oak,' Hammond interjects. 'A round of applause for Professor Solomon Oak.'

The applause is bare and Hammond is grateful for the acoustics of the hall.

'Let us move on to questions, then. Yes, please, you there with the brooch.'

The first question is about Ponden-Hall's use of beeswax. The second about Hugh DeLacey's posture. A third on composition; a fourth on brushstroke. They are courtesies – the tapping of a shell before ripping it open for the pearl.

It is Bromage who breaks from the pleasantries.

'And what will you do if you find him?' he demands.

'He belongs in Reading Gaol!' someone shouts.

'That he does – for tampering with souls!'

'If you find him,' says Bromage, 'he owes us all an explanation. This melodrama over the past sixty years. We deserve to know the truth. Why has he kept himself in the shadows? What is he hiding?'

'He hides nothing,' says Oak. 'His paintings are laid bare for all to see.'

'He's made a deal with the devil, he has!' A piercing voice from the back of the room.

Hammond mops his brow as the room erupts. Men jump to their feet, throwing their voices across the room to condemn Ponden-Hall for his secrets. One woman scuttles onto her chair and wields her finger like a sceptre, demanding that the doling out of life and death belongs to God alone. They are impassioned and shrill, this cacophony of voices, and it is a wonder that the mouldings and glass panes above them do not come crashing down.

'Excuse me, if I may?' This voice is calmer than the others. Authoritative. It belongs to Nicholas White, an old colleague of Oak's from his travels on the continent. Only begrudgingly does the audience calm down. 'Solomon was asked to deliver a lecture on this marvellous painting of Hugh DeLacey. He has done just that. We need not ridicule him for his opinion on Ponden-Hall's character.'

He turns to his old colleague, clasps his hands together and offers a slight bow. 'Thank you, Solomon. Perhaps we can end the evening in peaceable agreement. I do not think it farfetched to claim that Timothy Ponden-Hall was afraid of death. He shared this publicly many times after that tragic accident. To lose both of his parents in one fell swoop – well. Could anyone blame him?'

'Precisely why he has found a way to cheat death,' says Bromage. 'He was *obsessed*—'

'Mr Bromage, please.' Nicholas holds up a wizened hand. 'Timothy Ponden-Hall was never shy about his ambitions to find the elixir of life. He had more motivation than most, given the loss that he and his sister suffered. Did he ever find it? Who knows. Does such a thing even exist? We may never know. But perhaps, Solomon, there *could* be more to the paintings than beeswax and oil. And what marvels they would be if this were true.'

'You see, Oak.' Bromage's sneer cuts across his face. 'A sensible man here. Surely you cannot be so arrogant as to dismiss *any* possibility of unnatural meddling.'

Oak's face is impassive. He stands before them all, one hand balled into a fist by his side, the other resting in his pocket. He is still and cool as a stone.

'So what will you do when you find him?' Bromage asks once more. 'Perhaps you begin to see that he has much to reckon with.'

Oak coughs and takes some water. His voice is soft and gruff when he finally speaks – an instrument unoiled for so many years. 'I truly do not know where Timothy Ponden-Hall is. I should think that when he is ready to be found, he will be. What will I do if I should be lucky enough to meet him in these crepuscular moments of his life? Why, I shall shake his hand and say thank you.'

13

The frenzy that ensues at the end of the lecture is reminiscent of a children's treasure hunt. There is a flurry of hurried whispers as the young cling to each other and bound out of the doors in search of a pint. The elderly stroke their chins and invite each other to discuss these mysteries over a brandy or a glass of port. London is abuzz with the names of Ponden-Hall and DeLacey once more.

Alice stands to make her way to her father, and loses sight of him behind a portly priest and then the feathered hat of a dowager.

'What did you think?' Alice asks Lou without turning to face her. 'Thank you again for coming—'

But when she casts a sidelong glance, Lou is not beside her. She scans the crowd but Lou is nowhere in sight. Alice is grateful for her discreet understanding but feels a twinge of regret for their secrecy; how she would love to speak to her about the lecture, to elaborate on her own favourite parts of the talk and share with her other ideas that Oak did not present this evening, ideas that only she has been privy to, growing up as Oak's daughter. She will have to wait until their next delivery.

Alice spots Oak once more and pushes towards him, but before she can breach the final space between them, her arm is seized by a strong, bullish grip.

'Miss Oak, a good evening to you.'

Alice is stunned. Up this close, pulled under his heaving chin-neck, Edward Bromage is even more broad and boar-like than remembered. He smells of sweat and musk and neroli – his shirt cuffs clearly doused rather than sprinkled with some variant of eau de cologne. His hand loosens on Alice's arm but does not release it. 'We did not have the pleasure of properly acquainting ourselves in Oxford,' says Bromage. 'It is a privilege to see you again. What a lecture tonight from your father, eh? He is the king of the hour. That makes you a princess in my book.'

Alice attempts a smile and tenses to pull away. 'It is nice to see you again, Mr Bromage.'

Bromage bends low so that his mouth is mere inches from Alice's nose. 'I shall not beat about the bush, Alice. As you well know, my proposal to your father was not well received. He is making a mistake. Whoever your father has decided to work with is the wrong choice. I can promise you—'

'He is only working with the Gallery, no one else. He simply wants—'

Bromage's eyes roll to the glass above. 'Yes, yes, he wants to find Ponden-Hall to understand the paintings, we have heard this count-less times and it never ceases to be a bore. *You* have more sense than your father. *You* can recognise a deal.'

His jabs on Alice's shoulder linger.

'Your father is still caught up in his grief. He cannot recognise what is right and what is foolish. If Ponden-Hall has discovered a way to immortalise his sitters, the world should know about it. Men of science should know about it and understand it, and the Royal Society would be the most respectable keepers of the secret. They do not seek to harm or punish Ponden-Hall as so many others do.'

He leans in even closer, his smile rapacious. Alice can see a piece of food lodged between two of Bromage's teeth – a dark leaf of broccoli or cabbage from supper. It reminds Alice of a black key between the yellowing ivories of a pianoforte.

The paper that Bromage slips into Alice's hand is moist.

'Write to me. As your father learns more, keep us informed. We can help. There is compensation for you as well, of course. A woman of your age must have interests of her own… new dresses, perhaps? Fashionable hats?'

Alice crinkles her nose. 'Those are hardly enticing—'

'Just think, Alice. Your father could go down in history as the most famous art historian – the man who found Ponden-Hall and shared his narrative with the world. What a legacy he would leave.'

'My father no longer has interest in legacies,' says Alice. It is the line she has heard repeated so often over the past decade.

Bromage laughs. His stomach convulses, bursting out of trousers that have been belted much too tightly.

'Every man wants to leave a legacy, Miss Oak.'

He releases her arm and Alice is left dizzy with his scent; she can feel the imprint of his plump fingers through her coat and is surprised to find herself sweating. She does not stop to think as she pockets the note in her sudden desperation to find a glass of water, to step outside just for a moment and be sobered by the cool night air.

Meanwhile, Solomon Oak retreats to a corner of the hall where Jonathan Hammond and Sir Frederic present a platter of biscuits and pop a bottle of champagne. Stragglers linger around the podium and the now bare easel, for *Hugh DeLacey* has been swept away by gloved hands and already makes its guarded journey back home to the Academy, but Oak takes no notice of them. He replays the lecture in his head as his friends toast each other and dab their moistened foreheads and necks, relieved that the evening has concluded.

Out of the corner of his eye, Oak sees a swathe of purple at the closest doorway. He takes the platter of biscuits from Hammond and hastens after her.

'Miss Dodd!' he calls. He is out of breath by the time he reaches her. 'Just to offer my thanks once more for coming to my rescue this evening. I should think I would have coughed up a lung if I had relied on the others to bring water. I hope you did not mind the attention.'

'Not at all.' Grace breaks off a piece of the proffered shortbread and pops it into her mouth, allowing it to dissolve on her tongue. Her chewing is slow and delicate. 'And you confirmed the Sandwich Islands.'

'Yes. And perhaps more. I have a proposition for you.'

'Oh?'

'It would be indelicate to discuss it here, now. But I need your services.'

'My services?'

'As a young woman.'

Any warmth towards the historian dissipates in an instant and Grace's mouth hardens into a thin line. 'Really. We do not know each other well, Mr Oak, but I can assure you that you have misread me if you think I have any history with the Great Square of Venus – or any brothel for that matter. Whilst I do not judge women for falling into that trade, my own imperfect past has nought to do with it. And if you think my dedication to a purer life was a fickle decision, you insult me.'

'No, no, my dear, you misunderstand. Not services of that sort. Will you allow me to explain? Come to the Museum Library Wednesday. I have a reading room on the first floor.'

But before she can answer, Hammond is by Oak's side holding his arm. He nods to Grace but avoids making eye contact, stiffens and turns to his friend. 'Professor Oak, erm, a word, if I may?'

They retreat into a corridor where Hammond ushers Oak behind a potted plant.

'I say this with the utmost respect, Professor, but what are you doing?'

'I was thanking Miss Dodd for her assistance this evening. Ah, my Alice!'

Alice ducks under the spreading branches of the plant, which slap at her face; she tiptoes to kiss her father on both cheeks.

'Well done, Father. You were splendid. You truly were.'

'I could not be happier to see you, my dear. The train journey was fine? All in order? Missy walked you all the way into the carriage, did she? She was under strict instruction. And Jonny's assistant met you at Paddington? I hope he was there waiting—'

'I am here, aren't I? Jonny, it is so lovely to see you again!' She hugs her father's old student and bats away the hanging branch that seems to have taken to her plait.

'Little Alice, my, how you've grown!' Hammond holds her at arm's distance to look her over. 'The spitting image of your mother. You have her round cheeks… and her inquisitive eyes… just gorgeous—'

'Steady on, Jonny.'

'What are we doing skulking in the corner like this?' Alice asks.

'Oh, Jonny is worried for nothing,' says Oak. 'Biscuit, darling?'

'I was just expressing my concern over your father's reputation… what with his involvement with Miss Dodd over there.'

Oak and Alice follow his condemning gaze to land on Grace, who is talking with grand, animated gestures to two young gentlemen who wear notably bright cravats and pointed starched collars. When she notices them eyeing her, she offers a wink and slides a caramel into her cheek.

Jonathan Hammond's own cheeks burn, and in a fluster, he manoeuvres his beloved professor and the sweet, innocent Alice, and turns their backs to the crowd so they are now facing the potted fiddle leaf.

'How do you know her, Father?' Alice frowns. 'She is a bit younger than your typical acquaintances.'

'As I said at the start of the lecture: she is a sitter at the Academy, nothing more. She has helped me comb through a few articles these past few days.'

Alice is distrustful as she always is with anyone new who enters their lives, but siphoning through articles seems harmless enough. And her father does not sound particularly effusive. Even so – and she does note the billowing layers of thin muslin that float around Grace's bodice, surely too thin for this time of year – Alice sees no reason for her father to need such assistance. He has her, his own daughter, after all.

'And now you are asking her for further help,' rebukes Hammond. 'Surely, you can find a more respectable assistant. Mr Dawson can aid you at the Academy; I can help you here.'

'You are far too busy, Jonny. And anyway, it is her company that I find quite enjoyable.'

'I beg your pardon.'

'Oh no, Jonny, not like that. What do you take me for? She is a pleasant girl.'

'Who has a reputation as all sitters at the Academy do. If you are seen in the streets with her—'

Alice's ears prick.

Oak flicks his hand. 'I would not give a monkey's rump about what they think of me.'

'Professor Oak, she scrubs paintbrushes and primes the flax for Academy students and has extravagant, expensive tastes in dress. Do you know what they *say* about her?'

Alice turns and scans the crowd in search of the sitter. She has disappeared. Alice's eyes are bright and round as she appeals to

Hammond, 'What *do* they say about her, Jonny?' She has heard of these 'loose' London women, of course – mostly from her father, whenever she asks why she is not permitted to visit the city more often. But they are caricatures in her mind, wearing flouncy dresses, with cakes of rouge and devil horns, never real people.

'Well… you can imagine…' stutters Hammond. 'How do you suppose she can afford such luxuries?'

Alice's forehead wrinkles. 'Stealing?'

Hammond sweats. 'Yes, stealing and… other ways a woman might charm others.'

'Do you really believe she's a thief, Jonny? Of jewels and diamonds and such? How fascinating—'

'*Not* fascinating, young Alice. On the contrary, 'tis deplorable! Disgraceful.'

'Do you think she is hiding money on her person right now?'

'I really do not think we should fixate on—'

Alice pats her father's breast pocket for his watch, his spectacles. 'Do you think she has conned you, Father? Your necktie is missing.'

'Oh no,' says Oak, brushing shortbread crumbs from his chin, 'I forgot to put it on this evening.'

Hammond rubs his eyes in exasperation. 'Please, Professor, open your eyes, will you, and be sensible? You are a respected academic—'

'*Was* a respected academic. I am now an old man pursuing what is likely to be a wild goose chase. Oh, do not look at me like that, Jonny. Now, I appreciate your concern and I have heard you. She is a young woman who has presumably made some mistakes in her life. We have all fallen at some point; none of us are perfect.'

'I can assure you that most of us have not fallen like *that.*'

'Not yet, anyway,' chimes in Alice.

'She is interesting,' says Oak. 'And more importantly, she is interested. It is enjoyable for me to teach her about Ponden-Hall. She will be my final pupil.'

Hammond slumps as one defeated. 'Just do not be fooled by her amiable nature. 'Tis the sweet-seeming ones who are conniving beneath.' And then, in desperation to reach his friend, 'She is not Emma.'

Oak straightens at this. The thought has crossed his mind over the past week, of course, but speaking it aloud breathes life into its quiet and aching reality. His lips form a smile that do not reach his eyes and he places his hand on Hammond's arm. 'No. She is not Emma.'

Alice looks to her father and then to Hammond, who now focuses on the tips of his boots. It always bothers Alice that the mention of her sister is often followed by discomfort amongst others.

'Come, Alice,' says Oak. ''Tis late.'

And handing the platter of shortbread to Hammond, Oak pulls his coat about him and leads his daughter out of the hall, head down and shoulders hunched as if protecting what is within him. There is work to be done.

14

The next morning, in a quieter part of the country, a stonemason has risen with the sun. He kneels before the crumbled wall, bulged from ivy and undulating roots below. He begins to stack the honey-coloured stones. These mornings are serene and still, on the lip of a hamlet where his only company is soggy pheasants who bumble across the path. Most will not survive the shooting season.

Ah, but here he comes. For a fortnight now, the stonemason has worked on this wall. And every single morning, like the quartz mechanisms in a timepiece, a lone man appears from the door across the road – an imposing side door in a periphery wall that conceals the great house within.

The man walks at his own pace, sometimes swaying as if listening to a piece of music, at ease with the world. His age is indeterminate to the stonemason, for the man is always bundled in a long coat and layers. He does appear to stoop, although this may be to shelter his face from the wind.

And every single morning, the man walks from the door to the hamlet's inconspicuous and overgrown cemetery. The graves are old and faded and lean out of the earth like rotting teeth – smooth slabs eroded over time.

The man walks past the graves to a solitary apple tree, which stands wizened at the edge of the cemetery overlooking rolling fields. It is an old tree, dark and gnarled as if it has lapped up the land's salt and grief and aches of the past few hundred years. To this tree, the man walks every morning. Against the tree, the man leans sometimes for several hours, sometimes for mere minutes, before his return journey to the door in the wall.

This morning, it seems that he will linger, for he carries something in his hands. From his position across the road, the stonemason squints behind his piles of stone. Red. A small red box that he places in the grass. And soon, although the man faces away from the stonemason – faces the fields beyond – ashy puffs of smoke curl into the apples above, are absorbed by the knobby branches and licked away by the wind.

The stonemason forgets about the man for several hours. His hands are chalked and his back is bent as a willow by the time he pauses for lunch. Glancing across the road, he sees that the chap is still there, puffing away below the boughs of the apple tree, and the stonemason muses to himself, *This morning, he must have much to think about.*

15

At Paddington station, father and daughter hasten to the platform for Oxford. How many indecorous strangers have intruded on their journey this morning – bustling alongside them through Hyde Park fraught with questions, theories, even bribes about Ponden-Hall? One woman had nearly been cast into the Serpentine, knocked backwards by Oak's instinctive recoil when she waylaid them from behind a tree. Oak's knuckles are white from gripping his daughter's shoulders. Alice finds it bizarre and not without amusement. She has never witnessed her father's fame being of this magnitude before. How can there be so many who know of him? Who are *interested* in his life and work?

When they believe they are finally free of the 'unseemly zealots', a young man framed by mutton-chop whiskers and adorned in loud, piped trousers that bunch at his ankles taps Oak on the elbow.

'Mister Solomon Oak, it is an honour,' he wheezes with a bow. 'Forgive my disturbance but I wanted to commend you on yesterday evening's lecture—'

'Yes, all right, many thanks,' Oak replies without looking at him. 'Now I am really rather busy—'

'Of course, of course! I would never dream of wasting such precious, *precious* time.' The stranger inclines as if to whisper but his words flow out in a loud hiss. 'I just wanted to offer my services to Mister Ponden-Hall. You know, if he is still *experimenting*. I am a willing specimen. Very obliging. If you could please give this to him, he need only write to me at this address and I shall do whatever he wants.'

Oak flinches away from the scroll, which has been tied with a long black ribbon.

'For the last time,' he cries, 'I have no relations with Timothy Ponden-Hall! We are not in communication. We have never met. And I can assure you that if I were in his confidence, I would under no circumstance pass forward such a base and disgraceful offer. Good day. Come along, Alice.'

The stranger's eyes flick to Alice. 'Good morning, Miss.' He bows his head. 'Are you another *sitter* at the Academy?'

'Away with you!' spits Oak, his body seized in horror at such a thought. And shielding Alice from any residual offences, he ushers her forward at pace to the furthest end of the platform. 'How dare... I cannot believe the audacity... good heavens, what has become of everyone this morning?'

'I have never seen such a craze,' says Alice.

'Oh, this is just the beginning. Just you wait. It will be mayhem before long.'

Away from the crowds, Oak takes a deep, slow breath and steadies himself against a lamp-post. He can feel the threshing of his heart beneath his hand. He is also sweating, and cool beads of perspiration gather at the roots of his ungainly curls.

He tucks his newspaper under his arm and pats his pockets. 'Now then...' At long last, he manoeuvres his fingers into the space of an inner fold and produces a small wad of notes. 'For Missy and the food and the chores,' he says. He knows nothing of keeping a house – merely keeps a steady but humble sum available in the sugar pot for Missy to take when she needs.

'There is still an ample amount in the pot,' says Alice. She is equally hopeless at understanding the expenses of a household – has never, in fact, known the sums that dip in and out of the jar. On this occasion, Alice only knows that the pot is not lacking, for she has contributed her own coin over the past few weeks. She knows she should keep her own hiding place – one set aside for her Grand Tour ambitions – but she is not used to having an excess of money, certainly not money that is purely hers, and the safest place she knows is the sugar pot.

She pockets the notes obediently.

They have so rarely been apart for the past decade that neither one is adept at saying goodbye.

'Father, I—' begins Alice. 'Well. I just wanted to say again that I enjoyed the lecture last night. And for what it's worth, I'm proud of the integrity you have shown.'

Oak colours, glances sideways at his daughter before scrutinising the train tracks. 'Oh? Yes, well. What do I have if not integrity? Especially in the art world.'

Alice glances around them. She can feel a smattering of eyes peeking out from behind papers and over upturned collars, but most stand silent in their own thoughts. 'It seems that many do not share your opinion. Why, if any of them found Ponden-Hall, I do believe they would serve him to the papers on a silver platter with mint jelly.'

Oak grunts. 'No principles.'

'I think it is far more interesting to have principles.' Alice knows that she must remind her father that he has a daughter old enough to have such opinions. 'So... you will return to Oxford in four weeks' time then?'

'Yes, after the final lecture. Just in time for Christmas. But do not worry – I have already written to Missy and she knows to order the cakes and trimmings with plenty of time before the day.'

This is not something Alice would worry about, but she knows the effort her father expends every year to make Christmas a felicitous affair – the one time of the year where they might look like everyone else, with a wreath on the door and chestnuts on the grate. It was always her and Emma's favourite holiday. Her father's attempts to create a festive Christmas are a nod to their mother; he has always done his best to do right by his children, to create merry memories on important days as she would have done.

The conductor boards the train, making ready to set off.

Alice turns to Oak. 'I could stay with you, Father. So close to the end of term, I do not need to be in Oxford. I can make up the work over the Christmas holidays.'

'Don't be silly. You must finish your studies without distraction.'

'I can help you.'

'Alice—'

'Let me scribe for you. Or be a second pair of eyes as you trawl through articles.'

'My girl, I am fine here. I do not need assistance. You belong at home. In Oxford.'

Where the ennui will consume me, thinks Alice. 'I would not be in your way. I just want to help.'

Oak places his hand on Alice's shoulder and squeezes. It is an unfamiliar height for both of them – her shoulder is higher than he remembers, less bony. She can see his thoughts flickering, taking her in, and she imagines he notices that her hair is longer too, restrained in a single plait compared to the two ribboned ones she most likely has in most of his thoughts and memories.

'You are helping by staying out of mischief and taking care of our home,' he says. 'I have never seen this side of you, Alice. This desire to be helpful, this interest in my work.'

But it has always been there, Alice thinks. Her father has retreated too far into himself to have seen it.

'Yet you are seeking further help from Miss Dodd,' she states. It is a low blow, she knows this, but she is determined.

Oak sighs. 'That is different, my dear. She may be able to access something that I cannot. Miss Dodd's unique skills could be most useful in acquiring some rather important information. That is all. I promise you.'

Alice cannot conceal her disappointment. She nods and offers a pacifying smile, but the dejection weighs upon her entire body as an insipid and sullen few weeks loom before her.

'However…'

Oak bumbles in front of her and takes both of her hands in his. When she looks up, Alice can see a new merriment in his cheeks; there is a flush of excitement about them that was not there just moments ago. He purses his lips and opens them, seals them again in a swift back-and-forth with himself.

At last, he resolves to divulge: 'I have been eager to share this with you, Alice, but I wanted it to be a surprise. I had hoped that I could impart the joyous news to you and Missy over Christmas, but it seems you need a spot of cheer right now, and well, why withhold such happy tidings any longer?'

This is a surprise. Alice is at a loss, with no idea what her father refers to.

'It is about your prospects after spring, once you have finished your exams,' he continues.

Could he possibly know of her plans? Alice searches his face for any hint, any clue that he has observed and understood her after all. Has he felt her restlessness? Has he seen the collection of Europe maps and museum pamphlets on her desk? Oak is positively aglow with enthusiasm, and there is no other conclusion, no secondary possibility that could inspire such pleasure aside from the staggering, though perhaps painful, realisation that of course Alice must be set free. Her father has seen her after all. Alice could burst with gratitude.

'Do you remember Magnus Bird?' he asks.

'Bird... the name sounds familiar but I cannot place a face.'

'You were very young when he was a pupil of mine.'

A student of art history. One, perhaps, with connections to Paris or Florence, thinks Alice. How enticing.

'He is a banker now,' says Oak. 'A rather important one. Very successful.'

Alice does not see the connection to her tour but her father's grin is broad and exuberant.

He squeezes her hands tighter now. 'My darling Alice, I have arranged for you to be a governess in his house for his two children! A safe and secure position on the coat-tails of your final exams. Can you believe it? A coveted post for any respectable young woman!'

But for Alice, the world has gone black. An inky coal black that seems to stopper her vision and hearing.

'Magnus was most impressed with your capabilities. Of course, we have always had a respectful relationship, he and I, so he was only too thrilled to offer us – offer *you* – the position. He was particularly pleased that you could teach his daughters both Latin and French in addition to writing. I did tell him your sewing skills and talents for cooking were not strengths per se, but I do believe your aptitude for geography makes up for this—'

But Alice does not hear him. The air about her is ashen and stifling, and all she can hear through the heavy, cold vacuity is the word *governess*. It is not possible that her father has been so mightily blind to what his daughter needs, to who his daughter is. And yet he rambles now about lessons on deportment and drawing, on globes and inkwells. Alice releases Oak's hands and brings her own to her chest. The motion inspires Oak to stop prattling.

'Father, I…' Alice takes measured breaths and cannot look him in the eye, for if she does, the tears will come. 'A governess position?'

'Are you pleased?'

It is sincere, her father's excitement. Alice searches his face for doubt or apology but all she can see is hopefulness and the desire for her approval. This naivety is heartbreaking but it also helps to sober her mind. She will reckon with the chasm between them another day. Right now, she needs only to board the train without disappointing her father. She needs time to think.

'Well?' he presses. His smile falters but a little.

'What news!' Alice manages. She puffs her chest as bravely as she can. 'I am only shocked, that is all. What a surprise. And here I had never expressed an interest in… Well, you and I have never discussed what I would do after studying.'

'I know we have never broached the subject, but you will be most comfortable with Magnus, and his daughters are young so your position will be secure for some time.'

The stone in Alice's throat swells. Only the furious desire to quit London as soon as possible keeps her tears at bay. She must return home. She must speak to Missy. Or to Peter.

'Perhaps we can discuss the details later, Father. The train is about to leave.'

'Of course! I only wanted to share the news with you.' He rocks back on his heels. 'And, well, there is plenty of time to consider the details.'

He is deflated, Alice can see, and for this, she is grateful. His nature is not so unseeing towards her own sentiments. Perhaps it is not too late. She can alter the course of this arrangement yet; she only needs time to think.

As London disappears behind her, her dreams of visiting the continent seem to likewise diminish. She has never before felt so shackled.

16

The following evening, Alice waits for Lou at the lamp-post as she has done every Wednesday. Her father's news clouds every waking thought, but she has now had a chance to air the proposition. Perhaps working for Magnus Bird would not be so dire, Missy had suggested, for at least Alice would be in London. But the confines of Portman Square would not be London – not truly – and the thought of spending her days teaching drab songs on the pianoforte to spoilt little charges is a depressing prospect at best.

Alice sighs and pushes stones with the toes of her boots. As she bends down to rub a scuff, she notices for the first time an arched space beneath the post. There is an envelope there, alone and unwrinkled. Upon looking closer, Alice can see that it is addressed to Lou. *How curious*, thinks Alice. She peers over her shoulder before pulling the note from under the lamp and tucking it into her sleeve.

It is impossible not to think of her father and the glumness that weighs on her heart. Although she has been kept near him, she has not been truly close to him since Emma's death – no steady hand on her back when balancing on the park wall, no sweeping away of hair for a kiss on the forehead at bedtime. Never will she earn these moments shared between her father and Emma and she accepts this. Alice understands the delicate wall that has been built to help preserve them both from grief – or worse yet, from the despairing love each holds for the other, for they are now all each other has. But never before has Alice felt so starkly *unseen*. Despite their rigid routines and eating, studying, even snoozing next to one another for a decade, she wonders if her father knows her at all.

He is not one to coddle, reasons Alice. Has she not been cared for? Private tutelage in her own sitting room; a favourite breakfast of malt bread with butter and honey whenever she wishes; any piqued interest instantly pursued – a shiny violin, raised vegetable boxes in the garden, a calligraphy set with the finest nibs. Only her curiosity about shooting was diverted (to a season of fencing lessons), which was just as well, for Alice has no stomach for retrieving the shot pheasants or wringing their necks if the pellets have not been merciful. No, there is no doubt that Oak provides for his daughter, albeit quietly, from the wings.

She must look disheartened, for when she boards the hansom, Lou studies her with a dramatic squint before driving the carriage onwards.

'I found this,' says Alice, retrieving the envelope from the folds of her coat. 'Under the lamp-post.'

'Ah.' With one hand, Lou breaks the seal and scans the letter. 'A request for runner-bean seeds. This will be from our charge on St Michael's Street.'

'The cottage near the church?'

'Yes. He is blind, you see, but has an ardent passion for gardening. It is difficult for him to acquire seeds of a high quality. Can you believe that he was once in charge of the grounds at a great estate in Warwickshire? But once he lost his sight in his old age, he was turned out and has been on his own ever since, quite forgotten.'

'How terrible.' The thought makes Alice feel sick. How could one be so easily discarded from an established life? She thinks about Missy years from now when she might be too frail or slow to keep up their house. The thought of chucking her into the street appals her indeed and she makes a note to speak to her father about how helpful Missy is – how they need her and should recognise the thankless job she does.

'Yes. Well anyway, I am pleased that his postman remembered my secret spot. If you ever need to contact me, you can always leave a note there under the lamp-post.'

Alice nods, only half-hearing. Sensing her grumpiness, Lou presses on.

'I very much enjoyed the lecture on Monday,' she says. 'Your father is an impressive speaker.'

Alice sighs. 'Yes, he is. I lost you after the lecture. I'm sorry we could not speak afterwards.'

'I thought it best to sneak away before getting swept up into a controversial discussion.'

'I wish you had stayed on just for a little,' says Alice. Her voice is flat. 'The vultures descended – even on me. That man I pointed out to you. He was offering… well, it doesn't matter. I shall be happy to stay well away from it all.'

'For what it's worth,' says Lou, 'I agree with your father's stance. All of this prattle about immortalising souls and elixirs of life. I do not believe in any of it. Death is death. And if souls do exist, it is not our place to tamper with them.'

'That is exactly what my father says.' Alice rubs her face, tired and agitated. 'You really would get along with him.'

'I do admire him. I respect him for focusing on the art, especially when nobody else is interested in doing so.'

When Alice does not respond, Lou nudges her with her knee. 'Are you well?'

Alice is embarrassed that she is unable to conceal her foul mood, but it is no use. The gloom is like a leech upon her.

'To be frank with you, not really, no.' Alice pulls at a loose thread on her scarf. 'My father and I spoke about future arrangements, for when my exams are finished.'

'Ah, the tour. Was he very cross with the idea?'

'If only he were! Lou, he has arranged for me to become a governess! In London for the daughters of one of his old students.' Alice's fingers and palms are cold upon her face as she gives in to the despair. 'I know I should probably be grateful. And I am becoming increasingly aware of how at odds I am with other girls of my station. Perhaps what I want is too unconventional.'

'Your father is also unconventional.'

'Well, precisely!' Alice puffs her cheeks. 'A governess? I cannot bear the thought.'

'Did you tell him this?'

'Well… no. He seemed so pleased with the idea and I was taken by surprise. I only wanted to escape him and have a moment to think, but no solutions have presented themselves. I cannot imagine how I can break the arrangement.'

'But of course you can. Why, it has yet to begin. You must simply tell your father that you are grateful for the prospect but you are not interested.'

'It is not so simple.'

'Why not?'

'I… do not want to upset him. He believes this will keep me well provided for. It is a safe option. After losing my sister, you can understand why he would wish to secure such a path for me.'

But Lou is not deterred. She is gentle when she presses, 'But your father wants what is best for you, does he not?'

'Of course he does.'

'With all due respect to the governesses of the world, your life, Alice Oak, is bigger than that of a governess. To restrain you as one will only cause strife and frustration. Your father should know this.'

A twinge of pride flutters in Alice's belly; she is flattered to hear this from Lou of all people. 'He should know this,' she says quietly. 'But he has not spoken to me – not truly – for many years. He has kept himself from knowing me at all. Perhaps it has been wrong of him, but I do understand why.'

Lou pulls the hansom to a halt for their first delivery of the evening.

'You must show him, Alice. *Show* him that yours is a life of action. Prove to him that you have more to offer – that it is more appropriate for you to pursue long-lost explorers beside him than count beads on an abacus with children. 'Tis in your nature to combat him, is it not? And then when he is used to the idea – and only then – tell him about your passion for the Impressionists.'

Alice snorts. Perhaps it is time to show her father that she is no longer just a little girl or a sister to a more interesting child, but a young woman with her own curiosities.

As her mood returns to one of good humour, Alice re-notes the letter to Lou, which lies crumpled on the seat between them. A request for runner beans. She smiles within herself.

'These deliveries we do,' she says. 'They're helpful, aren't they? They're for people who need help.'

'Well, I hope so,' says Lou. 'We go to a lot of effort for nothing if they are useless.'

'It's… well.' Alice laughs. She cannot help it. 'For a while, I thought you were conducting deliveries of disrepute.'

'It depends on what you think is dishonourable, I suppose. If runner beans and books and obscene amounts of fudge are unsavoury commodities, then we are a shady pair of couriers indeed.'

Alice enjoys it when she is playful like this. 'You cannot blame me. What was I to think when we go about this business in the dark of night?'

Lou smiles. 'As I said, our charges live in the shadows of society. They are invisible to most and have grown accustomed to getting by on their own. If I can help in some way, however small, I am happy to do so without shining an unwelcome light onto them.'

Or onto yourself, thinks Alice. How easily Lou can blend into a room or disappear in a crowd. She, like her charges, favours invisibility. Alice can see this now although the reasons behind it are still unclear.

She considers for a moment before offering shyly, 'You know, my mother had a heart for charity. She volunteered under Louisa Twining, visiting the workhouses.'

'For Louisa Twining? Your mother?' The surprise and awe is genuine upon Lou's face and Alice is proud.

Alice nods. 'She kept a journal where she logged all of her visits. I keep it on my bedside table. It is my most treasured possession from her. She was most fond of visiting the orphan children.'

'She sounds like a most impressive woman.'

'Yes, I think she was.'

Lou gathers her coat about her. 'I lost my mother when I was very young too.'

'Oh?' An unexpected divulgence.

'But I do not think she was involved with charities.' Lou shivers. 'Take this extra hat. 'Tis mighty cold this evening. And if you could start with the crates on the right, I will follow you.'

Alice is fitter and stronger than she has ever been. She has noticed, too, that she has begun to shift more parcels than Lou in an evening's work, and for this, she is pleased.

Lou continues to be a source of bafflement and intrigue, and the more Alice learns of her, the more she feels a growing admiration. Alice has never had a close friend before. The few classmates who might have developed into friends seemed to step back after Emma's accident, awkward and unknowing in their youthful inexperience of death, before fading away altogether. There is Peter, of course, but that is different. And she cannot help but wonder: if Emma had lived, would it feel like this between them? Is this sisterhood? This closeness, this informality and honesty that inspires ambition and excitement and support? It is all a bit confusing and Alice will not think too much on it, will not think too closely about the delight she feels three times a week, the simple joy and anticipation she feels in her chest before an evening of manual labour and delivering parcels with Lou.

17

On Wednesday morning, although the doors have not been open for even an hour, the reading room in the British Museum is stacked with books. The sole reader in the room beavers away, leafing through a tome of Egyptian runes before opening a bound collection of *Punch* cartoons, then an old log from the Bristol docks.

Oak scrutinises all of them, absorbing more useless titbits of information than helpful ones. He tries to tether himself to the theories – to Ponden-Hall's work and the world around it – but it is too easy and too amusing to meander down the different rabbit holes.

Most woodpecker tongues possess an assortment of barbs near the tip in order to dislodge ants and larvae which have burrowed deeply into the wood. A woodpecker has a hyoid bone which wraps around its skull to protect its brain. Male woodpeckers may drum over five hundred times until a female responds. Persistent, thinks Oak.

All of this is useless knowledge to most. It would inspire no stimulating conversation at a supper party; it would, on the contrary, garner looks of mock interest or nods of sympathy as if encouraging a child who has given the wrong answer. But for Oak, learning new knowledge – any knowledge, even the minute details of a woodpecker's tongue – sparks pure joy. He is, indeed, happier now than fifteen minutes ago from the simple acquisition of facts.

How he has missed academia.

The door is cracked open and Grace Dodd backs into the room. Her arms are inundated with books: heavy tomes of atlases, histories of horse breeding, and archived newspaper articles from the past fifty years.

'Any interesting developments?' she asks.

She heaves the stack onto the desk and collapses into a chair. The bodice of her dress clings to her, and the film of sweat she has built up renders the muslin cloth nearly sheer in some places where it is tighter around her curves. Although she wears darker colours in the autumn – rich navy and green, elegant taupe and scarlet – the layered material is light so it flounces around her as she moves. Most men would not dream of seeing Miss Dodd in such delicate attire hefting books up and down stairs and across great expanses, with opportunities ripe for tearing or tripping. Most men would not notice what she carries in her arms in the first instance, for their eyes would certainly fall elsewhere, particularly in her current pose – exhausted and arched over a chair, fanning herself with a pamphlet on antiquarian Bibles. But she has an audience of one, and Solomon Oak does not take his eyes off his notebooks as he addresses her warmly.

'No developments. But I have learnt some fascinating information on woodpeckers.'

'The man at the desk has a stack of articles from *The Times* over the past sixty years. Some Lord has offered them to you for perusal from his private collection.'

'Mm. It will not do. But thank you – I shall have a quick flick through after I finish scrutinising the death records of the Mortimer family. DeLacey's butler's family – John Mortimer, you remember? The second portrait that appeared.'

'What are you searching for?'

'Any hint of where succeeding Mortimers might have been buried. It could give us insight into where the family might be now.'

'I see.'

'This was all thoroughly scrutinised at the time of death, of course. John Mortimer's family was based north of London in Cuffley. His mother and father died in the 1840s and were buried in the Cuffley churchyard. His brother Oliver died in a railway accident and was buried next to them a decade later. No descendants. A tidy end to the Mortimer family line.'

'So why are you looking at the records now?'

'Cousins, second cousins. Perhaps a branch of the family further removed has living relatives.' Oak pushes his spectacles atop his greying mop and rubs his eyes. 'There is, in all honesty, probably no point,

Miss Dodd. 'Tis a wild goose chase – I said this from the beginning. But it is something to focus on, I suppose.'

'Do not lose heart. Ponden-Hall is out there and wants to be found. I am sure of it.'

Oak smiles. 'Yes, I think so too.' He has always been charmed by the optimism of youth.

'I know I am new to this Ponden-Hall business,' she continues, 'but I can feel it. Why else would he resurface after all these years? Why not pass away from this world in peace and solitude? God knows he has suffered scrutiny in the public eye and will only be prodded more once he is found.'

Grace opens a bound collection of newspaper articles. It is a labour to lug open the hefty cover.

'Why would *The Times* articles not do?' she asks. 'That paper would have covered every whisper having to do with Ponden-Hall.'

'Precisely. Every obvious fact and theory will have been published. What I am interested in – and I never thought I would say this – are the gossip columns and society papers. I want the bric-a-brac: the nonsensical articles of people spotting DeLacey's ghost on the beach, the sighting of one-eyed horses in the dead of night, hearing woodpecker cries on the south bank by the river's nooses. It is all balderdash, of course. However, I never thought I would say this, but perhaps such fabrication was based on something more.'

'But no one would keep such rubbish. Why, such papers would line the bins by supper time.'

'Yes. I thought perhaps the museum would have a record of something, but it looks unlikely.' Oak sighs and surrenders to a yawn.

'You look exhausted, Mr Oak.'

'I did not sleep well last night. 'Tis nothing.' But as Oak rubs his temples, he regards the sharp woman before him and reconsiders. Aside from Missy, he has never confided in anyone about Alice before; he has never needed to. But this next chapter of her life is too important, and he is not too proud to seek council on how to anchor it. 'Actually, Miss Dodd, 'tis about my daughter, Alice. She is disappointed in an arrangement I have made for her. You see, I have secured for her the position of governess with one of my old pupils, in an impressive house in Portman Square. She did not seem thrilled with the surprise.'

'Did you discuss this with her?'

'Well, no.'

Grace rolls her eyes. 'What does Alice want? She is eighteen, you say? She is bound to have opinions on how she wants her life to unfold. I certainly did at that age.'

'I have never asked her what she wants to do after her studies. I am trying to ease her path.'

'A kind motivation. And let us be frank: the world turns and there are more opportunities now for women than before, but we are still limited. Alice is lucky to have your connections and to have such an opportunity on offer. But it is no good if it is not what she wants. She will suffer. I suggest you speak to her.'

Oak is silent for a moment with wrinkled brow.

'It is no good if it is not what she wants,' he repeats. 'But she does not know what she wants.'

'Or perhaps she does know, but you have never—'

'A brilliant idea, Miss Dodd. Alice needs to *know* what the position entails. She does not understand the full picture of a governess's programme.'

'I think most people can guess what a governess's day looks like—'

'A meeting. I will organise a meeting so that Alice can meet Magnus Bird. Next weekend, even. And she will adore another visit to London, I am sure of it.'

Grace lingers, undecided as to whether she should be more candid about this plan, but Oak is already writing to Magnus Bird and detects not a smidgen of Grace's doubts.

With renewed zest and the promise of securing his daughter's sheltered employment at the weekend, he turns to Grace. 'Now then. I want to speak about the proposal I mentioned at the lecture.'

'You said you need my help.'

'I do. I cannot think of anyone better suited.'

'Then I am properly intrigued,' she says. She holds up a finger as if to reprimand a child. 'And you understood me before when I denied involvement with the houses in Soho?'

'I understood you at the museum, and I can assure you I hear you now. In short, Miss Dodd, to confirm a somewhat controversial idea I have, I must have access to a set of files. And to get them, you must secure a position in an office of sorts—'

'I am no daily help, Mr Oak.'

'It is not for the position of a daily. Rather, a sort of assistant which may require you to clean occasionally or make a cup of tea. It is mainly, I gather, organising papers.'

This sounds no different from the stints of irregular, dull and cheap work she did before she ventured into conning – before she made any proper money.

'It is lucky that I was taught my letters,' she says with a wink. 'My father was a teacher. When he wasn't drinking, anyway. Who, may I ask, would I be working for? And what does this have to do with Timothy Ponden-Hall?'

Oak smiles, folds his hands together and leans on the desk. 'This is where it becomes interesting, my dear. Do you know much about Elizabeth Ponden-Hall, Timothy's grandmother?'

'Only what the public knows, I suppose. She came from a wealthy family. Aristocratic.'

'Yes. A suitable match for Julien Ponden-Hall. What a lot of people do not know – or if they do know, they dare not speak of it – is that Elizabeth was frequently unwell. Oh, she was physically fit as a fiddle. But she suffered fits of anxiety. She alludes to it in interviews she gave after the shipwreck, and acquaintances of hers that I have met over the years have confirmed it.

'Her parents, believing in traditional ailments and remedies, did not want to entertain such ideas of an unrested mind. The young Elizabeth, however – just a teenager at the time – kept insisting that she needed to see a doctor, so in the end, they brought her to Dr Walter Jahn. Dr Jahn was a well-respected physician amongst the aristocracy but was unique in that he was interested in cerebral development and nerves – we would call this neuroanatomy today. So Elizabeth would meet with Dr Jahn whenever she felt these bouts of anxiousness and it seems he was able to help her, for she never visited another doctor again, even when she suffered from other, more common ailments.'

'A good relationship with one's doctor is paramount.'

'Indeed. Dr Jahn was Elizabeth's physician until his death in 1810. After that, Elizabeth saw his son, Dr Frank Jahn, but their relationship was never as close. By then, Elizabeth was in her fifties and she had two very young grandchildren – Timothy and

Adelaide – whom she doted upon. Her visits to the second Dr Jahn were sparse.

'He, like his father, had also taken an interest in neuroanatomy, but became fascinated with phrenology – that is, if you are unfamiliar with it, the study of lumps and bumps on the skull to predict behavioural and mental traits. As you can imagine, phrenology has fallen out of fashion these days. Discredited by a few lofty scientists now. But back then, its intrigue was at its peak. Even the Queen sought out a phrenologist when searching for a wife for her son. Anyway, it is highly likely that the Ponden-Halls did not want to be associated with increasingly debunked methods, so Elizabeth's visits to Dr Jahn would naturally have tapered off.

'Frederick kept the practice running at the same location as his father, and eventually, his daughter, Miss Elke Jahn, would take over as a rather unpopular and ridiculed phrenologist. As it happens, Miss Jahn has been looking for an assistant for the past two months. She has not filled the position as the advertisement is still posted on her window.'

'Two months is quite a long time.'

'She is very picky.'

'You know her, then?'

'Not exactly. Many years ago, I appealed to her father Frederick to ask if I could access old documents. I had made a name for myself by then so he knew who I was. He would have considered my request if Elke had not interposed. Association with someone like me would not do the family business any good, she said; they were already being mocked for their phrenological enterprises, and any further publicity would bring more harm than benefit. So he turned me away. Even though it has been an age, I am certain that Miss Jahn will remember my enquiries, so I dare not approach her myself.'

'Which is where I come in.'

'Precisely. You see, my dear, it was not until recently that most physicians kept records of their charges. But Dr Walter Jahn, being the meticulous man he was and having an interest in a novel science, would have kept notes on each of his patients, Elizabeth included. I believe these files will be buried somewhere, long forgotten, in the boxes of the phrenology parlour's storeroom.'

'So I am to somehow find these files.'

'Yes. But I believe it will be easier than it sounds. According to a neighbour, Miss Jahn is selling the parlour after all these years. And she is looking to hire someone to help her clear out a century's worth of documents.'

'I see. And what makes you think she will hire me, Mr Oak?'

'Elke never married. She has never trusted men and she is fond of young women with spirit. And… you are, well…'

'A nobody. I am inconsequential in social circles and pose no threat in the exposure of family secrets.'

Oak shrugs, a cheeky glint in his eye. 'I do believe this increases your appeal.' He pauses. 'It is a rather big ask, I know, Miss Dodd. And if you are uncomfortable at the prospect of assuming false pretences or acting deceitfully on my account, well, I would understand completely—'

This is not the first time that Oak has delicately alluded to her past. The swiftness with which she has grown to trust Oak has startled Grace over the trajectory of the past few months, especially given his status as an academic. Oak's interest in and support of her is so different from that of the don's.

'Mr Oak,' she says, 'I am sure you can piece together my very simple past. I have nothing to hide from you, so let me share it plainly. My father taught me to read and write; he was a teacher of Latin and literature. Unfortunately, he was also a drunkard. When it became too unbearable, my mother fled to an almshouse and took me with her. She did not stay long. She was very beautiful, my mother, and so caught the attention of many paying men… not for any official brothel, mind you. Eventually, she was kept by quite a wealthy landowner in Greenwich. She offered to take me with her, but by then, I resented her for taking me away from my father, and I had found comrades amongst some of the clever, albeit dishonest, inhabitants of the almshouse. For a while, she sent me extravagant gifts – she always had an eye for fashion, you see, and now she could finally afford it. The gifts stopped in due course and I know nothing about her current whereabouts.

'In short, Mr Oak, I grew up poor and largely alone, but was more educated than an average person of my station thanks to my father. I do not know what has become of him either; I would be very surprised if he were still alive. People at the almshouse taught me the tricks of thieves and swindlers and I was an eager and talented pupil. Even more recently than I care to admit, I have benefited from the skills they taught me.' Grace sweeps up her cape, which is thrown across a stack of books, and lays it before Oak. 'Look at this gorgeous cape with its high collar. These trims of jet beading and this fur. One year ago, this was the most sought-after piece of fashion in London and abroad. How does a sitter like me afford such luxury?'

Hammond's warnings are soft echoes in Oak's memory but he has never heeded them; Grace has never given him cause to.

''Tis bad luck to have refined taste and be poor,' she says. ''Tis even more bad luck to have a talent for deceiving those in the most wealthy, sophisticated institutions in the city.' Grace leans back in her chair and hugs the cape. She will leave it at this: the conning of the spoilt and wealthy, the duping of the insufferable rich who would not realise if a ruby necklace – or mink cape, for that matter – went missing. These are easy deceptions to stomach. Grace will not divulge the more common tricks she has played, for the bitterness upon her tongue is thick as tar when she thinks about them. Even the most forgiving of men do not look favourably upon thieves of orphanages and poorhouses.

'But I no longer do it,' says Grace. 'Deceive, I mean. I suppose the lustre wore off.'

Oak studies this woman, his lips pressed in a neutral line. She is proud and determined, Oak thinks, but there is a vulnerability here too.

'It is difficult to give up one's life and start again,' he says. 'What, may I ask, inspired you to change?'

And this is the story that Grace is ashamed of. She can stand being judged for thievery, for how many in this world have resorted to such means to survive? She can even tolerate being judged for weakness or for fear; how she wishes she had given up her old life owing to a moral battle within her, a dramatic feud between good and evil, only to have good persevere in a dramatic awakening, to give up all sins and moral corruption for a chaste and honest existence. But she did not pivot the course of her life for any such purifying enlightenment. It was much more simple, and being so, much more deplorable.

'What inspired me to give up that life?' she repeats tartly. 'A man.'

She has come this far and indeed, she has nothing to hide from Solomon Oak. If he judges her now, how can she blame him? She still judges herself. She has nothing to lose in telling him.

'Last autumn,' she begins, 'I found myself outside the Academy, and wandered into the foyer to escape the cold. An assistant was ushering women into a room to start the first lecture on sculpture. It was one of the few art courses available to female students and only the very wealthy could afford it – this was plain from the clientele milling about. I slid into the cloakroom, pinched the most ostentatious hat I could see, popped it onto my head and walked straight in.

'I left the lecture brimming with questions and awed by these Renaissance masters. There is no other way to put it, Mr Oak: I had never been stirred – stimulated – in the mind before in this way, not since those early days with my father when he first introduced me to books, and my brain was abuzz with questions. It was a weekly class and I eagerly attended each one.

'A few weeks in, I met a man in the foyer after the lesson. He said he had seen me leaving the past few classes and had found my enthusiasm charming. I always left the classroom scribbling notes, you see, my head down, engrossed in whatever we had been discussing. It turns out he was a history professor and was using the lecture room at the Academy to deliver a crossover course on the Industrial Revolution and its impact on design. He invited me to stay and sit in on his lecture.

'Well.' At this, Grace scrunches her nose. 'You can imagine the clichéd months that followed. I would attend the art course every week, followed by the history lesson, and then the don and I would spend long, passionate evenings in his flat on Marylebone Road. He was so interesting, Mr Oak, so fascinating. And so knowledgeable – not only in history but in literature, philosophy, geography. I soaked it all in. And because I was clever with conversation, I held my own. I really did.'

Oak can picture this, of course – can imagine the burgeoning love between them and the excitement, thrill, that Grace experienced with the mere act of learning. Of course Oak understands this only too well. He is aware of the passionate affairs hidden in academic circles even if he does not partake of them himself. And before Grace needs to tell him, he can also see how it ends.

'At the end of the second term, he offered to help me apply for one of the department scholarships. Of course, when he searched for my name in the registry, it was nowhere to be found.' Grace sucks on her lip, examines her fingernails. 'I did not think he would feel so betrayed.'

When she offers no more, Oak says gently, 'Perhaps the disappointment for him was too much. If he was so concerned with status, you are better off with someone more purely interested in—'

'No disappointment or betrayal can justify how he made me feel, Mr Oak,' she says bitterly. 'He lashed out, debased me. It was not that he made me feel stupid. That would be too simple, comprehensible; I am very aware that there are countless things in this world that I do not know or understand. But he made me feel *hollow*, devoid of any knowledge or intelligence altogether. The look of utter disgust he cast upon me when he discovered that I was not a student at the university – had not been formally educated at all – rendered me completely vaporous. Why, I felt more brainless and more insignificant than a flea.'

She looks Oak square in the eye now. 'I will never allow anyone – especially a pompous and privileged man – to make me feel so small ever again. I simply refuse. I will never again be made to feel worthless. I will earn my own keep. And I will not be ashamed of the patchy, perhaps unorthodox education I have sought for myself.'

There is the tiniest upward twitch of Oak's lips before he adjusts his glasses and returns to the book. He is unfussed, unrushed when he says, 'You have nothing to be ashamed of. In fact, I think your means of acquiring knowledge so far has been admirable.' Oak is sincere in his conviction. He has always known that Grace's background was disreputable in some respects, but was never inclined to prod. He is and always has been most interested in a person's character, the malleable and messy development of simply becoming.

Grace is thrown by this kernel of blind acceptance and refusal to judge. 'I… all right, then.' She gathers herself up and resumes an air of professionalism. Inside, what is this she feels? Gratitude? Relief? Acceptance.

There is a knock on the reading-room door. The chief librarian himself bears a note.

The pink in Oak's cheeks flares up into cherry splotches as he scans the message.

'Bromage has appealed to deconstruct the new painting. He claims that his team can do it safely with an extraction from a folded corner of the canvas.' Oak crumples the note and throws it onto the desk. 'That will still require dismantling the frame and risk warping the picture.'

'They will ruin it, certainly!' exclaims Grace. 'Surely it will not be approved. Sir Frederic would never dream of doing such a thing.'

'I'm afraid he will have no choice. Bromage has the financial support of the right bullies. And enough of the public will support this endeavour with their own selfish curiosities in mind.' Oak pounds the table with his fist. The thought of the painting being cut fills him with nausea. He would rather see it burn than dissected by the hands of these cruel and selfish henchmen.

'When does he hope to do this?'

'Shortly into the new year.'

'Why, that is mere weeks away!'

Oaks presses his palms into the table and stands, pushing aside *Systema Naturae* with its taxonomy on Eurasian woodpeckers. 'We have much to do, Miss Dodd. I have spent too much time indulging in gratuitous enquiries. It is crucial that you find these documents, and soon. They could give great insight into Ponden-Hall's family history. I am sorry to put excessive pressure on you, but it is the truth: I *need* these papers.'

'Then I should visit Elke Jahn's office at once.' Grace is already standing, gathering her things. 'I shall… do some research. I need to know this woman if I am to secure the post. And then I shall assist her in decluttering her family's practice. I am to take note of any recordings of Elizabeth's fits of anxiety?'

'Oh, no,' says Oak. His knuckles remain pressed upon the desk but he relaxes as he leans forward, speaks in a quieter voice. 'I am not interested in the neuroanatomy of Elizabeth Ponden-Hall.'

'No?'

'No. I would like to read the notes on the birth of her son. A confirmation of a theory that has germinated in my old brain. Now listen closely.'

18

For once, Lou is late. Alice shoves her mittened hands into her coat; the air has turned icy within the past week – a swift pirouette from autumn to winter, even though it is only November. How she wishes she had a cup of warm chocolate with cloves to warm her hands and belly.

She recognises the hansom's soft-bobbing lamplight when it finally approaches. When Lou pulls up to the corner, Alice is surprised to see her disembark.

'Good evening, Alice.' She is breathless as she skirts the wheel. 'We must take a slight detour tonight.'

'A detour?'

'To the other side of Oxford, beyond Magdalen.'

For Alice, Jericho is the other side of Oxford and her stomach wobbles at the thought of more dark alleys and canal paths. And yet, there is also a nip of intrigue, of excitement. These evenings with Lou have emboldened her indeed.

When Lou faces her, Alice can see from the red in her eyes and the puffed skin beneath them that she has been crying. In this vulnerable state, she appears even slighter than usual, her face pale and small in the yellow lamplight.

'My dear friend, Mary – the one who has been terribly ill – she has worsened.'

Lou's countenance quashes any rise of worry or confusion in Alice. Someone is ill and her friend is anxious; Alice knows her part in this. She is not experienced in many matters of the world, but her empathy would rival the most virtuous knight and she is a master of keeping her chin up, for herself and for those she loves.

'I understand,' she says. 'What can we do to help?'

Lou stops Alice from climbing into the driver's seat. Alice can feel her quivering beneath her gloves.

'I need you to ride with her. She is inside. Please.'

Alice is surprised. This she would not have expected, for it means someone else knows about Lou's world of night drives and shadowed deliveries.

'She is so weak,' says Lou, who reaches for the lever to release the door. 'I have told her to lean against a cushion so she might stay upright, but she is burning with fever and can barely keep her eyes open.'

Although the cab is suitably small compared to a Growler, without its usual load of crates and parcels, the interior with its padded leather seats and upholstered half-doors appears the picture of comfort. Its cosy quarters prevent Alice from seeing the passenger, for Lou's silhouette blocks most of the door; she strains to move the heavy body before her, tucks a blanket round the arms and legs as if she is pinching a pie. Alice hears soothing noises permeating the frosty air and she cannot help but notice it is the most tender she has ever seen her. She has never considered Lou in this way before – that any side of her could be soft, gentle.

Her thoughts are aptly disturbed by Lou's backside, which collides into her as she reverses out of the cab.

'She is still burning up but her breathing has stabilised. I have put a cool cloth on her forehead. If you could dip it into the bowl to refresh it—'

'Yes, of course.'

Lou grasps Alice's hands in her own. 'Thank you, Alice. The doctor is not far. He is called Amos Barrie. Perhaps a half-hour's journey at this time of night.'

'My father's physician lives on Talbot Road. I am certain that he would not mind—'

'Thank you, but no. Dr Barrie has treated her before. Whilst he is retired, he is still the best there is. In you go.'

The step into the cab is steep and slippery from the rain, and Alice nearly falls back into the street after seeing her charge. Cast in the middle of lamplight and shadows, she is plump and round like a bantam hen with skin as black as the night outside. Her hair, pulled back by a cavalry of pins, is as white as cream by contrast and glistens in the light with perspiration.

Alice perches next to her – knows she should introduce herself but has been abandoned by all words.

'Mary, this is Alice Oak,' says Lou from the door. 'A friend.'

They are secured in the hansom and Lou's whip can be heard from above and behind them. Already, the cushion falls from behind the old woman's head and Alice reaches to reinstate it. Her shoulders and arms are soft and warm, and although she is a stranger to her, Alice feels no discomfort leaning into her as she fluffs the down, pushes the tassels aside.

'Are you comfortable?' she asks.

The woman's speech is slow and measured, and although there is a rattle in her throat and she struggles to breathe, her voice is as smooth and deep as a horn. 'Thank you, Miss Oak. I am afraid I have scuppered your plans for the evening.'

'Not at all,' says Alice. 'I am so sorry that you are unwell, Mrs...'

'Whipple. My name is Mary Whipple. But please call me Mary.'

'You are shivering. Here, let me wrap another blanket around you.'

She does not protest. As the journey goes on, Mary's breathing slows and her muscles relax. Alice knows that she must not stare – that even though Mary's eyes are closed, it is rude. But stare at her, she does.

She has met black gentlemen and gentlewomen before, but never has she conversed with one so closely. Although Mary is old, as evidenced by her flour-white hair, her skin is remarkably smooth and taut as a drum. Alice wonders what job she has at the estate – perhaps a housekeeper or a cook or a housemaid. She does not know much about the duties of these positions, only that the days are long and monotonous, according to Missy, who claims she will always choose a quiet, small-house position over one in a country manor. Whatever this Mary Whipple does, it will be laborious and exhausting. How impressive she is, Alice thinks, to undertake work like this at such an age.

Mary's eyes are still closed when she says, 'I am very grateful to you, Miss Oak. Lou has told me many things. She says you are a firecracker.'

At this, Alice pinkens and cannot suppress a nervous hiccup. She is glad that the hansom floats in and out of lamplight like a chequerboard. 'A firecracker…?'

A low, rumbling rattle pervades the carriage and Alice realises that Mary is chuckling.

'You have energised her,' she says. 'You and she are not so dissimilar.' Mary coughs and braces herself against Alice, grips her hand under the blankets until the fit passes. When she is calm once more, she does not release it. 'She needs someone to take care of her,' Mary continues. 'She cares for so many and deserves to be cared for. I am glad you did not let her down.'

Alice is unsure of what she means by this last part. She would like to ask – to talk more about Lou and who she is, how they know each other and came to this part of the world, but by the time she musters up something coherent to say, Mary is breathing deeply and resting her head upon Alice's shoulder. Her hands, which have escaped the confines of the blankets, rest like molehills on her lap. Even in the throes of her illness, her apron strings and waxed plaits and roundness of flesh exude peace and comfort. And she smells of bread. It is unmistakable: the familiar and tangy scent of warm bread freshly baked on a stone. *Motherly* is the word that Alice cannot summon, but she is precisely this.

When they arrive at the doctor's cottage, Alice and Lou strain to carry Mary Whipple from cab to cot. Lou strokes the old woman's head before they depart, and exchanges hushed words with the gentle physician before ushering Alice back out into the night.

Perched in the driver's seat together, they retrace their journey back into the centre of Oxford at a relaxed canter. The rain has subsided into a fine mist which leaves their faces cool and glistening like buttercups at dawn. As they cross onto the smaller back streets of Jericho, the horse's trotting echoes off the slick bricks. No lights frame the curtained windows. There is a noticeable absence of stray tabbies. The city has put itself to sleep early.

'She will pull through,' says Lou. 'She is strong.'

'Of course she will.' Alice knows nothing about Mary's disposition – knows nothing about Mary Whipple at all aside from the fact that she is important to Lou, which is enough to prompt her comforting.

In front of the anchor doorknocker, Lou pulls the hansom to a stop.

'I have known her for quite some time. She is like a mother to me.'

'I see.'

'She manages the estate.'

'Oh?' At this, Alice is baffled, for she has never known a woman of colour to be held in such esteem as to run a house.

'The master of the house employed her as domestic help long ago. Mary's mother was born in west Africa and enslaved by Portuguese traders. Eventually, she was brought to London and hired by a wealthy family as a scullery maid. Mary was born and was taught her mother's trade before the family no longer had need of her. Fortuitously, a great house in Oxfordshire was in need of a maid, and its master – unlike most at the time – was of the mind to pay all staff an equal wage regardless of skin colour. So Mary began her first proper post at the estate and never left. I believe she has worked there for over sixty years.'

'An incredible story,' says Alice. 'A lifetime at one house. Such loyalty.'

'Yes. I do not know what I would do if... I cannot imagine the estate... Well.' The breaking of her voice is poorly concealed. 'Never mind. There is no need for such thoughts.' And Lou draws herself up as bold as she can like a singing bird.

Before Alice can spew any awkward reassurances, Lou is climbing over her to alight.

'Thank you, Alice.' It is a quiet statement said in passing, her head down and already moving ahead to the task at hand. Alice understands then how exposed Lou feels, how uncomfortable she is to have needed her help. And she knows she should not feel this, but no small part of Alice is grateful for her vulnerability, for she feels closer to Lou now than ever before, and she seems for the first time tangibly human.

CHEMIST TO RECREATE PONDEN-HALL'S ELIXIR; REBUKES PAINTER FOR WASTING SOLUTION ON 'BEASTS'

Weekly Dispatch, May 1836

The chemist of St James, Samuel Reynolds, pupil of famed perfumier and chemist Pierre Gantillon, has made a public business proposition to Timothy Ponden-Hall. Reynolds desires to replicate Ponden-Hall's elixir and sell it in what he claims would be 'the most lucrative business venture of the century'. Reynolds studied perfumery in Paris for five years under M. Gantillon, an education which inspires great confidence in his abilities to recreate any substance with only a small sample to work from. He claims, 'My customers spend an absurd amount of money on all mixtures of lavender, honeysuckle, rose… any pleasing fragrance in fashion. They are hungry for the next beauty trend. They would pay extravagant sums for their very own bottle of the elixir of youth. Ponden-Hall need only give me a sample of the vial and I will do all the work. I would even name it after him: *Timothy Toujours*. And fifty per cent of the profits. He would be a fool to turn me down.'

Reynolds is not afraid to sling criticisms at the explorer. Of Ponden-Hall's recent portraits, *Prince − A Spaniel*, *Gentle Polyphemus − A Piebald*, and *The Three-toed Woodpecker* (or *The Trio* as they have been christened together), Reynolds is disparaging: 'He is DEBASING himself by painting these beasts. Why he chooses to waste the elixir on immortalising common animals is beyond my realm of comprehension. I do believe he has gone a bit mad.'

There has been no response from Ponden-Hall to Reynolds' offer, though an overwhelming number of prominent members of London society have already placed orders for *Timothy Toujours*. If Ponden-Hall agrees to this deal, it promises to make Reynolds one of the wealthiest men in Europe.

19

It is quite impossible to imagine Magnus Bird being enthralled by the chiaroscuro of paintings or the drapery in Renaissance sculpture; quite inconceivable to picture Magnus Bird enraptured by anything, in fact, for he appears to be one of the most sterile and soulless creatures that Alice has ever met. Draped in beige (his waistcoat and silk puff perfectly matched to his sack coat), he is the embodiment of a breathing tea biscuit. He has droned on for at least one hour now on the challenges of old-age pensions.

'Alice?' There is a rattle of teacup on saucer as a knee bumps the table. 'Did you hear Magnus, Alice?'

The voice is talking to her – her father's voice – which tugs her vision of the room back into focus. She had been daydreaming of pantaloons. What a bore it is to be back in cinched dresses and weighed down with pleats again.

Alice blinks out of her daze. 'Yes, Father. 'Tis very interesting, Mr Bird. My apologies. I was momentarily distracted by the rude rumbling of my stomach.'

Magnus leans back and pats his own sturdy middle; he releases a short series of deep, terse barks, which Alice realises is a stiff sort of laughter.

'Very good. Anyway,' he continues, 'I will always be grateful for your father's tutelage. He taught me how to be passionate about something—'

A liberal use of the word 'passionate', thinks Alice, as Magnus repositions himself into his rigid stance: hands clasped in his lap as if bonded by magnets, spine aligned with the back of the armchair which is also, coincidentally, beige. His daughters do not need lessons from *me* on how to acquire perfect posture, she snips to herself.

'—and whilst I discovered quite quickly that my own devotion would not be towards art, I found myself gripped by the compelling system of bi-metallism. Now did you know that if you do not coin gold and silver to a fixed ratio—'

'I am just going to help Missy with the sandwiches,' offers Alice. 'Please do continue though. It is all rather fascinating, Mr Bird.'

The grumpiness about Oak's mien is pointedly directed towards Alice, but this she ignores with a turn towards the sideboard, which has been laid with cakes and cucumber sandwiches.

To Missy, who is brewing a fresh pot of coffee, Alice whispers, 'I think our doormat on Mansfield Road has more spirit.'

'Now Alice, don't be rude.' But Missy has to steady her hand as she suppresses a titter.

'And you want me to live and work in his household? I shall die of apathy.'

''Tis not a position of absolute permanence. His children will grow up.'

'They are three and five, Missy. Why, I shall look an old maid by the time I am twenty.'

The late autumn sun spills into the flat, which is a cruel reminder that, if circumstances were different, it could have been an enjoyable day in London of reading, nibbling and researching. Perhaps an afternoon snooze for her father whilst Alice took a wander round St James's Square. A game of backgammon before supper as they teased through ideas on Ponden-Hall. This is the weekend that Alice has daydreamed about since receiving her father's letter. Fine, the invitation was primarily to meet Magnus Bird, but this she could suffer for half an hour. Now that she has met the man, and he sits snugly before her with hours, it seems, of discourse on minting silver and gold, how can she endure the day?

The weekend is not yet lost, thinks Alice. There is still time to aid in her father's research – to be useful and prove that her life is bigger than that of a governess. If Magnus Bird would only bid them adieu, Alice could salvage the morning and show her father that as *pleasant* as Magnus Bird is, she is not the ideal addition to his household, for really, a governess of such a house should be versed in stocks and bonds.

They are refreshed with coffee, dainty sandwiches and shortbread, with the promising new topic of bookkeeping on Magnus' docket, when a knock upon the door causes all four of them to jump.

'Oh, good morning! You must be Missy.' Grace's voice infuses the flat with the warmth and energy of a parakeet. Her attire is just as bright, for she wears a silk velvet coat of the richest emerald green lined with lambswool; her sleeve cuffs and collar are thickly plumed. She is, on every account of colour, texture and appeal, the complete opposite of their morning guest.

'A pleasure to meet you, Miss Dodd,' says Missy, who is compelled, much to Alice's horror and Missy's own surprise, to curtsy.

Alice, startled to see Grace again and in such vibrancy, studies her closely. She recalls Jonny's comments about her, and scrutinises Grace's coat and scarf, which looks to be made of the softest of cashmere, and her fur hat, which she has shed to unleash the thickest mass of dark ringlets. In such close proximity, Grace is arresting, to be sure. Alice trusts her not an inch. She eyes the bundle of notes on the mantelpiece and stands to hide them, pretending to be interested in the worn painting of a Labrador that hangs above.

'Good morning, Miss Dodd,' says Oak, rising. 'Today is the day. A cup of coffee?'

Today is the day. When Alice thinks about it, her father *has* appeared rather nervy since their arrival early this morning: several glances at his diary, huffing to himself as he twiddled the chain of his pocket watch, incoherent grumblings as he sifted through wrinkled notes. Alice had assumed that his jitters were in anticipation of their meeting with Magnus Bird, but Oak is most at ease with him. And who would not be? The banker's presence is that of a dim lamp in a perfectly bright and luminous room.

'Thank you, but no,' Grace declines. 'I am only popping in. I am off to my interview with Miss Jahn.'

'It is good of you to go early.'

'Any final tips I should know? I have conducted a bit of research myself, mind you. I know how important this is.'

Oak displays a breeziness that Alice knows is only half sincere.

'I have no doubt that you will charm her,' he affirms. 'Miss Dodd, you have not met my daughter. This is Alice.'

'A pleasure, Alice.' Grace beams. 'How beautiful you are. Why, you look much older than I imagined. With the way your father speaks about you, I had assumed you dressed in woollen skirts and school stockings.'

'How funny,' says Alice. 'I am eighteen. He has not mentioned you.'

Missy snorts.

'Oh, I am no one to mention,' says Grace with a friendly shrug. 'I am merely aiding your father with one affair.'

'And Miss Dodd, this is Magnus Bird, an old pupil of mine,' says Oak. 'He is now an important banker on Lombard Street.'

'A pleasure. Oh, no, please—' Grace's ringlets bounce about her face as she waves her hand. 'Do not stand up. I shall be on my way presently. I just wanted to assure Mr Oak that all is in hand this morning.'

Perhaps it is Magnus Bird's stuttering response and the blush upon his cheeks – the first sign of vitality throughout the long morning – or perhaps it is Oak's plaudit for Grace's efforts, an assured air of confidence in her success in whatever important trial he has trusted her with; one or both of these insults inspires outrage and anguish in Alice's bosom, and although she is desperate to keep a calm cast about herself, determined to remain cool and unfussed, her plight is remembered afresh and she is too young to disguise her heart. A lip wobbles.

And she knows that Grace Dodd has seen.

Alice avoids looking at her but she can see in the margin of her eye how the sitter sucks on her lip and notes the scowl on Alice's face.

She must like her better for it, for the grin on Grace's face is unabashed, curious – just for a moment – before she turns with serious countenance to Oak.

'And I came to request Alice's help,' she says. It is a statement rather than a question.

'I beg your pardon?' asks Oak.

'Me?' Alice is startled.

Grace nods. 'The more I think about it, the more sense it makes. Just to ensure I secure the position.'

'You need *my* help?'

'Yes. Come with me.' Grace holds out her hand as she would to a child.

'Um, I do not think that is necessary,' interjects Oak. 'Alice is quite busy here, you see—'

The cosy sitting room with its stacks of books and trays of short-bread and tangerines and half-eaten sandwiches is a picture of comfort. Magnus Bird blinks in his armchair.

''Tis nearly midday,' says Grace. 'I had assumed that this *meeting* would have been over early this morning. Was I wrong to assume that Alice would be available now?'

'Well, I think Magnus was just getting to know her—'

Grace smiles as she fetches Alice's coat, which hangs on the peg behind her. 'If it is a good fit, one knows immediately, yes? Perhaps if such a long meeting is necessary, 'tis not the best nor most obvious arrangement.'

Alice is stunned. Only Grace's wide eyes and conspicuous nod to the door impel her to cross the room.

'It will not take long,' says Grace. 'Three hours at most and she will be back to help with your critical work.'

'Three hours!' cries Oak. 'Do you know what could happen in three hours in the city?' The shake of his head is vigorous. 'Alice is not versed in city life, Miss Dodd.' And remembering Magnus, 'But she *will* be, of course. Certainly by the summer. She has not had the opportunity to know London yet.'

'I shall be with her the entire time,' assures Grace.

'I'm afraid it is not possible, Miss Dodd. Alice is needed here. Now best of luck with your meeting.'

'Father…' Alice is careful with her wording. 'I would quite enjoy a turn about the neighbourhood. Get some fresh air. I am always asking you to see London and if Miss Dodd is here to accompany me on a short walk—'

'You see? She wants to come.'

'This is a terrible idea, Miss Dodd, and I must implore you to put it out of your mind. Can you fathom the dangers a young girl of

Alice's age might face out in London on her own? The pickpockets, the kidnappings—'

'She is eighteen, Mr Oak! And 'tis the middle of the day!' Grace's laugh rises to the vaulted ceilings like the merry tinkling of bells. 'Do you know what I was getting up to at Alice's age in the city? Why, I was—'

'No, no! No, no. That will not be necessary, I'm sure—'

'Mr Oak, may I have your assistance, please?' pipes Missy from the kitchen.

'Not now, Missy.'

''Tis urgent, sir. An issue with the clotted cream.'

If Missy cannot mollify him, no one will. Alice is certain that Missy will be an ally in this. If anything, her departure with Grace will expedite the close of Magnus Bird's visit. As her father grudgingly shuffles to the kitchen, Alice turns to the banker.

'It has been a pleasure to meet you, Mr Bird. I am very grateful for the opportunity to be employed as your children's governess, but I will understand in the fullest if you would prefer someone of like-minded tastes. I am afraid I have bored you this morning.'

'Terrible quality in a governess,' adds Grace.

Alice bites her lip. Her rosy smile is the first sincere look she has bestowed on him all morning. 'Please help yourself to another sandwich, Mr Bird. Or perhaps some cheese. We brought this cheddar from Oxford. It is my father's favourite.'

In the kitchen, Oak is met with a piping hot scone topped with a perfect dollop of fresh clotted cream and raspberry jam.

'What is the issue, Missy?' he asks, confused.

'What do you suppose will happen if you keep Alice holed up in sitting rooms all of her life?' Missy hisses. 'You mean to send her to live with Mr Bird? He may be a gentleman, sir, but even the coffee loses its pep when he speaks! If this is your grand plan for Alice, why, you might as well have arranged a marriage for her and signed her life away.'

'Now, Missy, please – marriage, you say? Is she old enough to think about marriage? Do you think Alice would like that?'

'Mr Oak!'

'I jest, Missy, calm down.' Oak glances about the galley and then to the scone in his palm. 'This has naught to do with clotted cream. Is this ready to eat?'

'I have told you time and time again, sir, that you must let her go. Just a little. You can discuss the matter of her employment later, but right now, just a quick wander around a square or two. What harm would it do?'

'Now is not the time, Missy.'

'She is clawing at the walls, sir. Pulling at her hair.' Missy lowers her voice. 'She has offered to help with the cooking again.'

Oak's eyes widen, the fear plain upon them.

'I do not mean to restrain her,' he says, rubbing his eyes with the butt of his free hand. He swoops a finger-lick of cream and exhales. Shakes his head. 'Why is she not content with books—'

'Because she is not Emma.'

'No.'

Professor and daily stand before each other in the narrow kitchen. Alice is all they have – they both know this, allow the weight of this shared responsibility to settle upon them like a dawn fog. Only Missy can begin to understand Oak's anxiety, his irrational fears of losing his remaining daughter, the lone treasure of his life. It is moments like this when Oak yearns for his wife. Just a moment, he often thinks, to seek her counsel, her comfort. She would have known and understood their daughters more fully and naturally than Oak ever could – would have known what was best for Alice right now.

'Perhaps she can begin to explore Oxford more in the first instance.' It is a soft, forlorn plea and Oak already knows that he will yield. 'Not London.'

'With all due respect, sir,' says Missy, pushing another scone into his hand along with a linen napkin, 'if she were to be accompanied by anyone in this city, I reckon few could hold their own or know their way about more than Miss Dodd. That woman can take care of herself.'

And Oak knows she is right. Even so, his misery is not allayed.

Upon stepping out of the door, Alice revels in the thrill of their collusion. It is a long walk from South Kensington to Cecil Court, but Grace leads Alice at a swift pace and nips down quiet alleys to avoid the congestion of Brompton Road. They walk arm in arm as if they are bosom friends, and strangers nod to them, tip their hats.

'Thank you for helping me escape,' says Alice. It is a quiet but sincere regard. 'Mr Bird seems a nice man but… well, my father and I are not united in this plan for me to work for him.'

'He is beginning to see that, I think. You intrigue me, Alice Oak.'

Whilst this is meant to be a compliment, it is most unsettling for Alice. What *intrigues* does a woman like Grace Dodd have?

'And my swooping you away is a bit selfish,' continues Grace, 'for I believe that you actually *can* be of help to me. There is tremendous pressure on me to acquire this position. We must ensure that I succeed.'

This unnerves Alice even more, but she can only be whisked forward. She is overwrought, overwhelmed by the hawkers and clip-clopping of carriages on Leicester Square, which liken their counterparts in Oxford to gentle pedlars and children's wagons. There is no mistake that Grace is surefooted as she weaves them through London's back streets and passageways, yet Alice cannot stop thinking about Jonny's allegations. She had been fascinated, certainly, by this caricature of a woman whom her father had unwittingly befriended. But now that she is out rambling the streets of London with her, Alice is not compelled in the slightest. She is nervous. And as Grace taps her arm and nods to each historical building, each monument of royalty or literary prominence, Alice notes that she has never felt unsafe with Lou. Are not the slinking canal paths of Jericho and the dark lanes of Oxford's seedy underbelly more dangerous than the pulsating capital in the midday sun? Never has Alice questioned her security with Lou. Even in the pitch of night, with Lou, Alice feels guarded from harm.

'Now do not be fooled by these smart shopfronts,' says Grace, pulling Alice close. 'They may be brilliant now but once upon a time, this street was rife with robberies and forgeries. And about one hundred years ago, a great fire razed this half to the ground.'

'How awful.'

'An alleged Mrs Colloway, who owned a brandy shop and brothel here, emptied her barrels and set the entire stock alight. Women are not to be trifled with, eh?' Grace winks at her horrified companion. 'Ah, we are here.'

The phrenology parlour is hidden amongst the printers and public houses and shopfronts of London's finest tradesmen; one would miss the discreet door on the corner of the narrow, easily missed passageway leading off St Martin's Lane if one was not in need of Miss Jahn's services.

'Now.' Grace faces Alice and places her hands on her shoulders. ''Tis imperative that I am chosen for the position. I should think our chat will take half an hour. Perhaps more, perhaps less, depending on how Elke takes to me and if I have done well in my research. Regardless of how our conversation develops, we cannot risk her choosing someone else. And that is where you come in.'

'I do not understand.'

'There will be others coming to meet her about the position.' Grace squints an eye as she tries to recall. 'Two others if I saw correctly. The window was foggy yesterday morning when I visited and so the diary upon her desk was obscured. No matter. Two, three, four – you will see to anyone who comes.'

Alice starts. 'I will – what?'

'You will wait here,' Grace says as she gently guides Alice around the corner into the back lane. 'And as each woman appears for her appointment with Elke, *before* she can knock upon the door, you will intercept and inform her that the position has been filled.'

'I cannot do that!'

'Of course you can.'

'I cannot!'

'But you must.'

'No, Miss Dodd. Truly, I am a horrid liar.'

'Then tell them… that you were her old assistant and that Elke is a brute of an employer and that they should escape her clutches whilst they can.'

'That is a worse lie than the first.'

'We do not know that. Why, she could be a terrible witch. You will be doing them a favour.'

Alice crosses her arms and peeks around the corner to Cecil Court. 'And what if someone sees me? What if someone figures out what I am doing?'

Grace laughs. 'You are truly not from London. We mind our own business in the city. If anyone pays you attention long enough to realise what you are up to, they are probably targeting you for a trick. Our scheme will not matter to them in the slightest.'

Alice pales.

'But I shall be right inside and keeping an eye on you. So not to worry.' Grace pats her cheek and then retrieves a pocket watch from the layers of her coat. 'She will be expecting me now. I shall be quick. Just turn them away. Whatever you have to do.'

Alice grabs Grace's hand as she turns to knock on Elke's door. 'Must I do this?'

Grace's dimples are deep and her squeeze is sincere. 'Do you want to help your father acquire the information he seeks?'

That is *all* Alice wants. Perhaps this is her opportunity to show her quality. There is, deep in Alice's belly, the shade of a thrill about it.

'I shan't be long,' says Grace. And she knocks three times with the charm and confidence of a fortune-teller.

Elke Jahn smells of pipe tobacco and has evidently just arisen from bed. She sits behind her desk, silhouetted in the bright midday light that streaks through her office's sash windows, and rests bony, inter-twined fingers upon the knot of her silk dressing gown. She drinks from a mug that smells of cinnamon and something acidic; it cuts through the space between them and causes Grace's nose to twitch.

'But you are not familiar with the practice itself,' Elke repeats. Her voice is gruff and heavy. Grace cannot place the accent.

'Not the *details* of it,' corrects Grace. 'But of course I know a touch about phrenology. And to be honest, I am rather intrigued by the art, which is why this is an attractive position.'

''Tis a *science.*'

Grace lifts her chin and smiles. 'I believe it can be both.'

Elke grunts. 'And you have had experience in organising an unwieldy collection of files? There are roomfuls of them on the bottom floor – the scribblings of two generations of doctors. Meticulous. You can imagine the mess.'

'That does not intimidate me in the slightest. I once served as an assistant to a very well-respected and coveted history don. And whilst he might have been a genius, organised he was not. In fact, he was quite slovenly. Sometimes when he was done with a book or a collection of papers, he would stuff them under the sofa. Just like that – with the dust mites and biscuit crumbs. And do not get me started on the towers of teacups that would collect in the bathroom and behind the cushions.'

Grace enjoys spinning yarns like this about her former lover. He was, in fact, obsessively clean, but she relishes the thought of him living like a swine in his own muck.

'Yes, well. They are like that, men.'

Even Grace, who can hold court with the most stuffy of company, cannot tell if she is charming Elke Jahn or not. Her responses garner no colourful reactions and her stories inspire no pricks of the ear or upturns of Elke's pursed lips. Grace is confident that she can convince the phrenologist of her skills but this will not be enough to secure the job. She has tried drumming up a dialogue on potted plants, having noticed Elke's windowsills are crowded with succulents, but this was futile ('I wish they would perish,' Elke had shrugged, 'but they live and live and live'). Then Grace had asked about the dark leather volumes in the glass case behind Elke's desk ('An impressive collection of Christopher Marlowe's works – surely these cannot be first editions?'), but Elke had rolled her eyes and scoffed, claiming that Marlowe had been her grandfather's favourite playwright despite his clear inferiority to Shakespeare. No bite. Grace will not allow herself to feel nervous just yet, but the room grows warmer and she loosens her lace collar.

Out of the corner of her eye, she sees Alice through the window stepping in front of the shop door to cut off a tall woman wrapped up in scarves. When the woman tries to peer into the window, Alice grabs her arm and points to something down the lane.

Grace has one final card to play. Next to Elke's diary is a framed programme of sorts. Through the window during yesterday's snooping, Grace could make out the larger print: a few names, a date and *Das unterbrochene Opferfest*. A quick chat with the German cheesemonger in the shop below her flat had revealed the title's translation.

'Now forgive me, Miss Jahn, if this is rude or intrusive,' appeals Grace, leaning forward, 'but I have to ask... your surname is of German descent, is that right?'

'It is.'

'I thought so. Ah, how jealous I am. You see...' Grace opens her mouth to speak but changes her mind. She closes her eyes and shakes her head with vigour, causing her ringlets to bob about her face. 'I told myself I would not disclose this, but I am too curious! Miss Jahn, if I am to be perfectly frank with you, I am truly interested in the position to assist you – and indeed I am certain that I possess the right skills and experience – but even more than the job, I was most interested in meeting you, with your surname being so unique here in London, on the most obscure and coincidental chance – knowing the respectable circles that your family must run in – that you might somehow be acquainted with my favourite actress… Mathilde Jahn.'

Elke shifts. Elongates her spine.

'She is a German actress, you see, and the *one* time I visited the continent, I was lucky enough to attend a performance of… now here, I am going to butcher the title. My German is terrible, you see. In English it is *The Interrupted Feast of Sacrifice*—'

Elke's papery hands abandon her lap and are placed flat on the desk. '*Das unterbrochene Opferfest*,' she recites in a soft, triumphant clip.

Grace clasps her hands together. 'Yes! Do you know it?'

For the first time this morning, Elke Jahn's lips curl at the corners. Her right eyebrow arches, which betrays surprise, delight. 'Miss Dodd, Mathilde Jahn is my first cousin.'

If Grace has learned to stroke an ego over her many years of deception, she has also mastered the act of meek, intimidated awe. How brilliant she is at making one feel revered and special.

'Your cousin?' Grace repeats in quiet admiration. She brings her hands to her chest. 'What talent. What presence. I have never seen such spirit on stage.'

'Oh, she is one of the best.' Elke's fists ball and she nods with feeling.

'Oh, she is *the* best! Why, I thought perhaps you might have heard of her or even knew a friend of a friend, but to be *related* to Mathilde Jahn… I never would have dreamed. 'Tis an honour to meet you, Miss Jahn.'

'Look at this.' Elke reaches for the framed programme and turns it to face Grace. 'From her debut performance. Sadly I was here and not able to attend, but she sent me the programme that very week.'

'May I?' Grace holds the frame in veneration.

Elke scrutinises the young woman before her and replaces the frame with care. Her voice is lighter when she says, 'What a charming surprise. By the look of you, I would not have thought that you were interested in *real* culture.'

Grace ignores this backhanded compliment and scrunches her hair, reshapes it around her ears.

'Now tell me honestly,' Elke continues, 'who do you believe to be the best soprano on stage these days? I know I am biased but I do believe Mathilde would contend for the choicest position.'

'I beg your pardon?'

Elke throws her hand to the ceiling. 'The top soprano. Perhaps Mathilde is no Adelina Patti, but I do believe she is sensational. Who would rival her voice?'

Ah. So *Das unterbrochene Opferfest* is an opera.

Grace maintains her plastered smile. She is no enthusiast of the opera. On the contrary, she finds the pitches and vibrato of these human instruments most unnatural and grating to the ears.

'There is no rival, of course,' she says. 'Mathilde is unmatched. Superior in every way.'

Elke chuckles. 'But of course, you are biased too! I want to show you something. Or rather, *play* you something.'

The phrenologist stands and crosses the room to a table with a pale blue silk sheet cast over its bulk. She pulls at the sheet dramatically to reveal a most bizarre contraption: wooden and brass with a rotating mechanism and what appears to be the golden, bloomed horn of a tuba.

''Tis a phonograph,' says Elke. 'Have you ever used one?'

'I have not had the pleasure,' responds Grace. She has seen a phonograph before, in an office in one of the university halls, but never has she heard it sing.

'You will not believe your luck today, Miss Dodd. Look at this.'

In a chest beside the phonograph, Elke reveals an impressive collection of brown, waxen phonograph cylinders – rows upon rows of them in various shades and grooves.

'I have nearly every song my cousin has ever performed in this chest. Mind you, some of them are quite lengthy so they span two or three cylinders, sometimes four. But can you believe it? We may not be able to hear Mathilde live before us, but we can enjoy and savour her talent as much as we want! Over and over again.'

'How... marvellous!' The lilt in Grace's voice runs flat.

'Shall we listen to one now?'

Any quickening of Grace's nerves that was inspired by her clever success quickly dulls. Outside the bay window, she sees Alice speaking with great zeal to another woman. They are so engrossed in conversation — several impassioned arm gestures towards the shopfronts and wares in their windows — that Alice does not bother to stand between the woman and Elke's parlour at all. If Grace did not know any better, she would have thought that Alice was rather enjoying herself. Indeed the young Miss Oak throws her head back in laughter too often to be playing a part. Grace smirks. Here is the fun and the fire she had discerned in the girl's face.

'A cup of tea whilst we listen?' offers Elke.

Solomon Oak will be much displeased, for they will be late back to the flat. But has she not bested the first challenge of their plan? They might acquire this precious information yet, especially if Elke holds Grace in high esteem. And anyway, Alice is being taken care of. Grace has always been one to ask for forgiveness rather than seek permission.

'A cup would be lovely,' she says to Elke. 'A splash of milk and two sugars, if you please.'

20

Preparation for Lecture Two: The Animal Portraits

No. 3 *Prince – A Spaniel*, 1832, The National Gallery
No. 4 *Gentle Polyphemus – A Piebald*, 1835, The National Gallery
No. 5 *The Three-toed Woodpecker*, 1836, The National Gallery
No. 8 *Bluebell – A Dairy Cow*, 1837, The National Gallery
No. 9 *Peacocks*, 1839, The National Gallery

Their histories are just as important as their compositions, Oak reminds himself. *Just as important*. His lecture notes on the animal portraits are notably sparser, scruffier than those on Ponden-Hall's human subjects. They were, perhaps unsurprisingly, the favourites of his children. He has delivered this lecture on many occasions, trying it out on Emma and Alice over figs and toast in the garden; as he trawls through his notes and walks through his delivery now, their small voices pierce his presentation like a bell.

'*A dog, a horse and a woodpecker. Two pets and one anomaly, Father.*'

'*Not an anomaly,*' says Oak, '*because you see that three years later, the peacocks are a similar indulgence. But in the first batch of animal portraits – The Trio, as it has come to be known – yes, the woodpecker is the only one that was not a family domestic.*'

Prince, the Ponden-Halls' spaniel: bought for Timothy and Adelaide one Christmas by their grandfather. He was spotted with Timothy in Hyde Park most mornings whenever he was in London. A sound gun dog.

Polyphemus, DeLacey's horse. DeLacey was a keen rider, which does make the public speculate; he had the finest bred stallions at his fingertips and this is the one he kept as a pet. Polyphemus would have spent many years waiting in the paddock whilst DeLacey was at sea.

He is Emma's favourite of the trio. The horse is at least seventeen hands – a bay Clydesdale with white feathering surrounding his hooves. He stands erect in profile, sedate and old with no bridle, saddle or martingale to imprison him. Layers of beeswax have trapped the paint to create full, red-brown textures as rich and ridged as hazelnuts; the horse's flanks are rounded and full from the technique, as if lungs expand beneath the ribs, and the feathering around each heel and hoof appears soft and silky to the touch, for every single hair has been pulled through the wax in an act of great patience and precision. There are thousands of wispy locks just around the horse's cannons, never mind its mane.

But most surprising is the horse's face: it is missing an eye. It is unsettling. Repulsive, actually. Where the eye should be is a crater of black scarring, enhanced with baubles of wax that deepen the hole. But once this ugly disfigurement has been acknowledged, the painting as a whole can be appreciated. He is, in all other respects, a stunning creature.

He is Oak's favourite of the animal portraits, too.

'Poor beast,' Emma says.

'But quite lucky. Most would have had him put down.'

'Do you know what happened to him, Father?' asks Alice.

'No. But look at the white hairs around his muzzle and eyes. The depressions around the empty eye socket and wrinkles around the scar. It happened long ago and, still, Polyphemus lived to a fine old age. DeLacey must have adored him.'

'Gentle Polyphemus.'

'Indeed. It is the only painting whose title speaks of character. A great contrast, especially, with the three-toed woodpecker that followed it.'

'An animal from one of their excursions.'

'Mm. Most likely Sweden, from the very same expedition that would eventually bring them to the kraken. You see, they swept the Baltic Sea before heading north.'

Oak must remember to bring a map, for the audience finds it most satisfying to have a visual reminder of their course.

The woodpecker perches on an invisible branch.

'There is an empty bird cage in the portrait of DeLacey,' Emma recalls.

He pats her cheek, sticky from fig seeds. 'Very good. When this painting first appeared, many made the link as you have, my darling; a sort of fore-shadowing. Beautiful, is it not? The yellow crown shows that it is male.'

His clever girl. How can he deliver a lecture on these portraits without thinking of his children – without thinking of her? Emma lives within these paintings as much as the sitters do, but there are no rumours of her immortality, no praying for her soul or weighing up a devil's bounty. For the first time, Oak wonders why he has not returned to these masterpieces sooner. He cannot be close enough to them, cannot inhale too much the sugared tinge of wax and balmy oils, cannot grow tired of the little voice who satiates his thoughts with her questions and playful observations. He can only absorb each brushstroke as if they are the bones of a ghost – the fibres of a cherub too sweet and good for this world.

21

Even nearly a week under the employ of Elke Jahn, Grace Dodd finds herself staring dumbly fascinated – mid-box, mid-stack – at the multitude of wonders in the phrenology parlour basement. She is here to aid Oak, she reminds herself, to find these documents on Timothy Ponden-Hall's grandmother so they may chip further into the mystery; the extra coin is also an attractive incentive. But these motivations are often overshadowed by simple and sheer curiosity, for the parlour is unlike any space that Grace has ever seen. Scrolls upon scrolls of phrenology charts litter the floor and balance in precariously heaped pyramids; bronze craniometers and callipers – round, oversized forceps, as if fashioned to pluck the moon out of the sky – poke out of crates and medical sacks like spring grass; animal skulls caked with grime are stacked forehead bones to jaws across a table and serve as bookends to large, unwelcoming tomes.

But most captivating to Grace are the phrenology busts that line the shelves. They glisten, bald and ceramic, in the dull morning light that filters in from the street windows above. Some are divided by contours and organised by different dyes; others are region-labelled in tiny, meticulous script – patches of *hope*, *destructiveness*, *causality*, *sublimity*.

How could anyone have believed in such base diagnoses? Grace has peeked through enough notebooks and has rattled off a thousand questions to Oak to know that this *science* is questionable. Even so, she wonders if there is merit in the correlation between lumps on the side of the skull and selfishness. She finds herself prodding her own head, feeling for bumps or dips through her hair that hides it all.

Grace is startled from these ruminations when Elke's heavy tread is heard upon the stairs.

'Still enjoying *Fidelio*, are you?' the phrenologist asks. The phonograph has been tucked in the corner between two busts. It plays so constantly that Grace hardly notices it any more; so absorbed in her work is she that the trills and vibrato are as drab and ho-hum as the whistle of a tea kettle. In fact, when she dares to admit it, Grace finds herself on the brink of enjoying the baritone.

'Break for tea?' Elke asks. Her accent is Austrian, Oak has clarified, despite being brought up in England.

'Thank you. I was just admiring the busts again. That one is interesting. The sections all seem to be labelled quite negatively.'

'Ah, yes. One of Gall's earlier models. He studied the skulls of inmates in prisons and lunatic asylums. It is no surprise that criminal traits dominated their heads. You see the depressions here? Means a lack of benevolence. And here? Lack of spirituality.'

The tea is always too weak but Grace is grateful for the break. She is also supremely intrigued by Elke, who has taken to conversing with her for long hours every day.

Elke eyes the girl over her steaming cup. 'I will read your skull,' she says. 'No fee.'

She has offered several times, yet Grace has always declined.

'No thank you, Miss Jahn,' she says before sipping her tea. 'It is a fascinating talent you have, but I am afraid I have no need of it. I already know that I lack a sufficient amount of cautiousness and that I am a tad selfish.'

'But you do not know the details. The shape and unevenness of one's skull shows us which cerebral organs have developed particular aptitudes and character traits.'

'It is a kind offer, but no thank you.'

It is nonsense, of course, but a part of Grace – the same part that ties a black ribbon around her wrist after a death, the same part that covers her mouth whilst yawning to protect her spirit – is afraid of what Elke will discover. Does she not have similar protuberances around her ears as these criminals? Does she not share the same indents on her temples? She has worked so tirelessly recently to give up an unsavoury life that the thought of such a fate imprinted into her very biology is intolerable.

'Some advice then,' says Elke. 'You are still young enough to be in want of a husband.'

'I do not think—'

'This is what to look for. You see the shape of his head?'

Elke unfurls a scroll and spreads it across the table. It is a print that showcases the profiles of two men: 'A Sincere Husband' and 'A Disingenuous Husband'. The genuine husband's head is nicely rounded, whilst the disingenuous husband's head is lumpy and angular. His aquiline nose hooks upward to a forehead that is as straight and long as a cliff face.

It takes all of Grace's willpower to withhold a guffaw. She thinks back to her nights in Marylebone with the don when she would wake in the night and watch him sleep. Was his head rounded or angular? She feels a prick of satisfaction when she imagines it to be knobbly beneath the thick curls.

'Weak in conjugality,' says Elke, pointing to the disingenuous husband's quadrate profile. 'Insufficient Parental Love. Strong in Acquisitiveness. No, no. Not for you.'

Grace is no stranger to acquisitiveness but Elke is not privy to her previous life.

Their exchanges are so bizarre, so entertaining, that Grace must actively remind herself of her task. She has unboxed and filed hundreds of patient reports so far with no sign of Elizabeth Ponden-Hall. The boxes are endless, though; they seem to multiply in the night and each subsequent crate brings her further back in time by a week, a fortnight, a month. Grace will persevere in her search although the pads of her fingers are worn and her hands seem perpetually coated in dust. She is also the most financially secure she has ever been since pursuing an honest livelihood, for Elke Jahn pays a generous wage. Oak offers to pay her as well, but this, Grace has decided, she will decline at the end of her tenure. How empowering it will be to turn down payment – to pursue a curiosity of one's own volition and savour the ability to do so.

22

Preparation for Lecture Three: The Orphan Boy

Lecture notes, Solomon Oak
No. 6 *Harry – An Orphan Boy*, 1837, The Royal Academy of Arts

The portrait of Harry appeared on the doorstep of the Academy just three days after the orphan died from a chest infection at the Clerkenwell Workhouse.

He was nothing special, the papers blare over and over like a morning trumpet. This makes the already shocking portrait – 'a string of animals and then an *urchin*?' – more remarkable. The boy was shy and quite unskilled, which is a feat considering he was merely sorting bottles. So the papers report.

How Ponden-Hall became aware of the ragamuffin remains a mystery to all, even to this day. The boy was a shadow of a shadow, parentless like the rest of them and exceptionally small. A runt of runts.

Which casts the portrait in a curious light indeed.

Ponden-Hall's use of light is extraordinary, for most of the frame is cast in grey-blue shadow. Notice how the boy himself is illuminated by the one strip of light; the sun arcs over the dilapidated bricks and throws its beams on Harry alone. He does nothing, simply stands, but in doing so basks in quiet triumph in a moment of warmth.

Our eye is brought round: from the loose chestnut curls that hang past his eyebrows to a protruding collarbone left exposed by dark linens much too large for his frame. He could be wearing a potato sack; this is how shapeless and begrimed his garments have become. And yet—

All is not hopeless, for the boy holds a chunk of bread in one hand and what appears to be a blood orange in the other. We are intrigued by these details, first drawn in by their textures and careful prodding of the wax to make them look positively edible; but then we wonder: a blood orange? On Coppice Row, London? Are these not the treasured fruit of Sicily, that sun-drenched island on the Ionian Sea? The orange is bright and pure: Ponden-Hall uses the mineral crocoite here, a bold punch in the centre of the painting. The leaf, a delicate detail but also piercing, is most likely a mixture of malachite and linseed oil.

The boy is no orphan, no poorhouse runt to be whipped for dropping a bottle, for he possesses the fruit of princes and is crowned by the sun. He looks out at us with confidence. You see his lips? The soft upturn of the corner. Some interpret this as arrogance, but I disagree. I believe it is a look of forgiveness. Even if we are not sorry for his mistreatment in this world, we are forgiven for it.

He was only six years old.

Oak's own children eat runny eggs and rye for breakfast as he walks through his notes from across the table. The yolks leave thick, streaky tendrils across their plates.

'He was younger than I am now,' says Alice. 'Yet he was born so many years before me. What a strange idea.'

'He has been immortalised at six.'

'If I died now, I would be eight years old for ever. Surely, Father, you would like that. I could remain a little girl and never be burdened with growing up. You say yourself that being old is a challenge.'

'What nonsense,' says Emma. 'We must all grow up. The joys far outweigh the challenges. Isn't that right, Father? Why, if you had not grown old, you would never have met Mother and you would never have had us.'

'That is true. But I wish I could have both: the wisdom of old age and the carefree nature of youth.'

'Well. If I had a choice to remain eleven years old for ever or grow old with the brittlest of bones and the whitest of hair, I would age in a heartbeat. How limited my life is as a little girl.'

'Grow old, my darling,' say Oak with a chuckle. 'But not too fast. I would like to savour you both like a cup of Christmas punch.'

Oak is dozing in the armchair, his notes scattered upon his lap, when there is a tap-tap-tap at the door. He is agitated at first and in his hazy state between dreaming and wakefulness, he believes it is another Ponden-Hall enthusiast who has stalked his steps, who has had the gall to intrude upon the comforts of his private quarters. It has happened too often recently. But as he comes to and notes the time, Oak realises that this tapping comes not from a zealot but from Grace Dodd. It is her usual time for popping in, after her work at the phrenology parlour and before a sitting stint at the Academy.

'Do not let me disturb you,' she says. 'I am just dropping off another stack of articles from the museum. These have been acquired from a bookkeeper's on the south bank.'

Oak rubs his eyes, ruffles his papers together into an unwieldy bundle. He sees the articles' drab titles and winces. 'More of the same.'

'One of them compares DeLacey and Ponden-Hall's relationship to Romeo and Juliet's.' Grace scrunches her nose and points her tongue in mock disgust. 'A forbidden love. What a rubbish comparison. Mind you, I have never been a fan of the original. And what he says about names — how silly. What is in a name? Why, everything. Imagine if I was Ann Dodd or Sue Dodd. Those are sounds, not names. A name must have some weight behind it.'

'You do surprise me, Miss Dodd. How daring of you to criticise Shakespeare.'

Her hands lock on her hips. 'I know Shakespeare quite well, if you must know.'

'Another course you sneaked into?'

'Yes. And quite easily too. 'Tis a wonder what one can achieve with a high collar, ankle skirts and a perfectly pinned-up bun.'

'If only the don could see you now.'

He is less painful to think about these days. 'It was he who taught me how to write and form an argument properly,' she says flippantly.

'I do not think young people need to be taught how to form an argument. I think you especially rather like it.'

'Take this article, for example.' She tosses the bottom paper onto Oak's lap. 'It claims after the orphan boy died, the smell of oranges around the workhouse and surrounding streets was overwhelming for weeks on end. Sounds ludicrous, yes? Well, if you did just a smidgen of research, you would find that at the end of one of these streets was a canning factory, particularly known for its production of marmalade owing to its owner having a Portuguese mistress. January is the month for making marmalade. Of course it would smell like oranges. And bloody delicious too.'

Oak's laughter is unrestrained. 'My, you are an angry detective. Exceptional attention to detail, my dear. If we had the time, I would encourage you to disprove as many of these ridiculous publications as possible.'

Grace blushes and recomposes herself. 'You know, I almost had an article published once.'

'Oh?'

'Just in a student press. The don submitted it for me. I think he was quite proud of me. It was not chosen in the end, but just the consideration was enough for me.'

'And what was the article about?'

'It was on Mary Shelley and how cruel readers were to assume that Percy wrote most of the text.'

'An article before its time.'

'I suppose. I just felt compelled to defend her. And it was something to argue. You are right, Mr Oak. I do love to argue.'

23

Alice eats her lunch as she pores over her biology notes, but it is no use. She has read the same page no fewer than eleven times. Darwin's theory of evolution with its discussion of animal species and natural selection is a blur (what is phenotypic variation? reproductive isolation?). She does not process these terms, these ideas, for her thoughts funnel to one memory only and the contemplations that surround it.

Alice remembers the first time she saw Emma cry. She was hiding in the broom cupboard hunched over the waxed lid of a jar. When she crouched down beside her, her sister tilted the lid to reveal a squashed spider, its legs stiff and flimsy, its tiny body cracked with dried globs of blue blood.

'It startled me when I walked into the larder.' Emma sniffled. 'I screamed. Father came running and I pointed to it – trapped in the corner – and asked him to kill it.' Her lip wobbled. 'So he did.'

Alice could see no cause for weeping here. She did not understand and said so. *How brave and wonderful of Father*, she said. But Emma only shook her head and began to bawl more. 'I wasn't thinking,' she choked between sobs. 'It had done nothing wrong. It had done nothing to me. I was only frightened is all, in that moment. I should not have asked Father to kill it.'

Alice, still bewildered, offered, 'But 'tis only a spider. I can find you a new one.'

'That is not the point,' Emma sniffed. The red splotches on her face burned and glistened in the low light.

'Come.' Alice tugged at her sister's sleeve. 'We will tell Father off for killing it and he will say sorry and you will feel better.'

'No, Alice. This is not Father's fault. It's mine. I asked him to kill it. I thought too rashly.' Emma straightened then and dabbed her eyes with the cuffs of her sleeve. After a deep breath, she turned to Alice. 'Father must not know I have been crying. He would think me foolish.'

'Is it not foolish to cry over a spider?'

'I do not think it is ever foolish to cry.' Emma stood up, shielded her head from the hanging buckets and towels. 'Will you bury it in the garden with me?'

And of course Alice did. In the garden, beneath the rose bush, they used Missy's trowel to dig a shallow hole. Emma cried the entire time – a disproportionate amount of tears shed for an inconsequential, skittering creature, and Alice simply could not understand. She knew that Emma was grieving for something invisible, more weighty than the eight-legged corpse in the dirt, something to do with guilt or disappointment or something utterly mystifying that only eight-year-olds were mature enough to comprehend. Alice certainly could not. All she knew was in that hour of Emma's sorrow, the world ceased to move. Her brave, clever sister diminished to tearful heartache. And their father could not know, but she could. Alice loved her sister more after that.

Now Alice thinks of Lou and the night they took Mary Whipple to the doctor. She wonders how the old woman is doing. She remembers her smell, the tangy comfort of fresh bread and the feverish heat she exuded. She must have been returned to the estate by now. Alice plays these scenes over and over in her head – Lou's plea for help and the vulnerability she was so keenly unused to exposing. Since that night, Alice has struggled to reconcile this familiar feeling that creeps into the space behind her ribs, seeps up into her throat. Guilt. There is no use in denying it. She has no right to feel such protectiveness, such empathy and adoration for this woman who bears no relation to her. This loyalty, this sensation of warmth that permeates her belly – also coupled with a twinge of… competition? Awe? Such sentiments are reserved for sisters, are they not? Alice tugs at her plait, rubs her temples. But of course, she cannot know.

It is unfair to compare them, Emma and Lou.

Ten minutes past two o'clock. Was it not two o'clock several hours ago?

Alice stands to stretch. Perhaps some air will help her refocus. She is to have a final examination on this material before the term ends. Yes, a turn about the neighbourhood will do her well.

In the entrance hall, she catches her reflection in the mirror by the coat stand and pauses. Alice has never thought twice about her appearance, yet now, she wonders how others might behold her... how Lou might see her, how Grace might see her – as a fellow woman. She lifts her chin – turns it this way and that. She has her mother's nose and eyes. Beautiful. Soft. This is how family friends have described these features in the past. She tousles the stray hair around her forehead and examines the dark waves straining to break free of the plait, wiry and disobedient. This part of her, she knows, will never be tamed. It would erupt like a lion's mane – just like her father's – if she let it.

And why doesn't she? She draws herself up, straight and puffed like a soldier and turns sideways to examine her profile, places her hands over her flat chest. Then she unties the ribbon and pulls the hair loose. It tumbles about her shoulders, not quite as long and groomed as Grace's, and not quite as wild as Lou's, but there is something of a goddess about her. *Even I can look like a young woman*, Alice thinks. But before she can descend into any embarrassing poses – a jutting-out of her backside, a pout on her lips – Missy sneezes from the pot of damp tea leaves that she has sprinkled on the corridor stones.

Alice jumps.

For one moment, they regard each other.

'I was just... I am popping out for a brisk walk,' says Alice, grabbing her coat. She dares not turn around but guides the heft of the door to close softly until the latch clicks.

Missy kneels next to the basin of water and soda and begins scrubbing the floor in sweeping, circular motions. Her little Alice. Missy and her husband do not have children of their own. They have suffered alongside Oak with every tragedy. And here is Alice, still a young woman facing the trials of growing up, questioning what it means to be female. Missy never believed she would see the day. She continues to smile to herself and speeds up her work; she will finish the corridor and disappear into the study by the time Alice returns.

That night, the Jericho almshouse is full and they must be careful not to get caught sneaking beneath its north-facing windows. Lou rubs her hands together and pats both cheeks. She is paler than usual in the swaying lamplight and her eyes are red-rimmed and sunken from a pesky cold that she cannot shake. Alice bounces between both feet as if performing a jig.

'With these temperatures the river will freeze soon,' Lou says. 'Do you like ice skating?'

This is a tricky question, for Alice remembers the thrill of gliding across a lake only to be followed by cracking ice, a frosty gasp and the wet gulp of flailing mittens, bobbing plaits.

'It has been a long time since I have tried,' she says. 'Not since my sister had an accident once. She was fine in the end but it gave us all a fright.'

She has not mentioned Emma since their first outing, but the calm, thoughtful manner in which Lou receives this admittance, the way she does not stiffen or blush from fear of overstepping, suggests that she has not forgotten.

'We should go.' It is not an insensitive request. 'You should try it again. When the river freezes over, let us go skating together. It has been an age since I have done it too.'

In truth, Alice does not know how she feels about this, about skating itself and the memories it might conjure up. But the prospect of spending an afternoon with Lou is intriguing.

'All right, yes,' she says after a measured moment. 'I would like that.'

On the north side of the almshouse, the widow keeps a candle burning on the sill – a soft glow through the fog like a lighthouse beacon that Lou will follow. It is their final delivery of the evening: a large crate, heavy; Alice cannot help but notice how its contents slosh about whenever it is moved. Lou struggles to lift it now and takes deep, raspy breaths with the effort. Alice has, in fact, carted most of the boxes this evening, allowing Lou some respite so her illness does not worsen.

'Allow me to do this one as well,' she says.

But Lou shakes her head. ''Tis too dense tonight and the furrows are a trial at the best of times. I can manage. Best if you wait in the carriage.'

In the dense, syrupy fog that seems to thicken by the minute, the journey to the widow's window would be nothing short of perilous. With her hands on the crate, Lou takes pause.

Alice can see that she is sweating – tiny, glistening flecks of perspiration on her nose, on her cheeks.

'Or perhaps we could return with this one tomorrow,' proposes Alice.

A stray hair falls across Lou's eye with the slightest bow of her head. She breathes through her mouth.

'No. I will not be long,' says Lou, and half-lifting, half-dragging the parcel, she is swallowed by the fog.

Alice releases the catch and climbs into the hansom, a welcome break of shelter from the numbing cold that has latched onto her face and ears like a mask. Since the night with Mary Whipple, Lou has eased in appearance: she has not bothered to wear her top hat. She holds the straggly bits of hair back from her face with a ribbon – a small bow at the nape of her neck. Alice likes how stray, unruly strands wriggle out of place to dance about her head as she moves, how the silken rim of her hat does not quite fit round the mass of waves when they are not slicked with bandoline and nipped tightly into a small bun. She continues to wear a man's livery, this is true. But Alice cannot help but feel that Lou has relaxed around her, a privilege that she has not experienced with many others in her life.

The cab's windows, all a-fog, are completely white, which makes the sudden rapping upon them all the more startling.

'Hello? 'Tis mighty cold!' a muffled voice calls out.

A drumming at the window again.

Alice trips the latch and peeks out.

A tall man in a long black overcoat with layers of scarves wrapped round the bottom of his face hunches over, shivering in the mist.

'I nearly missed ye in this haze. Thought it was unlike Lou to be late.'

From the shadows, as if in a conjuring trick, he produces a small wooden chest. He dusts it quickly with one of his lapels and presses it into Alice's hands.

'I… is she expecting this?' asks Alice.

'Aye. From London. For the master of the house.'

'I do not have payment. She will return soon—'

'It's been taken care of.'

'Perhaps you would like to speak with her—'

'I am only the courier.'

As are we, thinks Alice. It is the first time that they have been on the receiving end of a parcel.

'Do not tip it,' says the man. 'A good night to you.'

And before Alice can question him further, the man is gulped up by the fog.

In the light of the candle lamp, Alice inspects the peculiar box. She shifts it from side to side, careful not to tilt it as instructed. She hears no clinking or swilling within. If not liquid, what threatens to spill out?

A copper cross slots into a loop which holds the chest closed, but it is not locked. It would be helpful to know its contents, thinks Alice, if only to direct how it should be handled. Any private matter would come with a lock, surely.

She slides the cross along the wood and there is a gentle pop as the lid is freed. It is difficult to see at first. When Alice moves the chest below the lamp and peers inside, she is faced with curious innards indeed. Six small bowls, deep and wooden, filled with heaping piles of vibrant pigments, ground to the finest powder with not a lump in sight. Even in the dim, flickering light, Alice can see their vitality: rich ochres and burnt carmine, cinnabar red and dark yellow of gallstone, logwood black and violet. Names that only the daughter of an art historian would know. The pigments are so perfectly ground that one's first instinct is to press a finger into the mounds, soft as fresh snow and infinitely more delicate.

Instead, Alice closes the box and supports it upright with cushions on the leather seat. She will not entertain the thought now. Strands of an idea meet inexorably but it is too mad, too impossible to consider. *For the master of the house*. Not just any man would covet such a package.

Alice hears Lou before she sees her.

Upon opening the door, the string of profanities cuts through the air, robust and infuriated. Alice glances towards the almshouse, suddenly paralysed with worry. What has happened?

Lou herself materialises out of the haze with a most unnatural limp.

'Good heavens! What happened?'

Alice springs to her aid but Lou brushes past her to lean against the cab and examine her ankle. Alice is horrified to see that the tips of Lou's top coat are spattered with dark red, as are her breeches and boots.

'Are you bleeding?' cries Alice.

'No. 'Tis port.'

'Port?'

'And Spanish wine.' Lou slumps against the wheel of the cab and fumbles with her buttons in an attempt to remove the coat, but her entire body pulses with frustration and the furious jerking and tugging of a sleeve at odd angles only unbalances her even more so it cannot be done. She is at once both sickly and enraged: her lips and the hollows of her eyes grey as she vigorously rubs her ankle and curses herself with the most debasing of names.

Alice watches, horrified. She fumbles with her own scarf. 'We should wrap your ankle—'

'There is no need to fuss,' snaps Lou.

At last, she is free of her coat. She casts it to the mud. Her hands and her breeches and the carriage wheels are all covered in mud. Her breath escapes in strained, white puffs and Alice is sure that Lou will cry or shriek or scream, for only such an eruption would suit this ferocious and uncharacteristic behaviour.

But Lou only leans her head against the wheel and closes her eyes.

Her breathing slows. She licks her lips. She appears to feel the cold once more, for she crosses her arms and succumbs to a shiver.

'An utter waste,' Lou says softly. 'Every single bottle broken. A complete and utter waste.'

'What happened?' asks Alice, surprised by this impassioned, furious response from Lou, so unbefitting of the error.

'I could not see where I was going. In my state, I... well. Perhaps I should not have undertaken it after all.'

''Tis just a bit of wine,' Alice consoles her. 'A little accident, that is all.'

But Lou shakes her head. 'I have seen darker and foggier nights than this. How foolish to trip. And with one measly crate at that. Why, I have ferried dozens of bottles in half the time and barely soiled the toes of my boots. I am not so… I do not make such mistakes.' And then softer, 'I am hardier than this.'

It is more a quiet protest to the dark than to Alice.

'We should go,' Lou says at last.

Then Alice remembers. 'A parcel has been delivered for the master of the house,' she says.

'Oh, good.' Lou barely acknowledges the chest as she secures the latch and struggles to hoist herself into the driver's seat.

Alice is unsure whether she should pursue the matter.

'I have propped the chest between cushions,' she offers. 'Do you know what is inside? Do you know what he is expecting?'

'Nothing different than the usual delivery, I imagine.'

Lou grips the reins in her hands but does not whip them. She stares into the dark, lips strained in a taut line, and Alice wonders once more why the night's mishap weighs so heavily upon her.

'I think… they are pigments for painting.'

Somewhere up ahead in the tavern across from the almshouse, a raucous laughter erupts. It is a merry night of drinking for some.

'The parcel for your master,' continues Alice. 'They are little bowls filled with coloured powders. Beautifully boxed. Did you hear me, Lou? I think they are for painting.'

'You should not have opened the box.'

Alice colours. 'I did not linger. I only peeked inside so I would know how to place them in the cab. I was not trying to be nosy.'

'Well. Next time, do not.'

The cold is icy on their cheeks yet still, Lou does not urge them forward, lost in her own deliberations.

And then – it is a meek affirmation, just audible above the horse's breathing and creak of the carriage: 'I am hardier than this.'

'Yes,' says Alice gently, 'you are. You have said this already.' It is more a matter of pride, then, than the bottles themselves. Still, thinks Alice, it will not do to dwell on the blunder, so she tries to lessen the tension. 'Perhaps… some time away from these deliveries,' she says. 'Just until you are recovered. 'Tis gruelling work at times, carting these crates about. I am sure your master would not mind. The way you have spoken of him – why, he sounds rather absorbed in his own life, the way he allows you to go where you wish and whenever you want. He sounds quite relaxed.'

'That's enough, Alice.'

The pitch of Alice's laugh is sharp. 'And eccentric too, mind you. I cannot imagine many masters permitting their coachmen to ride at their leisure.' When Lou does not engage, she presses on, emboldened by the numbness in her fingers and her close proximity to Lou, pressed next to her atop the cab on this biting cold night. 'Why does he remain at home the way he does, Lou? You told me on the day we met that he no longer has need of a driver. Does he ever leave the manor?'

'Not now, Alice.'

'Does he wonder where you go in the evenings? Does he know about your deliveries?'

'Alice, truly—'

'And, well, this parcel only makes him that much more curious. It is the strangest little box, you must admit. The finest little bowls… why, they must be pigments of the topmost quality. To have connections with such merchants, he must be—'

'For God's sake, Alice Oak, stop talking!'

The reprimand is engulfed by the fog that presses in upon them. It is both piercing and heavy and lodges itself upon Alice's breastbone. Somehow, this snapping is more fierce than her rebuke at the sweetshop – more exasperated, less controlled, her patience abraded.

'I… Forgive me,' entreats Alice. She cannot shrink into herself enough. 'I was being fanciful. I meant nothing by any of it.'

When she finally whips the horse forward, Lou's rigidity endures. She does not soften as the journey progresses, does not apologise or make amends in any manner. It is as if Alice is not there at all.

At the corner of Mansfield Road, Lou does not look at Alice as the girl alights.

'We will take a break from deliveries next week,' she says. 'Do not expect me.'

'Lou, please, I—'

But Alice's apology is lost on the wind, and she is left feeling a torrent of remorse and fear, for she cannot bear the thought of losing Lou. Only the cold stops her from crying.

It is two weeks, in fact, that pass before Lou collects her at the station again. They do not speak of their quarrel. The deliveries resume as if no pause has been taken. Lou's health is restored and she is just as chirpy, just as chatty as before, and Alice throws herself into the work with a ceaseless fervour. She promises herself that she will never again offend her friend, will not breach the subject of Lou's master or pry into any parcels for the rest of her tenure. Any questions she has, any curiosities around Lou's employment or the nature of their work, Alice will swallow. For she will never again risk losing this friendship.

24

Preparation for Lecture Four: The Potter's Daughter

No. 7 Anne – *The Potter's Daughter*, 1837, The Royal Academy of Arts

The seventh portrait left by Timothy Ponden-Hall appeared wrapped in butcher's paper and twine on the doorstep of the Academy on the wettest day of the year. By the time it was discovered in the late morning, the paper was so saturated with rain that it was all but smeared off the canvas it was meant to protect.

The toddler sits naked at the base of a potter's wheel with only a cloth tangled round her soft and rolling baby thighs. See how he has painted her perfectly balanced – the light heft of her torso leans back, yet she remains upright in the sweet, off-kilter manner of toddlers. Above her, wet and glistening, is a half-thrown formation of clay soon to be a pot for basil or perhaps a pitcher for summer flowers. The stable door opens onto a yard; the space once held ponies or cows, as evidenced by the hay scattered about, but it is now an artist's sanctuary. Dried and glazed creations line the back wall, all of them empty.

She is content, this sweet babe, mid-giggle or -babble. The mother is close by. We are not meant to worry; she has not been abandoned.

The scene is a glimpse into country life. This is an artisan's child, poor and merry. And again, the textures of the wax, the vivacity of the umber and gallstone elevate the piece to one of great wealth. Gallstone itself – see the dark yellows here in the light filtering in through the window – was prepared in the gallstone of an ox; incredibly expensive when this was painted, at five, ten shillings a cake. Memorialising little Anne's death, according to Ponden-Hall, was worth the expense.

How was he familiar with rustic village life, the scenes of peasants and lowly artists who might have been more akin with Shakespeare's fools than with his heroes? There is no mockery here; the painting is no veneer to cover judgement of the peasantry or working class. On the contrary, Ponden-Hall depicts the poorer characters of life as if they are Renaissance nobility, and just as beautiful; perhaps, daringly, more worthy.

It is no surprise that Anne the potter's daughter is often paired with Harry the orphan boy in university lectures and scholarly articles. What ties did the great Timothy Ponden-Hall have to such young and gritty creatures? Why, out of all the world's wonders and beautiful humans he encountered on his adventures, did his heart soften for these children?

Aside from DeLacey and his butler, this seventh portrait is the one we know most about, largely and humbly thanks to a private interview conducted by Solomon Oak himself. He was twenty-two, on the brink of fame already after a prodigious few years at university.

'I will not see anyone,' says the potter. She has opened the door only a couple of inches, just enough for the art historian to hear her refusal.

'I am here only to pay my condolences,' Oak says.

'Like the rest of them at first, before they go on to ask where my daughter is buried or if I believe in the elixir of life. It has been ten years since she died and my door is still newly sanded from all of the knocking.'

'I am sincere, madam. I only wished to offer my comforts and set eyes on the mother of such a beautiful girl.'

'And? What do you see?'

It is a cruel question, for as his flattering answer balances on his lips, Oak notices in that moment the collection of walking sticks leaning against the doorframe, the indentation of a stick-end zigzagging through the mud from the road to the porch, the blind green eye that stares blankly at him through the crack of the door.

'As I said,' the potter says gruffly, 'I will not see anyone. Good day.'

As she moves to nudge the door closed, Oak leans forward and offers in the quietest of voices, 'I have brought you some money, madam, if you will take it. It is from the Academy.'

At this, the potter is still. She is poorer than she has ever been after a decade of slow, sometimes stagnant productivity as she wallows in her grief. She needs money, there is no doubt, and yet: 'I may live a life of grieving, sir, but I am a principled woman. I will not be bribed.'

'No, madam, please let me explain. There has been an infinite queue of viewers to see your daughter's portrait as of late. This is largely due to a recent paper I wrote about it. The public is simply obsessed with Ponden-Hall and his paintings; they have travelled from across the country and even abroad to see his masterpieces. As a result, the Academy has acquired a small fortune and, well, discussions have been had and it was decided that you, as the girl's mother, should have some of the share. Finally.'

Could this be true? The potter exhales. She opens the door a bit wider. She must be no older than thirty. Her ears cock for the sound of any eavesdropping neighbours or passers-by.

'Come in for a cup of tea,' she says.

She moves about her cosy kitchen as if she is not blind at all. Collections of pots fill the room – on the windowsill, under the table, overflowing from the larder.

'Is this true?' she asks when she sits opposite him with a steaming kettle. Not a single droplet of tea is spilled as she fills the cups. 'I have never known institutions to be considerate or generous.'

'Sadly, I think you are correct in most cases,' says Oak. 'But this is a unique matter. The painting is owned by the Royal Academy as it was left on the building's doorstep. Such laws of ownership have been applied to all of Ponden-Hall's works. The difference with this one is that little Anne was a child who left behind a living mother. It feels like an uncomfortable exploitation for the Academy to reap such a fortune from the portrait of a child when her own grieving mother receives nothing.'

Oak withdraws an envelope from his coat pocket and places it beside the kettle. 'I must request though, madam, that you keep this quiet. Whilst the Academy has every right to distribute funds to whomever they wish, if the public knew of this… this gift to you… well, you have seen how stories attached to Ponden-Hall run rampant in the most sinister of ways. The keeper of the Academy is a friend of mine and I assure you that there are no ulterior motives to this gesture; they only wish to help a grieving mother and offer their condolences. And ten years late, they do admit.'

The potter places her hand on the envelope. It is thicker than she had imagined. Should she accept this? In the depths of her heartache, she can lose nothing more.

At last, she says, 'Thank you. Please thank them. I shall say nothing to anyone, of course.' And then she offers, 'I truly have no answers for you. I was just as surprised as everyone to hear that he had painted my daughter. I wish I could see it. Though of course, I would not know how successful he has been in capturing her likeness.'

'The villagers say it is a marvel. She is perfect.'

The potter frowns. 'A portrait of my daughter in London. Who would have thought? It does not make sense.'

'How might he have known you and your daughter?'

The potter shakes her head. 'When Annie was born, a string of villagers always helped me with the house chores. Could he have been amongst them? Sometimes they watched Annie, you see, whilst I threw. I am a widow. The pots are my only means of income.'

'You are a talented craftswoman,' says Oak. 'True artistry.'

'These words would not mean so much from someone else, but I know who you are. Even I have heard your name, Solomon Oak, out here beyond Staffordshire. Your name is already attached to his.'

'He must have come round. He never… introduced himself? Made himself known?'

'Not by that name, anyway. I am as flabbergasted as you are. Imagine that he has been roaming these parts at his leisure. So far from the sea too.'

'It makes perfect sense,' says Oak. 'He does not wish to be found.'

'Perhaps he is not as wild as they say he is. For how could a lowly potter and her child ever hold the attention of a man like Timothy Ponden-Hall?'

25

Just one week before Christmas, the river has frozen over. Its banks are lined with frost-tipped brambles, and the heartier families of Oxford and its surrounding villages hunker down with blankets and winter picnics, their baskets laden with mince pies and sugared almonds, bottles of damson vodka, and bread wrapped in tea towels with rounds of cheese and chutneys.

In the midst of these jovial gatherings, Alice awaits Lou, who has gone to the river to test its sturdiness. She has strapped on the blades, a perfect fit.

'Beautiful conditions,' says Lou. Her cheeks are already crimson from the cold and she pulls her rabbit-fur hat tighter about her head. 'Even the centre appears to be as solid as stone. But just to be safe, let us stay close to the edge.'

After tightening their leather straps, they hobble to the river and tenderly step onto the ice. Lou leads and Alice follows. At first, they progress awkwardly by dragging the blades on the river top, arms jolting in every direction like broken clock hands.

Gradually, they hit a rhythm, shoop, shoop, shoop, and they glide along the Thames with no plans, no purpose, as if they will skate all the way to London.

Alice is pleased with herself, wobbly as she may be. She feels her quadriceps and hamstrings tighten and release with each stride, and she knows that they will soon begin to burn. She will feel this tomorrow, every push, every bump, every jerk reaction to correct herself from falling. She imagines Caravaggio's angels hovering above her, lifting her arms for balance, blowing a friendly wind behind her knees. *They will watch over you.* For how can she not think of Emma and her mother in these moments?

Ahead of her, Lou skates slowly but with remarkable ease. She is so measured, so graceful in her gliding as if she has done this for one hundred years. The pain in her ankle from those weeks ago at the almshouse is all but forgotten. A flicker of competitiveness is kindled in Alice's belly. She quells this, the memory of giggles and shrieks of goading never far from her thoughts in the winter outdoors.

'Come on then!' Lou calls behind her. 'There is a cosy spot under a willow up ahead.'

The distance between them lengthens and Alice cannot help but feel a pang of panic. There is no need to feel this way, of course. They are not racing. She is not chasing. Yet the peach stone in her stomach grows with each of Lou's perfect strides, and Alice's own become more frantic and imbalanced. Up ahead, Lou is pointing to something in the middle of the river. A buoy of some sort. A lone tree branch that has frozen vertically like the mast of a sunken ship.

Please do not go to it, thinks Alice. It is too familiar, this jutting piece of driftwood. Provoking squeals of *Faster! Faster!* ring in Alice's ears; she is always the one behind, half desperate to catch up, half thrilled to spur the quicker one onwards with threats of capturing, even if it means hounding her forward to delicate, unchecked patches of ice.

She must catch up with Lou, but the quicker she tries to move, the more her legs flounder, the more her arms windmill. She has witnessed this scene before, has relived this scenario too many times in her innocent, impressionable brain.

Of course it is not the mast of a ship! she wants to shout. These are the imaginings of a child's daydreams, the dangerous ideas of storybooks and pretend. How marvellous to see the thing protrude from the ice like a narwhal's tusk, like the lance of a seafaring knight.

Please do not skate out to it! Alice believes she has called out, has warned her. But her tongue feels like cotton wool and still, Lou skates onwards.

Please, she thinks. Just wait for me this time and we can approach it together.

But Lou does not hear her and Alice is confused because she has never been skating with Lou before. Yet this feeling of being left behind, this nausea, this desperation to catch up is as familiar and as old to Alice as the bones in her flailing arms. In this moment, she knows that the centre of the river is wafer-thin and that even the light-footed tread of a sprite, of a cherub, of a sister, is heavy enough to crack the delicate surface. And here she is, recalling it once more, falling like the first time. Reaching out to her like the first time as the ice rises to meet her chin and shatter her baby teeth into a million shards of frost across the river. The cold is striking on her cheeks, on her nose, around her eyes – a sharp contrast to the warm blood that pools about her gums. And then she hears the spluttering, through a hazy veil of ice and hair, sees the strangers pull her sister out of the frozen river with a tree branch, feels the bulk of her father dash past her, clumsy, slipping, to envelop his daughter who is blue but alive, coughing and gasping. The relief is immense.

When she looks up, Alice scans the river frantically for the hole. For the muff on the ice, which looked like a dead rabbit.

But the branch remains intact, whole and undisturbed, jutting out of a pristine sheet of ice; she runs her tongue along a perfect row of teeth; she is not bleeding. In fact, she feels no pain at all splayed out there on the frozen river.

'Are you all right?' calls Lou, several paces ahead.

She skates backwards now, framed by the bare branches of an imposing willow that hangs out over the river from a knoll.

'You lead too much with your left. That's why you toppled over.'

Alice comes to. Yes, of course. Who is she to disagree? She is no master skater.

On the bank, Lou lays out a blanket and widens her satchel to reveal a stash fit for a shooting party's elevenses: seasoned cuts of sole and salmon from Wales, two apple tarts bespeckled with cloves, a bundle of roasted walnuts and the brightest tangerines that Alice has ever seen. She scoops one up and admires it as she would a ruby.

'From the kitchen garden,' says Lou.

'How wonderful.'

'I will take you to the estate and show you around one day.'

She speaks like this, lately – casual invitations to the house, assumptive statements that suggest it is only a matter of time before

Alice visits the master of her employment. Of course, Alice does not pursue such crumbs.

'I'm sorry about what happened back there,' she says to Lou. 'When I fell, I mean. I was reminded of my sister's accident. She was fine in the end but it was a horrifying experience. She would die a few weeks later of scarlet fever, completely unrelated to the accident, but I have always linked the two in my mind.' She shakes her head and says quietly, 'I suppose I was reliving it a bit.'

'It makes perfect sense. Especially if you have not been skating since.'

'We have not done many active things since she died.'

Lou sucks on a clove. She withdraws it from her mouth and examines the bud between thumb and forefinger. 'They were very close, weren't they.'

'Yes. The three of us were close, actually. But they were more similar in their interests. And in their temperaments.'

'Was it fun to have a famous father? You must have felt quite proud to see him lecture in grand, important halls.'

Alice considers this. 'It was impressive to see him lecture, but I think we had the most fun back at home in the quiet of our study. It was there, you see, away from the crowds and an audience, that my father could tell us the stories of Timothy Ponden-Hall, unencumbered by theories or technicalities of the art.' Alice pauses. 'My father cares deeply about those paintings, but I would venture to say that he cares even more about Ponden-Hall himself. My father appreciates art because it reflects man's experience. And I believe he thinks Timothy Ponden-Hall's experience in this life is unique and important.'

'How poignant,' says Lou. Whilst she focuses on the river before them, Alice can see that her mind is elsewhere.

'He did not want to take part in this new search,' says Alice. 'When the pig appeared, he declined to help at first.'

'Oh? I would have thought that the new painting would be an invigorating re-entry into Ponden-Hall's life.'

Alice shakes her head. 'Not for my father. You see, he had promised Emma that they would uncover the truth behind Ponden-Hall's paintings together. It would be his greatest professional achievement, telling Ponden-Hall's story at last. When Emma died, he lost all hope

and motivation to complete the work. I think he feels guilty pursuing the project without her.'

Lou is quiet for a moment, picks at the edge of the picnic blanket.
'Well. It would be quite the tragedy if the great Solomon Oak was
not the one to uncover the story at last. It makes me sad to think
about that possibility.'

Alice is surprised by this emotional divulgence.

'After hearing him speak, I mean,' adds Lou. 'He exuded such
passion at the lecture. It would be such a waste if someone else
finished what he began.'

'I agree.'

Lou turns to her. 'Do you think he will pursue this to the end? Is
he committed to finding Ponden-Hall even without Emma?'

Her eyes find Alice's and she is confident in holding her gaze.

'He is committed,' Alice says. 'And I really believe that he will find
him.'

Lou remains still, studies Alice for a moment longer before she
smiles and the tension dissipates.

'I have something for you,' she says.

From the bottom of the satchel, Lou fishes out a gift wrapped in
tissue paper. A sprig of holly and a curled cinnamon stick are tied
elegantly with a green ribbon.

'Ah! And I have something for you as well.' Alice remembers.
From the inner breast pocket of her coat, she fishes out a small,
crumpled parcel of waxed paper. 'You first.'

With care, Lou unwraps three grainy, brown lumps which have
fused to the paper. A coating of brown sugar sticks to her fingers as
she turns them before her nose.

''Tis ginger fudge!' boasts Alice. 'I made them this week. I tried
my best to grind the ginger down but I am afraid there might be a
few chunks. Do try one.'

Even a conservative nibble is overwhelmingly pungent and
peppery, but Lou is adept at concealing its potency. ''Tis delicious,'
she says, uncorking the wine. 'How thoughtful.' When she has
finished chewing and has taken a long swig of the bottle, she pushes
her gift towards Alice.

Based on its shape and heft, Alice knows that it is a book. Its
contents, however, are beyond her realm of imagination. With the

tissue paper discarded, Alice holds in her lap an Italian language text-book, leatherbound, with an uncracked spine.

At first, she is speechless.

'I have never – I did not know a textbook existed for Italian. Schools only offer German and French.'

'They wouldn't offer Italian, would they? The country itself has only recently adopted it.'

'What do they speak otherwise?'

'Oh, dialects mostly. It depends on where you are. But do not worry – the cities you will visit will most certainly speak Italian. It is based on the Tuscan spoken in upper-class Florence. And you will spend much of your tour in Florence.'

Lou is more certain that Alice's plans will come to fruition than Alice is, and again, Alice feels unsettled. She also feels indebted to Lou, for this is no ordinary gift.

'I am certain that this book will be offered to students in the next decade,' Lou continues. 'The world is wide and growing smaller, Alice. You will do well to explore it before its wildness is lost. Here, let's eat before we skate back. We should go soon before this chill settles upon us.'

Alice cannot think of an adequate way to express her thanks. Instead, she bites into the apple tart and also sucks on a clove, all spice and sugar, and wonders how this coach driver, this woman, has acquired knowledge that crosses oceans; she questions how she has come into possession of this new publication before her tutors have – men of Oxford and Cambridge, no less; and most of all, Alice wonders why Lou has taken an interest in her, and listens to her ideas and ambitions, not as if they are the wispy, hollow dreams of a sheltered sibling left behind, but as if they are real and only need life breathed into them.

26

The coffeehouse near St Paul's Cathedral is aptly stuffed with old books and a vast barrel, purely decorative, filled to the brim with discarded inkwells. It is a favourite haunt amongst the capital's literary enthusiasts and book publishers and often, as on this occasion, its historians and authorities on art.

It is clear that the name Solomon Oak carries weight here, for Grace has been admitted into the shop – crammed into the dimmest corner, this is true – but admitted nonetheless, despite being a woman. She waits for Oak now, sipping Turkish coffee that is rich and thick and as dark as soot. The cane sugar leaves a film on her teeth and the coffee itself leaves a bitter, grainy coat on her tongue; Grace cannot decide if she likes it or not, this novelty of proper coffee, so different from the blackened water of coffee pots and kettles at home.

She waits for some time, alternating each sip with the swipe of a finger across her front teeth. The men cast sidelong stares from their tables, from behind their books and pamphlets of publications, and Grace is reminded once more of how she and Oak will appear to the public. Yet Oak does not care – does he even notice, she wonders? – so why should she?

Twenty minutes past the hour.

She hopes that he will arrive soon, for in a rare moment of vulnerability, she is feeling quite unsettled. Why had she given in to Elke Jahn? For weeks and weeks, she managed to politely decline. Her curiosity – ironically not one of the prominent bumps on the geography of her skull – had got the best of her. Silly. And now in a quiet moment of reflection, she mulls over the phrenologist's words, chews them over like a salted toffee that refuses to melt away. What is it she feels? Disappointment? Pride? Perhaps shame? No, it is simpler than all of this. She is, more than anything, surprised, and knows not how to respond to the reading. *True goodness of the mind*, Elke had said. A misreading, perhaps. Surely. She will not think on it now; she will ponder it another time.

A crisp wind pushes into the coffeehouse as Oak struggles to control the door. His hat is blown off and rolls across the floorboards, his glasses askew upon his nose. His hair, wild at the tamest of times, erupts from his head as if galvanised.

'Mr Oak! Come in, come in!' The attendant swoops him away from the door.

Grace springs up to collect Oak's hat.

'Looks like a storm,' says the attendant.

'It will pass. The clouds look still.'

'May I take your coat, sir?'

Oak holds up a gentle hand and shivers in his scarf and woollen layers. 'That won't be necessary, but a hot coffee would be most welcome. Thank you, Louis.' And turning to Grace, 'My dear, forgive my tardiness. I was pulled into a rather intriguing account of the Greeks and their urns and lost track of the time.'

'Not at all, Mr Oak.' She is indeed pleased to see him and not just for a distraction; he has become a sort of comfort for her. Is this feeling of warmth and peace what most daughters feel around their fathers?

'Are you well? You look a tad peaky.'

Grace pats her cheeks. 'I do not like the cold. Once upon a time, I would have powdered extra rouge to pinken my face and neck. Now I have quite accepted the look of a gaunt skeleton in the winter.'

There is something else the matter, to be sure, but Oak is clumsy with nuance, has never been skilful at recognising the layers of his own emotions, never mind the emotions of others.

'I have news for you,' says Grace, the pep returning to her person as she fishes out a notebook from her bag. 'I have reached the 1700s in the archives, and who do you suppose has a hefty file – two folders bound together, in fact – but Elizabeth Ponden-Hall! It is just as you predicted: records upon records of every appointment with Mrs Ponden-Hall. Dr Jahn was a man of meticulous detail.'

'Oh, I knew he would be!' Oak balls his fists and lightly shakes them, sits up like a euphoric child. 'Tell me more. What have you found?'

'Now, do not raise your hopes too much. I have not yet come across what we are looking for. But listen to this. It is all positively fascinating.'

Grace reads aloud the records that she has copied into her notebook, going backwards in time: spells of confusion and sadness ('A weakness in temperament, Dr Jahn calls it. When the brain needs calming.'); bouts of illnesses, some diagnosed as common sniffles and coughs ('Often treated with a simple mustard plaster, imagine!'), some more serious like a mild case of influenza; more than a few entries on Elizabeth's overall moods – how she flipped between feeling calm, content, joyful, to experiencing strong fits of paranoia, anger, melancholy.

'When were these "weaknesses of the mind" most frequent?' asks Oak.

'Most of her life, it appears.'

'She was a complex woman.'

'We all are, Mr Oak.' Grace points to a boxed note on the page. 'Some of Dr Jahn's final entries on Elizabeth focus on the birth of Timothy. She was immensely proud of her grandson... What did the notes say? Ah, yes, she loved him with "a fierce pride" and claimed that he was "the jewel of the family – the best of them all".'

Oak nods. 'Her adoration of him was no secret.'

'But this is where I will let you down, Mr Oak. In all of Dr Jahn's notes, I have not come across the birth records of her own son, Andrew. I went through the files twice and have found nothing.'

Oak's sip of coffee is long and measured. He stares at Grace's notes but she can tell that he is thinking of something beyond the pages.

'It doesn't mean that I won't find them,' she says. 'Of course, I will keep looking. Perhaps he kept birth notes in another folder.'

'How far back have you gone in the archives?'

'Until... 1770. Elizabeth would have been eleven, twelve, then.'

'And you are certain that between 1770 and Dr Jahn's death in 1810, there are no records of a birth, no notes on her son?'

'No. But perhaps she went to a midwife or a specialist doctor—'

Oak shakes his head with vigour. 'She was loyal only to Dr Jahn. In fact, she refused to see other doctors — better doctors, most likely — when her parents proposed them. You are certain there are no other notes? A third file perhaps?'

'I am certain. The subsequent files were on a Miss Price and a Mr Pratt.'

'What about notes on the pregnancy? Records of nausea? Swelling?'

'Nothing of the sort. What are you suggesting, Mr Oak?'

Oak dabs the dark coffee from his lips. 'Andrew Ponden-Hall would have been born around 1779. Elizabeth only accepted the care of Dr Jahn, and yet there are no records of her pregnancy or delivery by a man who took copious amounts of notes for every patient.'

'She must have seen another doctor—'

'Julien Ponden-Hall returned from an expedition in 1779 — the expedition with Captain Cook, we now know. He had married Elizabeth four years previously when she was only sixteen. The couple were happy to reunite and start a family immediately, so it was no surprise that Andrew was born not long afterwards. I have always accepted this timeline.'

'What are you saying?'

'I am proposing, Miss Dodd, that Julien Ponden-Hall was not alone when he returned from his expedition, but brought with him a bastard son.' Oak leans back against the booth and drums his fingers on Grace's notebook. 'The idea flickered in my mind after your clever observation of the map in the DeLacey portrait. I thought of it again mid-way through my first lecture. And you have confirmed it for me today.'

'I still do not understand. What does any of this have to do with the map in the portrait?'

'I presume you are aware that Captain Cook never returned from this third expedition. John Gore took command and brought the crew back to London as Captain Cook had died in a violent exchange with an island people. Where do you suppose this took place, Miss Dodd? Why, no other isles than the Sandwich Islands. Here is our confirmed link to the painting. Elizabeth allegedly gave birth to their son Andrew nine months after Julien returned from the Sandwich Islands, but no record of her pregnancy or the birth exist in Dr Jahn's notes. I am certain that this suggests that Andrew was Julien's son from an island native. The affair would have been scandal enough for families of their repute; Andrew's mixed blood, if known, would throw his entire credibility and inheritance into question. So they kept it secret and passed Andrew off as their own legitimate firstborn.'

And Grace understands. 'Which means Timothy Ponden-Hall is of mixed blood too.'

Oak nods. 'And based on the painting, he has hinted this from the beginning.'

Grace places her hands on the table. She has wanted to tell Oak for some time now, but fear of his anger or disappointment had always held her tongue. Or worse – what if he feels he no longer has need of her after hearing this admittance? Still, she resolves to go on.

'I am certain that he wants us to know this about him,' she says. 'The map went unnoticed for so long. And you see, whilst I would love to take credit for this discovery, I was not altogether without help.'

'What do you mean, my dear?'

'I was fed the information about the map, Mr Oak. There was a letter.' From the hidden breast pocket of her coat, Grace produces the note she received from the milkman. So much has changed over the course of these curious, exhilarating two months. Grace cannot bear the truth of her initial motivations: a pouch of coins, a connection with the famous Solomon Oak for a course application. She is pure of heart and motive now, but what if he doesn't believe her?

Oak reads the letter in silence. By the flick of his eyes, she can tell that he rereads every word with hunger.

'There was also a pouch of money,' Grace divulges. She cannot help it. All must be in the open so that she may make amends. 'But I do not want any of it. You may have it, Mr Oak. 'Twas really a message for you in the first instance.'

But Oak is not listening. He is rummaging in his satchel for something.

'And my original interest in your work was selfish, Mr Oak,' Grace continues. 'I… had hoped to make your acquaintance so that it might aid me in acquiring a place on an art history course. But my curiosity, I assure you, was sincere from the start. From that first evening at the Academy, I was in total admiration of you and your scholarship. I did not expect... well, I could never have dreamed... in short, Mr Oak, the past two months have been the most *alive* I have ever felt, and I simply cannot believe that I have the privilege of assisting you in this mystery. I promise you, Mr Oak, that I am with you on this venture until the end.'

Oak's smile is a mixture of warmth and giddiness. 'Miss Dodd, have a look at this.'

Laid out on the table is a lithograph of *Hugh DeLacey* and Grace's note.

'Look at the writing,' says Oak. 'Here. *Someone will come for the portraits of Ponden-Hall.* Look at the penmanship of your secret author and the signature of the portrait.'

And it is unmistakable. Whilst the *Ponden-Hall* is smaller, less bold in the letter compared to its peer in the corner of the painting, the curve of the *P*, the spacing of the letters, even the flow of the double *l* at its tail are indisputably the same. Grace would never have thought to compare them. But here it is before their eyes in plain, effortless print: a letter written by Timothy Ponden-Hall himself.

Oak laughs. 'I take heart in this. Ponden-Hall wants to be found and his lineage revealed – and he has chosen *us* to tell. You are as swept up in this story, in these riddles, as the rest of us, Miss Dodd.' Oak is thrilled at the thought, feels closer now to the painter than he ever has before. 'Keep this quiet for now as the pieces settle into place. Bromage and the Society are still planning to move forward with their deconstruction. This discovery could delay them, yet. But it must be revealed with delicacy, and we still have much to learn.'

27

Preparation for Lecture Five: Woman in a Sunhat

No. 10 *Woman in a Sunhat*, 1840, The Royal Academy of Arts

Adelaide Ponden-Hall was a mute. Two years younger than her famous brother, she was his opposite in every way. Whilst he was gregarious and could infuse any gathering with his spirit and charm, Adelaide was painfully shy and kept away from parties. He was striking and she was plain. He could speak French and German in addition to his polished English and she created sounds that her grandparents likened to the hum of lightning bugs and flies.

Timothy took risks and possessed the luck to survive grand adventures, whilst Adelaide was susceptible to any ailment carried on the wind and was often too poorly to step outside the front door. Once, the papers report, when the family gathered at the Thames to welcome Timothy home from an expedition, Adelaide was bedridden with heatstroke from walking Prince around the garden. It had been an overcast day.

At the one celebration she did attend – the revealing of the kraken leg at the British Museum – she wore a woollen hat and was covered from head to toe in layers of silk and satin. It was in the heart of summer.

'Was he very cross with her?' Emma asks. *'For missing all of his achievements?'*

'Oh, no,' says Oak. *'You see, despite her frail disposition, Adelaide Ponden-Hall was Timothy's favourite person in the world. He loved her*

more than any treasure dreamed into existence – more than Aztec gold, pink diamonds, the leg of the kraken itself. Addie was his greatest gem.'

They are hunkered down in the study as it is stormy outside. Emma fiddles with a train set and builds a track around Alice, who has fallen asleep in the drowsy warmth of the fire.

'Mind her toes,' Oak says, peering over his glasses.

'His favourite person was his sister? You're just saying that, Father, so I am nicer to Alice.'

'I promise you it's true. He loved her immensely. He understood her. Some say they had their own language between themselves. It is a pity we did not know more about her. This painting was most revealing. It was Timothy's way of sharing her with the rest of us. She was, perhaps, not as feeble as her parents and the press let on.'

Not as feeble and not as plain, for the woman in the portrait has a quiet, unfussed beauty about her. Adelaide sits outside, framed by a sky of azurite blue. Her eyes are light, and there is nothing stunning about her cheekbones or nose, this is true, but the expression captured is undoubtedly a smile – a timid one of pale, upturned lips. The public was shocked by this, for Adelaide Ponden-Hall was known to be a sorry, pitiful creature. Yet there is no Mona Lisa trick of sfumato here, no wily shadow; her smile is as certain as the moonrise.

She wears a large sunhat made of straw, laced with flamboyant begonias and sweet peas that frame her pale blonde curls. Notice how the flowers in her hat perfectly counterbalance the basket of flowers slung over her arm. The hat should feel heavy for her and for us, with its size and the wide brim that curls up to reveal Adelaide's face, but it does not. On the contrary, compared to the weight and vibrancy of the peonies and peach dahlias that seem to erupt from her basket and splash across her apron, the hat sits upon Adelaide's head as lightly as goose down. It protects her from the garish sun so she can enjoy a day in the garden despite her sensitivities.

Her opposite arm is hidden by the wingtips of a kite. Embroidered with a milky moon and stars along its spine, and flanked with elegant knots of ribbon, turquoise and purple, it is the work of a skilled kite maker, the envy of any carefree spirit who flies kites on the beach or on the windy bluffs of a cliff.

Could Adelaide Ponden-Hall possibly find joy in flying a kite? The rumours of her weakness would have her snap in two at the gentlest gust. Yet here she poses, surrounded by vigorous blooms and a toy of mirth and freedom.

Now. The composition is most interesting. The kite – see where it is positioned and how it balances – is reminiscent of a shield. It is not only held but wielded, another protector from another angle, this time not from the sun or the cold, but from whom?

In this, Adelaide remains a mystery to all but Ponden-Hall himself. Whilst she is pale, ghostly even, between the scintillating petals and peduncles that surround her, her skin and chest pulsate like living flesh. See how tints of blush-pink at the curves of her cheeks and the hollows of her clavicle contribute to this verisimilitude. He has discovered Adelaide in the wax and oil and has breathed a new life into her that cannot be snuffed out. Her energy is undoubtable, her beauty pristine and calm as a pearl.

'I cannot imagine losing Alice,' says Emma, placing her hand on her sister's foot. Alice slumbers on, undisturbed by the bridge that arcs over one of her ankles for the windup locomotive. 'How did she die?'

'Nobody knows. She was a recluse at the best of times, but in the years leading up to her death, not a whisper had been heard of her. It is speculated that she died quietly at home from one of her many ailments. The Ponden-Halls made no public announcement. Perhaps because they knew that Timothy would commemorate her in this way. She was only thirty years old.'

'So young.'

'Yes, though I suppose given her nature, it is a wonder that she lived so long.'

This is Grace's favourite painting, Oak remembers. The thought of Grace following a memory of Emma inspires a prick of discomfort. What is this pang in the hollow of his ribs? Grief? Despair? Of course, it is guilt. For he is undeserving of having a second chance with a second daughter; and herein lies another dollop of guilt, for she is not a daughter at all – well, she is someone's, but not his. And would he not give up every breath spent with Grace to have his own child, so curious, so like himself, building train sets beside him and butting under his hand like a spaniel?

The guilt is felt threefold just minutes later when Oak remembers that he has such a child! His daughter, he has a second daughter. He loves this one most of all – so much so that he has placed her in the treasure box of his mind and keeps the key between his toes where it is forgotten, mistaken sometimes for a pebble. The love he has for Alice would quell a monsoon, but he must keep it quiet, keep it safe. He is proud of his restraint, and in being so, does not realise that in addition to whoever he believes he is fooling – God, fate, the lamp-lighters outside his window – he also deceives Alice herself. Alice must know how much she is loved, thinks Oak. She must understand that this is why she is so judiciously protected. Oak loves this daughter, yes, but does he enjoy her? They must know one another for this to be possible. *I would like to know her,* Oak thinks. But this terrifies him, for it risks growing the adoration that he already possesses. Is he robust enough to bear this risk? His cowardice is, he knows, yet another imperfection in his tenure as a father.

28

As Oak watches for his driver from the window, there is a soft tap at the door. He must walk between his travel trunks and briefcases to release the latch; he is surprised to find himself a touch wistful seeing his belongings packed up for the return to Oxford. The flat itself he will not miss, with its single-paned, rattling windows in the winter cold. But the buzz of his work, as tired as it makes him, has revitalised his appetite for study and discussion. An addiction, at the core of it all.

Grace is ushered into the flat, shivering under her furs and hat.

'A quick goodbye before you're off,' she says. 'And something small.'

She presses into his hands a little square parcel. Upon unwrapping the linen cloth, Oak finds himself holding a finely knitted scarf – dark green like holly with flecks of grey.

'A trifle, really,' says Grace.

''Tis perfect. I am in need of a scarf. Always, actually. I tend to lose them in every room I enter.'

She is pleased and helps him arrange it around his neck.

'And one final thing,' she says. 'I have felt a bit of a fraud in my work with you, and as it's Christmas, I should like to be wholly, thoroughly honest with you at last.'

Oak stiffens, for he cannot fathom what she means. His cheeks freeze in a nervous smile.

'I will just say it,' says Grace. 'I believe in Ponden-Hall's pact. Whatever deal he has struck with the devil, with God, with whomever, I believe he did it for love and I am positively tickled by it. I think he has built a world for himself and Hugh DeLacey: their butler, their favourite animals, the children they could never have. Timothy Ponden-Hall could never have all of this in real life, so why not in art? I hope he *has* found a way to immortalise all of them, and I hope he can join them soon with whatever schemes he has planned in this final chapter of his life. What do you think of that?'

Oak laughs, is both utterly relieved and bewildered, for this divulgence is not what he had expected.

'Oh, I know you think it is all balderdash,' says Grace.

'Do you know, my dear,' Oak says, 'I shall be honest with you too. I do think the stories are all drivel and exaggerated nonsense, but a part of me wishes that I could believe in some of it. Because what an extraordinary thing to hope for – eternal life for those we love. For those we have lost and things we have never had.'

Grace kisses him on the forehead.

'Happy Christmas, Mr Oak. Thank you for a most illuminating and intriguing past few months.'

When she has gone, Oak takes stock of the flat once more, and adjusts his new scarf more snugly around his neck. It has been a productive stint in London. Enjoyable, in fact, and he is pleased with his decision to deliver the lectures. But now, he is ready to go home. He misses Alice and his house and the cosiness of his study. A bit of peace and time to reflect on the past few months is exactly what Oak needs, and with this to look forward to, he putters around latching his suitcases and resolves to make one more cup of tea before his driver arrives.

On Christmas morning, 15 Mansfield Road is a picture of festive splendour. The tree, a freshly felled evergreen, is bedecked in beads and jewelled baubles and basks beneath an array of paper stars that hang from every beam. On the mantelpiece, a miniature village with powdered snow is interspersed with candles and bundles of cinnamon sticks. The windows are suitably frosted. A wreath hangs on the back and front of every main door, each one inundated with berries and oranges and the shiniest tinsel that would attract magpies from across Oxford. Even the doorknobs are wrapped in knots of red velvet. Like every year, Oak has spared no expense. Christmas was always his children's favourite holiday.

When a knock at the front door interrupts her breakfast, Alice gathers herself up for a castigation. She has become adept at handling these bold visitors. They come with letters for her father or for Ponden-Hall, or they come with gifts: sweetmeats, painting materials, flowers – once, a creepy handmade puppet in the likeness of the giver's deceased mother 'for inspiration'. Alice buries them all in the waste pile before her father can see them.

But on *Christmas day*? This is audacious indeed.

Alice throws open the door, a reprimand on her lips, and is surprised to see Peter Bridge on the bottom step looking up at her.

'Good morning, Alice.' His cheeks are flushed from the cold and his hands are clasped behind his back.

'Peter! What are you doing here?'

'I… well. I have come to say goodbye.'

'Goodbye? Come in, come in, it is positively freezing.'

But Peter shakes his head. 'My father will be waiting with the carriage. We are off to London for the day.' Here, a pause. His chin dimples in the slightest frown. 'And tomorrow I set off for France with my uncle.'

Alice has not heard him correctly. She leans the door upon the latch behind her and shivers her way to the bottom step.

'What do you mean, tomorrow? I thought you were leaving at Easter—'

'Yes, that was the original plan. But my uncle wishes to be in Paris for the new year. And, well… I do not have much say in the matter.'

The cold is cutting but Alice does not feel it. Her dress is thin and her feet are bare in the winter chill but it is a space within her that grows most numb.

'And you're off to London now?' she asks.

Peter nods. He steps closer and raises a mittened hand but then drops it awkwardly. 'But… we shall see each other on the continent,' he tries. 'Right? In the summer.'

They both feel the lightness of these words, the husk or mere outline of a dream.

'How exciting for you, Peter.' It is difficult to say without casting her eyes to the pavement. She crosses her arms and summons up her best smile. 'You will have a few more months to scope out the best spots before I arrive.'

'And I bought this for you.' From behind his back he reveals a small package wrapped in brown paper and red ribbon. 'Happy Christmas, Alice.'

Peter leans in and kisses her on the cheek. It is the lightest of touches, his freckles and the deepening blush around them so warm, so close to Alice's nose, and she can only swallow, lick her lips that have become chapped in the frigid air as he turns from her. He is already across the road by the time she looks up. His coat is just a touch too big for him so the tails billow a bit behind.

It is only Peter, thinks Alice. *An assistant in a bookshop.* There is no need for this heaviness in her chest. But as he recedes down the road, she has the urge to run after him. She would like to go with him, to London, to Paris, to anywhere, it does not matter, for Alice cannot be left behind.

It is *only* Peter. But he is all she has left in her small world. And before he rounds the corner, she calls out to him, 'Safe travels, Peter Bridge!'

He turns to her with a grateful smile. His wave lingers, suspended as a Christmas star that Alice can admire, but not yet pursue, and then he is gone. She hugs the ribboned gift to her chest.

In the early afternoon, Missy bustles around the kitchen, glazing a tart on the windowsill and stirring a pot of mincemeat on the stove. The table is stocked to feed a banquet of kings: bowls of candied peel, platters of jellies and cakes with icing; roasted goose with plum pudding, honeyed chestnuts and salted kippers; pitchers of currant wine and rum punch, of which the lemon juice, sugar, rum and brandy remain out on the sideboard for the ease of mixing up a second, third, fourth batch as the day progresses.

With the sheer amount of food, never mind the quality of the ingredients and the branding of liquors and meats, one would expect to see the extended family of a grand house gather for the feast, for a day of merriment and drinking and carols around the pianoforte. Instead, it is only Oak in his favourite jacket with holes at the elbows; it is only Alice in a silk dress too short in the sleeves, for she has grown since it was purchased at the beginning of summer.

They sit together at one end of the table and for once, have much to say to each other. It is strange to be in the other's company again after a long six weeks apart. Even though they have lived as a pair in this very house, most of the time in this very room, for the past ten years, their reunion pulses with an energy that seemed to be extinguished long ago.

Between mouthfuls of pastry, Oak tells stories about London and snags his jacket on a fork tine in his vigour. Alice asks questions and does impressions of her tutors. They laugh freely – deep belly laughs that are foreign yet familiar, like a long-forgotten friend.

As Oak wipes his eyes and pours another glass of punch, Alice helps herself to another slice of cranberry pie.

'I went skating the other day,' she says, 'on the river when it froze.' She is curious to see what her father's reaction will be, is uncertain about how he will feel. She has thought about withholding this from him, but the merriment she felt on the day – and the feeling of returning to something fearful – is an experience she wants to share.

'Oh?'

'I enjoyed it. I wasn't sure I would remember how, it had been so long. But I picked it up just fine.'

Oak takes a moment to consider this. He, too, is uncertain about how he feels or should feel. At last, he smiles. 'How wonderful.'

'There was a surprising rush of relief to see that I could still do it,' says Alice. 'And I was thinking that perhaps you could understand – the way you have returned to your work and to lecturing.'

Oak slices a triangle of cheese and spreads it onto a biscuit. 'That is an apt comparison,' he says, popping the piece into his mouth. 'And do you know, it has been thoroughly enjoyable. Energising, even.'

'Yes! That is exactly how I felt.'

'And, well…' Oak strays onto delicate ground, 'as you know, I thought it would be… *difficult* to return to my work since your sister had been so involved. To my great surprise, I did not feel grief but a familiar excitement. Almost as if she was with me.' It is not as painful to say this as he might have expected. In fact, sharing this with Alice brings solace. *Is this the first time they have spoken about Emma together?* Ten years. It has taken him too long to brave the subject. It is no wonder they have lived like this for so long.

'Me too, Father,' says Alice. She is smiling. 'I felt her too. Although I did fall once.'

Oak laughs. 'Perfectly understandable. I am truly happy to hear this, my girl. Fresh air and exercise are important. And you always loved skating.'

'And you, Father? Any new developments around Ponden-Hall?'

'In fact, there has been one.' Oak glances about the room to ensure that Missy is out of earshot. 'To remain between us for now, yes? There is good reason to believe that Andrew Ponden-Hall was Julien's bastard son from his journey with Captain Cook.'

Alice puts her fork down. 'A bastard?'

'Mhm.'

'But that is incredible. I have never heard this rumour before.'

''Tis no rumour. I believe it is very much true and has been a well-guarded secret all of these years.'

'Elizabeth raised him as her own.'

'She did. And based on her medical notes, it was not easy for her.'

'You have always said that she was a very proud woman.'

'She was. This would have tormented her. She comes from a staunchly traditional family. Just the thought of raising a child born out of an infidelity would have been inconceivable. Not to mention that they would most likely have seen the baby as impure. It is a stroke of luck that Andrew was fair and his children were blonde.'

'Or else what?'

'Who is to say?'

'So Timothy Ponden-Hall is of mixed blood.'

'Yes, and I am convinced that this plays a part in his story – his hermitage, his mystery after Hugh's death. Exactly what, however, I have yet to discover.'

'And nobody knows about this?'

Oak shakes his head and peels a tangerine. 'Just you and I. And Miss Dodd, of course.'

There is the slightest pause of Alice's fork as she presses to break through the pie crust. The forceful stab of metal on porcelain causes the table to wobble.

'I did not realise you were still seeing her,' she says.

'Oh, she is only helping me with bits of the research. It is she who gained access to Elizabeth's medical notes. You remember the job she interviewed for with the phrenologist? It was this information we were seeking. She unearthed the files at last.'

'How clever of her.'

Alice has another bite of pie.

'You will remember the map of the Sandwich Islands in the DeLacey portrait,' Oak continues. 'Ponden-Hall is telling us something — has been since the very first painting. It is a wonder that these details have not been brought to light until now.'

'I see.'

'I have a few more ideas. More paths to pursue.'

'And you will continue this work in London?'

'I think it makes sense to return for a week or so in the new year.'

The wine bottle clinks forcefully against Alice's glass. Had she herself not offered to stay in London to help? Had she not requested to aid her father in this integral opportunity of his life's work? The wine goes down smoothly but Alice does not taste it. The food on her plate and on the surrounding platters is suddenly unappealing and unforgivably ostentatious. Had her father not confirmed that Grace would aid in one small matter and nothing more? What meetings and discussions have they shared these past long weeks? Alice feels sick.

Oak, too, has remembered Alice's offer to help and his promise around Grace's involvement; he springs to make amends.

'Of course, it seems that Grace would not have secured her crucial position with Elke Jahn without *your* help, my darling,' he says. 'She has told me repeatedly of how critical your role was on that day.'

Alice takes another sip of wine, though now it proves difficult to swallow.

'And there is much reading to be done,' Oak continues. 'I shall have to learn more about Cook's expedition, and I wonder if we should revisit old articles on the family around the time of Andrew's childhood. Perhaps you could join me in London for a bit if your studies allow a break.' He smiles hopefully and pours Alice a cup of punch. 'I would be most appreciative of an extra pair of eyes.'

Alice stands to fetch the Christmas pudding, the dense sphere of raisins, currants and candied orange that was mixed from east to west and boiled in a cloth five weeks ago on Stir Up Sunday. She has salivated over its aromas of cooked sugar and nutmeg, has admired Missy's care to keep it moist in a weekly bath of brandy. Now, she carries it to the table and does not notice the scents of lemon zest, cinnamon and cloves that rise from the platter. The sprig of holly stuck into the pudding's cap looks ridiculous, like a fatuous toupee on a bald man.

'Yes, I'm sure I can come to London for a few days. If you would like me to.'

Oak clasps his hands together. 'Splendid!' And then, after noticing her slight frown, her downcast eyes, he adds, 'Forgive me, Alice. I did not know you were interested in helping me on this matter. I did not see. 'Tis one of my… *many* failings over these years.'

Perhaps it is a start. He has never acknowledged such shortcomings in the past.

'And I have been thinking,' he continues, 'that perhaps you could delay your employment with Magnus Bird until the autumn. We could spend the summer together pursuing Ponden-Hall. Here, in London, or wherever you would like. Perhaps we could even make a trip to Cornwall.'

Oak's eyes twinkle but Alice can only stare at him. He is so expectant, waiting for – what? A torrent of gratitude? Sounds of intrigue, approval? Alice can feel her frustration wind up taut as a whip and top.

'You… still want me to work for Mr Bird?' she asks at last.

Oak is startled. 'Well, yes, that is the arrangement.'

All is still.

'But… you saw how the meeting went in London.' Alice's voice wobbles and it rises in pitch despite her best efforts to steady it. And she cannot hold back any longer. 'Father, I have *no* interest – not a drop – in working for that man. In working for *anyone*, for that matter, as a governess. How can you be so blind? This has never been what I have wanted. Missy sees it. I am certain that Mr Bird saw it. Why, even Grace Dodd, whose opinion you seem to value so highly, has tried to aid in my endeavours to make you understand!'

Oak is dumbstruck.

Alice would like to tear at her hair, shake her father out of his incredulity.

There is an entire bowl of brandy butter, freshly whipped and hardened into decadent peaks. Alice scoops the spread over a hearty portion of pudding. She has wondered if her father's return to academia – to his life's work on Ponden-Hall and his unfinished story – would rekindle the spirited, eye-twinkling father of their childhood. The hope was there, Alice admits to herself, for she misses her father. The Solomon Oak she has lived with for the past decade is merely a shell.

Yet now that her hopes are realised, now that life has been revitalised and there is a human behind the blood and bones, Alice discerns a deeper truth: without Emma, Alice will never be enough. Alice has never understood Oak as she did. Emma was not only her father's daughter; she was his pride and light. Without Emma, Alice is a stream without a current.

But she has tried. Has she not remained as loyal and eager to please as a hound at his tired master's feet? Alice has only ever craved the chance to show Oak that she, too, can help establish his legacy – perhaps not as well as Emma could and not as naturally, but she is capable and curious and alive. She has tried to be visible for years, to show Oak that she has her own curiosity and spirit, only to be patted and turned away from, and now to be packed off to work as a governess.

'Actually,' says Alice, 'I don't think I will be able to join you in London after all. I am needed here. I have taken up a job over the past few months.'

'A job?'

'Yes.'

'What about your studies?'

'I do both. The work takes place in the evenings mostly.'

Oak steadies his hand so the brandy butter spoon does not shake. What constitutes the evening? How could his daughter possibly not be indoors, safe and warm, after dusk? Oak's face grows hot.

'What type of work takes place in the evenings? How did you find this job? Who is your employer? Since when... *why* have you taken a job?' Oak has so many questions. 'You are a student. You should be devoting all of your time to studying.'

'I do, Father. And once I have completed my exams, I will not have time to work as anyone's governess because I would like to see a bit of the world that I have studied so diligently for so long. That is why I have taken a job. I am saving money to go to Europe for a tour.'

'A tour! Come, Alice. Why you are but—'

'A capable young woman who is not appeased by mere books.'

'Nobody does grand tours any more, even young men. They are out of fashion. How you could possibly think this is a good idea—'

'I couldn't care less about fashion and I know you couldn't either. I want to visit Paris, Geneva, Rome – all of them. All of the places you loved when you were young. I want to see the art we grew up hearing about. I thought you would be pleased.'

But Oak is not pleased. Surprised and confused, yes, but more than anything, terrified.

'This is an asinine idea. Do you know how dangerous it is to travel abroad on your own as a little girl? Do you know how expensive it will be?'

'I am not a little girl, and expense is not an issue. My job is lucrative.'

Oak is as purple as a beet. He dabs his forehead; there is no concealing the perspiration that glistens on his temples. He sees his daughter slip away before his mind's eye. This he cannot allow.

'This is a foolish dream, Alice, and you know it,' he says. 'You aren't worldly enough to undertake a journey like this. Why, we haven't travelled to the continent in years; I no longer know anyone out there who can help you. You don't speak any of the languages. You don't do your own laundry!'

'I am going, Father. There is no need to attempt to convince me otherwise. And you can stop the insults as well. I am much more capable than you think I am. My life is bigger than that of a governess in Portman Square and you would know that if you only showed the slightest bit of interest in me.'

Alice pushes her uneaten pudding aside and walks out in silence.

Upstairs in her bedroom, she trembles in rage and dejection. She had not planned to tell her father in this way. In fact, a quiet part of herself had hoped that perhaps he would join her on the journey. Now, Alice seethes at her desk, head in her hands, and wishes that she was abroad already – without Oak, without the ghost of Emma, without this caricature in her mind of a sitter-turned-scholar who has taken her place and will celebrate Oak's legacy with feasts and heaps of gifts.

Her elbow knocks the crumpled ball of brown paper from Peter's present. Alice takes the bound collection of Dumont's essays in hand, places her palm and fingers flat upon the cover. She bends to it, smells the leather and pulls away before a tear can cross the bridge of her nose to drop upon it. She places the collection next to her mother's old journal. Her mother, who volunteered in workhouses for a decade through two pregnancies whilst playing the organ and studying frescoes; her friend, not yet nineteen, who orders books from abroad for important scholars and is off to Europe to learn languages and admire the works of masters. And here is Alice, left in her bedroom, alone with papers and ghosts.

Only once in her life has Alice succumbed to overpowering raw emotion. On the night of Emma's burial, she sat in her father's lap and cried until her eyes were so swollen that she could no longer see. Her entire body was drained of water, sapped of salt, tears and saliva, raw and cracked like a desert floor. Now, she surrenders to raw emotion again, this time to jealousy, anger and above all, loneliness. For that is what she is: irrevocably alone. A memory rises to the surface of her mind: strong scents of bergamot and neroli, a dried scrap of cabbage stuck between yellowing teeth, a folded piece of paper sticky with sweat. In a daze, she retrieves the address from her coat pocket and writes to Edward Bromage. She would bare every secret in the world at this moment to prove to her father that she, like Emma, like Grace Dodd, is invested in this mystery too – would divulge all the secrets around Timothy Ponden-Hall if she had them, just to seize her father's attention. But there is only one secret that Bromage will be interested in. And in this impassioned moment, Alice wants most of all for her father to feel the pain and rejection as she does. In her letter, she holds nothing back.

29

Christmas night rolls on and on like a sluggish sea. The wreaths, ribbons and tinsel – tokens of revelry just hours before – seem to loiter with stale cheer, and the remnants from Christmas lunch have been covered, picked at, spooned through and re-covered.

Oak does not leave his study. The quiet is a terrifying preview of the months to come. He had heard Alice stomp out of the front door shortly after lunch. She had returned but then left again – heaven knows where to – and came back around half-past seven. Too dark, too cold. Now, at the creak of a floorboard in Alice's room above, Oak tenses, feels relief that the girl is indeed still at home, before such reassurance descends into an intense and resilient grump. Oak forms an apology for his behaviour, stores it in his cheeks, but knows he cannot bring himself to release it. *She wants to leave me. I have failed her as a father.* So he locks himself away and does not go to her but instead continues to read about Captain Cook's excursion and fruitlessly scours the pages for any mention of Julien Ponden-Hall until he retires to his bed.

Alice avoids her father for a different reason. It is true that they are not privy to apologies. But she also fears that the second she sees her father, she will burst into tears like a remorseful child, for more than anything, Alice is consumed with a guilt that has gnawed at her belly since the late afternoon. The letter, she hopes, will not have been collected from the pillar-box in Park Town today. Aside from the usual Christmas morning delivery, the postmen should not conduct their typical duties. Still – the risk is too great. What does Alice know about the mail system?

At her desk, Alice buries her head in her hands. She had regretted writing the letter as soon as she dropped it into the box – had lurched her hand in after it, in fact, in a futile attempt to catch or retract it. She had paced the streets after this, chastising herself for succumbing to her anger, appalled and ashamed at her disloyalty. She had even returned to the pillar-box in the darkening evening to try once more to retrieve the letter. All she took away was a bruised and scraped arm.

She will return in the morning to intercept the postman. Do they collect post on Boxing Day? She will wait for as long as it takes so that Edward Bromage does not receive her letter.

So the hours crawl onward and the prospect of a lazy Christmas evening is neither appealing nor promising, as it should be. It is not until the middling hours of the night that father and daughter drift to sleep in their own quarters, more distant from each other than before.

In these same dark hours of Christmas night, staff at the manor in Oxfordshire bustle about in quiet purpose. They empty every hearth of its ashes, a superstitious but satisfying task to symbolise the sweeping away of the past year's ills. The tree in the hall is watered, pruned and dusted; it will remain on display with its baubles and strings of nuts until Twelfth Night, despite the gloom that settles about the house. The entire estate, buzzing as of late, feels heavy and sombre, sighing its grievances into the long grass and across the hills.

At three o'clock in the morning, the click of the lock reverberates through the corridors like the summoning groan of a conch shell. The door is pulled open. Light from hundreds of candles spills into the hall as if daylight itself has been contained in the chamber beyond.

They come to help – have been waiting for this moment for the past few days. The painter has hidden away since before Christmas Eve. Trays of cold meats and wine have been left at the door, exchanged for biscuits and bonbons as the hours pass. New wicks, freshly dipped in beeswax, accompany the food, for there is always a flickering glow behind the door and they dare not leave the painter in need of light.

Now with the grand door propped open, they enter. It is a majestic sight, the books and maps and nautical instruments bathed in candle glow. Vials and glass pitchers of oil reflect a thousand combinations of pigments, powders and wax heaped in bowls, some spilling onto the great table, some knocked onto the floorboards.

And in the middle of it all is the new painting. The housemaid suppresses a sniffle. The butler rests his hand on his chest. The gardener bows his head.

And they get to work. The painting is wrapped in brown paper and tied with twine. It is carried through the great house with reverence, down the staircase, past the drawing room and through the servants' kitchen to the stable yard. Here it is loaded into the hansom where it is protected on all sides by cushions, snug against the buttoned leather seats and cashmere throws, to be transported like royalty. And like its predecessors, it will be delivered to its final destination by an invisible hand before daybreak – given over to the world, surrendered like a story.

PART TWO

A Housemaid

FOR SECRET, UNCHARTED WATERS IN
CARIBBEAN SEA,
THE FINE BRITISH-BUILT SHIP BEATRICE
B. PATOC, MASTER

Shipping and Mercantile Gazette, July 1839

Wanted: sea-hardy gents to brave unknown waters of Ponden-Hall, DeLacey's final journey, rumoured secret island between Jamaica, Nicaragua. Intended to sail from London 1st August, eight years following TPH, HDL excursion.

Experienced sailors only; potential for high reward.

Apply to: BONNEVILLE, Shipbrokers

1

The pounding is furious. Oak is jolted out of his half-dreams and props himself up on his elbows. He looks this way and that, cosily sunken in his goose-down bed with the pillows and blankets piled about him. No sliver of light outlines the curtains; it is still black outside.

Yet someone raps upon the door as if he is being whipped from behind. And what is he calling out? Oak sits up, shakes away remnants of sleep and strains to hear beyond the stone walls. Why, he is shouting Oak's name. He will wake the entire city, the fool.

Grumbling, Oak throws on his dressing gown. The clock in the hall reads six-thirty in the morning.

'What in God's name—'

'Solomon Oak? Mr Oak, you are needed at once!' The disturber of the peace is a young man, perhaps Alice's age, crimson cheeked and underdressed in the sparse snowflakes that have begun to fall.

'What is the meaning of this? Do you know what time it is? You will wake the neighbourhood!'

'My apologies, sir, but I was told to bring you forthwith. A new Ponden-Hall, Mr Oak! Appeared this morning out of nowhere. In brown paper and twine just like the last one – just like the pig.'

Oak comes to himself as if slapped, feels the cold afresh as the words break through his sleep daze. 'Another Ponden-Hall. Are you certain?'

'I seen the signature myself, sir. In the bottom right corner.'

Oak already begins to untie his dressing gown, fumbles through the keys and pile of post that has collected on the sideboard in search of the railway timetable.

'When is the next train to London? I shall go immediately.'

'There is no need, sir.'

'What do you mean?'

'The painting is here, sir. In Oxford.'

This is most startling. Here in Oxford. It is almost implausible. Every Ponden-Hall painting has surfaced on the doorstep of a museum in London. Why has he broken the pattern now?

'You have seen the painting,' says Oak. 'You are certain it is authentic?'

'I'm no expert, sir, but 'tis the most beautiful work of art I have ever seen.'

'Who found it?'

'A morning attendant at the Ashmolean. Came across it by accident, in fact. Nobody is due to work today, of course. He has a stiff leg, you see. Went on his usual morning route and happened to walk by.'

From a coat pocket, Oak fetches a handful of coins and presses it into the boy's hand. 'For your pains,' he says. 'Tell them I follow you. I will be at the Ashmolean within the hour.'

'There is one more thing.'

Oak is already closing the door. 'Go on.'

'The painting is… for you.'

'Whatever do you mean?'

'There is a note tied to the corner of the painting. "For Solomon Oak", it says.' The boy grows paler. 'No one dares touch it further until you arrive.'

Oak is unresponsive. He hears the boy's words – can sense the fear interlaced between them and better understands the depth of urgency. For him? Oak's knuckles are white from gripping the door. A note. Timothy Ponden-Hall has left a new painting. For Solomon Oak. It is all too much to take in. So much, in fact, that Oak will not believe it until he sees it with his own eyes.

'I will follow you,' he finally says. 'Thank you. I will be there shortly. Thank you.'

Oak needs time to think. He pauses, one hand on the doorknob, the other on the lock. It cannot be. What madness is this to bring old men into the world's light? When he turns around, he is startled to find Alice at the bottom of the stairs hugging the banister. In this moment, they mirror each other: two faces of abject wonder and shock, as their anger and guilt fall away like the flurries of snow outside.

'Come,' says Oak. 'We must not keep them waiting. Let us see this newest masterpiece.'

They are the only ones on the street. The city of Oxford slumbers on as Oak and Alice hasten to the museum. They hunker into their scarves, heads bent against the chill, and try their best to look nondescript. Beneath his coat, Oak quivers with anticipation. An attendant welcomes them at one of the side doors.

'This is where we found it,' the man says, gesturing to the inconspicuous archway to the right of the main entrance. 'Meant for us first and not the public. Only we attendants would use this door.'

Inside, they are greeted by the museum's keeper, Sir Arthur Evans. His face is flushed, positively pink around his handlebar moustache as he licks his lips too frequently, out of nervousness or like an animal anticipating a juicy feeding.

'Thank you, Mr Oak, for coming so swiftly. She's just through here.'

'She?'

Sir Arthur Evans nods and whisks them through several doorways. 'A housemaid this time.' And glancing at Oak, '*Your* housemaid.'

Into the office of Sir Arthur Evans himself they go. The painting perches on the mantelpiece of a high-ceilinged study decorated with polished wood and fine marble angels. Oak does not need to scrutinise the piece before confirming that it is real; it is a feeling more than visual verification – a presence in the room, a fragile balance. He brings his nose to the bottom right corner. The signature, bold and textured, is as familiar to Oak as the handwriting of an old friend and is just as comforting.

In his twelfth painting, Timothy Ponden-Hall has returned to the human form. It is a portrait in the most traditional sense: she sits at a three-quarter angle, her chin upturned so her features are clear and distinct as she faces her painter. Characteristic of Ponden-Hall's more recent portraits, there are no bells and whistles, no props or frivolous backgrounds to distract from the woman herself in her pins and ruffled apron straps. She is round and hearty. She exudes warmth and deep, rich laughter. She is even perhaps mid-laugh, the way her lips pulse, the way her eyes crinkle. Through the wax and oil, she comes alive, her voice rising from layers of gesso and paint, for it will not be constricted or bound by a canvas.

'My, my,' mumbles Oak. For Ponden-Hall has outdone himself. The housemaid's skin is unlike anything he has painted before: buffed coats of vine black – charred desiccated grape vines and stems, inter-mixed with shades of lamp black, soft soot from oil lamps, and bone black – the bluish charring of bones. Her complexion is smooth and regal, accentuated by and starkly contrasted with her white hair pulled into a taut bun.

Sir Arthur Evans comes shoulder to shoulder with Oak and coughs shyly. He bends close to the painting, then stands back, looks from the portrait to the observing Oak and back again as if watching a tennis match. 'Who is she?'

'A housemaid, you say,' says Oak. His eyes do not leave the painting.

'Well, yes. But who *is* she, Solomon? You must know her.'

'And why should I?'

'The note, of course. She has been left for you. We thought that perhaps… she was an acquaintance of yours. One does not always make public his relationships with women, particularly women of this colour…'

At this Oak straightens and turns to the keeper. 'I beg your pardon. Are you insinuating—'

'No, no!' Sir Arthur Evans exclaims. The suggestion that Oak has had an inappropriate acquaintance with this woman is exceed-ingly offensive. The pink of Evans' face now surpasses the red of a raspberry. 'I could only presume… well. You could understand our curiosity… You do not know her then.'

'No indeed. And I am just as baffled as you are as to why the painting has been left for me.'

'She is called Mary. Was called, I should say. See here on the back.'

No. 12 *Mary – A Housemaid*, 1890.

'And the obituaries? Any listings?'

'Not yet – not over the past few days that we have found. They will come pouring in, I assure you.' Sir Arthur Evans' smile is as wide as a hanger, for such attention, such mystery, such *scandal* is too often reserved for society in London. The Ashmolean will be the centre of gossip for months to come. How thrilling. 'Ah, and your note. Here.'

It is a folded piece of linen paper as ordinary as a receipt from the butcher. Yet there, across its crease, is Ponden-Hall's bold script, all in capitals, *FOR SOLOMON OAK*. Oak holds the note in both hands, runs his fingers across the text lightly before withdrawing them like a naughty schoolboy. He has touched this paper, thinks Oak. How casually he has scrawled this instruction and how dramatically it alters the painting's message. Suddenly, Oak is overwhelmed; he feels a closeness to the painter that was, up until this moment, askew, for his respect and admiration has naturally been unrequited all these years. Could it be that Timothy Ponden-Hall trusts Solomon Oak? *How much does he know about my career, my life's work centred around his creations?* And Oak is overcome by gratitude and humility. It is exaggerated tenfold, for he shares this special moment with his daughter.

'Look, Alice,' he says. He pulls her close and shows her the note. 'He is trying to tell me something. *Me*. Perhaps we are fated to learn his story after all.'

Alice nods, swallows the bile that has risen in her throat, and commands every fibre in her body to be still. She leans into her father, which is interpreted as an act of camaraderie, a motion of closeness and understanding, when really, it is all she can do to remain upright as she catapults back into Lou's hansom in all but body, feels the weight of Mary's figure on hers, hears her shallow breathing that falls into step with the galloping on wet stones as they tear through Oxford towards the doctor's cottage. 'Who is she? Who is this Mary?' Alice hears through a fog. Her father and Sir Arthur Evans marvel at her stance, her lips, her eyes – more alive in the painting than she was that night, in many ways. Alice needs air. She must get out of this room where Mary's presence is suffocating. She cannot bear the questions any longer, cannot suffer how they speculate where Mary is from, how Ponden-Hall knows her, what kind of person she was.

Her name is Mary Whipple! She wants to shout. *Of a great house in Oxfordshire.*

She must tell her father. *Mary Whipple worked for Timothy Ponden-Hall and I know someone who can lead us to him.* This is what Alice can share; has she not yearned to help her father with this mystery? She has suspected for some time now that Lou was connected to the painter. She will divulge this information immediately – this and her moment of weakness in writing to Bromage. As soon as she and her father are alone, she will tell him.

But right now, she needs air. Somehow, she manages to excuse herself. Relieved that all attention is on the portrait, Alice staggers to the door; her legs are jelly as if she sways at sea. And as she crosses the threshold into the imposing hall, she is stopped short, glances over her shoulder as if someone has passed her. Did no one graze her elbow just now, touching her long unruly hair that springs out of its ribbon like bindweed? But the air is still and she is alone, inhaling deep breaths to steady herself, and she cannot ignore the undeniable aroma that wafts around her as if someone has brushed by at pace – a warm and yeasty tang of baked bread that drifts to the rafters above, the malt and salt of a loaf fresh out of the oven. The smell transports her back to the hansom, to Mary's head leaning on her shoulder, to her warm, bantam-like body exuding comfort like a mother, the savoury scent of flour and milk, of dough perfectly baked, leavened and crisp.

Oak spends the entire day with Sir Arthur Evans making plans of how best to display the new painting. As the owner of *Mary – A Housemaid*, Oak must approve every decision around its where-abouts. He could keep it in his own home, of course, but this, Oak knows, would be unwise and even dangerous, given the craze of Ponden-Hall's admirers and enemies. 'It must be displayed,' he had told Sir Arthur Evans. 'A new painting would never be kept secret for long, plus its reveal is crucial to Ponden-Hall's story. Timothy will want her shared with the world.'

Journalists were called immediately, and posters were ordered to be printed by the following morning.

Upon his return to Mansfield Road, despite the late hour, Oak plans to pore over the paintings – now twelve – for any previously unseen messages around family, heritage, bloodlines. When Oak enters his study, he is startled to find Alice there, sitting before the etchings of Ponden-Hall's paintings, which have been laid out across the floorboards.

Alice springs to her feet.

'Good evening, Father.' She clasps her hands behind her back as if addressing a headmaster. 'I wasn't sure when you would be home.'

'A long day,' sighs Oak as he removes his coat, his scarf. 'I am exhausted. And I… did not sleep well last night. And you? Are you well?'

'I, too, struggled to sleep last night,' says Alice. The ghost of their argument lingers between them. 'I was just revisiting the paintings again in light of the new portrait. I thought perhaps we might have missed something to do with his family or lineage.' There is something else too, tiptoeing on Alice's tongue. She will burst if she is not unbosomed soon.

'I was, in fact, coming to do that very task,' says Oak. He is proud of Alice's like-mindedness and says so.

'I was about to make myself some tea,' says Alice. 'Would you like a cup?'

'Tea would be lovely. I am too restless to sleep any time soon.'

But Alice does not move. The truth of her disloyalty weighs upon the room.

'I have done something horrible, Father.' The confession spills out of her. Although her voice wobbles, there are no tears, for this visceral worry and guilt are worse than weeping. 'I have written to Edward Bromage about Julien's bastard. I am so sorry. I cannot apologise enough. I hated myself as soon as I dropped it into the pillar-box, but by then, it was too late and I couldn't reach in to retrieve it. And I had intended to go back this morning to intercept the postman, but then there was the new painting, and my head has been swimming ever since. How I have suffered since our quarrel, Father. But I was just so furious with you. For not listening to my plight and not recognising my restlessness. And jealous of this woman who you have known for all of two months and trust more than me to help you with your work. I know it does not justify my vile behaviour but that is why I did it. I am ashamed and sorry and do not know how to make amends. And now this horrid man will know about your discovery and who knows what he will do with the information.'

They stare at each other, old man and young woman. At last, Oak walks forward and places his hands on his daughter's shoulders. He will never be used to raising his hands so high – will never be adept at nuance or in expressing himself to the one closest to him.

'My darling girl, my greatest mistake has been in keeping you in the shadows; I was only trying to protect you. In turn, I myself became blind and I made you feel as if I have not needed you. In truth, after losing your mother, your sister, perhaps I need you too much.' Oak swallows. 'I will speak to Magnus and tell him that you are no longer available for the post. He will understand.' Oak offers her a sad smile. 'So Alice, it is my own fault that Bromage will learn of that information.'

And neither knows what to say.

It is easier, then, to look away from one another – one final squeeze of the shoulders, a deep breath, a grateful, close-lipped nod.

But before she goes to boil the kettle, Alice pauses once more.

'Father, there is something else.'

All day, Alice has thought about Lou and Mary Whipple. She mourns for the old woman in her own way, but more than this, Alice aches for her friend, for she knows what Mary meant to Lou. At the Ashmolean that morning, all Alice wanted to do was share her knowledge with her father, tell him that she knew Mary Whipple and that her own connections could potentially lead them to the painter.

But now Alice is less sure. She remembers the night at the alms-house and Lou's icy detachment after Alice's prodding. If Lou wanted her to know about Ponden-Hall, would she not have confided in her by now? Lou is protecting the identity of her master for a reason unknown to Alice. She can only trust Lou in this decision. And without confirmation of the truth, what good would it do to tell her father half-formed ideas and premature conclusions? They would not be helpful to Oak – not yet. Alice also feels a loyalty towards Lou that she has not felt for anyone else; whether this is warranted is yet to be seen. But loyal to her, she is.

Oak waits for his daughter, quiet and expectant.

Alice shakes her head. 'Never mind,' she says. 'An idea for another time.'

She will tell her father, but she will write to Lou first. In the morning after breakfast, she will write with her condolences and ask for the truth. Only after she hears from the coachwoman will Alice bare all for her father. And anyway, he has more than enough to think about with this new painting for now. With this plan, Alice's conscience is appeased.

A tray of tea is brought in and placed on the floor. Together, they sit before Ponden-Hall's eleven paintings and the licking fire that blazes behind them; soon, a twelfth etching will be added to the collection. With their tea and shortbread fingers, they could be having a winter picnic, the likes of pretend games once played out in this very room with animals and wooden saucers. They could be playing draughts by the way they study their pieces before pointing, moving the twelve pictures about as they ruminate, question, sometimes laugh. It is well into the late hours of night and morning that they work, father and daughter cycling through Ponden-Hall's paintings like the two hands of a clock, an endless regime, a united persistence.

3

They keep an eye on the papers. Mary Yelland of Kent, a seamstress; Mary Sophia Simpson of Belfast, mother and instructor of the viola; Mary Loosley of Cambridge, domestic servant. There is an excess of deceased Marys in the following days but none are reported as a housemaid, and none are women of colour. Oak trawls through the gossip presses too. Mary Smithing of Windermere, housemaid, suggested by grieving family most upset by disappearance of the body after a house fire; Mary Eloise Markette of Cornwall, housemaid, death by ocean after leaving farewell note, intimate relations with T. Ponden-Hall in his seaside years. The stories compete to exceed all other papers in content, entertainment and above all, lunacy – they cannot believe that Ponden-Hall has painted a black woman.

Over her father's shoulder, Alice monitors the papers as well, even though she knows that Mary Whipple of Oxfordshire will never be lamented in print.

Lou does not respond to her letter.

One week into the new year, on the evening when their work is meant to resume, Lou does not appear. Alice's note is still under the lamp-post. She writes to her again and leaves the second letter atop the first.

On 11 January, a most compelling article graces the cover of *The Times*. Alice discovers the paper on the dining table when she ambles down for breakfast closer to midday than morning. She has taken to lie-ins, a luxury she has never embraced in the past, but whilst her studies are on hold and with no word from Lou about work, Alice slips into a timeless rhythm that is indifferent to the moon or the sun.

Groggily, she pours a cup of coffee. The paper is open to the article next to a tart of raspberry jam. She has barely swallowed the first sip when she registers the headline, sees the name of the author.

'The Bastard of Julien Ponden-Hall' by Edward Bromage, the Royal Society.

The coffee sloshes over the rim and into the saucer. So here it is. Alice trembles as she pulls the paper close and reads about her father's secret that has been unleashed to the public like a rabbit amongst stoats.

It has been confirmed by reliable sources that Andrew Ponden-Hall, father of Timothy Ponden-Hall, most famed explorer and painter of the nineteenth century, is in fact the bastard son of Julien Ponden-Hall, who journeyed with Captain Cook to the Sandwich Islands (now known as the islands of Hawai'i) in 1778. It is posited that Julien returned from the expedition under the command of Captain John Gore and bore with him an infantile son whose native mother remained on the islands. This astounding discovery comes just months after Ponden-Hall's biographer, the elderly and reclusive art historian Solomon Oak, confirmed that the map in Hugh DeLacey's portrait is not a mere symbol of maritime exploration as has been widely accepted, but a crude depiction of the Sandwich Islands – a hint from Ponden-Hall that he wishes his heritage to be known. How does such information colour our understanding of his already fascinating body of work? Of course, Ponden-Hall is on everyone's mind as a twelfth painting has appeared on the doorstep of Oxford's Ashmolean Museum only last week.

Her letter to Bromage had been so sparse, so minimal, yet the article is ripe with feeling, inundated with emotive adjectives and ludicrous assumptions about Ponden-Hall's motivations and movements. What did she expect? Such a stunt from Bromage is unsurprising, his intentions calculated with every word and purposeful full stop. The summary of Ponden-Hall's work is shallow and the facts are cherry-picked.

Alice turns the page. The article builds to its volcanic apogee, an appeal to Timothy Ponden-Hall himself:

To all of this, I offer one message: Mr Ponden-Hall, I speak on behalf of the Royal Society – on behalf of the nation! – when I say that we accept you and admire you. If you have hidden in the shadows after all these years in fear of judgement for being impure or for having mixed blood, rest assured, dear soul, that we are a progressive and forgiving people. Come forward. Lay the rumours to bed and share with us your secrets. We are one species, Mr Ponden-Hall; we live and we perish. We as a people are far more interested in your discoveries around immortality. What elixir have you tampered with? What souls have you preserved? There will be no judgement from your fellow men – only gratitude and admiration. We are completely blind to your bloodline. Trust us, Mr Ponden-Hall, to protect you and your exquisite secrets.

As a follow-up to our announcement at the end of last year: the Royal Society has been granted permission to deconstruct a small fraction of the *Kunekune Pig* portrait to further understand its composition and search for traces of the famed elixir. A date has yet to be confirmed. Whilst rumours have circulated about a retraction of this grant following the appearance of *Mary – A Housemaid*, we are certain that the dissection will go ahead. More soon.

Alice's stomach roils. What is meant to be a comforting message is a gross and offensive oversight. Bromage reverts to his own desires like a boomerang. Head in hands, Alice laments the article and cannot bear that her father's discovery has been announced in this way.

She casts the paper onto the table as she considers what to do, and notices the jam tart once more. It is her favourite snack from a particular stall in the market. Her father has seen the article then. And he has left it for her with this peace offering – a reminder that they are united in this and that there is nothing to forgive. It is a small consolation.

The paper is knocked to the floor in Alice's dash from the kitchen. Yet her father is not in the study nor in his bedroom. All is quiet. Alice descends the short stairwell into the laundry closet where Missy stirs a boiling pot for shirts.

'At last you're awake,' the daily says cheerfully. 'A message from your father. He has gone to London for the day – an impromptu journey. He will return after supper. What would you like to eat?'

But Alice is already on the landing, fetching letterhead from the desk so she can pen yet another letter to Lou – one that may redeem her mistake and put the macabre rumours to rest.

4

The few hours Oak spends in London are both fleeting and dense. He sits with Jonathan Hammond in one of the hidden consulting rooms of the National Gallery and they talk animatedly between themselves, drawing their heads together with a hush when they remember the content of their conference. Hammond shirks his museum duties for the day. Their teacups are bottomless yet still their throats are dry from discussion. Just like old times, thinks Oak, when we were both younger, having squabbles about the Dutch Golden Age.

Midway through, an attendant escorts Grace Dodd into the chamber. Her hair is pinned in an extravagant bun and she wears a lace chemise as if attending a summer luncheon in the country; these surface details do not conceal her fury.

She tosses the *Times* article onto the table before them.

'Are we *reliable sources* now for this Society goon? I was not under the impression that we were working for anyone, Mr Oak.'

Oak pours her a cup of tea. 'Two sugars?'

'And what does he mean by this? *Completely blind to your bloodline?* Such arrogance. What nonsense.'

'Oh, Edward Bromage is a coxcomb,' says Oak. He takes a handful of walnuts and dried dates and places them on his own saucer. 'Do not take this article to heart. Almond biscuit?'

Grace is dumbfounded. She searches his face for any hint of irony, any flicker of rage. 'Are you not angry about this? He has published *our* discovery and taken the credit for his own!'

Oak bats away her words with his handkerchief. 'I do not know about you, Miss Dodd, but I certainly want no credit associated with this man. I am grateful, to be sure, that he has not portrayed us as accomplices.'

'He describes you like a worn-out dishcloth.'

Hammond snorts. 'The one factual clip of information in the entire piece.'

'He has shared our discovery with the world, yes,' says Oak, 'but such secrets never remain quiet for long. I am convinced that Ponden-Hall's family history would have surfaced quite soon in the midst of this revitalised interest in his work. Think nothing of Bromage's article, my dear. It is a sensationalised headline with emotional writing meant to appeal to a simpleton population. I am disappointed that *The Times* agreed to publish it in the first place.'

'Competition is ruthless these days with all of the presses,' Hammond sighs. 'Anything to sell papers.'

'Ah, and—' Oak holds up a triumphant finger, 'the wheel turns in our favour. Bromage cannot threaten to come for this new painting – cannot even dream of it – because it has been left for me. He will be stewing in his boots. Even if he means to move forward with his appeal to deconstruct the pig in these coming weeks, his case will have fewer supporters. The public will certainly note that Ponden-Hall's most recent piece has been left as a message of sorts to me, and everyone knows how I feel about touching the paintings for experimentation. I do believe Ponden-Hall's little gesture has bought us some time.'

Grace scowls and slumps into a chair. 'So you will do nothing.'

'I didn't say that. Why do you think I have come to London? I have an idea – one that Jonny is on the cusp of agreeing to.'

'I just don't know,' says Jonathan. 'I have never been one to call in favours.'

Oak turns to Grace. 'Bromage has made a grave mistake in his article. He is a dog with a bone. He is so consumed with this immortality poppycock – with acquiring this supposed elixir of life – that he has misinterpreted Ponden-Hall's motivations completely. Bromage believes that Timothy hides in shame and only seeks acceptance from the public to come forward. Ha! On the contrary, I do not believe Ponden-Hall wants us to know about his bloodline just so he can sweep it under the floorboards.'

'So you think he is proud of his family history?'

'Proud? I cannot speculate. If we attach unwarranted emotion to the information we know, we are just as ignorant as Bromage. But I am certain that Ponden-Hall's link to the Sandwich Islands will colour the rest of his story and his body of work. We need only learn what this is.'

'What is your plan then?' asks Grace.

'Well. I have asked Jonny to call in a favour with his brother-in-law, who works for the *Daily Telegraph*. I would like them to publish an article: an interview with myself on the gravity of this discovery. What could this lineage mean? How could it have impacted Ponden-Hall's art and his hermitage after all these years? A scholarly piece, grounded in history.'

Hammond rubs his eyes. 'It could end up being quite a heavy article, Professor.'

'Mm. It is impossible to discuss such mixed bloodlines without considering uncomfortable ideas: the domestication of the exotic, this idea of "the West and the rest", this unspoken rule that aristocratic breeding supersedes differences of colour.'

The crease on Grace's brow deepens. 'You mean that someone like Timothy Ponden-Hall, although of mixed blood, would outrank me socially because of his family name and my own lowborn origins.'

'Perhaps. The fate of a mixed-blood child has always depended upon how his British relations accept him. Take the Milliner family, for example: Milliner had a Guyanan lover overseas and brought a son back to England. The grandmother insisted that he remain apart socially from her "pure" English grandchildren. So the boy was accepted, but lower down in the social hierarchy – though still more respectable than, say, a common cobbler or stonemason.'

'And how do you suppose the Ponden-Halls accepted Julien's bastard?'

'This is the story we must unearth. We have already seen glimpses into Elizabeth Ponden-Hall's psyche. I wonder how much of this societal acceptance plays a role in his art.'

'He wants us to understand,' says Grace. She has begun to understand, herself. 'Unlike Bromage, who will ignore the discovery in pursuit of furthering science.' She turns to Hammond. 'And your brother-in-law will write this article if you ask him to?'

Hammond and Oak glance at each other before Oak turns to Grace, eyes aglimmer.

'I was thinking,' he says carefully, 'that you would write the article, Miss Dodd.'

'Me?' She is astounded.

'You were, after all, instrumental in uncovering the truth of Julien's child. And you have written in the past – quite compelling copy, if I remember correctly.'

'For a student press,' says Grace, 'that was not published in the end! And nothing close to the reputation or readership of the *Telegraph*.' She thinks about the article – how proud she was of the draft and how she had sat on the don's lap as he complimented lines, scribbled comments above others. An amateur article produced in the giddiness of a new romance. No, not high-calibre at all compared to a proper publication.

'There is another reason,' says Oak. His lips twitch in a smile whenever he pokes fun at himself. 'Even the most widely circulated paper in the world will not satisfy its audience with a boring subject. People do not want to read more of my ranting about the focus on his art, the focus on his talent, now the focus on his life. But. Perhaps the interview is conducted by Grace Dodd – intelligent, opinionated and wildly controversial, given your... well, let us be frank, given your reputation as an Academy sitter and your unorthodox education. You would be a surprising voice. Fresh. These benefits are secondary, of course, to your own talent in spinning a story.'

Oak slides another article across the table.

'Read this. 'Tis an interview published in the *Pall Mall Gazette* a few years ago. See how the writer intersperses the interviewee's answers with his own ideas.'

Grace scans the piece, lips pursed. It has been a long while since she wrote anything of substance. Is she capable of writing with eloquence and flair without the scrutinising eye of a teacher? In this moment, Grace cannot decide if she is grateful or annoyed with herself for mentioning this interest of hers in the library all those evenings ago.

'It makes for compelling reading, does it not?' Oak asks. 'Sensationalised a bit, perhaps, but with no pretence. You do not need to pretend to be something you are not.'

Grace licks her lips as she skims the final paragraphs. When she looks up, she has assumed her usual poise and charm. 'Why, that is all I have ever wanted.'

5

That evening, with Solomon Oak returned to Oxford and Jonathan Hammond off to supper with his brother-in-law, Grace Dodd soaks in her bathtub and ponders the liminal. The tub is old and made of porcelain, stained and chipped from years of use by generations of tenants, most of the disagreeable variety. Grace moves her big toe from one blackened nick to another. Usually, she grimaces at imperfections. It is so easy to conceal blemishes, to fix or hide an aberration, that to ignore doing so suggests laziness or a lack of care. Such an attitude will not progress one in life. These black dents in the bathtub, however, are a great comfort, and she would not dream of having them repaired. She knows them well: the cluster of chips near the drain where she has dropped the metal plug from too high too many times; the large dent under her right shoulder from when she and a lover fell in, grasping for each other as the tub filled, and sent the champagne bottle crashing down. She finds them endearing, like her increasingly stubby fingernails and the ever so faint lines that sometimes linger on her forehead.

Next to the tub on the windowsill is a stack of old periodicals. She sifts through them with care, pinching the covers with thumb and forefinger to mitigate the spreading wetness. This particular collection from the library is a heap of social weeklies from the early 1800s: the *Cheltenham Looker-On*, the *Poor Man's Guardian*, the *Journal, Cleave's Penny Gazette*. She searches for articles not necessarily on Ponden-Hall but on the concept of mixed-race families – how this was portrayed in cartoons or editorials at the time. There is little to see, aside from one drawing of a hall in East London: it depicts a blending of classes and cultures as sailors, wealthy Londoners, a black woman and an Asian fiddler cavort together for an evening of dancing. Charming and idealistic, to be sure, but Grace imagines Elizabeth Ponden-Hall witnessing this scene in the East End and can only see her gazing on, appalled.

The idea of a mixed lineage admittedly baffles her. Black children and white children have set positions in society. Mixed children have no clear place at all. What should become of them? And if they are to be placed on a social pyramid of sorts, why should not everyone be placed according to who they are?

I am the same, thinks Grace. A thief has her place, as does a lady, as does an honest woman who works an honest trade. What of the women who have been two or more of these? What should become of Grace Dodd, an ex-con turned portrait sitter? An aspiring scholar?

She shifts in the tub. 'Tis silly to think of such things – to label herself as if she is defined by such titles.

She remembers Elke Jahn's reading, then. Elke's bony hands had truly ground into her skull, exploring the geography of her head, searching for answers like a gypsy at a crystal ball. Grace raises her own hands to her head now, water droplets pit-a-patting about her face. The median line of her forehead: *an intuitive knowledge of character*. This was unsurprising. Grace has always read people with her gut – men who appear polished and civilised but cheat on their wives with girl grooms and evade paying taxes with silver tongues; women of frail dispositions who look timid and shy but have the skill and audacity to slice off a hand with a butcher's knife if they are slandered. Grace has never been fooled. This intuition of character is what has kept her alive.

The bone plate in the upper back of her skull: *underdeveloped*, Elke had said as she slid her fingers across the sutures. *Your self-esteem, Miss Dodd*. This had inspired the phrenologist to raise an eyebrow. *A strong woman like yourself?* At the time, Grace had said nothing. Now, she massages the spot and has many questions. Is self-esteem the same as a lack of pride? Or self-reliance? Do such readings reflect *late* development too? For she does not believe that her self-esteem is lacking; on the contrary, she errs on the side of cocky, if only when it comes to her own value. She is right though, thinks Grace, in that I was not always so confident. The pain of losing the don was extinguished long ago, but the shame he had made her feel had lingered long after. She frowns at the thought of a stranger pulling secrets from nothing, from the nonsensical curve of her head.

It was Elke's final comment that left Grace most unsettled. Upon prodding the upper part of Grace's forehead, Elke had nodded and clicked her tongue – in approval or in a tutting way, it was difficult to judge. *Benevolence. A wide, attractive portion, Miss Dodd. True goodness of the mind.*

Well. The phrenologist was bound to get it wrong at some point. Although Grace has tidied up her life and no longer lurks in the unsavoury wings of society, she is certain that she is not good. She knows the stock from which she comes. Grace endeavours to live honestly these days, and she desires a simple life – though not boring, God willing! But good? She has never been good. She is too selfish to merit such a quality.

Mr Oak is right, of course, thinks Grace as she smooths her hair from her face and sinks deeper into the tub. Phrenology is tommyrot. She has wasted too much time on the reading already. To think that phrenology parlours were once sought out by the upper echelons of England is almost unfathomable. How funny we humans are, thinks Grace. And she does not deign to give it another thought. Reaching over the rim of the tub, she pulls forth another periodical. This is what she will focus all of her energy on: hierarchies of blended races, dated political cartoons, rumours and gossip and impassioned claims to Ponden-Hall's paintings – any thread or clue to prise the mystery open, to bring clarity to a story steeped in hearsay, a story that Grace has come to care more about than even her own.

6

Alice waits for the postman on the porch step, as she has done every day for the past four weeks. She is no longer solemn or compassionate towards Lou's silence. As days have blended into weeks without the slightest whisper, Alice's patience and empathy have stirred into irritation (is a quick note to assure that she is indeed all right and only grieving too much to ask?). Eventually, this irritation funnelled into worry. What if Lou is so overpowered by grief that she has become ill herself? Perhaps Mary died of a disease that has spread through the house like a red wind and Lou is fighting for her final breath as the space beneath the lamp-post fills with Alice's silly letters. Or perhaps, without Mary to tether her, Lou has moved on in search of the next job, the next exploit.

Such thoughts bounce around Alice's mind like the silver bells of an infant's rattle. She then recounts their last meeting: had she said or done something to cause offence again? Had she upset the balance of their working relationship, crossed a line by being too familiar? These are illogical ideas if she pauses to consider Lou's character; Lou is strong and practical – and, Alice reminds herself, she is a woman of manners and class. She would not up and leave without a goodbye.

Yet grief is an unpredictable master. Doesn't Alice understand this more than anyone?

At last, the postman arrives with a comical tower of letters that leans this way and that as he ascends the steps.

'Good day, Horace.'

'More for your father,' he manages as he struggles to balance. 'From all over the country. Even one from Paris by the looks of it.'

Alice receives them, allows the stack to tumble onto her chest. The number of letters has not dwindled; some write who claim to know Mary, whilst others write with deals to study the painting and its materials in exchange for immortality once discovered; still others write to condemn Oak to hell for fraternising with Ponden-Hall, and a few write with obscene offers of money to purchase the painting for their private collections. Most of the letters are burned before they are fully read. Some of the letters – the hilarious, unpalatable ones – are used as coasters or cutting boards for particularly smelly cheeses.

'None for me, then?'

'Sorry, Miss Oak.'

'Actually, Horace. Are you allowed to… could you confirm if *any* letters are being sent out from – I do not even know the name of the house. Somewhere north of Oxford is all I know. A grand house. It must be, from what I know of it and its master.'

Horace presses his lips together in a frown. 'I'm sorry, Miss Oak. I would need to know more information than that, and even if I did, I really couldn't tell you where the post comes from.'

'I understand.'

The house's master, thinks Alice, is most tenaciously pursued by nearly everyone in England. The list of questions she has for Lou is limitless, the most pressing being, 'Why has Timothy Ponden-Hall left my father a painting?' She is certain that Ponden-Hall is Lou's employer, for how else would he know Mary, and why would he paint her if she was not an integral hand in his staff? Mary's employment as a black woman makes perfect sense, too, knowing that Ponden-Hall himself was of mixed blood; of course he would hire a staff of varied races. The small circle of people in Alice's life are somehow unpredictably linked, yet the silk of the web that links them remains fibrous, translucent. If she could only speak to Lou…

And there is one final piece that niggles at her mind: what have become of Lou's deliveries? Do the parcels continue to float up the canals from London? Who sorts through the chests, and divvies up the books, leathers, fine silks and tweeds from Bond Street? Who delivers them in the dead of night to the seedy back doors of Oxford's forgotten and ignored?

Alice has mulled over this for some time and comes to the conclusion that, daringly, the answers to these questions are, in fact, attainable if only she is willing to pursue them.

In a decisive sweep into the house, she dumps her father's pile of letters onto the armchair in the study, pulls her coat about her and steps out of the door. She glides down the street, trying to keep her thoughts from solidifying, for if she thinks too closely on what she is about to do, she might turn right around and retreat to the parlour, the kitchen, her bedroom – safe but bored, how she has remained bottled for the past ten years, over half of her life. She feels a wink of fearlessness which is, begrudgingly, reminiscent of her excursion with Grace Dodd. Despite her initial reservations and the slight jealousy that ensued, Alice admits the stubborn truth to herself: she quite likes the Academy sitter. How thrilling, how *bold* that afternoon on Cecil Court had been. This bravery simmers in her chest once more.

The city is quiet. Even St Giles feels sleepier on this morning, with fewer carriages than usual being trotted into the centre. Alice crosses into Jericho before realising that she has done so. The neighbourhood is so different in the daylight.

Miss Grant's cottage is stark and silent. Even the wisteria in its mid-winter hibernation looks like a climbing knot of white, bloodless veins across the stones. The entire building has been sapped of life.

Alice taps the anchor doorknocker twice. In the darkness, quivering in the cold and fearful of what lies in the shadows, this act is more urgent, making it more natural in many ways to deliver secret parcels in haste; no lingering, no words. Here in the daytime, Alice feels exposed. The knock seems to reverberate up the street and down the alley to the canal. It is a summoning for – who? She is visible for neighbours, passers-by, boatmen and punters.

There is a click of the latch and the door is pulled open just wide enough to see an eye, a nose.

'Miss Grant?' ventures Alice. She whispers although no one else is around.

The woman behind the door squints as if she is not used to the light. There is a flicker of recognition but she says nothing.

'My name is Alice Oak. I am a friend of Lou's.'

The door is opened further and Miss Grant pokes her head out, scans the road and the alley before ushering Alice inside.

'You should not come here in the daytime. With a coat like that?' She nods towards the canal. 'There are always looters about. You will draw attention to yourself and to us. I hope you haven't brought a parcel now?'

'No, no, I do not have anything.'

'Rupert, you can come out, darling.'

The boy, eight or nine, emerges from the closet, glances at Alice once before seating himself at the table and resuming what looks like a page of calligraphy. Alice did not know there was a son; of course, he would be sleeping during their nightly drop-offs. The closet, Alice sees, does not have a basin at all but is crammed with stacks of books – and not tatty copies, but spines of shiny leather, inlaid with gold inscriptions. She has never seen the books unboxed but she has felt their heft, has suffered from lifting them awkwardly and ferrying them with stiff arms from boat to hansom.

'You will accept my apologies for being cautious,' says Miss Grant. 'He was seen the other day reading by the canal. A sordid-looking fellow. I am certain he will have noted the book – a new publication. I have told Rupert off countless times for taking books outside.'

Her speech is refined and polished and her hair is pinned back in elegant plaits. The boy, too, is dressed in smart breeches and a linen shirt. They are more suited to a fine country house than this thread-bare hole at the edge of Jericho.

'I'm sorry to disturb you,' says Alice. 'I only wanted to enquire about… Have you continued to receive… Well, really what I am trying to glean is whether or not you have heard from Lou?'

Miss Grant frowns. 'No. Not since before Christmas.'

Alice cannot conceal her disappointment.

'And the packages?' she asks. 'Have they continued?'

'Not a single one. I had begun to worry that perhaps I did something wrong. It is most unlike her not to write.'

'I've not heard from her either. She hasn't responded to my letters.'

Alice can feel Miss Grant studying her, can sense her bewilder-ment. And then, as if she has confirmed to herself that they are indeed a strange pair of women but does not care enough to probe further, Miss Grant offers, 'I would not worry. In the short time that

243

I have known her, Lou has always lived by her own rules, in her own time. If I never saw her again, I would still be eternally grateful for what she has done for us.'

'The books, you mean?'

'The novels, the pens, the schoolbooks.' She watches Rupert scrawl across the page. 'He will not be properly educated, you know. Not at a school around here. Lou has given him the opportunity. I am fortunate enough to have had a respectable education myself so I could teach him just fine. But I could never have afforded the resources.'

'And the boy's father?'

Alice reddens. She regrets the question as soon as it airs. She is *Miss* Grant, after all.

But Miss Grant is unruffled. 'A very well-to-do gentleman with a pretty wife and three legitimate children between them.' Her smile is unapologetic. 'My son should not suffer for my transgressions. Thankfully, one other person in this world agrees. Mind you, keeping such a collection here is just asking for us to be robbed. She never gives us second-hand. They are always new. Fresh, unbroken spines from the London publishers.'

Alice recalls her own Christmas gift – the satisfying crack of the spine, how the engraved leather still smells of cow. 'She is most generous.'

'In a straight line, darling. Pick up the nib without dragging.' Miss Grant models a perfect *f* next to Rupert's lines before folding her arms and turning to Alice. 'Do not worry about your friend. She will reappear when she's ready.'

So the deliveries have stopped. Alice does not know what she was expecting – that Lou would have sent them by another courier? Found someone else to deliver on her behalf? No, no. Lou has retreated into the shadows and in doing so has paused her existence and involvement with everyone in her life.

And yet. Were these parcels not important to her? For how long has she run these rogue deliveries in the dead of night, risking her safety and reputation to get these parcels to the nobodies of Oxford? They mean something to her, thinks Alice. And who knows the consequences of their sudden termination, even after only four weeks?

Home in her bedroom, Alice is underwhelmed by the platter of buttered bread, kippers and walnuts on her bedside table, and by the cup of Earl Grey whose steam curls past her nose and up into the beams. Her schoolbooks, ignored since before Christmas, are stacked on her chest of drawers.

And Alice's attention falls on her mother's journal. How many times in the evenings has she thumbed through these pages? She has read every entry hundreds of times – logs of her mother's visits to infirmaries and orphanages, never sentimental, but stoical records of this important charitable work. Alice has always had a benevolent heart like her mother, but never has she had the opportunity to use it in her small and quiet life.

It will not do. With a cursory bite of bread, Alice dashes up the attic stairs two at a time. They are in one of the chests – not the dressing-up one with pixies etched into the sides. It does not take long to find them: old exercise books with notes on Henry VIII, rows upon rows of times tables and sums, the same poem scratched out – 'Daffodils' by Wordsworth – ten, eleven, twelve times. Alice's teachers criticised rote learning, which she had actually preferred. She would fall asleep every night with the chants echoing through her head like bleating sheep. Her father, however, had favoured the pen, and so Alice and Emma mastered penmanship in addition to criticism.

All of their notes are here: on geography, history, Latin. Jars of seeds, etchings of monuments, the odd rock – Emma had always been a collector. And there at the bottom of the chest are new inkwells, spare pens and stacks of paper, browned with age but crisp and uncurled – tools of learning that Alice has always taken for granted. The daughter of an academic would never know such trivial barriers to education.

All of these she puts into a basket. The exercise books are not new; the Latin texts and history volumes are not freshly printed; in fact, their spines are frayed and one book's cover remains limply attached by a few meagre threads. They are scruffy cousins to the gifts that Lou bestows on Miss Grant and her son, but Alice hopes that Lou would be pleased. Surely shabby resources are better than none.

She will deliver the basket this evening, on foot, so she will not be able to carry much. She will not think too closely about Jericho's looters and drunkards. She has seen the beast in the light and it is not so terrifying. And anyway, the risk inspires a heady buzz. Is this not what she has wanted all these years: a bit of adventure, a chance to be helpful?

Alice resolves to recommence Lou's other deliveries as well. She is neither connected nor wealthy, and she is only privy to slices of these people's lives through the parcels she has received with Lou. But she will do her best. For the daughter of the ailing dairy farmer, does she not have old belts, riding boots, a riding jacket that has been worn only once? They are collecting dust at the back of her wardrobe. For the orphanage, does her father not have spare copies of *Wuthering Heights*, *Silas Marner*, an anthology of the Romantics? There is even an entire set of Dickens on Emma's old bookshelf in the entrance hall beneath the coats. Her father will never notice that they are gone.

And so Alice takes on the role of provider and delivery girl for Lou's motley group of beneficiaries. Provisional, of course. Temporary. Only until Lou returns and can do the job better, as she has always done, which Alice hopes is soon, for she misses her and feels strangely unmoored.

7

A few weeks later, back in the wintry comforts of the Kensington flat for a few days, Oak has laid the etchings out across the dining table. He peers over them with a cup of coffee, paces back and forth, pauses. As a series, even with the two new paintings from the past year, there is no clear thread that holds them together.

No. 1 *Hugh DeLacey*, 1831, The Royal Academy of Arts
No. 2 *John Mortimer – Butler*, 1831, The Royal Academy of Arts
No. 3 *Prince – A Spaniel*, 1832, The National Gallery
No. 4 *Gentle Polyphemus – A Piebald*, 1835, The National Gallery
No. 5 *The Three-toed Woodpecker*, 1836, The National Gallery
No. 6 *Harry An Orphan Boy*, 1837, The Royal Academy of Arts
No. 7 *Anne – The Potter's Daughter*, 1837, The Royal Academy of Arts
No. 8 *Bluebell – A Dairy Cow*, 1837, The National Gallery
No. 9 *Peacocks*, 1839, The National Gallery
No. 10 *Woman in a Sunhat*, 1840, The Royal Academy of Arts
No. 11 *Archibald – Kunekune Pig*, 1890, The National Gallery
No. 12 *Mary – A Housemaid*, 1890, Ashmolean Museum

These twelve masterpieces are the milestones of Oak's life. He smiles at this thought. Is this what art historians are: the experts – the keepers – of others' achievements? Are we historians and scholars because we are not talented enough to create great works of our own?

But no. Oak has never desired to be an artist. There are too many exquisite paintings already in existence with too little recognition.

Even if he did possess the genius to walk amongst titans, adding to the pile would be wasteful. Superfluous. Yes, Oak is content with his life's work – is proud that he has championed and advocated for the skill and artistry of a modern master in Timothy Ponden-Hall, even if it means that he is unpopular amongst the people. Once again, Oak has sacrificed favour for integrity.

And his daughter respects him for this. In Alice, he will leave a small legacy; Oak recognises this now. His children, though late entrants in his life, are his cherubim in a Renaissance masterpiece. They appear to float or dance around the protagonist of a painting, yet who is the protagonist without them? They bring focus to the selfish hero, frame him and help develop perspective and depth. And my, are they not the most beautiful babes ever depicted, in a perfect twist of the torso, a flawless pointed toe? The cherubim do not idly flutter about as one might initially assume; they are not decorous for the sake of space or frivolity. No, they protect the mortal protagonist and whisper comforts in his ear, remind him that they will live on long after he has stepped out of the light, will uphold the stories of many more painted heroes.

Oak thinks, then, of Grace. She is not his daughter, but she has inspired a wildness in his thinking that was lacking before. What was it she said at one of their earlier meetings? The weight of a name. How bold she was to criticise Shakespeare.

He stoops now before one of the paintings and sees it, miraculously, anew.

Taking up a pen and paper, he writes to Grace – measured, unhurried. There is one possibility that he has never considered, but to pursue it will require much digging and a heavy stroke of luck. And so to Miss Dodd, once more, he pens a very odd request.

On the first of March, Alice snoozes in the armchair of her father's study, mid-luncheon, mid-history revision. The cold chicken and asparagus sit dully on the platter like ashen lumps. She has begun revising for her exams. In the day, she recites dates: the Battle of Hastings, the sealing of the Magna Carta, the arrival of the Black Death. Alice writes and recites and writes some more.

And in the evenings, she has taken to sneaking out for long, post-supper walks where she delivers modest parcels around the seedy dens of Oxford: a book, a candle, an old telescope, an apricot seed. She only takes what she can hide in her pockets or under the brim of her winter hat. She never lingers after knocking. She has no idea if these little tokens are desired or not; most likely not, she thinks, not compared to the generous treasures that Lou once left for them. But no one has told her to stop, so she continues.

But on this first of March, Missy taps Alice awake with the urgency of a sprite.

'Alice, wake up. Alice, wake up, I say.'

She nearly knocks over the lunch tray in her startlement.

'I'm so sorry – is something the matter—'

'Is this the letter you've been waiting for?' Missy asks.

It takes Alice a moment to shake the sleep from her eyes. Between Missy's fingers she can see her name written in bold pen, the familiar long tail of the *A* that extends just a hair too far. She snatches the letter and brings it close to her face. It even smells like her, she thinks – a mix of earth and rain and rosemary as if she has ridden the back of the wind. It does not really smell like her, of course, but seeing her handwriting instigates a rush of relief; Alice's heart could burst.

'Thank you, Missy, thank you. When did this arrive?'

'The postman's just left.'

'Thank you,' she says once more and embraces her before moving to a stream of light in the window.

She nearly tears through the first words in her eagerness. The message is small, on an entire page of letterhead:

Alice,

You have been a dear friend.
We have much to talk about.
I would like to invite you to the estate for a night. I would be most grateful
for your help in the greenhouses as we are short of staff.

A coach will collect you from the station on Monday.

Yours,
Lou

Every fibre in Alice's body could spring to the beams above, and indeed, she finds that she has thrown her arms up and her head back in a giddy, exhilarated stretch. Her friend is all right. And she is going to see her again — tomorrow, in fact. *You have been a dear friend.* So Lou knows that she has continued her deliveries.

More than that, Alice is certain that she will learn about Timothy Ponden-Hall. Perhaps… dare she dream that she might meet him? She feels a shift in the painter's story, can feel it deep in her femurs and through her toes. Alice will play a role in her father's magnum opus, after all. Just the thought compels her to bring the letter to her chest in gratitude and fear.

With no time to waste, Alice hastens to her room to pack her satchel.

8

The next day, Alice rocks between heel and toe at Oxford station. A sweet warmth spreads through her limbs as if she has gulped a thimbleful of sloe gin. She has told Missy that she will be back late, needing to attend an evening biology lecture with her tutor. Missy had scrunched her nose; she has no stomach for dissections and the sinewy muscles of frogs pinned down in silver trays. Alice feels guilty for lying to her – hopes that Missy will not check on her until the morning, or better yet, lunchtime. By then, Alice hopes to have returned, apologies aplenty, her behaviour justified – revered, even – for cracking the mystery of Ponden-Hall on her own. If she is caught, Missy will be furious, but there is no time to entertain this probable outcome for now.

When Lou's hansom rounds the bend, its bobbing lanterns obsolete in the morning light, Alice is unsurprised but disappointed nevertheless when she sees that it is not Lou who drives it.

Jacob is heavyset and burly and fills the space of the driver's seat like a dense sack of potatoes. His whiskers, whilst tidily trimmed, cover his cheeks, jowls and chin – a distinguished grey with flashes of auburn.

'Good morning, Miss Oak.' His voice is gruff and even like a gravel road.

And they are off. The coach ride itself lasts under thirty minutes but Alice is disoriented as soon as they leave the city. The hills and twisting roads that snake between them are beautiful and bewitching. So close to Oxford these country roads wind, yet Alice feels a sense of adventure and wide, limitless space that is both invigorating and unsettling. Perhaps Timothy Ponden-Hall himself has ridden down this road — a path fit, then, for brave heroes and explorers. The checkerboard hills are majestic even on the coat-tails of winter, and there is promise in their frosty fields of a vigorous awakening. Alice has daydreamed about this estate and its master, of seeing them in stone and flesh, for countless hours over the past six months, and yet now that she approaches them, she is anxious.

The coach slows to a trot and stops, at last, in a clearing.

'This is the back entrance,' says Jacob. 'This road's in no condition to accommodate a carriage, I'm afraid. We'll walk the rest of the way. She wishes to meet you in the kitchen garden.'

Here, in the middle of the Oxfordshire countryside, where the hills roll like rippled buttercream and the horizon is framed by the silhouettes of tree lines, Alice is stunned at how tiny she feels. She breathes deeper and walks taller. She finds the crunch of her boots on the uneven path romantic — the clicking of her heels on half-buried stones is what she imagines an adventurer's footfalls would sound like.

She follows Jacob down the meandering path, straddling the edge so she may walk in the sun. It is only March but the sun is high and generous and feels nourishing on her skin.

Before long, Alice notices that to her left, just beyond the row of trees that lines the path, there is a high stone wall. Unlike others that are waist-high to pen in sheep or cattle, this one stands heads above her own. It is a long wall; it continues along the path as far as she can see, and she is surprised to have only just noticed it. It is ancient: its honey-coloured stones, whilst immaculately stacked, bulge in sections where ivy has curled through the cracks.

The wall conceals vast grounds, that much is clear, and Alice is certain that in its midst lies a grand estate that belongs to a wealthy family of great importance. And somewhere in its stables or orchard or workers' cottages, is Lou. She walks on, gliding her fingertips along the stones.

'Miss Oak?' Jacob calls from below. He has rounded the bend and is no longer in sight.

Like a hound responding to its master, a breeze picks up then and ushers Alice onward, onward, until her jelly knees are bounding downhill, her pathetic satchel hanging from one arm.

'The back drive is over a mile long,' says Jacob, 'but we aren't going to the house. The greenhouses are just around the bend.'

At first, the scenery is more of the same – tall conifers flanking a gravelled drive, the trees blocking out most of the sun. But as she crests the small slope, the trees and brush and lichen-laden stones are left behind and Alice is struck by the sprawling land before her. Even the masters would struggle to capture this, she thinks. Meadows, sea-like and undulating, are interspersed with thickets and old stone walls.

The house looms even from a great distance, and although Alice is not close enough to see the sconces and timber sashes of the windows, it is clear that all of its curtains are drawn and that no fires are alight within; not a single one of its grand chimneys is smoking. It is one of the most elegant estates that Alice has ever seen. To its left, a small labyrinth of box hedges; to its right, an archway that leads to an orchard. Beyond, pastures upon pastures to a horizon of trees, their silhouettes as fine and precise as if etched with a scalpel.

And she is certain, more and more, that in the midst of all of it, hides Timothy Ponden-Hall.

Lou is upon Alice before she sees her – a tangle of rumpled tail-coat, linen smock and the faintest hint of horse muck. Lou hugs her tightly, and even in Alice's relief, her exhale, her comfort in reciprocating the embrace, she can feel that there is less of Lou than before, as if her bones have become as delicate and brittle as a dove's.

When at last Lou pulls away to study her friend's face, she is pleased to see the rosiness of her cheeks. Alice's face has thinned just in the past few months, the baby fat all but skimmed away, and her hair is no longer constricted by a sleek plait but is instead loosely bound in a half-bun at her collar. The shadow of a woman dances upon the edges of her profile, soft and blurred, the perfect sfumato.

Lou, though, has never looked more haggard. If Alice's health is a satisfying sight, Lou matches this in sickly ardour. Alice is stunned to see her this way. Although she grins, Alice cannot help but notice how gaunt Lou has become, how pale and tight her skin clings to once striking, now skeletal cheekbones. Lou's hair hangs ragged and wild about her ears and chin in a lion-like bob. Even in this poorly state, she commands an intimidating beauty.

'We have much to talk about,' Lou says. She squeezes Alice's shoulders. 'And there is much work to be done, I'm afraid. We are all stretched too thin around here.'

'I – I was so sorry to learn of Mary's death.'

'Yes. Well, she lived a long life. And I do believe she would agree that it was an extraordinary one. Come. Let me show you around the garden.'

Beyond the entrance is a sight to behold. Alice drops her satchel.

This is no antiquated kitchen garden at the back of a farm cottage, nor is it the skinny kitchen gardens that stretch out behind the manors of Marylebone. There are at least three acres here enclosed in the red stone walls, every inch of it pristinely and efficiently purposed to grow fruit and vegetables to feed a household and sizeable staff.

'The amount of produce here could feed a village.'

'And often did,' says Lou. She gathers a pair of gloves from one of the wheelbarrows. 'In its golden years, Abbotswood had a staff of eighty if you include the gardeners and gamekeepers. This garden fed them all, along with the Abbot family. And its surplus was brought to the surrounding villages, always without payment.'

'But no longer?'

She frowns. 'The scope is there but there are not nearly enough staff to consistently turn over such quantities. If you look closely, many of the beds are not in use. Maybe a fifth of them are used for growing now. The rest lie untouched and are used the following year or the year after for crop rotation.'

'How many staff are employed now?'

'There are ten of us. And we all do everything – the gardening, cooking, household, all of it.' Even Lou, who suffers no conceit, says this with pride.

As she registers the size of the kitchen garden, Alice understands why even one absent body is sorely missed.

Aside from the odd trill or coo from the birds that flit about and the soft rustling of the leaves on their branches and vines, all is quiet here, which magnifies the space even more.

'I have never seen anything like it,' says Alice. 'It is positively enormous.'

'You have not even seen it all. Come. It's a bit of a shame for you to see it for the first time now. Everything is still sleepy from winter.

In a few months' time, it will be transformed – a real garden of Babylon. You will see.'

Lou guides her to the very back wall where there are two rows of fruit trees that span the acre. Whilst not all of them bear fruit in the current season, they are all there as Lou points out each one: plum, damson, fig; quince, cherry, pear; and the apples – twenty in a row, each of a different kind, some for cooking and some for plucking off the low-hanging boughs for a snack before reaching the shade of the next tree.

They are all twisted and gnarled with bark that looks as ancient and wise as elephant skin. Whether they have truly born fruit for centuries as they appear to have done is a mystery, but there is peace and faith here that the trees are more constant than the men who tend to them and that they can be counted upon to produce a bountiful harvest year upon year.

'It is south-facing,' explains Lou. 'The fruit trees are closest to the back wall so they may soak up the heat from the stones even after the sun has set.'

Inward from the trees are rows upon rows of berries, sheltered from the hungry beaks of birds beneath a finely woven net. Raspberries, blueberries, gooseberries, honeyberries. Alice would not be able to distinguish between the leaves but Lou rattles them off like a nursery rhyme. And then come the raised beds of vegetables and herbs: pepper, beetroot, carrot.

Tomato, green onions, shallots.

Spinach, kale, coriander.

Rosemary, thyme and basil.

The potatoes have their own wide expanse, which seems to take up a tenth of the entire garden. The garlic, too, has its own bed in pride of place with its long, papery stalks jutting out of the ground like straw. Alice has only seen garlic in bulb form poked into roasted meats or ground to a powder for soups and stews; the stalks flop light and long across the soil here whilst their familiar heads remain submerged as if they have burrowed beneath, stinky and shy.

As they ramble between the beds, Lou points to the blight on this leaf, pulls a weed from the base of that bulb.

And where is the master of the house? Alice would like to ask her.

Why did Mary Whipple mean so much to him?

Why have you disappeared over these long winter months?

Why in heaven's name did Timothy Ponden-Hall leave my father the painting?

But she must be patient.

'Here is the greenhouse where we'll spend the day,' says Lou.

It is another sight to behold, the greenhouse. With glass on three sides and a glass roof, it is a marvellous vast room that backs onto the potting-shed walls, which are stoked and warmed from behind. The heat emanates from within, a stifling heat that swells and pulses and would rival the hottest day of the year. It is a clever piece of architecture.

And inside are more trees.

'Figs, apricots, peaches,' says Lou, pointing to the bursting foliage within. 'And banana, although as you can see, that has been less successful. We've not been able to replicate the African conditions in which they thrive best.'

Even so, the trees here certainly have a foreign feel to them – huskier barks, strange hanging vines, palm fronds that ruffle out of their trunks like pineapple crowns.

'You enjoy Windsor brown soup,' recalls Lou. 'This is a date palm. Where do you think the dried dates come from?'

Alice has never considered this, of course.

'It comes from Egypt and Morocco. We are lucky to create a similar sanctuary here.'

In a back room of the greenhouse, they settle.

'Hold out your hands,' says Lou. 'That's it. 'Tis too early to begin planting outdoors so we begin by seeding in the greenhouse. These are cauliflower seeds. Fetch that potting soil, please. We'll be out of the way here.'

They perch on rickety stools and line up miniature clay pots in rows of ten. Alice is in charge of laying the base whilst Lou follows behind her and folds in the seeds, pats down the soil with firm fingers.

How can this be the same woman who decries high street shopkeepers for mistreating their staff? Who has manoeuvred gondolas down Venice's snaking canals, who skates backwards down the Thames and recites Petrarchan sonnets to pass the time? Lou's energy, her zest for such pursuits, extends even to gardening. She possesses in her fingers – these petite, slender fingers – more purpose and knowing than Alice has in her entire body, Alice is convinced of this. For Lou presses and prods the soil with skill and affection, and she is just as content sowing seeds as she would be at the helm of a ship or the elbow of a violin maker.

As Alice follows suit – mimics the prodding and patting and dusting of the soil, for she is keen as ever to learn and impress – she cannot help but feel that her job here is inessential. She is reminded of afternoons in the study when the three of them would do rebus puzzles; her father and Emma would decipher the most difficult words and leave the obvious pictures for her. And when most of the phrase was cracked, they would ask Alice to complete it with ceremony and celebration. An assured victory. A job of charity.

This is how Alice's role in the greenhouse feels. A job of charity.

'You do not really need my assistance, do you?' she asks. It tumbles out of her like the final crumbs of potting soil. She is not offended by this; she expects Lou to admit that perhaps she has just missed her company, or that even simple work is made lighter with two.

Lou plants the final cauliflower seed and brushes her hands together. She hands Alice a new sack of soil and slides a jar labelled 'squash seeds' off the shelf.

'No,' Lou says, eyeing her. 'I do not *need* your assistance. But you have known this for some time.'

Alice is surprised at her candour. 'What do you mean?'

'The deliveries, of course. Parcels on doorsteps. Do you think I needed you for that?'

It is impossible not to feel the sting of this.

'You can put more soil in these pots,' Lou continues. 'These will remain in the greenhouse longer than the others.'

'Well—' Alice begins. But she knows not what to say – is startled by Lou's honesty and her nonchalance about their time spent together. She was referring to this morning's work and had not considered the deliveries at all. 'Well,' she bristles, 'to complete so many deliveries in one night could have proved challenging on your own—'

'We were most likely slowed down by two of us squeezing crates into the carriage.' Lou's laugh is not unkind. 'Do not feel so disappointed, Alice. They were always lonely, those nights. Your company made a tremendous difference. And in fact, as I… grew more tired in those weeks leading up to Christmas, you were a genuine help. Ah, here, there's a hole in the sack. Tuck it inside this other one.'

'I would like to think this was not utterly one-sided—' Alice heaves the sack onto the table in a grump. 'Perhaps I should just leave, then. It is you who invited me out here, remember, knowing very well that I don't have the faintest clue about gardening.'

Lou continues to move down the line planting seed after seed. 'After Mary died, I needed you then, Alice. Truly, I did. And I am in your debt for taking care of my charges. I never would have expected... Well, you have been a greater friend than I could have ever imagined.'

Alice colours at this but her humiliation is not lessened. 'So my entire employment has been a ruse.'

Lou pokes in each seed with the precision of threading a needle.

'Not at all. The purpose of your employment was very clear and always has been. It just wasn't what you thought it was.'

'What was it then?'

'Why, to learn about your father, of course. It was the only way we could understand Solomon Oak's pure intentions. His motivations. Without speaking to Solomon himself – and that would have given the game away – how could we confirm his sincerity? It had to be through you, Alice.' She purses her lips. 'I am sorry to have deceived you. In all honesty, I did not expect to make a friend.' She pauses in her planting and moves to find Alice's eyes. 'A true friend. I... do not have many.'

The revelation should not be so scalding, but alas, will it never be possible to emerge from her father's shadow? Lou's words turn over in her mind, begin to sink through Alice's gullet and chest like a wide, cumbersome stone. She has treasured every moment with Lou. Alice's face burns as she recalls how she has thought of her often, has felt guilty, even, for likening her to a sister.

She steps back from the table.

'So you have used me.'

Lou exhales. 'No, Alice. Perhaps it seems that way, or perhaps it started that way – but I am sincere when I say that I never meant to be deceitful. We needed to learn more about your father and his intentions and so I asked you about him. I never tried to hide my interest in him.'

'But you were not forthright either!'

The sympathy upon Lou's face only angers Alice more.

'Do not pity me,' she snaps. 'And all of this time... how stupid of me to think you were sincerely interested in my life.'

'Alice,' appeals Lou. Her hands are small upon the hulking workman's table. 'You were so kind and open about your father and the losses you suffered together. In those conversations, all I ever meant to be for you was a friend. Truly. This was unforeseen... I did not expect to care so deeply.'

Alice softens at this and resents herself for it. She crosses her arms to maintain her resolve.

'I am not a fool, you know,' she says. 'I know who your master is. I know Timothy Ponden-Hall hides somewhere within these walls and that you are keeping him concealed for reasons I do not understand. And all this time I have kept quiet. I have bitten my tongue out of respect for you – so I would not anger or upset you again – and trusted that you would reveal it all when the time came. And here I come to discover that you have been spying on my father through me with no intention of confiding in me whatsoever.'

'But I have confided in you, Alice. My deliveries. Mary. Do you think I often spend my days ice skating and having picnics amongst the families in Oxford? I would have thought you'd know by now that the circle of people in my life is very small. Tiny, even, now that Mary is gone.'

Alice thinks the coachwoman looks more weary now than she has ever seen her.

'I did not expect to make a friend in you,' Lou continues. 'And I am sorry that it started out as a job. And that my motivations were not plain.'

And Alice knows that she will not walk away.

'I would like the truth, Lou,' she says at last. 'I deserve to know it. And so does my father.'

Lou only offers a tired nod. She looks up at the hazy, veiled sun.

'You are right, Alice. You deserve to know the truth. In fact, 'tis the main reason I have invited you to stay. But the daylight is fading fast, and it would be most helpful if we could finish the potting. Will you help me? I will answer all of your questions in due time, I promise.

Please trust that it would have been difficult to reveal more than I already have before now. But I will explain everything. I promise.'

Alice does not fully understand why – for she could walk out of the greenhouse there and then, could return home where her uselessness is not so brazenly exposed – but she begins to sweep the discarded soil from the worktable into the little pots. She carries them in fours and adds them to the ends of her rows.

In silent gratitude, Lou continues to plant and pat, poke and pat. And although Alice has resigned any hope of impressing or helping in any profound way, she cannot help but think that Lou's shoulders are more relaxed, that her spine – so often rigid and upright to uphold crisp jackets and long coats – is somehow softer and more forgiving in these moments of quiet toil. Indeed Lou leans towards her as they work alongside each other, and when she has seeded every pot and must wait for Alice to fill more, Lou stands beside her in silence, so close that her arm rests against Alice's. Like old friends, old comforts. It is enough to reassure Alice that perhaps it really has not only been she who has missed Lou over these long months.

Supper is served in one of the workers' cottages. Alice has been given a room upstairs with a little casement window replete with views of the rose garden. Although it is only a servant's quarters, the room is more expansive than her own on Mansfield Road. It is simply decorated, and clearly uninhabited for much of the year aside from the odd guest cousin or friend of a staff member, but there is still warmth in the walls and Lou has made the effort of collecting a bunch of daffodils to put in a vase next to her bed.

After a bath, Alice enters the kitchen, which is filled with smells of thyme and parsley and pepper. It is a comforting smell, one with onions and garlic at its base as Alice has learned from Missy over the years. An array of candles are dotted across the dining table and windowsills. It is bright and cosy, and if Alice was not already tired out from a day of labour, the heat from the stove and the mix of smells drifting from the simmering pot are enough to make Alice sleepy and warm.

'Nearly there,' says Lou over her shoulder. 'Wine is on the table.'

'I forgot to tell you,' says Alice, sidling onto the bench. 'I saw the Malay boy last week. Whilst out buying some cheese. He is working at the cobbler's now – your friend.'

'Oh, how wonderful!' she beams. 'This cheers me indeed. He will be taken care of there.'

Lou pushes her hair away from her face and stirs the pot. Alice is still not used to seeing her with this bird's nest of hair. *Not unlike my own*, Alice thinks, *with its unruly waves*, and this satisfies her, for although it is a shallow similitude, it inspires some sort of kinship in Alice's mind.

The window has begun to fog up along its edges, and through it, Alice can see the courtyard and soft light glowing from what must be the kitchen and bay windows of the other cottages, where Jacob and the other hands are also sitting down to their own suppers. *And somewhere in the main house, perhaps Timothy Ponden-Hall sits at his own table.* All will be revealed soon. Lou has promised, and Alice can feel it.

'*Poulet au vin blanc*,' says Lou.

The small table is crowded with little platters of potatoes, bread, a mix of sprouts and carrots. There is also cheese, chocolates, a bowl of pears, a dish of nuts. An eclectic spread that does not obviously complement the chicken dish that Lou has placed before her, but Alice can see the care that has gone into the presentation.

'It smells delicious.'

'It is very simple. White wine, lardons, mushrooms and more brandy than you'd think.'

'I suppose I should not be surprised that you are, amongst every-thing else, a skilled cook as well.'

'Oh, no. It looks more impressive than it is. I learned to cook this dish in the countryside in France. A girl taught me one evening after a long day's work in the vineyard.'

Alice smiles through a mouthful of bread and shakes her head. 'You see, I am right. You are certainly more successful than I am in the kitchen. Although Missy does finish every last bite of anything I make.'

As she sits across from Lou and listens to her stories about France, Alice feels a contentment that she has not felt in a long while. She feels, in this moment, that she will have until the end of the world with her. There will be time. The wine is rich.

'You will visit all of these places on your tour,' says Lou. 'Assuming, of course, you make the effort to venture beyond Paris. Which so many silly young men neglect to do.'

'It does sound absurd to stay in the city after hearing these tales of yours.'

'Silly indeed.'

Lou pours herself another glass and pops a bonbon into her mouth.

'You asked me once which of the Ponden-Hall and DeLacey stories was my favourite,' she says. 'I told you I couldn't pick one. Having thought about it, though, this isn't true. I do have a favourite.'

'Oh?'

Alice's head is dreamily fuzzy. She feels as though she has consumed a king's feast and she is not used to drinking wine.

'Acquiring the black pearl,' says Lou. 'It is not the most adventurous story but it makes me laugh.'

'The black pearl. I must know the story but I cannot recall it at this moment.'

''Tis one of the lesser-known ones. There's not much to it really. They were sailing around a group of islands in the South Pacific Ocean. They anchored at one of them – not the largest, not the smallest. There was a market near the docks which the crew happily browsed, bartering with the natives for fresh fruit, trinkets made of shells, carvings of bamboo and wood.'

Alice shakes her head. 'I do not remember this one.'

'Well, Timothy only had eyes for one thing: the grandest black pearl he had ever seen. The seller was practically a boy – probably sixteen, eighteen at most. Timothy offered him an outrageous sum for it. The boy politely declined the offer; the pearl, he said, was to be given to his future wife so that she would be wise. If he parted with it, it would only be for a trade, and for something truly magnificent. They say the men had to drag Timothy away as he offered up sack upon sack of gold for the silly thing. No oyster or pearl, no matter its size or its shade, was worth that much. But Timothy persisted. He offered his swords, his compass, his clothes. The boy shook his head to all of them.

'And then he noticed Timothy's pocket watch. Full of jewels, it was a stunning piece. The more jewels there are on a pocket watch, the less the gears grind within – did you know? I doubt this boy knew anything about the mechanics of timepieces, but this was the trade he wanted.

'It was the only belonging on Timothy's person that inspired pause. The watch had only just been given to him by his grandfather – an heirloom that had already been passed down for five generations. What could he do? He had to decline. So with a heavy heart, Timothy boarded his ship and the crew continued on their journey across the South Pacific.'

'And how long did it take him to change his mind?' asks Alice. She truly does not know this story – strange, for she knows the tales better than anyone. But she knows enough about Timothy Ponden-Hall to understand that he is stubborn as an ox.

'Unfortunately for the crew, *three days*. And when he finally coerced the crew into turning the ship around, they realised that they had no idea which island it was on. There are hundreds in that part of the world. They must have revisited dozens to find that market and that boy. But they did.'

'And he traded his family's pocket watch?'

'All for a black pearl.'

Alice grins. 'I suppose it makes sense. Black pearls are meant to come with blessings of long life and prosperity. Another talisman against death for him.'

'Yes, long life. And did you know that Chinese legends say that black pearls are formed in the brain of a dragon? What wonders. Layered and layered in a skull of cunning and wit. But he did not keep it for himself. When they returned to England – ten days later than planned thanks to his escapade – he hung it on a fine gold chain and gave it to his sister.'

'He gave it to Adelaide?'

'He did. The quiet one who never asked for a single trinket or treasure.'

'I cannot imagine his grandfather was very happy.'

'Nor his grandmother. But I believe he would have given anything for a gift for Adelaide. He loved her very much.'

'Yes, my father always made this very clear.'

A heavy pause. It is the glass of wine in her hand – or perhaps the previous one – that emboldens Alice to press on.

'And you… well, I suppose… it would have been incredible to hear the stories first-hand,' she says.

She expects Lou to break eye contact, to brush past the comment as if smoothing a wrinkle on the tablecloth – to stiffen, at least, for Alice has frozen in her own surprise at saying it out loud.

Of course, Lou does none of these things and tops up her glass.

'Yes,' says Lou. 'It was.'

Alice could weep. She is overwhelmed. Wine sloshes over the rim of her glass and she mops it up with her sleeve. *It is confirmed then,* she thinks. *He is really here.* She fumbles with the bottle and Lou's glass, for she has knocked both in her clumsy excitement.

'Alice,' Lou breaks into her reverie. 'I promised I would tell you more about Ponden-Hall. I would like to show you something. Early tomorrow morning. Meet me at the gate of the west wall.'

'No, not tomorrow morning,' protests Alice. 'Where is he? Can we go to him?'

But Lou is ferrying dishes to the basin.

'How do you know him?' Alice presses. 'Where did you meet him?'

'Tomorrow.'

Alice is not finished with this conversation, but her tongue is fuzzy and it is so warm in this kitchen, in this cottage. She feels Lou's cold hands in hers, feels her delicate frame support the stout heft of her own, guiding her all the way up the stairs and down the corridor that smells of lavender.

'He is here, isn't he?' Alice hears herself as if from afar. These walls absorb sound and colour – perhaps this is what it feels like to be a pearl enclosed in an oyster, or in the pockets of a dragon's brain. 'In the manor,' she continues. 'That is why it is all closed off. This is why nobody knows who the master is. He is really here.'

But Lou only says quietly, 'Tomorrow.'

Alice hugs her then, in relief and gratitude. Lou returns the embrace, is lying her flat, lowering her onto cool silk and goose down, and Alice remembers no more.

9

The next morning, Alice awakes with a head of wool and thunder. A pitcher of water and rosemary sits on the bedside table with a ready glass. She sips with tender swallows. The faintest grey light is cast upon the windowsill. She has not overslept. It is a wonder that she remembers Lou's instructions.

She is waiting, as promised, at the west wall of the estate before an unassuming door.

Alice shivers in the coolness of the dawn, appreciates its sharpness as it sobers and numbs her.

'Good morning,' says Lou, taking her arm. 'We are not going far.'

In the nook of her other arm, she cradles a red wooden box.

Out onto the sleepy country road they go, where a fog lingers about their legs. It is not far indeed, for they only cross onto a field where the long grass sparkles in dew and climb over a broken gate into a tiny cemetery before Lou stops.

'I come here every morning,' she says. 'It is one of my favourite places in the world. Come with me.'

She leads Alice past the tilting slabs that have eroded over time. Few names are still readable – Helan, Browning, Hill. The dates are anyone's guess, faded etchings on stones reclaimed by nature and time. Why she has brought her to a graveyard, Alice does not understand. Her head still throbs from last night's supper and her many questions continue to swirl within it with no respite, yet she does not say anything. She has never been one to appreciate the quiet or calm of burial grounds – in fact, she finds them eerie – but already she can feel that this is a place of peacefulness. The skeletons are snug at rest; there is no desire to clatter or haunt.

Lou leads her to a solitary apple tree at the edge of the cemetery overlooking fields upon rolling fields. It is perhaps the ugliest tree that Alice has ever seen, dark and gnarled. But it looks strong, and she is unsurprised when Lou tells her that it yields hundreds of apples every season.

When Lou gestures for her to perch next to her on one of the tree's knobbly roots, Alice is more confused than ever. The fields are beautiful, certainly, but not more special than any other fields in this part of the country, and the grounds of the manor within the walls are far more impressive.

'Now I hope you will not be repulsed by this,' says Lou. Out of the red box she pulls two cigars. 'Have you ever smoked a cigar in the morning?'

'I have never smoked a cigar in my life,' laughs Alice. A morning of surprises this is turning out to be.

'This one pairs well with coffee.'

The cigar is foreign between Alice's fingers and the smell is pungent, heavy with pepper and spice. Lou explains the rolling process to her — how women on Caribbean islands flatten and roll the leaves on their bare thighs with one hand. Lou cuts the tips of the cigars as if she is snipping roses for a dinner bouquet.

'Do not inhale,' she instructs. 'Hold the puff in your mouth.'

Alice coughs, of course, and she can only mimic how she thinks it should be done.

'You smoke a cigar every morning?' she asks.

'Yes.'

'Those red boxes delivered on the canal, then, were yours.'

'Yes.'

'You are truly a bafflement.'

Lou shrugs. 'It is difficult to find these particular cigars in this part of the world. And, as you know, I have helpful friends in London.'

'And on the continent.'

'Yes.'

'I suppose I had started to think... well, I thought they were for your employer.'

'I know,' says Lou.

Alice does not notice how her shoulders have stiffened, how even under the oversized hunting coat, it is clear that Lou's spine is the only straight line between the twisted apple tree and these crooked gravestones.

'You're going to tell me everything, aren't you, Lou?' implores Alice. She is giddy at the thought. Excited to be here with her, to be the receptacle of a closely guarded secret. 'That's why you asked me to come, isn't it? You do work for him – for Timothy Ponden-Hall. Will I get to meet him? Can you imagine what my father will think?'

Lou taps cigar ash onto the grass and tries to smile.

'Alice,' she says, 'did you know that some people say when a body is buried under a tree, the tree's roots curl and follow the lines of the body's bones? They fill out and unfurl like little veins. That is what some people say.'

'I have never heard that before.'

'I do not think it's true. I do not think the tree would harmonise with a decomposing body like that. But I like the idea. I like to think that the roots have ensconced him – every bone, every fibre, in a bespoke cocoon. I will never have the heart or stomach to see for myself, of course.'

'What do you mean? What – here?' Alice draws her legs into her chest. 'Good God, is someone buried here?'

And now she notices Lou's ashen face. Alice looks at her, lips parted. Is that a tremble? She does not seem to draw breath.

'You have been asking about the master of the estate.'

'Yes. Timothy Ponden-Hall – it has to be.'

'Alice. There is no easy way for me to tell you this.'

She does not understand.

'Alice.' Lou's breath wobbles. So unlike her – to wobble, to falter. 'Alice,' she says, 'Timothy Ponden-Hall died sixty years ago. He was buried here beneath this very apple tree.'

And in that moment, Alice feels the earth shift; every skeleton in its clay and mineral tomb convulses – arches itself so its mandibles are cast heavenward in a cruel and mocking laugh. It cannot be as she says.

'You are mistaken,' whispers Alice. It is she, now, who can barely breathe.

'He died after complications from the shipwreck.'

'No. This is impossible.'

'I wish it was. But I promise you it's true.'

'A preposterous theory you have heard from someone—'

'How could I make up such a thing?'

'Everyone else does!'

Alice is on her feet. The cigar, forgotten, is lost amongst the grass. 'Alice,' says Lou, 'I... I didn't know any other way to tell you.'

Alice, unseeing, balls her fists at her forehead, pulls at her hair. 'Sixty years ago? But that is before even the first painting appeared at the Gallery!'

Lou does not remove her eyes from Alice's face. 'Yes.'

'So we have all been deceived. Here is my father's life's work obliterated in a single moment! The rumours, the new discoveries – all for nothing! And here I came to you hoping to meet him – expecting you to reveal that this cryptic, elusive painter has been master of this house all along—'

'But Alice—'

'You led me to believe that... and we thought that he chose my father—'

'Alice, please listen to me.'

But she cannot. She shakes all over, can barely keep upright as she paces back and forth amongst the roots of Ponden-Hall's grave.

'Alice,' says Lou. It is the closest Alice has seen her to crying out. 'The painter of the portraits *is* the master of this estate. All these sixty years. Every painting from Hugh DeLacey to Mary was painted right here by one artist. But he is not Timothy Ponden-Hall.'

Alice throws her arms up, exasperated. 'Who is he then?'

'The painter is...' Lou swallows. She licks her lips and finds Alice's eyes. Alice regards her with a clenched jaw, nostrils flared; she dares not breathe. Lou's voice is rough and shaky when she finally says, 'The painter of these portraits has always been his sister. Adelaide. She is the master behind every painting.'

Alice studies her, eyes narrowing. She crosses her arms as if to guard herself from any further onslaught of nonsense. Is Lou mad? Has she heard her correctly? 'Adelaide Ponden-Hall?' Alice asks, a hint of mockery in her voice. 'The deceased Adelaide Ponden-Hall. The Adelaide Ponden-Hall who Timothy painted in his tenth portrait?'

Lou shakes her head. 'That portrait...' It is a frustrated appeal: 'Alice, Adelaide Ponden-Hall never died.'

Now Alice shakes her head and closes her eyes. 'It was in the papers! It was confirmed.' Her heart pelts her lungs and ribcage with fury. Her head begins to throb. 'Where is she, then?' She throws her arm towards the house that towers behind the wall. 'She has hidden in there for sixty years, has she? This estate, these grounds – they're Adelaide Ponden-Hall's, are they? Your master is Adelaide Ponden-Hall? Let me meet her then. Let me see her face to face if I am to consider if anything you've told me is true.'

'Alice.' Lou stands now. 'I have wanted to tell you. Like I said before, I never imagined that we would become friends or that you would... that we would grow close. I never intended to appear so deceitful—'

Alice's mind is addled by this non sequitur.

'—and this is why I had to be certain of what your father's true motivations were around my paintings.'

Of course, Alice has misheard her.

'What did you say?' Alice scrutinises her, brow wrinkling. 'What did you just say? What are you implying?'

Lou steps towards her but Alice backs away. Lou is so small in this graveyard, so tiny amongst the trees and fields and tall, tilting slabs of stone, and yet there is something unsettling about her as she tries to come closer.

'I am her,' Lou says, her voice breaking.

'You are who?'

Alice continues to walk backwards. Lou's hands reach out to her – hands she once would have eagerly, hungrily, cupped in her own – but she recoils.

'I am Adelaide Ponden-Hall.'

For one moment, all is still and silent as if they are rooted in silt at the bottom of a pond, facing each other beneath the suffocating, unbearable weight of icy, paralysing water.

And then Alice begins to laugh. It is high and shrill as she catches her breath. She searches Lou's brow, her eyes, any twitch of her lips to confirm her jest – an ill-timed joke. But there is none. All she sees on her face – her delicate and elegant face that betrays few years beyond Alice's own – is worry.

'You are mad,' Alice whispers, not a trace of the laugh on her tongue. 'How could I have thought—'

Alice moves faster now, backs into the corner of a gravestone, stumbles over a root.

'You are just like all of the others,' she spits. 'Wild claims. Delusional truths. You are worse than any of them if you truly believe—'

She cannot finish the ludicrous thought. This is not the intelligent, sensible woman she has come to know over the past year.

'Alice, I wanted to explain everything,' says Lou. 'But after Mary died, the house was in a state and I fell ill, and on some days, I could not bring myself to get out of bed. Alice, I grow weaker by the day. Please don't go!'

Yet she must. She must leave this tiny hamlet and get as far away as possible from the manor and its horrible mysteries and delusions and Lou. She does not even return to the cottage for her satchel. She will not see Lou again, for how could she? How could she lead her like this to the falsest of hopes? Lou is misinformed. A sorry believer in conspiracies and embellished stories, just like the rest of them.

PART THREE

Ponden-Hall

PRINTER BESEECHES PONDEN-HALL TO PAINT DYING DAUGHTER AS THEY RETREAT TO SEASIDE FOR FINAL DAYS
Morning Chronicle, June 1840

Printer Gabriel Jones is publicly entreating Timothy Ponden-Hall to paint his young daughter, five, who is dying of a bronchial disease. Whilst multiple doctors have diagnosed the girl's case as terminal, one has prescribed sea air to ease her passing in these final days. As the family packs for Weymouth, Jones has been feverish in his ploy to commission Ponden-Hall for a portrait.

Jones states: 'We know Ponden-Hall is somehow immortalising his sitters. He has done this for two children already – no relations to himself. I beg him to consider painting my Maria. Please help us prolong her life. My own life will lack purpose when she is gone. I am in utter despair.'

Jones refers to Ponden-Hall's portraits of *Harry – An Orphan Boy* and *Anne – The Potter's Daughter*, both painted three years ago. As proposed, there are no known links between Ponden-Hall and these young subjects.

Jones' plea has received mixed responses from the public. Some have always judged Ponden-Hall for guarding his secrets, and these individuals echo Jones' entreaty for the explorer-painter to share his confidences and services. Others, somewhat surprisingly, have condemned Jones for being 'insensitive', claiming it is 'bad form' to appeal to Ponden-Hall during this time of mourning. It has been only one week since the portrait of Adelaide Ponden-Hall, Timothy's own sister, appeared on the doorstep of the Academy. It is well known that the siblings were close, and her death will undoubtedly have cast Ponden-Hall into a state of grief.

Still, Jones is persistent: 'My condolences go to Mr Ponden-Hall, of course. But we know that he has immortalised his sister in some way through the painting. What about the rest of us? I do not care what sort of sorcery or chemistry he is playing with here. All I want is for my daughter to be granted this chance too. He is a heartless man indeed if he ignores a suffering father's plea.'

There has been no response from Timothy Ponden-Hall.

TO PRINTERS: an advertisement for Jones' printing office can be found on page 1.

1

Late Spring 1891

'Pursuers of fame,' the sensationalised columns read. 'Particularly abhorrent for using their own daughter after her death.'

Grace thumbs through a long list of quotes from over fifty newspapers and penny presses. She has handwritten each quote herself in perfect, swirling script. She has also brought a few original articles, which she found in a dusty corner of the Gallery archives. The train rocks, which makes her queasy when she tries to read.

It is their third short excursion this month chasing leads from old sensationalised papers. The first – to a wizened gatekeeper in Sussex who had claimed to hear woodpecker cries outside an abandoned manor after the three-toed woodpecker painting surfaced – could barely remember his own name. When Oak asked him about his claims, the man had stared slack-jawed, then giggled behind his hand, claiming he had not a clue as to how a woodpecker might sound. The second – an old woman who had claimed as a young girl to be Harry the orphan boy's friend at the workhouse – admitted as soon as they arrived that she had made up her entire story. 'I thought the attention would help find me a home or at least get some extra food,' she told Oak. 'Didn't do neither.'

Such painful, wasted journeys are harsh reminders that the trail to Ponden-Hall cools by the day. Yet there are no other leads.

'This woman – the one that they claim is in *Woman in a Sunhat* – was called Eliza Bassington and she died from consumption,' Grace continues to read from her notes. 'So you can see why the presses had a time of it splashing the Bassingtons across their headlines. "Greedy, fame-seeking family uses deceased daughter in absurd painting claim"; "Vulturous family does not allow Ponden-Halls to grieve in peace". Not the slightest bit of interest in their actual claim about the painting, of course.

'And look at this article.' Grace lays the paper on the table and reads sideways, "'Covetous Bassington family claims that Ponden-Hall's most recent masterpiece, *Woman in a Sunhat*, belongs to them. The sitter, they claim, is not Adelaide Ponden-Hall, deceased sister of the painter, but their own daughter, Eliza, an unknown country girl living well outside of the London society that Timothy Ponden-Hall would be acquainted with. There have been several claims to Ponden-Hall's paintings, but no one has blatantly discredited the identity of one of his sitters"... and it goes on.'

Oak brushes the biscuit crumbs from his chin. 'I remember it well. I have to admit that their story at the time seemed too preposterous to consider. And there was, of course, the statement from Julien and Elizabeth. There was no reason to doubt it.'

'No, there wouldn't be.'

'What do you think, Alice?' asks Oak. 'Perhaps I have overlooked something.'

Nearly six weeks have passed since Alice's visit to the Oxfordshire estate. The days have felt long and agonising. Lou's claims about Adelaide continue to cloud Alice's mind. Another story from a gossip press. But her divulgence around Timothy's death? Alice has considered proposing this possibility to her father but always decides to keep silent. Why should she say anything? There is no proof. Just bold words of a country coachwoman and a hideous apple tree.

And yet Alice knows in the core of her belly that Lou – the Lou she has come to know over the past several months – is an honest woman. Did it not pain Lou to tell her? This truth Alice has still not been able to face, for if what Lou claims about Timothy is indeed true, how can she tell her father? What does this mean for his life's work? And there is still the revelation of Ponden-Hall's mixed bloodline. How does this play into the story? Alice has more questions now than at the start of this saga. If she cannot yet speak to her father, perhaps she should confide in Grace – get the sitter's opinion on the matter and proceed from there. Yes, this is what she will do. She will air the absurdity with someone her father trusts and see what she thinks.

Until then, she finds it difficult to look Oak in the eye or talk much about Timothy Ponden-Hall at all. She feels guilty for this, for the company she has kept with her father as of late has been unreserved, productive, *happy*. And here she is, retreating like a hermit crab as in the past.

Oak interprets this behaviour as a response to their conversation one week ago. Talk of Alice's tour on the continent is a common topic now, and they have started to plan her route. In the next week or two, they will buy her ticket. Oak remains distressed, of course, but he keeps this quiet now. He understands his daughter's restlessness and enthusiasm at the thought of new lands, new cities. Which is why he should not have offered to send Missy or one of her tutors to accompany her on the trip. Alice had prickled and then rightly accused Oak of not believing that she could do it on her own.

Oak sighs, ever lost in the wily and battering storms of parenthood. A positive development which brings him relief and joy is that Alice and Grace get along very well; any vestiges of jealousy on Alice's part seem to have faded with the change of season. Aside from Alice's aloofness, this excursion to Potters Bar with the two of them is a pleasant affair indeed. With any luck, it will also be fruitful.

Oak excuses himself to order a pot of tea in the dining car. Alice feels horrible for allowing her father to feel this way, but having him suffer for what he believes is a silly offence is much kinder than suggesting to him that his entire life's work has been a lie.

'Would you like me to talk to him?' asks Grace. She does not look up from her papers. 'About your tour, I mean. It was rather silly of him, what he offered last week. As if you would want to explore Vienna with your daily!'

Alice cannot help but snort.

'Let us not be rude about Missy,' she quips. 'She would be really rather lovely company.'

'I jest, of course. I bet there is a handsome young tutor at the university who would happily accompany you abroad.' Grace sneaks a glance over the stack with an arched brow.

Alice cringes. 'Thank you very much but I cannot think of anything worse.'

'Good girl!' Grace drums the table once with her fist. 'They are a bore, university men.'

'He would explain every painting to me – probably inaccurately – as if I were a wooden spoon.'

'Indeed.'

'And he would pronounce Botticelli with the most pompous accent.'

Grace laughs. 'Oh, it makes me wince to think of it!' She fluffs her hair and returns to her work. 'But truly, your father is excited about your trip. He has told me so.'

'I am hoping for him to meet me somewhere for a section of it. But I should like to venture out on my own just for a little while. Keep him busy, will you? I am sure there will be an excess of work to keep him distracted from worrying about me.'

'Ha! He will never stop worrying. And I should think he will want you around for any significant developments on Ponden-Hall.'

At this, Alice's temperamental good humour is dashed once more. 'Sincerely, please do not feel that I wish to be more involved. I did at the start when the pig appeared, but quite honestly, I am tired of it all. As of late, especially, I have heard some ludicrous theories.'

The coach door is slid open and Oak appears, chewing a toffee.

'They wouldn't give me a pot,' he says. 'We are here, anyway.'

Potters Bar is an easy hour from King's Cross. The village is quaint, with white-painted brick buildings and thatched roofs. Although it is midday, the inn is buzzing with chatter and clinking glasses; the alluring smells of sizzling meat and potatoes linger about the garden gate and even though they are not hungry, all three of them – even Oak, who has given up saltier dishes in his pudgier years – wish they were here for pleasure rather than work.

So they press on to the cottages that line the village's narrow roads. They are not as tall as the homes in London, and the chic uniformity of soldier-like townhouses is replaced by outlines of brown beams that form checkerboards and arches across the bricks. Wisteria has begun to bloom and there is no shortage of it climbing up cracked walls, garden obelisks and along doorframes.

'How very sweet,' says Grace.

''Tis this one,' says Oak. 'Tidbury Cottage.'

A dog barks for several minutes before the door is flung open.

'So sorry! I've burnt the buns! Come in, come in!' Margareta Bassington shouts over her shoulder.

The spaniel sniffs them as they enter, grows bored within seconds and totters after his master. He is adorned with a thick wool collar – bright magenta and fuzzy – which makes him look like a jester of sorts, with his head resembling the tip of a powder puff.

Upon looking around, they see that the collar is no anomaly, for there is an endless array of knitted paraphernalia scattered about: woolly cushions on every sofa, a nest of scarves in the corner, scalloped blankets draped over every chair arm and back in sight. It is not a large cottage, so the wool creations fill the room with their rainbow frills quite aggressively.

Margareta herself wears many knitted layers – a sweater beneath a pinafore under an apron – and Alice wonders if these garments are, in fact, unfinished, for it seems that long tassels of unknotted yarn drag along the floor at her feet.

'I think I've scraped off most of the burnt bits,' she says, plonking a steaming basket of hot cross buns on the dining table. 'I know Easter has come and gone but I have so many leftover currants and raisins, it seemed a shame to waste them. My son is usually home to eat them, you see, but he has stayed in Bristol this summer to work at the docks. I'm very proud of my Stephen but he is so far away. "Mother," he tells me, "you must move into a city – much more civilised," and this and that, but I know he misses the country. He misses my cooking, that I know for certain. So eat up, eat up! Butter is there and I can bring out the honey if you'd like.'

'It smells divine, Mrs Bassington,' says Oak. 'You are very kind to have us to tea.'

'It is an honour, Mr Oak! Oh, I've told all the neighbours – I hope you don't mind. It's not every day we have someone of fame come to visit. I hope none of them pop by – that would be frightfully embarrassing. Though I did make extra buns just in case.'

'Well, we shall endeavour not to take up too much of your time. This is my daughter, Alice—'

'A pleasure, darling girl.'

'And this is Miss Grace Dodd, who has been helping me with recent research.'

'Well, you are just gorgeous, Miss Dodd! My apologies – what a forward thing to say, but you must hear it all the time. Why, you should be in the theatre!'

Grace flashes her dimples and winks at Margareta. 'You are very sweet. But for now, I am most interested in helping my friends here.'

'Yes, of course. Now which press is this for? I have to admit, Mr Oak, I was a bit taken aback by the notion that you with your prestige and reputation had descended to the penny presses, but then I thought, "No, no, Mags, you mustn't judge the man. I'm sure he has his reasons—"'

'Ah, Mrs Bassington, you are a dear to hold me in such esteem. The hope is for an article in the *Telegraph*, but we are far from going to print. For now, in light of the recent developments with Ponden-Hall's whereabouts, we are simply retracing all possible pathways. Overturning a few pebbles that we perhaps overlooked in the past.'

'Well, my parents did their best to share our wee bit of knowledge about the family, but as you know, nobody was interested in taking them seriously.'

'And for that, I apologise—'

'Tut, tut, no, no,' says Margareta, waving her forefinger in Oak's face. The rest of her fingers clutch a bun that's still steaming. 'I want no apologies from you. Nor from anyone, really. I am nearing seventy-five years old, Mr Oak, and if I've not learnt how to let go of a grudge by now, well, I wouldn't be wearing such bright and happy colours, eh? And anyway, it was the newspapers who were horrid to us. Never anyone of actual merit, you see. The newspapers saw to that.'

'I have been rereading the old articles, Mrs Bassington,' says Grace. 'As many of them as I can find, anyway. It seems they were far more interested in the supposed falsity of your parents' story than in the claim they had to the painting.'

'Well, of course! Nobody wanted my parents to have that painting. It was far more interesting to paint them as quacks desperate for fame and attention than hearing the human side of the story.'

'Which was their claim that the portrait was of your sister, Eliza, and not Adelaide Ponden-Hall.'

'It was the fact that my sister had just *died* and the papers took no heed of my parents' grief. Oh, it was awful. Her death was a shock to us all – consumption is a horrid thing. And when the painting appeared at the Gallery, my parents were so grateful to Timothy. He loved Adelaide furiously, as you know, and so it was beautiful to see him honour Eliza in this way. He knew that Adelaide and Eliza were very close friends. But no – the presses didn't listen. More important people believed the portrait to be of Adelaide herself, and so my parents were scoffed at, ridiculed for many years and eventually forgotten.'

Oak, Grace and Alice exchange glances. She is the most lucid of anyone they have questioned so far. Her fire and spirit are admirable, but perhaps such passion has coloured her memory.

'I understand your frustration, Mrs Bassington,' says Grace delicately, 'but Julien and Elizabeth themselves issued a supporting statement that the painting was of Adelaide.'

'Which was utterly ridiculous. You took note, I hope, that it was an entire week after the painting appeared. Articles in every paper, respectable and not, were written about the painting. I don't remember which identified her as Adelaide – it could even have been *The Times*... but the family did not correct them. And seven days later, Julien and Elizabeth thanked the public for their condolences and requested to be left alone with their grief for a time. What hogwash! Pardon my language. But it was such nonsense to perpetuate this lie.'

Alice's eyes flick to her father and Grace in turn. It is difficult to ignore the strings of yarn tassels hanging from this woman's hairpiece, the over-applied rouge on her cheekbones and nose. If Margareta's parents were anything like their daughter, it would have been easy indeed to label them as doddypolls.

Grace says what Alice is unable to, placing her hand on the table near Margareta's arm. 'With all due respect, Mrs Bassington, why would Julien and Elizabeth play along with this claim? They would have effectively been confirming their granddaughter's death – no light matter. And there are no records of Adelaide Ponden-Hall after the painting.'

'There were no records of Adelaide Ponden-Hall *before* the painting! The child was kept under lock and key for as long as I knew her.' Margareta sinks into her chair and puffs out her cheeks. 'To be honest, Miss Dodd, we were all baffled by this. I hate to say this out loud because it is a wretched thought, but the Ponden-Halls were not proud of Adelaide. They never were. I don't know why. Perhaps she could never live up to her brother, I do not know.'

''Tis quite a cruel extreme to lead everyone to believe she was dead,' says Oak.

Margareta scoffs. 'How anyone could think that is Adelaide in the portrait is beyond me. But you know, Adelaide was so rarely seen by the public, and even when she was, she was covered in layers of clothes and ridiculous hats and veils due to her "weak disposition". Ha! She might have had a few breathing problems but I have rarely seen a young woman with so much fire as Adelaide Ponden-Hall. But I suppose if nobody knew how she looked, assumptions could be confirmed as fact if nobody challenged them.'

'May I ask, then,' presses Oak, his voice soft, 'if the portrait really is of your sister, what became of Adelaide Ponden-Hall?'

The entire conversation makes Alice uncomfortable. She is resentful of Lou for planting this seed in her mind – this idea that the tenth portrait is not of Adelaide after all. Why is she here with her father and Grace discussing this implausible possibility with this nutty woman? Alice butters another bun so as not to appear too attentive.

'I have wondered this for most of my life, Mr Oak,' says Margareta. 'I suppose… I have always thought that she lived quietly behind the scenes, very much alone until her real death. Her family did not care for her except in relation to Timothy, and he was so often abroad. She died when the painting appeared, as far as the world knows. Her real death would have come and gone like an afternoon breeze.'

'Everyone says the two were very close,' says Oak. 'As someone who knew the family, would you agree with this?'

Margareta smiles. 'As far as I could tell, from the stories Adelaide would tell Eliza and me, she idolised Timothy and he felt an equally deep affection for her.'

Oak sips his tea, now cold. 'Do you know, Mrs Bassington, I have to admit that your parents' claims about the portrait held no credence for me all those years ago. Timothy's closeness to his sister supported the notion that he would memorialise her in one of his paintings. Julien and Elizabeth's statement left no room for doubt. And yet in the past year, it seems that all of my work, my research, all of the paintings I thought I knew so well, are revealing themselves to me in a most illuminating and curious way. Why, for some of them, it feels as if I am viewing them for the first time. *Woman in a Sunhat*, particularly.'

'And why is that, Mr Oak?'

'I am a fool to have only realised in the past few months – with the help of my daughter and Miss Dodd – that *Woman in a Sunhat* is the only human portrait that is not titled with the sitter's proper name. A foolish oversight, I know. With the whirlwind of articles at the time and Adelaide's name perched on everyone's tongues, it never made sense to question it. But now... I wonder, after all these years, if the portrait has been of Adelaide all along.'

Margareta claps her hands together and knocks the sugar pot to the floor. 'You are truly doubting, then! You are considering my parents' story.'

Oak's nod is slow as he turns to Grace and Alice. 'I do not know what this means in the grand picture of Ponden-Hall's life. There are many moving pieces.'

'But you are really considering the truth! The portrait is of Eliza, Mr Oak. I promise you. If we had not been so poor, we would have had miniatures painted of us and I could show you. The portrait is of my sister, to honour her and remember her. It would not have been out of Timothy's character to pay tribute to my sister because of her friendship with Adelaide.'

'Could you tell us more about Adelaide?' Grace asks Margareta. 'It seems you are one of the few who ever met her. What was she like? I only know of her what the newspapers wrote.'

'I will tell you everything I can remember. Mind you, I was only seven or eight at the time so my memory is patchy. They were five years older than me. I joined their games whenever I was allowed to. They played outside every day, rain or sun. I would watch them from the kitchen window if my parents didn't let me go out. This was in our old house, mind you, near Oxford. My family moved to Potters Bar a few years after Eliza's death. A new start seemed apt.'

'Near Oxford, you say?' asks Alice.

'Yes. I don't remember the name of the village. Very small. Eliza and I had our porridge in the kitchen every morning, and like clockwork, Adelaide would tap on the back door and beckon us to play. More often than not, she already had a game in mind. Whatever props she had with her told us where we would be transported for the day: the pyramids, a panther's cave, a castle in the clouds. At least once a week, a pirate ship.'

'These sound like the games Emma and I used to play,' says Alice. The words tumble out of her, quiet and nostalgic.

Oak nods. He remembers.

'Many of the games were Adelaide's version of her family's adventures. Coming from a long line of explorers made her a fantastic storyteller,' Margareta continues. 'There were always the two of them. Two heroes for every tale, just like her grandfather and his best mate, like Timothy and Hugh. I think they were happiest as their male selves; they refused to respond to Eliza and Adelaide in the midst of their games. In fact, Adelaide hated wearing girls' clothing. I remember her telling us once that she was much more comfortable in boys' trousers and jackets than in anything else.'

At this, Alice stirs. A twinge of discomfort within her.

'When I was allowed to join,' Margareta continues, 'I was often the squire or the cook or the stableboy. Mind you, Adelaide's imagination was boundless, and there were many stray cats and sheep who stood in for their villains.'

'Amusing,' says Grace. 'And did you ever see Timothy himself?'

'Never. Adelaide was only ever around during term time and Timothy was off at boarding school. Mind you, after a morning's play and lunch, she had her own instructor at home. She had lessons in the afternoons so we rarely saw her after one o'clock. "How extravagant," Mother would say, "for a young girl to have her own tutor!" Eliza did try a few times to be nosy and ask about the family, but other than the stories she shared about her brother, Adelaide only ever smiled politely and said they were all just fine.'

'So you never saw any of them?'

'Oh, no. I don't even know where her house was! Adelaide always came to ours. We first met her on the green along the river one day whilst having a picnic. She was by herself with a toy bear and a plum. We only discovered who she was and who her family were after several months when she mentioned that she came from a long line of seafarers and that she was under the care of her grandparents. It didn't take long for Mother to realise who she was. The Ponden-Halls have always been a source of gossip for this country, you see. Even before Timothy's adventures and his paintings.'

'That is for certain,' says Oak. 'I wonder, Mrs Bassington, if I might stretch my legs a bit? I'm not used to train journeys any more and if we are to board another shortly, back into the city, a little walk would be quite welcome.'

'Of course! Let us take a turn about the garden. It's very small, won't take longer than ten minutes. Bring that basket of buns, Alice.'

The garden is tiny indeed; the spaniel can reach the back gate in a few springy bounds and does so to spook a perched pigeon. Even so, slabs of stone have been laid to create a path along the humble perimeter, and Margareta has green fingers of sorts, for the colours and smells that envelop them in this little corner of Potters Bar make it feel like a miniature Eden.

The guests follow Margareta around the perimeter, hands clasped behind their backs and eyes raised in attentiveness as if they are taking a tour around Kew.

Grace bends to smell a rose. She is not used to rural settings like this and finds herself surprisingly charmed. 'Your sister and Adelaide,' she asks, 'did they remain close until she died?'

'I believe they did. As we grew older, Eliza started to take up work around the village. She eventually moved out to a cottage on the other side of the dairy farm so I didn't see much of her. Around the same time, Adelaide's lessons seemed to increase. We didn't see her nearly as much. I think perhaps she was in London more. This was when Timothy and Hugh were at the peak of their fame, just before the shipwreck. I never saw Adelaide after the wreck. I think Eliza did, from conversations I had with her. They must have remained relatively close for Timothy to paint her.'

'And Adelaide never reached out to you or your parents when Eliza died?' asks Oak.

'No. I suppose, upon thinking about it, it would have been appropriate to hear from her. But I wouldn't have expected to.'

'Why not, if they were such great friends?'

'Well.' Margareta stops in her tracks, which causes Alice to walk straight into her tangle of hair and yarn strings. 'She was never... emotional like that. How can I explain. She was the most extraordinary friend to my sister; she made her laugh and run freely and think expansively. But she was always very reserved in her own right. She never seemed very affected by things.'

'What do you mean?' presses Grace.

Margareta throws her hands on her hips. 'Oh dear, I'm not portraying her very well here. For example, I don't think I ever saw her cry. Or, to be honest, even upset herself about anything. I remember once when they were older, they were outside exchanging clothes and jewellery as girls of that age do. Adelaide had let Eliza borrow some beautiful silk scarves and necklaces. Adelaide's favourite costume piece was a monstrously large black pearl.'

'A black pearl?' asks Alice. There is a niggling in her stomach. 'That is quite a specific memory of a trinket.'

'Indeed. It was an oddity – its size, particularly. Anyway, Eliza balanced it on the wall of the well when she was wrapping her hair up in a headscarf and knocked the pearl straight in. Oh, she cried and cried for days, she felt so awful. But Adelaide seemed to forget about it in a moment. She must have frowned for a heartbeat when the jewel was lost, but after that, she thought nothing of it. Never held a grudge against my sister either, as far as I could tell.'

'How curious,' says Grace.

'Perhaps when one has experienced death and suffering at such a young age as she did, one becomes stoical,' offers Oak.

So different from myself, thinks Alice. Father and daughter are connected by this reflection for the briefest of moments, Emma's ghost lingering between them like a breath on their shoulders.

'Yes, I think so,' says Margareta. 'Please don't misunderstand me. I would never want my depiction of Adelaide – these hazy, half-blurred memories – to make her sound even the slightest bit cruel. She was a marvel. 'Tis what makes it so funny to hear how people speak of her, as this weak and frail thing deteriorating in her brother's shadow.' She claps her hands together as if clanging a cymbal. 'No. Forget what I said. Only take this away about Adelaide Ponden-Hall: she was a truly unique and spirited creature. Do you understand? It would be wonderful if the public knew this about her.'

'Indeed,' says Oak. 'I am adamant about discovering—'

'AH! And she was beautiful. She was absolutely stunning, and in an altogether different way from any other woman I have seen. I can't put my finger on it… something about her eyes and how dark they were. The shape of them. Real black pools, really deep. Nearly as dark as her gorgeous hair, which she always wore down, wild and long.'

'Dark hair?' asks Alice.

The three are startled.

'But the woman in the painting is fair-haired,' says Grace. 'She is blonde and light-eyed. Like Timothy.'

Margareta giggles. 'Well, precisely! This is what my family has been trying to say! The portrait is of my sister, Eliza.' She grabs a handful of one of her straggly plaits. 'Before I was grey, I was yellow as a dandelion. Eliza was the same, only a shade paler as you can see from the painting.'

'But Adelaide's hair was dark?'

'Nearly black in the winter. And as unruly as a swallow's nest. It lightened up a bit in the summer months. Her skin was gorgeous then, too. It seemed to soak up the sun. Like a Spanish princess, my sister used to say.' Margareta crosses her arms. 'Are you telling me you truly don't know how Adelaide Ponden-Hall looked?'

'Well.' Oak is speechless. 'I am certain I... I suppose I just assumed—'

'I have certainly always pictured Adelaide Ponden-Hall to be a fair little thing,' quips Grace. 'The painting would have inspired this image, I don't deny that, but her brother was so fair. Why, the two *could* be siblings – Timothy and the girl in the portrait. Your sister.'

'Genetics are funny, are they not?' Margareta leads them into the cottage once more. 'But that is my story, Mr Oak, and those are my greatest lasting impressions of Adelaide – that she was spirited and strikingly beautiful.'

At the door, there are many warm handshakes and good wishes. Halfway to the gate, Alice is summoned back, for Margareta has dug up a pile of knitted jumpers and aprons and stuffed them into a linen satchel. Peeking in, Alice sees that they all have flora or fauna knitted upon them – a deer on the left breastbone, a rabbit's head on the shoulder, a large daisy right across an entire front.

'My Stephen will never wear them,' she says. 'He conveniently forgets them in the boot room whenever he visits. I reckon they'll be a bit large on you but you might grow into them.'

'My many thanks, Mrs Bassington,' says Alice. 'And...'

She has refrained from asking her for the past hour. She is unsure of what she wants to hear. It is delusional, what she is considering – too absurd, this tempest of thoughts. For the past few weeks, Alice has failed to solve the riddle. If Timothy Ponden-Hall has indeed been long dead, Alice must admit to herself that so much of the torment she will suffer is not only because of the disappointment and failure her father will endure but because of the betrayal Alice herself feels by the closest friend she has ever had. The riddle's perfect answer would rescind the betrayal – would justify the past year and all its misleadings, and most importantly, reveal her friend to be as honest and sincere as she has believed her to be. Only in this past hour has the flicker of an answer, as unthinkable as it may seem, made itself known. And if it does indeed unlock the riddle, it challenges the impossible and births a thousand further questions.

'When they played their games of pretend,' Alice ventures, 'you said they only ever answered to the names of their male characters. What were they called?'

Margareta puffs her cheeks and exhales. 'It's been so long. Eliza called herself Jack, after our father, you see? And Adelaide...' She looks up at the sky to aid her recollection. 'Adelaide always went by the nickname her brother gave her. What did he call her... Addie-Lou. Timothy used to call her Addie-Lou. It was always Adelaide until those sorts of games. When we played pretend, she was only ever Lou.'

Alice feels these words more than she hears them, steadies herself as her heart hums beneath her ribs, can feel the palpitations in her knuckles, her ears, her churning belly that grows warm and knotted. It is not the conclusion she expected; she could never dream up such a story or hope to make sense of the winding course that led here; but it is somehow, perfectly, enigmatically, the only one that makes sense.

She is breathless when at last she tries to speak.

'I know—' she begins but the words stick and swell in her throat.

Grace touches her arm in concern.

'Alice?' Oak finds his daughter's eyes. There is something wrong. Something is amiss.

Alice grips her father's hands. 'I don't know how... I don't fully understand, but I think I know where Ponden-Hall is, Father. We have been mistaken all this time. We must get to Oxfordshire at once. It might still not be too late to set it right.'

2

After trains from Potters Bar to London and London to Oxford, they hail the first carriage at the station and Alice directs them to the manor. They are famished and withered from the journey. The driver shifts in his seat on arrival, glances around at the silent roads and holds out his hand for a quick payment; only as a courtesy does he ask if they are certain of their destination. He leaves them at a gallop.

'It is a wonder you remembered the way,' whispers Grace. 'I was utterly lost after the first turn out of Oxford.'

To their surprise, the gate is open, rusted and stiff on its hinges but unlocked and propped open just wide enough for a single person to slip through.

Oak and Grace are overwhelmed with curiosity and worry for Alice. They have been told fragments along the way, disjointed ideas that hop around; confusing, somewhat fantastical ramblings that make Alice pale and distressed. They gather enough to know that their visit is of the utmost urgency. Alice wipes tears away quietly with the butt of her hand as they walk up the long gravel drive.

The looming oaks that line the road are silhouetted in purple as the sun sets. Wafts of wisteria and rosemary drift amongst them on the wind, although the source is hidden. Again, as on Alice's last visit, the nature surrounding them is oddly quiet. Even the flick and shadow of a gliding blackbird is noiseless, as if it is a moving painting, no beat of its wings or shrill song.

Halfway to the house, the flicker of a candle emerges from the front door. The door itself is so grand and heavy and slow-moving as if through seawater, that it seems an illusion at first – that the doorknocker descends into shadow at all is a trick of the diminishing light. Yet here it comes, this quaint candle flame not quite necessary in the golden bruised sunset, come to welcome these unannounced guests who have brought nothing with them, who wish to enter the master's house with no notion of what the impending night will bring.

Alice recognises the easy gait before the figure is upon them.

'We hoped you would return,' Jacob says, clasping Alice's hand.

'I would have come sooner but I only just... Jacob, I do not understand—'

The groundskeeper squeezes Alice's shoulder.

He leads them through the stable yard, where the horses seem restless and agitated. They bob their heads and whinny, eyes rolling like black glass in the shadows.

In the courtyard, Alice turns to Lou's cottage. She is searching for a light on the bay windowsill where they accumulated bottles of wine all those weeks ago, seeking for the twitch of a curtain upstairs or the first puffs of smoke from the chimney. Alice is upon the porch before she realises that the others have not followed her but wait at the edge of the courtyard where stairs to the manor's formal entrance begin.

'She has moved back into her room in the house,' explains Jacob. 'There is more space to take care of her there.'

The reality and gravity of who she might be begins to weigh upon Alice's chest like an ocean. The manor is Lou's, of course. As are the grounds and the animals and the servants. How could she have found peace as a coach driver all of these years? Why remain hidden? To whom is Alice a friend – Adelaide or Lou? The questions tumble one after another through her mind with the swiftness and ferocity of an avalanche. And never mind the whale of a question that lingers on her lips: *how?* How is it possible for this young, sprite-like woman to have painted Hugh DeLacey sixty years ago? There is no trace, no whisper, of the macabre around Lou. Did she not tell Alice herself that such devilry and witchcraft is best left for novelists?

Alice cannot picture Lou's face at this moment – not the details, anyway. Is her hair as ravenlike as she imagines, or could speckles of grey be hiding amongst shadows and top hats? Is the skin around Lou's half-moon eyes and across those high cheekbones so smooth? Alice is not one to notice trivialities like crow's feet and spindly lines. She cannot remember; she cannot recall. She thinks of their

deliveries – Lou's strength, and the expertise with which she transported the parcels, although come to think of it, she did less with the
passing weeks as Alice did more. She remembers their day skating
on the Thames – Lou's agility and grace gliding across the ice, backwards even, when Alice herself could not keep her balance. *How?*
How is this woman the little sister of Timothy Ponden-Hall?

Inside, the house is taller and even more imposing than expected
with its untouchable ceilings and high sash windows. But instead of
feeling grandiose and fresh and regal, the space exudes loneliness. It
is a vast and empty crypt that lacks skeletons and ghosts.

Jacob leads them down the main hall through darkness, for the
curtains are closed and still and block out the purple evening throughout the house. Where the odd candle has been lit along a corridor,
within its shallow pool of light, glimpses of covered armchairs, dusty
console tables, empty shelves and flowerless pots slumber away as
if in hibernation. Some of the rooms, Alice can see in their swift
passage through, are entirely empty – a ballroom perhaps, or a formal
drawing room.

Yet there is life here. There is a draught, quite a cool one that chills
Alice's clammy face.

'Is there a door open somewhere?'

'Always,' says Jacob. 'The doors of the dining room are never
closed. They open out into the apiary.'

'I didn't know there was an apiary here.'

''Tis her most beloved part of the estate. Look here.'

Jacob raises the candleholder and goes to the wall. At first, they
see nothing, but as the circle of light glides forward, tiny, twitching
figures can be seen along the mouldings.

'Why, they are bees!' exclaims Grace. 'In the house?'

'There won't be many now – just the nocturnal ones,' says Jacob.
'But we never close those doors so they're free to roam about as they
please.'

'How extraordinary.'

'She is a beekeeper too,' mumbles Alice.

'Do you hear something?' asks Oak.

In the heart of the house, they pause and listen. Yes, low and rich
as if the bones of the house itself are humming, there is music somewhere within.

'Up this way.' And Jacob leads them on.

More candles are lit on the first floor and some source of vibrancy seems to emanate from a room up ahead. There is movement up here: the tinkle of a teapot, the shaking-out of a blanket. And louder now, each note more distinct with each step, is a cello being played.

Light spills out of the room into the corridor as it always does, a pulsating sun with its monstrous chandeliers. The cello music spills out as well, and for one moment, it feels as if they are about to enter a grand party. Soft hints of cinnamon and tangerine peels settle in the air. Alice does not know what to expect, what she will see upon entering the room. She feels her father's shaking hand on her shoulder, and like this, together, they turn in towards the light.

Although they all enter Ponden-Hall's studio at the same time, the professor, the ex-thief and the girl on the cusp of womanhood are drawn to different features of the room in the first instance.

For Solomon Oak, it is the seafaring paraphernalia: the framed maps and nautical charts, gold barometers and brass compasses. The shelves in this room are the opposite of bare, overcrowded by sextants and taffrail logs as if waiting their turn in the back room of Bonhams. Oak has seen these gadgets before in beeswax and oil, in his lecture notes, in his dreams. These are Timothy Ponden-Hall's instruments. They will have Hugh DeLacey's palm prints upon them, the dust of far-off sea cliffs and the salt of every ocean.

Try as he might, Oak cannot swallow the stone in his throat. It lodges there as he takes in the galley knots, the bowed wooden beams that make up the vaulted ceiling, which must have come from ships, the bones of a home inside a home. He does not realise that his cheeks are wet and glistening until Grace presses a handkerchief into his hand.

But Miss Dodd is not taken by these seaman's tools or the gold gilded books. For her, it is the mahogany table of elephantine proportions in the centre of the room, upon which sit pig bladders of paint, vials of pigments, jars of oil and varnish, metal tubes by the hundreds. And everywhere you look, wax. Milky white wax hardened in teak bowls, globs of wax spilt over onto the table and through its cracks to the floorboards below. It is a chemist's table, a magician's table; an artist's table would describe it too simply.

'Look, Mr Oak,' whispers Grace when she finds her voice.

The easel, simple and solitary, is as sturdy as a cross or a gallows.

The painting upon it is incandescent. It is perhaps the plainest of them all; no revealing setting, no clever composition or playfulness with light. Yet it is, most astoundingly, the most alive. Even without the signature, Oak and Grace know who this is. Her eyes are dark indeed – a deeper black than the wild, unbridled hair that falls nearly to her waist. She is striking, to be sure, with skin a mix of cream and olive and pink. A black pearl, strung in gold – the only jewellery that adorns her – sits on her breastbone between the ribboned V collar.

Oak can tell that she is meant to be imperfect, that the piece is not meant to flatter. He sees this with the rougher brushstrokes and lack of precision around the lips, the jawbone, the wrist. So different from the exactitude in *Hugh DeLacey* or even in the recent *Mary – A Housemaid*. But the imperfections only make the painting more real, and as a result, more arresting.

Grace brings her hand to her bosom and she feels Oak start to tremble beside her. His life's work has come to this moment – this finite and fleeting second where every riddle is answered by the slightly altered signature in the bottom right corner:

ADELAIDE PONDEN-HALL

'Father, I want you to meet someone.' Alice breaks into Oak's reverie.

Alice's own face is puffy and tear-streaked but the distress is gone.

She leads Oak and Grace to the far corner of the room where an inconspicuous truckle bed has been erected. Amidst the polished wood and refined flagstones, the bed is an eyesore. But it appears cosy enough, for it is heaped with cushions and throws of the finest cashmere, and a pitcher of rosemary water next to a tray of bonbons and plums is almost reminiscent of a May Day tea party.

Lou straightens herself on the bed of cushions as best she can.

'Father. Miss Dodd,' begins Alice. The words she is about to say still do not make sense to her; they are impossible yet ring true, and as inconceivable as they may be, they reveal the only ending that answers every riddle. 'This is my friend, Lou.' And although she wants to give an addendum with confidence, with conviction, she finds that her throat is dry, and her voice is quiet with doubt when she says, 'I think you know her better as Adelaide Ponden-Hall.'

Lou's smile is warm but there is a weight upon her eyelids, a fatigue about her that suggests she could fade away at any moment. Even in this corner sheltered from the brightest circles of the candelabras, Lou's beauty is clear. In half-shadows, she is a conundrum of youthful rosiness and slow, heavy movements. Alice holds her hand, afraid of her own evanescence. Whilst Lou's features are still striking, her body seems to have deteriorated to a delicate mass of skin and bones held together by a dressing gown. The vibrancy that is normally there – the gusto that emanates from the pads of her fingers, the tip of her nose that Alice is so familiar with – seems to fade before them, the final glow of an ember. This is a different Lou from the Lou of even five weeks ago; how has she diminished so rapidly?

Lou offers her other hand to Oak.

'It is a pleasure to finally meet you, Mr Oak. It is perhaps a bit self-indulgent to admit, but I am a great admirer of your work.'

Even the housemaid laughs as she pours three cups of tea.

'You know,' says Lou, 'we have shared much of the same lifetime, you and I. In many ways, we have grown up together, communicating through folds of beeswax and oil. And, well – my life's story is all there in the paintings, Mr Oak, but if you will grant me an audience, I would like to share with you the story that threads them all together. You see, you are the only one I trust to tell it. You are the only one who has focused most purely on the paintings.'

It is too much to take in. Oak is disoriented. He is overcome with relief and confusion all at once.

'I would like to hear your story,' says Oak, breathless. He cannot address her. She is a stranger to him, yet her familiarity is unnerving. He glances around the room once more – to Timothy's maps, his books, his seafaring instruments and framed knotted ropes. These are no props of theatres or museums. They are authentic and weather-worn from long months at sea, comforting tools and talismans in the cabins of great ships. They are all here, and yet, where is their master? Where in this deep, magnificent house are the explorers that brought these apparatuses home?

'Where is Timothy?' the old art historian asks at last. The air is heavy; his words sound slow and far away as if they push against a tide. 'Is Timothy here too?'

There is sadness in the subtle twitch of her lips as Lou studies this man. For too long did she feel inadequate as a child; for too long did she strive never to disappoint anyone again. These are familiar feelings that stir beneath her ribs. Where have they come from, having been buried so long? Contrition for not being more like Timothy; fresh grief – staggering, to be sure, after all these years – at the thought of having to relay, to accept, her brother's death once more. But no. Lou will manage these sensibilities as she has done for half a century. It is to *her* paintings that Oak has devoted his life. It is *her* mastery and *her* story that Oak has admired and coveted. He simply does not understand, not yet. And she can only hope to trust him.

'My brother is present in every corner of this room,' she tells Oak, 'in the same way that Emma is beside you when you look upon a painting.'

To hear his daughter's name now is discombobulating. Oak looks from Lou to Alice, who is herself grappling with something internal. *What does she mean?* If Adelaide Ponden-Hall really is the painter of these portraits, where is Timothy? Timothy Ponden-Hall, who Oak has believed in all of these years; Timothy, who he has championed as a modern master. *In the same way that Emma is beside him?* The grief on Oak's face could make a mountain buckle. What is more painful: that Timothy Ponden-Hall might be dead? Or that Oak, throughout his career as an esteemed academic, has leapt to erroneous conclusions? All of Oak's postulations have relied on Timothy's mastery as a painter and a categorical rejection of the supernatural. Here, on the lip of understanding at last, is he to be proven wrong on all accounts? 'Tis not Timothy's mastery at all but his sister's; and his alleged sister, this woman before him who has supposedly painted for sixty years, has lived through eighty birthdays – well. How can she look barely older than his eighteen-year-old daughter without some form of… without dabbling in…

Oak breathes deeply and studies the beams above him once more. He has never believed in elixirs of immortality. He is too old to start believing in them now.

'Please tell us.' It is Grace's voice that interferes with their thoughts, soft and careful. 'That is why we're here, isn't it?' She places a hand on Oak's shoulder. 'This is the story we have sought to understand, isn't it, Mr Oak? We have chased the wrong rabbit, it seems. Taken the wrong turn somewhere.' Her light-heartedness is ineffectual but still she goes on. 'Please tell us everything. We are a tired but eager audience and I assure you that no one would like to understand more than we do.'

Lou notes Grace's leg-of-mutton sleeves, the bell-like fall of her skirt. There is more to her than material and jewels, just as Lou had hoped. A woman like Grace will see the unseen, indeed, has already begun to do so.

'Of course,' says Lou. She motions for them to move towards the hearth. 'There is much to share but you must be famished. Let us say no more until you have had something to eat.'

3

Lou's Story

The hour is midnight. The cobwebs amongst the highest beams sway in an invisible current. A mouse scuttles out of a gap in the joinery, twitches his nose and after a pause, retreats. They all sit before the great hearth in Lou's studio, and although it is only late spring, the air, even at this hour, is drowsily warm. The fire is lit, for light and to ward off the chill that will creep in through the windows as the night progresses. There is a strangeness to the air as shadows hang at contorted angles, sharp and looming. They flicker with each lick of the flames. Subtle shifts.

Despite the late hour, the two housemaids bring in platters of cured meats and cheese, loaves of bread and biscuits and bowls of cherries, peaches, plums. There are carafes of wine and mint water. The maids fuss over their guests, bring them cushions for their backs and padded stools for their feet. The three are tired indeed, fatigued from their train journeys and suddenly hungry now that they are still. Yet Oak, Grace and Alice hardly notice the generous plates that are heaped and placed upon their laps. They have attention for Lou who sits weakly in the midst of them, petite and frail, wrapped in a shawl, propped up amongst pillows in a grand armchair. In the face of these lapping, playful flames, her face is at times shadowed, at times luminous in an ethereal glow.

'Please eat,' she says, taking a sip of wine. 'There is still time.'

Still time. Alice sits closest to Lou, her hand still resting on the arm of her chair after helping to lower her into it. Their evening coach rides flicker through her mind, woolly and lucid all at once. How careless she was with time then. And these past few weeks – even when she had felt betrayed, embarrassed, angry… has she not missed Lou? Clarity is what she needed. And understanding. But time? This Alice took for granted. How foolish she has been. Lou had tried to tell her under the apple tree. Alice is desperate to apologise, to explain herself and ask for her forgiveness.

But it is Oak who speaks.

'I… Lou,' he tries. 'Madam.' He cannot call her this name that she claims to be attached to. It is a sacred name for Oak; he has seen it splashed amongst falsities for most of his life and any truth claimed around it must be proven to him. He has earned this, at least, for who he is, how he has spent his life. He is flushed from the fire's heat or from the wine. Now that he has had a few more moments to take in this house, this studio with its recognisable trinkets and treasures, this stranger before him who feels unsettlingly familiar, he does not know how to quell the doubt that roils within him. How can he voice his confusion without offending? Now that Oak has put into focus this startling new claim, he cannot comprehend who Lou is – that this woman is the painter of the portraits that have shaped his career and the childhood of his children. That she is the master behind these works that are imprinted in the most cherished caverns of his mind. 'This is… all very extraordinary to me,' he says. 'I am stunned, to put it plainly. I do not know what to say except… well, I would like to understand. I do not understand any of this.'

Lou's smile is tired but warm. 'You do know more than you think. And thanks to a friend in London – the milkman, Grace – you were guided to consider the importance of the Sandwich Islands, which lie at the root of my story.'

'You did want us to know about Julien's affair then,' says Oak. 'He brought home with him a son.'

'Yes. When my grandfather returned to London from an expedition in 1779, he brought with him a bastard son.'

The air is still. They watch her, all of them, not daring to breathe as the fire crackles on. How long has this story simmered and changed shape in Lou's mind? How strange it will be for her to feel it upon her lips. She has returned to England – to painting – for this moment, but how strange indeed to finally speak it into the world.

This history, these memories, these feelings that she is about to share are more than just a story; they attest to her very existence.

'My grandfather brought home with him a bastard son,' she begins again. 'His wife Elizabeth never forgave him but agreed to raise the boy as their own, a secret they would both take to the grave. The boy's real mother was a native of the Sandwich Islands. Not a word about her was ever breathed in the Ponden-Hall house. They called the boy Andrew – my father. He looked like Julien, with fair hair and light brown eyes.

'Andrew would marry my mother, Martha Kipps, and they would have two children: Timothy – a gregarious thing, a pale-haired and light-eyed boy like our father; and two years later, me – a surprise in all respects but most shockingly in appearance. You see, unlike my father and brother, I looked like my true paternal grandmother: my skin was creamy but olive-tinted; the doctors believed I was jaundiced for the first few months of my life until they realised it wouldn't diminish. "An undercurrent of caramel toffee", my grandfather would say with affection. My hair was wild like kelp, ale-brown, and my eyes were as dark as pitch. "Black like the devil's tongue", Elizabeth would hiss, for she imagined savages from island nations to be unruly and bulbous and hideous.'

Lou scowls at the thought. 'Much to Elizabeth's chagrin, as I grew into the toddling years of my life, her friends started to comment on my unique features. I attracted far too much attention – the wrong kind for a family of our status, the kind that would expose our impure lineage. It was assured from that point onwards that I would never be seen by the public. "A frail disposition", they would repeat in the right circles. "Susceptible to ailments; will weaken in the sun."'

The exposure of an impure lineage. Oak recalls the periodicals and cartoons – the impassioned opinions on how those of mixed blood should be treated. The Sandwich Islands in the DeLacey portrait, Adelaide's erasure from society gatherings. It begins to dawn on Oak that this is not a story about death or preserving life or immortality; it is about being seen.

'When our parents were killed in a carriage accident,' continues Lou, 'Julien and Elizabeth became our legal guardians. Timothy was six and I was four. Timothy was sent to boarding school. I was sent out of London.'

'At age *four*?' Grace interjects. The shock is plain upon her face. She, too, has led an independent life from very young, but even she was not responsible for herself at such a tender age.

'For the rest of her life,' explains Lou, 'Elizabeth believed that I lived in a tiny cottage on the outskirts of an Oxfordshire village with a nanny and, eventually, my young maid; I was invited to family Christmas as a courtesy, and I was permitted to visit the London residence when Timothy was home, mainly to ensure that he would stay for a decent spell of time.

'Without Elizabeth's knowledge, though, my grandfather had bought me this small manor outside Oxford in the Cotswold hills replete with a small number of trustworthy staff. I had my nanny, yes, but also enough help to comfortably run a household with a kitchen garden and stables. From my tutor, I learned mathematics, Latin and Greek, classical poetry and modern prose. And I learned much about art history and the fundamentals of painting: composition, colour mixing, priming a canvas. Painting was my favourite pastime and I would spend full days in the library, which I had converted into a studio. Here, I experimented with oils, powders, pigments and, eventually, wax, thanks to the surplus of it from the apiary. I did not know if I possessed any talent when it came to painting; I had nobody to compare myself to except the masters in my books.

'Looking back, I believe the guilt Julien felt around this arrangement was enormous; my isolation was his doing, a long-winded outcome from his affair. I led a rich life but in complete secret, in complete isolation.'

'How revolting,' whispers Grace. She is so in awe of Lou before her – of the trials she has suffered – that for a moment, she forgets the absurdity of her story. 'Why, it's positively nauseating how they treated you. Can you imagine?' She turns to Oak, who sits beside her with wrinkled brow. 'It would be as if you hid Alice away, exiled her to grow up alone because her hair was a different colour from yours. 'Tis repulsive.'

But whilst this is a disturbing truth to consider, Oak is flitting through the files and notes and articles in his mind, piecing together these details from Lou's narrative with the information he has regarded as fact all of these past decades. Adelaide Ponden-Hall *was* hidden from the public, due to her *weak disposition* as was famously known. *She was a mute*, he thinks. *She was weak and needed to be cared for because she was easily taken ill.* Could it be that she was hidden for another reason? How cleverly she was concealed from the press. Were not the Ponden-Halls a proud family? Surely, even if Adelaide was susceptible to ailments, they would have enjoyed parading her on the odd occasion as the prim next generation. *She was never seen*, thinks Oak.

'Years passed,' Lou continues. 'A public obsession with my brother and Hugh ensued. Their travels and treasures were envied and admired. And every few months between expeditions, Timothy and Hugh would come to stay here, in this very house, with me. They loved each other,' she says, looking at each of them in turn, landing her gaze on Oak. 'The rumours were true. It was another thing to hide, another secret to keep within these walls.' She smiles, remembering. 'I felt so honoured, so happy, to see them with each other as their true selves. They would meld into this hidden and beautiful, secluded life of mine where the press felt far away. There was never special treatment from the staff; Timothy chopped wood for the stove and scrubbed the windows; Hugh cooked every meal and stocked the larder. And every evening, they told me stories – about the treasures they found, yes, but more interestingly, about the people they met along the way. How they ate, what they wore, the rhythms of their languages, the smells of their perfumes. The consolation of their long absences was that they were traversing the world, meeting more people whose stories I would hear upon their return. I missed them terribly, both of them at once, all of the time.

'The shipwreck would bring them more permanently home to me.'

'Forgive me, but—' Oak sits forward in his chair, sloshing his tea onto the saucer, onto the sheepskin rug beneath his feet. He is torn now between maintaining good manners as a guest, as a gentleman, and his will to push back against improbable assertions. 'You speak of these bygone days with Timothy and Hugh when they were at the peak of their fame over sixty years ago. Yet here… yet before us now…' Oak's stumbling only leads to more half-sentences and slips. 'What I am trying to articulate, madam… what I am trying to ask is quite simply: *how* can this be possible? You claim to have grown up with these men during the years of my own young childhood, and, well—' Oak offers an incredulous smile. 'Just look at us. How can it be that you are fifteen years older than I am?'

Oak's words fill the room as if the fire itself has lapped them up and cast them, bright and bold, into every dark and far-off nook in the chamber. Oak thinks of the bubble in one of Jean Siméon Chardin's paintings, delicate and iridescent, shimmering on the precarious tip of a little boy's straw. This is how it would feel for the bubble to burst, to pop and set free what is held within, what everyone is wondering.

In the fire's glow, they are all rosy. The shadows dance upon their cheeks, playing with their wrinkles and hollows of skin. The edges of their faces are soft and blurred. But they are not looking at one another. Once again, they focus on Lou. Her face is calm, her eyes tired but dark even in the face of the blazing hearth.

And Lou understands. *How indeed.* She, too, has been bewildered by her appearance for most of her life. She has never cared for mirrors, but when she has stumbled upon one and taken the time to look, she has only been flummoxed by the preservation of her youthfulness. Perhaps, on a far-off island in the middle of the Pacific Ocean, her real grandmother's hair never turned grey; perhaps her real grandmother's skin never sagged or succumbed to creases. *Haven't I felt my bones grow brittle?* she thinks. *Haven't I strained muscles and suffered twinges in my spine in these recent years?* And yet on the outside, she has remained unchanged. A perfectly preserved shell whilst the nut inside diminishes to dust. She has been able to ignore this strangeness all her life, living in the shadows, dressing in livery and pinning her hair under top hats; no one has examined her closely, including herself. And now here, at the end of it all, she is being truly seen. And it is unsettling for all of them.

'I do not know, Mr Oak,' she says quietly. 'I am perplexed by my own appearance.' She holds out one of her hands and then turns it, a slight tremble, to examine the palm. 'I feel weaker by the day, Mr Oak. I am shrinking into myself. I can feel my back hunch and my energy being siphoned away. I began to notice it one year ago. I knew when I returned to England from my last journey that I would not set sail again.'

'And yet...' Oak says.

Lou's face, whilst gaunt and riddled with exhaustion, still possesses the warm radiance of youth, a beauty somehow unspoiled. Oak is appeased by her honesty but is no closer to understanding the impossibility of her story. He still cannot believe it.

They consider one another in silence, frustration and puzzlement simmering in equal measure.

Grace's voice is a peaceable and welcome buoy. 'What happened after the shipwreck?'

'Oh yes,' says Lou. Breaking away from Oak is like emerging from a trance. Her hands are freezing, so she buries them beneath the blankets and huddles into herself. 'After the wreck, my brother and Hugh were rescued – absorbed – into the haven of my invisible life one final time. They were admitted to the Cornwall Infirmary on the evening of the wreck, and a few days later, in the dead of dark, I sneaked in to see them. Even in his broken state, Timothy was desperate to leave the hospital before the public could gather. He had something deeply important that he needed to protect, to keep safely hidden. So I brought them home.'

'So it was you,' says Alice. 'You helped them escape.'

Oak regards his daughter in astonishment. His daughter believes this woman. She has been taken in.

'Yes. Both of them had stabilised but were fearfully weak, beaten and almost unrecognisable from the battering they had suffered in the storm.' Lou fixes her eyes on Oak once again; she is solemn and gentle when she says, 'My brother would die within the week from his injuries.'

Oak's exhale is sharp. It is too much to bear. The walls he has built, not to mention the years he has spent, on the foundations of Timothy Ponden-Hall's artistry are razed to the earth. How is it possible? Oak recognises this feeling that creeps into his limbs, his skin; he has not felt it so acutely, so searingly in several years – the undeniable, relentless feeling of loss. The tales he knew, the stories he told Emma and Alice, the bedrock upon which he has built his life: they slip through his fingers like sand, like pigments ground to powder that leave only a cloud of dust.

'Upon his request,' says Lou, 'sick of fame and still estranged from our grandparents because of how they treated me, my brother was buried in a nameless grave. He is here, Mr Oak, beneath an apple tree in the village cemetery. He has been here all this time.'

When Oak says nothing, she continues. 'Hugh's system, too, had been weakened terribly by the shipwreck and his body was unable to fend off an influenza. He died just eight days after my brother did. In the span of two weeks, I found myself grieving for my brother, the one ally in my life, and for his lover, who had, over the years, grown to be one of my greatest friends.

'I isolated myself.' Lou shifts in her chair and casts her eyes to the ceiling where the shadows continue to stir. 'In this room I hid away. You would have thought that living out here in the middle of fields, my existence unknown to everyone beyond the garden walls, would have been enough to satiate this desire to disappear. But no. I withdrew from everyone – even Mary – and locked myself in this room without food, without drink, for three days. I had already endured the cruelty of neglect and prejudice in my young life, but grief was more debilitating than any of them. I was paralysed.' Here, she seeks Oak's eye and then Alice's. 'I know you have both suffered as well. I know that you understand this instinct to pull back and vanish from the world.'

Alice tries to hold her gaze but she cannot. She never can when Lou looks at her in this way, when she can feel the tears prick the corners of her eyes. This acknowledgement from Lou is a nod to their coach rides together – to their deliveries and skating and long evenings walking through Oxford's winding back streets. Lou has listened to her; she knows how grief has devastated their lives too.

'And I suppose you also understand how the most unimaginable lifeline pulls you back in,' she says. Her words are measured, soft. 'It palliates the grief by giving you a purpose. But you must break your isolation and re-enter the world. For me, this was painting.'

For Oak, ten years after Emma's death, it was a Kunekune pig. This lifeline, unthinkable and startling, has indeed brought him back to the world.

'I decided to paint them,' continues Lou. 'Timothy Ponden-Hall and Hugh DeLacey, as they were in the prime of life. I would memorialise the two people I loved most. My brother's portrait would be kept close to me in my studio; Hugh's would be given as a gift to his beloved favourite art institution in London.

'Wrapped in brown paper, the painting was left on the door-step of the Royal Academy of Arts in Hugh's honour to display in the lead-up to his sea burial. What followed was beyond my wildest imagination.'

'The portrait was hailed as a masterpiece,' says Oak.

'Yes.'

'The talent and refinement behind each stroke are the work of a genius,' Oak recites. *'The method of using beeswax and oil in this fashion is unique and peculiar.'* Oak buries his face in his hands. He knows what was claimed. 'It is all so familiar.'

'Such a buoyant reception of the painting was a shock to me,' says Lou. 'I had never known how good I was at painting – had certainly never dreamed of my work being praised and coveted by the public.' Here, a pause. 'But most shocking of all was that the public believed it to be painted by Timothy.

'I had signed my name in the bottom right corner as all artists did. In giving credit to my brother, my invisibility was solidified by the world.

'Hugh was buried at sea. The press crowded the docks, eyes darting to and fro for a glimpse of my brother amongst them. I stood at the front of the throng to say goodbye to my friend, completely invisible to them all.'

It is too much to hear the story from this side.

'All too familiar indeed,' says Grace quietly.

'I would go on to paint portraits *in memoriam*, all part of a fantasy built for my brother and Hugh – the life they would never have together: Mr Mortimer, Hugh's beloved butler; my brother's spaniel, Prince; Polyphemus, Hugh's favourite horse despite being robbed of one eye; woodpeckers and peacocks – special birds brought back from abroad, which reminded them of their adventures.

'I painted myself and my own loves into this life as well. What a rich and jubilant existence I dreamt of us sharing in these folds of wax and oil: Bluebell, my favourite dairy cow on the estate; Harry, a sweet boy I had come across whilst helping in an orphanage in London; little Annie, the potter's daughter who I had grown fond of on my trips to Staffordshire ferrying clay to and from artists' workshops there. Most recently, the dear Kunekune pig I brought home from the Maori people over a decade ago. And of course, I painted my childhood friend Eliza after her untimely death by consumption.

'When Elizabeth and Julien issued a statement in the paper to confirm my death and assert me once and for all as the woman in the portrait, it was more than I could bear. Of course they knew that the woman in the portrait was not me. But they took the public's assumption that Timothy's latest masterpiece was a painting of his beloved, frail and now deceased sister as a convenient opportunity to finalise the end of my existence for the family.'

''Tis vile,' hisses Grace. Her curls bounce as she shakes her head vehemently. 'And to think that all this time… well. Miss Ponden-Hall, I do not know why you desire to share your story at all. The public do not deserve you.'

Lou nods slowly. 'I felt that way for a long time. But you see, after their statement was published – after a decade of painting these memorial portraits – I had nothing left to mourn. I had lived through ten years of the public's increasing fascination, *obsession* even, with my brother: their bribes, their searches, their fixations on immortality and Timothy's alleged mastery of it. The theories made me laugh at first. And it felt gratifying to see the dearest people in my life celebrated by the public. But then I began to feel that these stories and rumours had become the focal points of the paintings rather than the sitters themselves. I had no desire to share my art any longer. So when Adelaide Ponden-Hall was known to be dead, there was no reason for me to stay hidden in the manor or sit still in the shadows any longer.

'I was free to pursue a life of freedom and exploration just as my brother, father, grandfather and great-grandfather did before me. I have boarded many ships and set foot on many lands. And, well… I know my time is limited, Mr Oak. I feel it with each passing day. And before I go, I would like to reclaim what was mine – what has been given to my brother, even if it was not his fault.' She pauses here to find Oak's eyes. 'Nor the fault of his admirers and champions.'

They stare at each other, art historian and painter, wrestling with a torrent of impossible questions. *Will he believe my story?* she wonders. For Lou, it is the first time that she has voiced herself into existence. He will recognise her story, she knows this. But it is a new, unsettling side of a familiar tale that in many ways renders his life's work a gross falsehood. There is her appearance to reckon with as well. Lou knows Oak's stance on the supernatural and the hurly-burly of elixirs and immortality. In this, she is with him. In this, she is an equal sceptic, which in turn renders her equally flummoxed by this unsettling, inexplicable appearance of hers. She can only hope that he can sense in his belly, in his chest, that she is who he has been looking for and that her story is his to share if only he honours it.

For Oak, it is too difficult to stomach. Has he not wished to understand this story his entire life? Has he not bent his life to align his own path with this painter's? Here, at the crux of it all, in this house where Timothy Ponden-Hall's presence is eerily indubitable, where a new painting looms before him with Ponden-Hall's familiar strokes and buffs and prods of wax and oil, Oak should feel relief and understanding. Instead, he understands less than before; he is utterly overwhelmed by questions and moved to consider that his life's work is nowhere near finality, is not at all what he thought it was in the first place.

And Oak begins to despair.

He cannot stop himself, for he is – perhaps at last – in the presence of a master whose genius he has admired his entire life. He despairs because he loves and knows this artist's work more than most flesh-and-bone friends who have passed through the years, and he despairs because at the end of his search, there is not clarity but an unlikely, tragic tale. His daughter believes that this is Adelaide Ponden-Hall. He can see that Grace begins to believe it as well. But Oak still does not understand, does not have all the answers, may never know all the answers and perhaps must find a shade of peace in this. He is a professor, an art historian. How can he draw conclusions based on inconceivable evidence? How he wishes he could believe her and understand. But he cannot. As much as he wishes to give credence to this woman's story, he simply cannot, and in not being able to do so, he feels lost and further from Ponden-Hall than he has ever felt before.

4

They are only there for one week.

All three of them – Oak, Alice and Grace – meld into the pulse of the house as if they have always been there. Oak kneels before the vegetable boxes with the gardeners, digs out the early potatoes and lovingly pats away the dirt; how charming their violet skins are, knotty and dimpled, and how fascinating that the purple disappears in the frying oil so that it is an ordinary potato in its final moments. Grace wanders the corridors with a feather duster. She scoops up piles of dust bunnies, manoeuvres the duster behind the most neglected corners of every room. It is a satisfying chore, to be certain, but the dusting also allows Grace an excuse to nose about the house. She finds herself walking on tiptoe, hands clasped behind her back, whilst she admires the large oil paintings in every room. The maids like her. She makes them laugh, for she dances as she cleans and withholds nothing when they ask her about other grand houses, and grand men, that she has seen. Alice mainly shadows Jacob. She putters around the stables and feeds the horses, takes pride in knowing how to harness them. They know Alice's touch.

And of course, they spend as many hours as possible with Lou in the precious golden hours when she is awake. She mainly stays in her studio. They sit before her in plump, soft armchairs and drink coffee, eat chocolate limes and ginger biscuits and bask in the sunlight that erupts through the tall sash windows. Often they take it in turns so as not to overwhelm her. She seems to become more fragile with each hour.

During his time with her, Oak finds that they have much in common. He is still doubtful about who she is, but the more time he spends with her, the more he discovers how interesting her life has been, and how knowledgeable she is about even the most obscure subjects. Oak is delighted to engage in conversations inundated with questions around Renaissance portraiture. Out of her three guests, Lou is most animated with Oak; for long hours on end, they talk over one another about humanism and piety, about Bellini and Raphael and how Donatello has been the most influential artist in the western world. And although Oak has a trove of questions that he has built up over his career to ask Timothy Ponden-Hall, he does not ask her a single one. Has forgotten about them, actually. They converse like old friends, understanding each other in quirks and unspeakable truths.

One morning, Lou brings Oak to a darkened corner of her studio. It is one of the few nooks in the room where the light does not reach; vertical piles of wooden frames and yellowed canvases huddle here, bound by cobwebs and slack string.

'I want to give you something,' she says.

Oak is startled.

From behind the other frames and canvases, Lou draws out with great care a painting hidden in the shadows. It is unframed and unmounted, vulnerable and naked. She slides it into the light and turns it towards Oak.

'My God,' he whispers. His breath catches as it so often does upon looking at her work, but this time, it is not only out of awe and veneration but also out of wonder and surprise.

Before him is an unfinished painting of Timothy Ponden-Hall.

'I painted him first, before Hugh,' says Lou at Oak's shoulder. 'Or I tried to, anyway. As you can see, I was never able to complete it. I did try. Many times.'

There is a familiarity about the piece, stylistic flourishes of Ponden-Hall's early works – the swatches of wax, the prods and pulls of the paint that leave the canvas more textured than flat. It is also a recognisable scene reminiscent of Hugh DeLacey's portrait: there is a desk with scrolls of maps laid upon it, shelves behind inundated with books and atlases and nautical instruments, a vase full of roses on the windowsill. Unlike Hugh, who sits behind the desk, Timothy stands, one hand resting on a pile of maps before him, the other casually in his pocket. The composition of this piece perfectly twins the portrait of DeLacey. They could even be in the same room, desks in opposite corners, and indeed the mouldings of the shelves behind could continue straight onto the other's portrait.

The uniqueness of this painting, however, is Timothy's face – or the hazy traces of it. The sketches of his eyes, his handsome nose and jawline are all there, but the rosy flesh that should give the face life and light is simply missing. Where pinks and creams should fill in his forehead, his cheeks, there is only a chalky, ghost-like layer. Timothy seems to glow, translucent and pale, amongst his more completed surroundings. Oak is reminded of DaVinci's *Adorazione dei Magi*, beautiful cadmiums, ochre and golden deep yellows set amongst dark browns and bolder strokes – apparitions, figures never finished owing to the artist's relocation from Florence to Milan.

'I must have painted his face twenty times,' says Lou, 'but I could never get it right. Nothing I painted did justice to my brother's lively spirit. It has sat here unfinished in this room for sixty years.'

Oak can only stare. He leans closer to the folds of wax and paint and retreats once more. And in this moment, he knows. It is all improbable – that Timothy Ponden-Hall died sixty years ago and is buried beneath an apple tree; that his sister, exiled for the colour of her skin and invisible to the world, painted every portrait with the precision and genius of a master; that the painter Ponden-Hall has returned after fifty years to find *him*, Solomon Oak, to tell her story. Unimaginable, all of it. But here, at last, in this quiet and private moment looking upon the unfinished painting, Oak knows in his stomach – can feel it in his heart – that this woman is the painter of the portraits. Adelaide Ponden-Hall. He still does not fully understand. But there is acceptance.

'I know it is not a masterpiece,' offers Lou, 'but I thought perhaps you might be interested in seeing it.' She touches Timothy's face. There is the slightest flinch by Oak; he is not used to such casual treatment of a work – of a Ponden-Hall. 'You have so kindly focused on the process of my painting,' she continues. 'I thought perhaps it would be illuminating for you to see a work unfinished. It is, I suppose, exposing my work in its rawest form.'

Oak swallows. ''Tis a vulnerable thing for any artist to share.'

'It is for you. It is yours.'

How can Oak not feel overwhelmed by this precious gift?

'Thank you,' he says at last — a soft croak from the depths of his belly. It is not enough, will never be enough. But what else can he say? What else can he do but swell in gratitude and hold her hand for just a while longer as she walks him through the compasses and tele-meters and brass octants that line Timothy's painted shelves, modelled from the very ones perched on the sideboard behind them. They walk the grey line between Lou's paintings and tangible, corporeal life. And Oak is more aware than ever before of how blurred this line is — this line between art and reality — and how the best artists straddle it, create a space where meaning exists on both sides.

One afternoon, arm in arm, Lou walks Grace around her studio. Lou needs assistance in walking now; she feels more like a summer shawl upon Grace's arm than a living, breathing person. She is so light, so weak. Lou points to this pigment suspended in oil and to that chisel which she uses sometimes to carve the other end of the paintbrush.

'And these,' she says, gesturing to ten teak bowls heaping with bright, finely ground powders, 'are my favourite colours to use. They are the base of most of my work.'

The bowls sit in the centre of the table, two crisp and tidy rows in the midst of more chaotic piles of brushes, water jars, bladders and trays of old resin and wax.

'My favourite paintbrush,' sighs Lou. 'The weight is perfectly balanced when I hold it.'

Her fingers graze this brush, a box of nibs, a jar of ink. She pauses at a glass vial, opaque and sticky from layers of dust.

'This was from my brother,' recalls Lou. She lifts the vial and brings it close to her face. As she turns it sideways, its milky remnants slosh to the lid. 'He brought it back with him on his final expedition. One of many gifts he had bestowed on me over the years.'

Lou twists to see the vial in clearer light. The sun's rays dance through the glass, permeate the milky substance only slightly so it is almost translucent, pearl-like and shimmering.

'This was from Timothy?' asks Grace.

'The last treasure he ever brought me. He and Hugh took great pains to ensure its safety after the wreck.'

It is this vial, thinks Grace, *the very vial that the world covets, the vial that perhaps holds the secrets to all of this.* It is an effort to keep her voice measured. She slows her breath to steady her heart for fear of Lou feeling it quicken; they are still arm in arm, so close to each other. It has taken a tremendous effort on Grace's part not to simply stare at Lou throughout these slow and precious days. Yet she cannot help it, for every strand of Lou's hair, wild and full, is darker than lampblack; the skin upon her forehead, around her eyes, across her elegant cheekbones is as smooth and perfect as the shell of a freshly laid egg. Grace remembers the rumours of the vial – an elixir that immortalises the soul, preserves the physicality of the human body. *This vial… could it be?*

If Lou senses Grace's awe, she does not show it, for she is calm and unsentimental as she holds it closer for Grace to see. In fact, Lou's expression betrays an innocent perplexity – the fibres in her mind reaching back to the day he cupped it in her hand. Did she ever believe the rumours? Had she ever been tempted by the contents of this vial, or had she kept it safe simply because Timothy had asked her to? She cannot remember what she thought sixty years ago, and now it is only an ornament on her table, once important but placed aside as life moved onwards and onwards.

'You know,' says Lou, 'shortly after he gave it to me, I accidentally knocked it over and spilled some into a bowl of wax I was using. I did not realise the stopper had come loose.'

They study the jar for just a moment more, this browned and uninspiring phial that has sat amongst her paints and brushes over these long decades.

When Lou places it back and moves on to a shelf of compasses, Grace does not move. She remains fixated on the tiny bottle and does not know what she feels compelled to do. *Smell it? A drop on her finger? Feel its weight on the centre of her palm? What does one do so close to immortality?*

The lightness of Lou's arm against hers pulls Grace back.

'I saw you a couple of times at the Academy,' says Lou.

'You – what?'

'In London. The Academy has always been one of my favourite haunts, and on more than one occasion, I saw you there.'

Grace blushes. 'Who was I sitting for?'

'Not sitting. You were scrubbing the brushes. That is why I knew you would help me. The care you took with the brushes… and the kindness you showed some of the other charwomen – there was a benevolence about you. And when I discovered you were interested in studying history of art – oh yes, Professor Fairbanks loves to moan to anyone who will listen, particularly in the foyer so he sounds important – I knew you would not take for granted the opportunity to meet Solomon Oak.' Lou's voice is soft. 'Though I am sorry for the secrecy in getting you here.'

Grace cannot speak, for she feels nothing but gratitude. 'There is nothing to forgive, of course,' she says at last. And she can turn away from the vial. Any sentiment or curiosity or moment of self-ish vanity is so astoundingly insignificant compared to this woman's story. Grace can live with this mystery, for it is Lou and not this vial who has brought her to this new life of writing and researching alongside a revered art historian. Dreaming of it, however, is not new at all – has in fact slowly grown and bloomed within her chest and head ever since her father taught her how to read and question things, and she will indeed never take it for granted.

Lou walks Grace to a cabinet of gemstones and tells her about Timothy, her brother whose treasures surround them in this room, who is with her in everything she does.

When they come to the newest painting, Lou's self-portrait, Grace once again finds her hand upon her chest.

'I have always loved *Woman in a Sunhat*,' she says.

'My dear friend, Eliza.'

'Yes. But this. You. This one is more exquisite than all of the others. It is an honour to see.'

'Thank you, Grace,' says Lou. 'It does feel like an accomplishment to have finally finished it.'

'Finished it? When did you start it?'

'I painted this self-portrait before I left for Europe fifty years ago. I was thirty years old. I had intended to leave it at the Gallery or the Academy like the others, but it did not feel complete. So I left it here in the studio and it has been gathering dust ever since. In the end, when I brought it forth a few weeks ago, I did not add much after all. It felt fuller somehow – and I am a different person now than I was when I first looked upon it.' Lou floats her fingers over the bottom right corner. 'The signature, though, is fresh. The final touch. And I hope it is not too bold of me to have written my full name this time.'

Grace's empathy wells in her throat. 'On the contrary,' she says quietly, 'it is about time the world sees your name.'

In her final excursion from the house, Lou is carried by Jacob to the graveyard and is seated gently on the roots of the apple tree one more time. Jacob wraps a blanket around her and with a tender nod, leaves her with Alice. It is before breakfast, before a peep has been heard from the other bedrooms. They have brought two cigars, one for each of them.

From her coat pocket, Lou draws out a small jar of honeycomb.

'I have heard that turning the end in honey eases the puff,' she says. 'I thought you should try it.'

They pour a glob of honey onto the lid of the jar and Alice dips the tip in, turns it round slowly like a ballerina in a clockwork jewellery box.

The taste is not much different and she coughs again, which makes both of them laugh – soft, hearty breaths of laughter that tumble onto the fields and wood beyond.

'Your father tells me that you will soon book your ticket,' says Lou. 'Your grand tour at last.'

Alice straightens with pride. 'Yes. And after some weeks, my father will meet me in Paris. We shall visit the Louvre together.'

'A marvellous idea. I have one final gift for you too. 'Tis a small thing.' Out of her breast pocket, Lou pulls a piece of paper, thick and textured, folded into quarters.

Upon opening it, Alice sees a long list of names: villages, streets, surnames from all across the continent.

'Some may be out of date now,' says Lou, 'but most will welcome you with open arms if you care to pay a visit. I have kept up correspondence with many of them. They knew me as Lou Whipple, you should know.' She smiles. 'I could not use my true surname, of course. Oh, Mary was tickled by this – the thought of her name in acquaintance with friends on the continent. They are not all grand houses – though some are, as you will see – many are the hovels of farmers or simple inns in the hills that surround the cities. 'Tis the poor who may show you how to live the happiest life.'

'You have been trying to teach me this lesson throughout the year.'

'Well. The few close friends who I have had the pleasure of keeping lived largely in the margins of society, like me. Eliza was the daughter of a poor farming family. I am for ever grateful for her friendship; I was alone so much of the time in my exile in this house and her family lived just on the other side of the wood. And Mary, as you know, came from a slave family. She was only a couple years older than me when my grandfather employed her as my maid. We had a lifetime to grow close. Her death has been most difficult to endure. I miss her so.' She pauses. ''Tis a strange reality to have been hidden away from my own family, my own blood, because my complexion was slightly darker than theirs. More akin to a milky tea than buttermilk, my brother once told me.' Lou laughs. 'He hated buttermilk, and milky tea was his favourite. Another reason, I hope you can understand now, why I conducted my deliveries at night. If anyone noticed my skin colour was even ever so slightly more brown, I would have risked drawing more attention to myself, and being a woman with access to privileged resources was risk enough.

'Anyway, it was Timothy and Hugh and these women, Eliza and Mary, who saw me for who I was, you see, and never turned away.'

To hear Lou talk about her life in this way, so close to its denouement, to hear her speak of these friendships, is a privilege. Alice knows this. But she cannot help feeling a twinge of jealousy – and for what? Their closeness to her? Their time together? She is jealous of all of it and feels the desperation of wanting to keep Lou with her just a bit longer.

'I wish...' but Alice lets the thought die on her lips. 'Well.'

'In another story,' says Lou.

Yes. *But that is a dangerous game to play*, thinks Alice, *dreaming of other endings*.

'I have been baffled by our own friendship, Alice Oak,' she says. 'I never thought I would meet another true friend so close to the end of my life. It has been a most rewarding surprise. Though I suppose, given who we are, it should not be so remarkable that we have become close.'

But at this, Alice is certainly baffled. They are like oil and vinegar in temperament, upbringing and experience.

'It's true,' Lou laughs as she studies her face. 'We are similar in many ways, Alice – our thirst for adventure: I, a Ponden-Hall, and you with the spirit of Solomon, Emma and your mother to whisk you forward. We have both been overshadowed by our siblings for much of our lives so far. And more than that, we have not minded the shadow – not really – because of our love for them. But above all, perhaps we can relate to each other the most because we understand the equal burden and privilege of outliving them.'

Alice has never thought of it this way before: this burden and privilege to outlive a most beloved sister. And Lou is right; no one else will understand this. Just the two of them, in this moment, in their own fellowship. And for this, there is a little peace.

5

**In acquiring NOTES for an article in the *Daily Telegraph*:
'An interview with Professor Solomon Oak on
the Invisibility of Adelaide Rose Martha Ponden-Hall'
by Grace Dodd**

On one of their final mornings at the estate, Oak and Grace sit on
the terrace and admire the fields of cow parsley and buttercups. They
drink tea. There is a surplus of shortbread and black grapes. Alice is
out walking the spaniels with Jacob, and Lou slumbers upstairs, her
breathing slow and deep like the unrushed rhythms of impending
summer.

'I think I will begin the article like this,' says Grace. She has
agonised over this beginning. How long it has been since she wrote
something for an audience – since she wrote something she cared
about. She clears her throat. 'To the family, she was always referred
to as *the girl*. Nameless, even formless, to all in the household with
the exception of her older brother, the girl led a quiet and curious
life amongst her soft toys, wooden castles and books until she was
removed to the countryside altogether. These were the bizarre living
conditions of the child who would eventually become the country's
most coveted painter.'

'An evocative beginning,' says Oak.

Grace scrunches her nose and sucks on the tip of her pen. 'Or
perhaps I should start with a vivid description of the apiary? Lead in
with the beekeeping and excess of wax?'

By now, Grace has asked Oak hundreds of questions, and finally it
is time to wrestle them into the shape of an article.

317

'Or I could just jump to this bit,' says Grace, flipping to another sheet. 'This is the lead-in to your interview.

'I have known many women in my life and I can say with great confidence that I have never met someone quite so striking as Adelaide Ponden-Hall. She possesses an intimidating beauty – dark and elegant, quiet and wise. And whilst she has every reason to harbour a sharp bitterness grown over a lifetime, she holds onto nothing – only a peace and a preference to be alone. There are many chapters in her story and these will be revealed, finally, in due course by one she trusts to tell it: the revered art historian, Solomon Oak. In the meantime, before the full book is published, I am writing this article to gently introduce to the world the muted Ponden-Hall, to replace the assumed "T" with a rightful "A" and show that whilst she may have been invisible all of these years, she was never silent.'

Oak nods. 'And the interview will commence then?'

'Yes. Just three questions, I think, to set the tone. A brief introduction to the real Adelaide.'

'A first question on her family life, then,' says Oak.

Grace rifles through her notebook. 'Yes. I think what she told us on the first day about Elizabeth's cruel disdain for her and how she grew up apart from everyone else.'

'It would be remiss to not address the issue of racial prejudice.'

''Tis true, but it would be so crudely rushed in an article like this. And you will most certainly devote an appropriate number of chapters to such injustice in the biography. I thought perhaps in the article, we could narrow the focus on how this unfair treatment of her impacted on the paintings. For example, focus on how her own invisibility inspired her to make others who were invisible *seen*.'

Oak thinks for a moment. 'Perhaps her greatest triumph, then,' he says, 'is her own liminal narrative, as she has given flesh and mystique to an utterly invisible life.'

'Yes,' says Grace. 'Exactly.' Her scribbles are furious upon the page. 'Perhaps a consolidated explanation, then, of each of the paintings: who they were to her and why she painted them.'

'That would make sense.'

'I have an obscene amount of notes on that,' she says. 'That should be simple enough. And what do you think of this ending?

'When we see PONDEN-HALL in the bottom right corner of a painting, we think of greatness; we think of mastery. Such adjectives are masculine in our minds. Adelaide Ponden-Hall signed her name at the bottom of a painting and thought nothing of it. It is only right for us to return her work to her, to recognise the true artist and celebrate this woman's life's work, which has captivated and bewitched us for over half a century. Ah—' She pauses and looks up at Oak. 'I had hoped to end with a clever twist of words around the supernatural. To close the door on the rumours once and for all.'

They regard each other in silence. These days have been so full, the hours with Lou so cherished. Oak and Grace have not yet spoken to each other, have hardly had time to reflect upon the truths that they have learned.

Grace places the nib of her pen on a fresh page.

'Mr Oak,' she says, thoughts of the vial flickering behind her own eyes. Grace knows what she believes, however inconceivable it may seem. She wonders if Solomon believes the same. 'You have met Miss Ponden-Hall and finally — after a life's work of searching for the unifying thread — you understand the truth behind the paintings. Can you address, one final time, the rumours surrounding the supernatural?'

And Oak pauses. His breaths are slow and measured as he considers. There is a linear narrative, yes, and this wild, unruly thread that he so desperately sought to pull straight has indeed become taut; the paintings are aligned like soldiers pulled into rank — satisfying, full of sense. And yet here at the end of the mystery, Oak is bewildered. An unforeseen tangle. In his conversations with Lou, she has conveyed the wisdom, grace and knowledge of a woman who has lived a long, enriched life. She has known cities as he has known them, through the eyes of hungry scholars desperate to know every painting, sculpture, fresco. She has worked in vineyards, music halls, farmyards and opera houses. There is a perceptiveness and tiredness in her voice that only the elderly possess.

Whilst Oak is a stubborn man, he is still first and foremost an academic, and it is this which prompts him to humbly question: *have I been wrong?*

It is a sobering consideration. How passionately he has defended his case — fought for the paintings to be remembered for their genius and not for some debasing foray into the occult. The paintings are triumphs. They are the works of a prodigy, a master. How fervently he has argued that in spite of the rumours, even if there was a smidgen of truth in these demeaning allegations around the supernatural, it would not matter one bit, would not matter in the slightest, because the paintings should be revered for what they are: a testament to human talent and the experience of what man is able to express through art.

And in this tangle of reflections, Oak's stance becomes clear – clearer than it has ever been before.

To Grace, Oak shrugs and offers an assured smile:

'Why would one need an elixir to immortalise anyone? That is what art is for.'

A full biography of Adelaide Ponden-Hall is currently being written by Mr Solomon Oak, her designated biographer, and Alice Oak, a beloved friend.

Epilogue

In the chilly morning darkness of 4 a.m. on 7 May 1891, nearly sixty years after the portrait of Hugh DeLacey appeared on the doorstep of the Academy, a hansom pulls up to Charing Cross station. It is a rickety stop, a bouncing stop that betrays its driver's unfamiliarity and newness of touch.

The clicking of the latch seems to echo down London's wider streets; it reverberates from the bronze gaze of the statue of George IV down to the Thames and its soupy fog, from the Haymarket westward to Hyde Park Corner. Even these expansive, well-trodden passageways of carriages and horseshoes and boots are eerily quiet on this morning.

Three figures alight from the hansom. There is a strange summer mist that hangs about them, clings to their coats as they move unsteadily in the darkness. One trips on the kerb as she returns to the carriage door – the smallest one, who moves with conviction and holds her head high, chin up, whose silhouette of hair is as ungainly as a pigeon's nest. She slides a large rectangular parcel out of the trap and with great care, proceeds to carry it down Charing Cross Road towards Trafalgar Square. It is much too large for her; it makes her teeter forward and sideways as she strains to see where she is going from behind the parcel.

The other two figures follow close behind. One stoops a bit in his top hat and gingerly takes the arm of the third, who is the most sure-footed of them all. Her silhouette is one of curves and curls even in these morning shadows, and she walks with her shoulders squared, with a slight lean of comfort towards the old man whose arm and hand she holds in her own.

They pass the subtle grey door amongst its gentlemen's clubs and brandy houses. Although the keepers will enter the museum through this door near the Barry rooms as they always do, the parcel in tow is more deserving of a grander view. Up the main stairway and onto the National Gallery's main entrance, Alice Oak, Solomon Oak and Grace Dodd bring Ponden-Hall's final portrait to be discovered by the world.

Alice props the portrait against the centre door. It looks out between the Corinthian columns onto the square and its fountains, and when the sun rises, Nelson's column with its guarding lions will be cast in warm, mellow light that extends from Trafalgar Square all the way to the river.

'Who will find it if we leave it here?' asks Grace.

'Perhaps one of the guards,' says Oak. 'But Jonny, hopefully.'

'You could tip him off, Father,' suggests Alice. 'To ensure it is he who finds it. I do not like it up here. It feels so exposed. Every carriage and working man in London will pass through the square in a few hours.'

'There will be less foot traffic here than along the side door. And the museum will open later.'

'And anyway,' offers Grace, 'she would not want this one to be treated any differently from the others. Let whoever finds it find it. It will make its way into the right hands just as the others did.'

She is right, of course, but Alice is still uneasy.

'Well. It is done then.'

But they do not move. Leaving the final Ponden-Hall portrait in the dark feels like an abandonment. To leave now means to surrender it to the world, as it was always meant to be surrendered, but it also means exposing the truth – speaking a secret out loud, untying an intricately knotted mask. For Alice, it is giving up a best friend.

She remains rooted to the spot. The remainder of the day plays out in her mind: they will ride home at pace to ensure they are back in Oxford when the painting is found. She will sit at the kitchen table with her father and a cold cup of tea, waiting for the telegram to arrive to summon them back into London. She will decline to accompany Oak. Instead, Alice will walk to the bank of the Thames where she and Lou – she and Adelaide – once had a winter picnic and sat under a willow, and she will allow the past year to wash over her like the pull of a river in spring. She will cry for Lou and for Emma and miss them both with a ferocity and fire she did not possess in the vaulted rooms of her tutors when she was a shade of a student who possessed no wants. She will take her Italian book to the river. She will smell its leather and pass her fingers over the crisp ink and take in none of the prepositions or conjugations. Who knows for how long she will ache.

Oak places his hand on his daughter's shoulder.

Together, they face the portrait wrapped in brown paper, so deceptively small for what it is about to reveal. Oak, too, imagines the day's events unfolding. The summons from London. The swarming journalists around his house, the Gallery, the Academy. His excitable pupil, Jonathan Hammond, appealing to him once more like a schoolboy for advice, for knowledge and the truth. The frowns and raised eyebrows of all involved as Grace Dodd glides into the offices and perches next to him, produces a notebook full of dates, quotes, article clippings and a sample of beeswax and ochre pigment on the leather cover. A furious, shiny Bromage bursting out of his buttons as he accuses the pair of manipulating him with false leads. 'Where is the elixir!' he will shout with globules of spit and others will follow suit. Oak and Grace will remain composed. At the afternoon's press conference, they will confirm that all will be revealed in due time as Adelaide Ponden-Hall has requested.

Perhaps even that evening in Grace's new quarters – a respectable neighbourhood close to Notting Hill – they will begin writing the biography on the most fascinating and influential portrait artist of the nineteenth century: her cultivation of beehives in the dining room, her process of prodding and buffing the wax with both sides of the paintbrush, her preference for painting on board rather than canvas. Maybe they will touch on the deep reverence she had for her brother; maybe they will share her great adoration for Hugh, Timothy's quiet, thoughtful love who became a second brother to her over the years. Muses tend to work their way into their artist's biographies, and Oak does not see the harm in this.

'It is far from done, my girl.' Oak squeezes Alice's shoulder. 'There is much to be written.'

'We should go,' says Grace. 'Someone may have already seen us.'

Oak and Alice walk back to the hansom hand in hand, which they have not done for many years. Grace goes before them, a protectress of sorts who will see them off before retreating to her own bed for a few hours of calm before the parcel paper is ripped free, torn like the page of a book opened in haste, a frayed margin. There are ghosts about them too – the loves of Adelaide's life and Emma with them – keeping to the shadows for just a while longer before they are cast into the dawn light and their stories are told for the sake of being told and nothing more.

Acknowledgements

It took me three years to write this novel, but it is the product of a much longer fascination with art and its role in immortalising people and stories. No doubt, I have been influenced by nearly a decade of teaching Oscar Wilde's *The Picture of Dorian Gray* and Mary Shelley's *Frankenstein*; I am grateful to my colleagues and students for the rich discussions around humanity and beauty we've had over the years whilst studying these masterpieces.

Sharing any work prematurely is a scary thing, but I was so fortunate to have these early readers who treated a young and messy manuscript with such patience, care and thoughtfulness: Laura Graham, Ashley Wright, Rufaro Maposa, Kristina McClendon, Blake Knight, Tess Hitchcock and Paul Kingsnorth.

My gratitude extends to the Limos, Heywood-Lonsdale and Bongard families along with Annie Randolph-Dyer for such pure, unwavering enthusiasm on this journey. My love and thanks to these friends who always believed I would write books one day and have shared in my joy with every milestone: Jen Levy Katz (and Rob Levy for the gold dust), Michelle Petty, Cassandra Coats, Ashley Walters Jahn, Karen Pang and Brandon Patoc. Thanks to New England Coffee House in Stow-on-the-Wold for keeping me watered with café bombons and the kindest company.

I entrenched myself in Victorian London and Oxford thanks to endless historical accounts, but I would like to offer a particular nod to the British Newspaper Archives, *A London Child of the 1870s* by Mary Vivian Hughes and *London Labour and the London Poor* by Henry Mayhew. *The Story of Art* by E.H. Gombrich was often at my elbow whilst writing, and it continues to be a great source of comfort and inspiration. Tom Heywood–Lonsdale let me pester him about trees and cigars, and Matthew Knight kindly gave me a lesson on walled gardens one afternoon in Kent. All errors, of course, are my own entirely.

A heartfelt thank you to Emily Ponsonby, who welcomed me into her studio so I could be the luckiest fly on the wall as she drizzled beeswax onto board and worked her magic. Her beeswax and oil paintings were the inspiration for the style of Ponden-Hall's work in this novel, and I am for ever grateful for her generous time and openness. I am in awe of her talent.

The team at Bloomsbury has left me brimming with wonder and gratitude time and time again. Emma Herdman's compassion and wisdom helped bring Alice Oak to the forefront of this story which truly allowed these female voices to sing. And Charlie Greig – with her sharp insight and generous spirit – helped bring the story home. My thanks as well to Francisco Vilhena, David Mann, Sarah Knight, Beth Farrell, Amy Donegan, Anouska Levy, Isobel Turton and Paul Baggaley.

My agent Olivia Maidment is an inspiring fount of support, knowledge and enthusiasm. I am for ever grateful to her and the Madeleine Milburn team for believing in this story.

Finally, thank you to my family: my selfless parents who have taught me so much, and my sisters Peest and Kreed who share a love of stories and independent bookshops, and who humoured my wild imagination growing up. Grazie to Leonardo and Hero, the most curious companions in art galleries, for their patience and grace when I have hidden away in cafes to write. Above all, thank you to Oli for taking my writing seriously from the very beginning – for giving me the time and space to pursue this dream, and for keeping our full and lively family life going with such brilliance and poise.

A Note on the Author

Dani Heywood-Lonsdale has paternal roots on the tiny island of Molokai, Hawaii – referred to as the Sandwich Islands throughout *The Portrait Artist* – and maternal roots in the Philippines. She is a Faber Academy alumni and teaches English Literature in Oxfordshire.

A Note on the Type

The text of this book is set in Bembo, which was first used in 1495 by the Venetian printer Aldus Manutius for Cardinal Bembo's *De Aetna*. The original types were cut for Manutius by Francesco Griffo. Bembo was one of the types used by Claude Garamond (1480–1561) as a model for his Romain de l'Université, and so it was a forerunner of what became the standard European type for the following two centuries. Its modern form follows the original types and was designed for Monotype in 1929.